THE HAUNTING OF TOBY JUGG

THE HAUNTING OF TOBY JUGG

Dennis Wheatley

WORDSWORTH EDITIONS

In loving memory of
MICHAEL TRAYLER
the founder of Wordsworth Editions

I

Readers who are interested in other titles from
Wordsworth Editions are invited to visit our website at
www.wordsworth-editions.com

For our latest list and a full mail-order service contact
Bibliophile Books, 5 Thomas Road, London E14 7BN
Tel: +44 0207 515 9222 Fax: +44 0207 538 4115
e-mail: orders@bibliophilebooks.com

This edition published 2007 by
Wordsworth Editions Limited
8B East Street, Ware, Hertfordshire SG12 9HJ

ISBN 978 1 84022 545 7

Typeset in Great Britain by Chrissie Madden
Printed by Clays Ltd, St Ives plc

INTRODUCTION

When Dennis Wheatley died in November 1977 the notice put in the newspapers by his son read simply: 'Wheatley, Dennis Yeates, aged 80 years. Sailor, soldier, airman and author.' That he was an author everybody knew; he had published more than 70 books. He had been a sailor in that, having been expelled from Dulwich College, his father sent him to complete his education as a cadet on board HMS *Worcester*, which was a training establishment for future merchant navy officers – not that Dennis had any intention of going to sea. He was a real enough soldier, volunteering and commissioned as soon as the First World War broke out, and serving for much of the next four years in France.

When the Royal Flying Corps was formed he did, in fact, volunteer to be trained as a pilot, but was rejected because he was colour-blind. Nevertheless, twenty-five years later he wore the uniform of a Wing Commander – not that he was any more interested in aeroplanes than in ships. What had happened was that, early in the Second World War, largely because of his wife's connections with MI5, he had begun submitting, to very senior people, detailed papers about counter-measures which might be tried if there was a German invasion, and, as an imaginative exercise, putting himself in the enemy's place and suggesting measures which the Germans might take. The result was an invitation to join a new planning section of the General Staff, involved chiefly in the development of Deception Strategies. It was to consist of a few picked men from all three services. Dennis was asked if he would prefer to serve as a civilian, which would have meant slightly higher pay in the beginning. He brushed the idea aside. Uniform was the proper costume for a gentleman in time of war, he said. So he was brought in as part of the R.A.F.'s allocation, and thus became, as he liked to recall, 'the only man ever commissioned direct from civilian life to serve in this strategic stratosphere'. He enjoyed himself enormously, meeting and working with very senior controllers of the entire war effort.

And this had happened to him, he mused, at an age when he might reasonably have expected nothing more than to be put in charge of guarding a reservoir.

With the R.A.F. itself he had no particular involvement, although he dedicated *The Haunting of Toby Jugg* 'To my friends, past and present, of the Royal Air Force'. The book was written after the war, and, apart from the wheelchair-bound hero, makes very little reference to the period in which it is set. There are, however, two episodes worth noting which were drawn from Dennis Wheatley's earlier life.

One involves the prep school to which Toby Jugg has been sent. In 1939 Wheatley wrote several chapters of what was to have been a new thriller. 'I had heard,' he says in his autobiography, 'about a school in Devonshire which was co-educational and run on ultra-modern lines. The pupils were allowed complete licence to attend classes or not as they liked, lie in bed all day if they wished and even abuse teachers that they disliked. It was rumoured that the pupils were encouraged to attend Satanic gatherings in a ruined church nearby.' Gregory Sallust, Wheatley's hero in some previous thrillers and subsequent spy stories, would have been sent to investigate. 'The book was never completed. But I used the idea many years later in *The Haunting of Toby Jugg*.'

The rumour about Satanist gatherings was almost certainly untrue, but the school was absolutely real, celebrated or notorious in its day. It eventually came to grief – perhaps predictably – amid a welter of scandal. The relevance in *Toby Jugg* is that Dennis assumed, no doubt correctly, that there would be no Scripture lessons in such a school and no Morning Prayers. Toby is therefore made to comment, in retrospect, that the school, as an institution, was indefensible. 'It is a terrible thing to bring children up as atheists – just how terrible no-one can fully appreciate until, like myself, they find themselves pursued by some creature of the Devil.'

The other episode involved Dennis himself, and was, he said, among the most terrifying experiences of his life. He recounts it, almost word for word, with only the names changed, in *Toby Jugg*, but it is so extraordinary, and so central to his beliefs about the supernatural (of which he normally said he had no personal experience) that it may be worth reprinting here the detailed uncensored account which he gave towards the end of his life.

He was nine years old at the time and had been dispatched to a boarding school in Kent, where it was thought the sea air would do him good. He was lodged, with three other boys, in a house run by the Headmaster's wife, Mrs Hester. 'We didn't care for her particularly but we adored her best friend, Milly Evans, who came to stay with her for long periods.' A boy called Bernie Arendt, whose father was head of the Great Eastern Railway's catering department, became Dennis's closest friend.

'The house was separated from its neighbours on either side by about thirty or forty feet, and behind it had a small garden. It was a square box, without wings or balconies. The front door opened onto a narrow hall. Further along it divided, the left half being a passage to the kitchen, the right a straight-up flight of stairs. On the first floor there were two bedrooms on either side of the landing and, over the front end of the hall, a bathroom. The staircase made a hairpin bend and continued up to the second floor, which also had five rooms, immediately above those below.

'As the youngest boys, Bernie and I always went up to bed before the others. Our room was the first on the right on the first floor. One night we went up side by side, he on the right, I on the left, next to the banisters. There was no light on the landing but we could see our way by that which filtered up from the hall. When we were three steps from the landing I chanced to glance to my left. At that age my head came only to the height of the banister rail. As I looked through the double row of banisters I found myself staring into another face within a few inches of my own. Beyond it was the dark outline of a man's figure. He was crouching low on the first few steps of the upper flight of stairs, and above his face one of his hands gripped the rail of the banisters. The face was round, white and horrible. I was petrified, struck dumb with fear, and remained rooted to the spot.

'Meanwhile Bernie had reached the landing. Opening the door of our room, he stepped inside and exclaimed, "Oh, what a lovely moon!"

'The sound of his voice released me from the spell. Turning, I gave a terrified yell. As I plunged downstairs, I caught a last glimpse of the figure on the far side of the banisters. It, too, had turned. Swiftly and noiselessly it was gliding up the stairs towards the top floor.

'Bernie darted out of our room, saw me tumbling headlong round the lower bend towards the hall, and came pelting after me, crying out "What happened? What's the matter?"

' "A burglar!" I shouted. "Help! Help! A burglar!"

'Mr and Mrs Hester, Milly and a man they had asked to dinner all came running out from the sitting-room. While the women sought to pacify me the men seized hockey sticks and went upstairs to tackle the intruder. There was no way out for him: no backstairs, no fire escape, no out-jutting lower roofs onto which he could have jumped, and from the top floor windows it was a thirty-foot drop. They searched every room on both the upper floors, but in vain. The burglar had taken nothing and disappeared without leaving a trace.

'They tried to persuade me that my imagination had been playing me tricks, but I was positively convinced that I had seen a man on the stairs and it proved quite a job to quiet me down. I was put to bed, comforted with jelly and cake and eventually read to sleep by Milly. Next morning, as it seemed that the only explanation of the burglar's escape was that he had shinned down the drainpipe, we examined the flower-beds round the house. But there was not even the suggestion of a footprint, so, for me, how he had managed to get away remained a mystery.

'Years later, during the 1914-18 war, I met Milly Evans again. While we were talking over old times, she asked me if I remembered the fright I had given them all by seeing a ghost. I replied that I had never seen a ghost.

'Upon which she said. "Of course you thought it was a burglar. But it wasn't. I remember now that we let you go on thinking it was because we didn't want to frighten you further; but it was some sort of supernatural manifestation that you saw, and from the description you gave us, a pretty nasty one. The Hesters were very keen on spiritualism, and two or three evenings a week we used to practise table-turning, and that sort of thing. As nothing was taken and no man could have got out of that house without our finding some signs of his having been there, we had no doubt at all that our séances had attracted some form of elemental, and it had begun to haunt the place. We were so scared that we gave up spiritualism."

'In view of my complete ignorance of psychic matters at the age of nine,' (Dennis continued) 'it is quite understandable that I should have taken a ghostly figure for a man of flesh and blood; and *the fact that I did* is irrefutable proof that I – the person who actually saw the ghost – played no part in establishing the intruder as a supernatural apparition. This personal and unsought experience has, in consequence, convinced me beyond all shadow of doubt that there are planes outside our physical world and disembodied intelligencies which in certain circumstances impinge upon it.

'Unfortunately, from the earliest ages, unscrupulous people have communication with their loved dead, and a very high proportion of them have, sooner or later, been exposed as charlatans. Materialists make much of that, but it really has no bearing on the question, for this is a case in which one swallow *does* make a summer. It needs only a single instance of indisputable communication to prove survival after death, and of the innumerable cases which have been vouched for by reputable people it is difficult to believe that every one of them is founded on either deception, hallucination or lies. My own experience cannot be taken as any proof that on dying the essence of our individualities leave our bodies to continue their activities in some other sphere, but it can be taken as proving the existence of occult manifestations, and the existence of one makes the existence of the other infinitely more plausible.'

Dennis Wheatley was not what highbrows call a 'serious' writer. What he prided himself on was something which highbrows hold in rather low regard – the craft of storytelling, and there were literally millions of readers to testify that he was indeed extremely good at it. However, his stories deal with matters serious enough; with wars and political movements, with grand sweeps of history, and with spiritual or religious things. It would be wrong to suppose that he did not take such matters seriously when they formed the underlying substance of his tales. On the contrary, the political analysis in his spy stories, and the ideological positions which his heroes represent, were simply his own; the history in his historical novels was always researched scrupulously, and sometimes indeed rather too solidly shovelled in; and his religious or spiritual philosophy remained quite consistent throughout his career. These may have been unsubtle, just as his storytelling technique was unsubtle, but they worked for him and they worked for his readers.

The Haunting of Toby Jugg fits this pattern. Far from being a religious or philosophic tract, it is a vigorous, almost melodramatic, thriller which happens to have a supernatural theme. It does, nevertheless, contain perhaps the most explicit statement of moral and metaphysical views to be found in any of his novels. He puts the exposition of those views into the mouth of his heroine, but they were undisguisedly his own. She – and he – believed in reincarnation and the law of karmic retribution or compensation. This belief is fitted somehow into an almost Manichean picture of the universe; a universe divided between light and dark, good and evil, God and the Devil, locked in perpetual conflict, but with the forces of light having an ultimately superior edge.

It is, one can see, a practical philosophy, and Dennis was practical.

He wrote books to please his readers and therefore to make money; which, starting with his very first novel, they did, in great quantities. He worked hard and became famous. He threw himself immediately, honourably and unquestioningly into two world wars, emerging unscathed and with distinction. His second marriage at least was a great success; he had a son, stepchildren and grand-children, all of whom flourished. He enjoyed almost every aspect of the world as he passed through it. Whether or not as a karmic reward, he was a lucky man.

ANTHONY LEJEUNE

THE HAUNTING OF TOBY JUGG

*I dedicate this book
to my friends past and present
of the Royal Air Force*

The Haunting of Toby Jugg

Monday, 4th May

I feel that the time has come when I must endeavour to face facts. These past few nights I have been frightened – scared stiff – really terrified. Ten months ago I was a sane, strong, healthy man; now I am weak, irresolute and, I fear, on the verge of going mad.

Perhaps I am only imagining things. But if I set down all that is happening here – or rather, that which I believe to be happening – when I look at what I have written again next day, I shall at least know that I haven't dreamed the whole horrible business overnight.

That is why I have decided to start keeping a journal. In it I intend not only to give an account of these strange experiences of which I have recently been the victim, but also make an attempt to rationalise them. If I can somehow argue matters out with myself until I reach a logical conclusion as to what lies at the bottom of my fears, I shall, perhaps, be able to face them better and save my sanity.

I used to enjoy writing essays, and the work involved in setting down my thoughts coherently should help a lot to keep my mind free from aimless, agonising dread of the night to come. I shall not write in the evenings, though, as the accursed shadows in this big room are apt to make me jumpy near sundown, and might lead me to exaggerate the facts. I'll work on it in the mornings, or afternoons, when the good, clean daylight, streaming in through the broad windows, makes me feel more like the man I used to be.

It is not so long ago since my friends nicknamed me 'The Viking', partly, of course, on account of my appearance, but also because I was credited with having a kind of 'devil-may-care' courage with which everyone is not blessed. I wonder what they would think if they had seen me as I was last night – a gibbering nervous wreck – frantic with fear of some ghastly thing that was hidden from me only by the blackout.

Still, fear of physical danger and of this sort of thing are entirely different matters. Some of my brother officers who were hard put to it to prevent themselves showing how badly they had the jitters would probably laugh at me now; while others braver than myself, and there were plenty of them, might be every bit as scared as I am. It would depend on their individual degree of susceptibility to the supernatural.

If anyone had suggested to me a few months ago that I was a psychic type myself, I should certainly have denied it. But I must admit to being so now, as the only alternative is that I really am going nutty. Rightly or wrongly I believe that I am being haunted by some form of devil – and I don't mean the sort that comes from knocking back too much Scotch. I mean one of those forces of Evil that are said to have been let loose in the world after Satan and his host were defeated by the Archangel Michael and cast down out of Heaven.

That sounds old-fashioned stuff, I know; but either something of that kind did actually happen when the world was young, or it didn't. There is no middle way about it. And, if it did, there has been no revelation since to the effect that these age-long enemies of man have been withdrawn to another sphere, or that their infernal Master has ceased from his efforts to corrupt and destroy the seed of Adam.

Satan has become rather a figure of fun these days, or, at worst, a bogey-man with whom wicked old women sometimes frighten children; but, all the same, he still remains our ultimate expression for the most concentrated form of Evil, and everything else that is evil must in a greater or lesser degree partake of his attributes. Therefore, in endeavouring to get to grips with my own problem, it may be worth speculating on him a little, and on the reasons for the apparent decline in his powers.

In this year of Grace – save the mark; I should have said this year of world-wide death and destruction, 1942 – how many people, I wonder, believe in the Devil? I mean as a definite personality with hoofs and horns and a barbed tail, waving a pitchfork and breathing brimstone over everything? I suppose a few very religious rather backward people do; lonely, timid spinsters living in remote country districts, particularly in Scotland and down here in Wales, and the older generation of peasants in Central and Southern Europe.

I can't myself. I think that all those accounts of monks and other characters coming face to face with the Devil in the Middle Ages were, as old Gibbon put it: 'The product of an empty stomach on an empty brain'; or else deliberate lying. In those days religion played such a large part in everybody's life that people thought of Heaven and Hell as only just round the corner; so the easiest way to obtain a little cheap notoriety was to come down one morning with your shirt on inside-out, and declare to a wide-eyed audience that the Devil had visited you in the middle of the night with some tempting proposition.

On the other hand one can never be certain – absolutely certain – that all such records are the ravings of unbalanced minds or pure invention. After all, why do we disbelieve them? Mainly, I think, because it seems improbable that such a V.I.P. as the Prince of Evil could be bothered to torment, or accept the homage of, quite ordinary people.

But his demons were said to be legion, and it may be that they sometimes assumed their master's form when appearing to the Godly, or attending a witches' sabbath as the guest of honour. That may be the explanation; for, while it must remain an open question whether any human being has ever seen the Devil, it seems impossible to doubt the existence of demons. Cases of demonic possession still occur from time to time, as any Roman Catholic priest will testify; and during the Middle Ages such happenings were regarded as almost everyday affairs.

The reason for their much greater frequency in the past is not far to seek. Life was so very different then, and everyone was so much more concerned with the things of the spirit. Whether they were in a state of grace or not was of vital importance to people, because they were daily reminded at morning prayers and evening Bible readings – as well as during the whole of every Sunday – that, should they meet with a sudden death, they would get no second chance, but have to give an account of their acts to date when hauled naked and trembling before their Creator.

Such constant preoccupation with thoughts of miracles and martyrs, angels and demons, must have made their minds much more open to supernatural influences than ours are today. It is, therefore, one thing to be a bit sceptical about the accounts of Old Nick putting in a personal appearance and quite another to brush aside as trash the whole vast literature dealing with Christian mysticism.

Here are innumerable accounts of people who became so obsessed with the question of the Life to Come that they gave themselves up to a special devotion to their favourite Saints, and as a result of their wholehearted fervour developed miraculous powers of their own. And of others, the bad-hats and natural rebels, who dabbled in witchcraft, Satanism and alchemy. It is certainly incontestable that there was hardly a village in Europe where someone or other was not credited with the power to cast spells and bring calamity on their enemies by ill-wishing them. The bulk of testimony to such happenings is overwhelming, and it simply is not credible that for hundreds of generations the whole population of Christendom was fooled by a succession of liars and lunatics.

Of course, in these days, there are plenty of sceptics who regard all accounts of occult phenomena as bunkum; and due either to people imagining things when in an abnormal condition, or to the machinations of rogues and charlatans who make a dubious living out of tricking the credulous.

But the opinions of such bigoted materialists do not prove anything. They are simply the outcome of the present widespread lack of Faith. It is only natural that people brought up, as I was, to believe that there are no such places as Heaven and Hell, should be strongly prejudiced against any evidence which might convince them of the existence of some fearsome Otherworld, inhabited by mysterious forces and the spirits of the dead. To accept it would compel them to abandon their comfortable philosophy – or lack of one. They would begin to get the wind up at the thought that they must have souls themselves, and the frightening question of what might happen to them when they die.

The extraordinary decline in the practice of all religions during the past thirty years no doubt accounts for the comparatively few people who now ever pause to ponder such questions seriously. Yet it would be absurd to assume that a fundamental change has taken place in the composition of human beings, and that because great numbers of them rarely think about their souls they no longer have them.

Moreover, the age of materialism has brought us no new answers to such riddles as: What took place 'in the beginning', and what is meant by 'the end of time', or, how did it come about that life started on our own small planet? Yet the more we learn of the universe the more apparent it becomes that everything in it is regulated by unchanging laws, and that chemical conditions alone are incapable of producing any form of life whatsoever.

Yet the origin of these mysteries has been questioned only in recent times. Previously, in every country and in every age since the beginning of recorded history, it has been the first article in the creed of man that the Creation was the work of a Supreme Intelligence. In addition, all religions also held in common that the souls of men were immortal, and that the unceasing struggle for them between the eternally warring forces of Good and Evil was all part of the Great Plan.

World-wide tradition asserts that these beliefs were based on a series of Divine revelations made for man's guidance; and, all modern thought having failed to produce any other tenable theory, it seems difficult, if not impossible, to reject them.

But to accept them carries with it an awe-inspiring thought; for it then becomes unthinkable that in the past hundred years or so any part of this vast and complex system can have altered. Therefore, although the Devil may no longer appear to people – even if he ever did so in person – he cannot have become inactive, and his power for evil must remain as potent as of old.

No-one has ever denied him intelligence, so it is reasonable to assume that he is clever enough to adapt his methods to suit every advance in modern thought. If wars, revolutions, the mushroom growth of the herd mentality and their resulting miseries can be attributed to a supremely evil intelligence working se etly upon the greed, fears and follies of man, he has good reason t ongratulate himself on the monstrous reaping of hate and vio ce that his sowing has brought him in the past quarter of a centu In fact, if looked at from that point of view, it seems that the gener ecline of religion since the end of the Victorian era has enormousl cilitated the Devil's age-long task of replacing order by chaos an at last, entering into his Principality of this World as the Lord of Misrule.

Even to suggest that he is now taking a personal interest in myself would be atrociously conceited; but, unless I am suffering from delusions, I can only suppose that either I or this room have recently become a focus for the activities of one of his innumerable lesser satellites. How otherwise can one possibly explain the shadow; or the stark terror that has gripped me, holding me rigid in a paralysis of fear, on each of the five occasions that I have seen it – and, God forbid, may do so again tonight?

Tuesday, 5th May
I could not write anything this morning. I tried to as soon as I was alone, but my hand shook so much that it would not hold the pencil firmly. Then, at half-past eleven, I had to go out with Deb.

It has been a lovely day and the bright sunshine in the garden restored me a little. Those sharp black eyes of Deb's don't miss much, though, and it is hardly surprising that she noticed how haggard I look.

'I haf begome quite vorried about you,' she remarked. 'I cennot t'ink vot is de metter mid you des pars' few tays. You haf develop' a nervous twitch an' you look zo peeky.'

That is an absurd exaggeration of her accent, so I shall not attempt further renderings of it. As she is quite an intelligent woman, and has been a refugee here since 1933, she actually speaks pretty good English for a German Jewess.

Naturally I don't want to put the idea into her head that I've got bats in the belfry, so I did my best to pull myself together, and simply said: 'You know quite well that I've been sleeping badly, lately. I'm only looking a bit off-colour because I had another restless night.'

What a masterpiece of understatement! With the aid of a triple bromide I got off all right; but I woke about half-past one, and I knew instantly that the Thing was outside the window again.

I wonder if I can bring myself to describe it? Anyhow I must try. But first I must explain how it comes about that I know it to be there in spite of the blackout.

Down here in Wales people are supposed to observe the A.R.P. regulations as strictly as elsewhere, but we are over three miles from the village, and there is no-one to enforce them. I don't think the Boche has ever dropped a bomb within thirty or forty miles of Llanferdrack, so when I came down here after two-and-a-half years of war I found that everyone had got pretty slack about such matters.

The room I occupy used to be the library – it still is for that matter – and I was glad that Helmuth had chosen it for me, as it makes a splendidly spacious bed-sitting-room, and as I am very fond of reading I like being surrounded with rows and rows of books. It must be close on forty feet long and has big bay windows at both ends. Those to the south have a glorious view over miles of wild country-side, and the middle one, being a glass-panelled door, gives me easy access to the garden.

All six windows of the room were originally furnished only with brocade pelmets, and hanging drapes that do not draw. On the garden side blackout curtains were added soon after the beginning of the war, but as the room was rarely used it was evidently not considered worthwhile to do anything about the north windows, because they cannot be seen from outside the building and look out onto a courtyard.

When Helmuth had the room prepared for me last March, as a glorified bed-sit, I suppose material was already getting scarce; so instead of having proper curtains fitted to each of the three windows on the courtyard side he had a big piece of brown stuff rigged up, which is drawn right across the bay at night. But it is a good six inches too short, so when there is a bright moon its light seeps in underneath and forms a broad band along the floor.

It is that damned strip of moonlight that gives me such appalling jitters. Actually it is three strips, as the mullions between the windows throw great black shadows that divide it into sections. Of course it is not the moonlight itself that unnerves me but – No! It's no good. I can't do it. I've broken out in a muck sweat at the very thought of what I see. I must think of something else . . .

Madagascar! There was good news today on the wireless. It is cheering to know that despite all Hitler can do we still have enough punch left, and a long enough arm, to land a blow so far afield. Ever since those filthy little yellow men overran Malaya it has been quite on the cards that they would have a go at South Africa, and if the Vichy French had let them occupy the island it would have made a perfect base from which to launch an invasion of the Union.

Thank goodness it looks now as if we have put paid to that one in advance. The report says that at dawn today British naval and military forces arrived off the north-west coast of the island, landed in Courier Bay, and proceeded inland across the neck of the isthmus towards the naval base at Diego Suarez.

Well, good luck to them. How I wish I were there, instead of here! Of course, naval aircraft must have been used to cover the landing; slow, unwieldy old kites compared with the types I used to fly. Still, I'd cheerfully take up even a Gladiator against the enemy, rather than have to face this loathsome, inhuman thing that haunts the courtyard, and has recently been trying to find its way into this room.

How do I know that? I cannot say. But something inside myself tells me positively that it is so. That something can only be a supersensory apparatus which, to give it its medical name, is called man's higher consciousness; but old-fashioned people would say it was my spirit – or soul – that, knowing itself to be in danger, sends me these frantic warnings.

As I was brought up to be an atheist, the last thing I should have admitted to, up to the age of eighteen, was that I had a soul; but since then my horizons have broadened a lot; and only yesterday, on arguing matters out with myself, I reached the conclusion that, logically, one must accept the eternal verities. That too, even in these materialistic times, is still a fundamental belief held by the vast majority of educated, as well as uneducated, people.

Judging by those I met during the two-and-a-half years that I was free of Helmuth's tutelage, genuine atheists must be very rare. Most of the young men I knew were pretty hard cases – they had to be or they would have cracked under the strain – but most of them became quite offended when sometimes, for the fun of getting up an argument, I suggested that they had no souls. To have agreed with me would have been to degrade themselves to the level of animals – or rather, a bag of salts and a few buckets of water kept going only by a series of chemical reactions – and, in their heart of hearts, they were convinced that they possessed some intrinsic quality which lifts mankind above all other species of creation.

That makes it all the more curious that most people these days rarely think about their souls. But, I suppose, if they did for any length of time it would interfere with the innumerable petty interests of their daily lives.

Nearly everybody will readily admit that they believe in some form of after-life. But they take it for granted that God cannot possibly be the sort of jealous, sacrifice-loving, tyrannical potentate depicted in the Old Testament, and that the fiery-furnace version of Hell was kept going by the Churches only as a convenient means of blackmailing the laity. When they do think of such matters they visualise the Creator as a nice old gentleman with a long white beard, who invariably speaks English, and confidently anticipate that when their time is up here they will be given a pretty reasonable deal as a start off in some new existence.

As for the Devil, they never give a thought to him at all – except when it comes to discussing possible costumes for the Four Arts Ball. Neither, I confess, did I, until I suddenly found myself in the situation of a rabbit who sees a ferret with red eyes and bared teeth coming after him.

One thing is certain. In these days, the vast majority of people live out their lives without bothering to propitiate the Deity, yet nothing of this kind ever catches up with them. Sooner or later, though, they have all got to die; and, maybe, when they do they will meet with a rude awakening. If so, perhaps I really ought to consider myself fortunate in being forced to thrash out these problems now.

All the same I would give anything, at the moment, to be one of those countless thousands who are entirely wrapped up in fighting Hitler, or even a charwoman scrubbing floors and queueing up for rations. But I am not. I am either going nuts or, long before my proper time, I have been brought face to face with the grim things that come and go on the borders of eternal night.

Later

I broke off to write again to Julia. I know that war charities and her billetees must keep her frightfully busy, and at the best of times she was never good about writing regularly; but I do think that she might have replied by now to the letter I wrote her early in April. That was just after the two consecutive nights upon which I first 'saw things'. I said nothing about that but asked her to come down to see me, because I wanted to talk it over with her. She is the only person I know with whom I could discuss such matters without her getting the idea that I am going mad. But after those two nights the visitations ceased, so I began to think that I must have been suffering from nightmares – until things started to happen again at the beginning of this month.

Why I didn't follow up my first letter with another, several days ago, I now cannot think; but I suppose this business has made my wits a bit woolly. Anyhow, this time I haven't minced matters. I told her bluntly that I believe this place to be haunted and that I am scared out of my wits. I asked her to keep that under her hat and to come down here as a matter of the utmost urgency. With luck she'll be here tomorrow; but I've still got to get through tonight. I must try not to think of that, though; so I had better keep my mind busy trying to prove to myself that I really am still sane.

I wonder why it is that, apart from practising Spiritualists on the one hand and professional fortune-tellers on the other, it is rare to hear of anyone these days who can claim to have had any actual experience of the supernatural?

The falling off in the practice of religion no doubt explains it to some extent; but I am inclined to think that the general decline in psychic perception is more largely due to modern conditions, in which the daily fight for existence compels the vast majority to occupy themselves almost exclusively with material matters.

In its waking state the human brain normally picks up and registers the thoughts conveyed by any voice within its range of hearing. Experiments have shown that while in a hypnotic sleep it will also react to orders whispered in too low a tone for it to catch when awake. And mental telepathy, examples of which are known to most people, show that it is capable of picking up thoughts which have not been sent out by the human voice at all. It is therefore clear that part of the brain consists of a radio receiving set.

But a radio will pick up from the ether only the signals given out on the wavelength to which it is adjusted. And anyone can appreciate how vastly different the mentality of modern man must be from that of his counterpart of a thousand, or even a hundred, years ago.

Perforce the minds of men and women of all ages have been largely filled with their daily occupations: food, sex, family and home; but to these in modern times have been added an immense variety of anxieties and distractions.

To begin with, people are now much more generally looked up to for their money than for their real worth, so more of their time is given to endeavouring to make a good income. Moreover, in order to give the appearance of being well off, it is the rule rather than the exception for them to take advantage of the modern credit system and live on anticipated earnings, so their worry over money is all the greater.

In the past the majority never left the towns or villages in which they were born; now a great part of the population shifts to new places of abode every few years, either on account of a change in employment or fluctuation in fortune. Each move brings the anxieties attendant on finding and furnishing new living accommodation.

Clothes were formerly mainly for utility and the same garments were often worn for years at a stretch; now even the masses regard a certain smartness of appearance as a necessity, but fashions are constantly changing and the average woman spends hundreds of hours each year harassed by the question as to how she can best dress well yet continue to live within her means.

The superseding of individual craftsmanship by the manufacture of machine-made goods has robbed the working classes of their security of employment. In the old days every youngster was brought up to a trade and a good honest workman could always be sure of keeping a roof over his head; now, in peacetime, the unemployed are numbered by the million, and for them there is the crushing anxiety that if they cannot somehow manage to find the rent they will be thrown out in the street.

Even the people who have jobs never know how long they will be able to keep them; strikes, lock-outs, foreign competition, new inventions, financial crises – all matters over which they have little or no control – are an ever-present menace to the security of managements and workers alike.

Then there are the countless time-occupying distractions that our forefathers never knew: a newspaper every morning to fill the mind with fresh ideas, cheap travel bringing the seaside within easy reach of every home, games taught at school and sport developed into a vast national industry, cinemas, theatres and concert-halls in every town, radio programmes blaring forth night and day, limitless fiction and cheap magazines, crossword puzzles and football pools – and now, of course, this accursed war.

Up to Napoleonic times, at least, comparatively small professional navies and armies did all the fighting that was necessary, while the bulk of the people continued undisturbed in their normal occupations; but now war disrupts the lives of whole populations and involves everyone in countless new activites, anxieties and tribulations, so that their minds become more heavily drugged than ever with what they consider to be the imperative necessity of the moment.

I have not been endeavouring to prove to myself that in the past people, on the whole, lived happier lives, although I think a good case could be made for that, and certainly for one that they enjoyed a far greater measure of security before the industrial revolution took them from the land.

I have simply set down my reasons for believing that up to about a hundred years ago they had ample time for quiet reflection and, in consequence, thought much more about the mystery of creation, of good and evil, and of the things of the spirit generally; so that the receiving apparatus of their minds was automatically tuned in to pick up those strange vibrations that come from the other side. Whereas most moderns seldom have the leisure to contemplate the eternal, and on the rare occasions that they do their apparatus is so illattuned, from lack of use, that it fails to register anything. And that it is this which accounts for so few people of the present century having met with any psychic experience.

Yet there are still occasions when some people suddenly find themselves tuned in to some dark station of the Otherworld. That is entirely contrary to all that I was brought up to believe. But I have got to believe it now. Somehow I have got to convince myself of that absolutely. I must – otherwise I shall end up in a strait-jacket.

The light is failing now. I had better ring for Taffy to draw the curtains. I wonder if Julia will come tomorrow? But, idiot that I am, how can she? My letter can't possibly get to her at Queensclere until Thursday morning. That means I have two more nights to face before there can be any hope of getting me away from here.

Oh, God! How can I bear it?

Wednesday, 6th May

I got quite a pleasant surprise when I looked in the mirror to shave this morning. My face was always on the thin side but it has lost that lean, drawn look it had yesterday; my grey eyes are bright again and the heavy pouches underneath them have entirely disappeared. They always say that the recuperative powers of youth are remarkable, and it is certainly wonderful what a good night's sleep has done for me.

Deb refuses to allow me to take more than one triple bromide, even when I have had a succession of bad nights; but last night I grabbed the bottle from her and swallowed a couple before she could stop me. Whether it was the effect of the double dose, or that the brute that haunts the courtyard decided to have a go at some other window, I don't know; but I slept like a log from ten o'clock right round till eight-thirty, and I am feeling a new man in consequence.

It is another lovely day, too. What fun it would be if I could go for a climb up the mountain; but that is out of the question. Helmuth used to take me climbing up in Scotland when I was a boy, and I loved it. He had promised to take me to Switzerland, and I was bitterly disappointed in 1939 when he decided that we had better go to Mull again instead, owing to the uncertainty of the European situation. As usual, he proved right, and the outbreak of war occurred while we were up there.

That last summer holiday was fun all the same, even though it differed little from its predecessors. There are grouse and quite good deer-stalking on the island, and mackerel fishing round the coast. Having our own boat always enabled us to go on exciting expeditions, and we got in some thrilling climbs on the mainland. I expect Helmuth misses his climbing too, but these days he is always so occupied with the estate, and gingering up the tenants to do better in the 'Grow More Food' campaign, that he doesn't get much time for anything else.

I don't know why I am rambling on like this, but I find it a pleasant occupation to put down my thoughts just as they come into my head. I only wish that they were all such pleasant ones. Unfortunately, I find it impossible to keep the bad ones out of my mind for long, and I am still damnably worried about myself.

What is more, I started this journal for a purpose, and I must not let the fact that nothing happened last night lull me into a false sense of security. I have still got to convince myself that I am perfectly normal, and that there really are other 'gaps in the curtain' through which people sometimes catch a glimpse of the unknown, as well as the one which has opened to disclose such a monstrous thing to me.

I think any reasonable person would agree that, while it is fair enough to question the validity of any particular supernatural manifestation, there is far too much evidence of the existence of occult forces to maintain that they are nothing but a product of man's imagination. To do so means not only the denial of a great part of the Gospels and all other sacred literature, as well as countless well-authenticated records of miraculous happenings in historic times – the admission of any single one of which as fully proven automatically proves the whole case; it also implies a wilful disregard of modern scientific investigation into the qualities and capabilities of the brain, soul, mind, spirit – or whatever one chooses to call it – that animates every human being and gives to each a unique personality.

But before I use the words 'soul' or 'spirit' again, perhaps I had better attempt to define what I mean by them. I take them as designating not only the something extra to the physical body that all religions teach lives on after we die, but also that part of our consciousness which leaves us in no doubt whether a course is right or wrong, and, at times, enables us to become perceptive of sights, sounds and smells outside the range of our normal senses.

Although scientists have not yet obtained conclusive proof that the soul survives after death, they have gone a long way towards it. Emotions can now be registered and emanations invisible to the human eye can be photographed, showing that while alive we radiate an intangible something which disappears at death. People's hearts have stopped beating during operations; others have been drowned or asphyxiated, and they have been pronounced physically dead; yet scientific treatment has brought them to life again. For a brief space something must have gone out of them but, on its home again being rendered tenable, it returned.

That means that, quite apart from faith and wishful thinking, there is a good case for survival; and there is a far better one for the existence of supernormal powers in the living.

Thought-transference is, I suppose, the simplest form in which the non-physical manifests itself, and with some people it is almost a day-to-day occurrence. Married couples who have lived in unity for a number of years often find that anticipating one another's thoughts becomes almost a habit; and it is by no means unusual for friends who have not seen one another for a long time each to write to the other on the same day.

Death warnings are also far from unusual. I remember reading a book by the great French scientist Camille Flammarion, in which he recorded scores of cases of people who, while employed in some quite normal occupation, suddenly broke off to exclaim that they felt convinced that a near relative had died, and the following day brought confirmation of their second sight.

Then there are the many instances in which for no explicable reason people wake up in the middle of the night with a feeling that something is wrong, and on going downstairs find that the house is on fire; although the sound of crackling and the smell of smoke could not possibly have been perceptible to their normal senses, even if they had been awake.

Again, there is scarcely ever a big railway disaster or liner lost at sea without someone who should have travelled on the train or ship having decided not to do so at the last moment. When questioned such people often assert that they had every intention of travelling and that having failed to do so caused them considerable inconvenience by upsetting long-standing arrangements; yet, on reaching the station or dock, they felt an imperative compulsion to postpone their journey.

Everyone must have heard of the case of that type by which the late Marquess of Dufferin and Ava escaped being dashed to death in a falling lift, while *en post* as British Ambassador in Paris. In that affair the unmistakably psychic nature of the warning was underlined by the fact of its having been conveyed to him by seeing an apparition. He vouched for that himself, and one can hardly question the veracity of such a man as the late Lord Dufferin.

From Saul's grim transactions with the Witch of Endor to the strange events preceding the death of the late Mr Justice Macarthy, history, both ancient and modern, gives innumerable instances of people seeing ghosts, many of which in recent times have been authenticated by doctors, magistrates and other trustworthy witnesses.

But why should I labour the point? It can be only because my unsettled mind craves so desperately for further support to a conviction that it has already formed. I really have no doubt that apparitions are at times seen by people who have never attempted to contact occult forces, or have even given them a thought.

It is possible that, owing to my present poor state of health, I may recently have become the victim of hallucinations. I admit that. But of one fact I am positive. I was perfectly sane and healthy when I was a boy, and at the age of eight I saw a ghost myself.

Must stop now – time for me to go out for my airing.

Afternoon

I have few dislikes in the way of food and do not take much interest in it, although my large frame calls for quite a bit of stoking up, so I have a very hearty appetite. Generally I demolish anything that is put in front of me and hardly notice what I am eating.

But I must say that I enjoyed my lunch today. Of course, down here in Wales, apart from tea and sugar, no-one even pretends to accept rationing. The home farm provides us with as much meat, poultry, butter, cream and eggs as we could wish for; the lake gives us fish and the garden an abundance of fruit and vegetables. If we did not use the stuff that is brought in the outdoor staff would only sell it to the local tradesmen – so what the hell! I lunched off duck and green peas followed by the first hot-house strawberries with plenty of fresh cream.

Anyhow, I'm feeling good – better than I have at any time since the recurrence of the trouble, which was on the night of the 30th of April. In fact, I am feeling so much fitter than I did yesterday that I have decided that I am now capable of making myself describe the Thing that makes me doubt my sanity.

I have already given an account of the inadequate blackout arrangements in this room, and of how the moonlight coming through the windows of the north bay throws three broad bands of silvery radiance on the floor, this side of the curtain that cuts off the arc of the bay at night.

I should add that after the second of the two visitations early in April, I asked both Deb and Helmuth to have the curtain lengthened so that it reached the floor. Deb said with some asperity that she had neither the necessary material nor the coupons to get any, and that anyway it was not her job, so I had better get Helmuth to give instructions about it to the housekeeper. My Great-aunt Sarah has lived here most of her life and her companion, Miss Nettelfold, does the housekeeping for us. Helmuth said that he would speak to her about it; but either he is so busy that he forgot, or else it is she who has forgotten to do anything about it.

On May the 1st – that was the morning after the second bout began – I reminded Helmuth of his promise; but still nothing has been done. Perhaps I chose a bad moment to bother him, as he seemed very offhand. He said he always slept with the curtains of his room drawn back, so that when there was a moon it often shone right in on him, and he really could not believe that a little strip of moonlight on the floor could cause me any serious inconvenience.

Since then I have not liked to mention the matter to him again, as I don't see how I can press for the job to be done unless I give the real reason why I am so anxious to have those extra six inches put on the curtain; and nothing would induce me to tell him that.

I have spent hours wondering how I could lengthen it myself; but the snag is that there is nothing here I could use except some of the cushion covers, the bed linen or my underclothes, and if I started cutting any of those up it would be taken as a sign that I was crazy.

So the curtain is unaltered and the moon still throws those three damnable splodges of light across the floor. The gap between the floor and the curtain is not much more than six inches, but as the light comes in at an angle the bands it makes are very much wider, and they reach to within four feet of my bed.

Thank God they come no nearer, or I should probably lose my nerve completely and scream the house down. Even as it is, it is all I can do to prevent myself from yelling for help. I would, if I were certain that whoever came to my assistance would see the same thing as I do. But the hellish part of it is that they might not. Then I should know that what I see is only a figment of my imagination, and that I really am going mad. Perhaps that is the case, but if so I am determined not to let anyone suspect it as long as I have a will of my own.

Now for the apparently absurd and mortifying truth. I have allowed myself to be reduced to a nervous wreck simply through seeing shadow. But what makes it? And why does it dance its devil dance on that accursed band of moonlight?

There are no trees in the courtyard, so it cannot be a waving branch that throws that animated black patch. It cannot be a person or a bird, as it is not the right shape, and its movements are unlike those that either would make. Yet something does. Something that comes out of the night and climbs up onto my window-sill, so that its dark bulk is silhouetted by the moon.

Owing to the comparative narrowness of the band of light I can never see the whole shadow at one time; but it seems to be thrown by a large ball-like body with a number of waving limbs. To be honest, I have come to the conclusion that it is an octopus.

I know it must sound as if I am a raving lunatic, to say that I believe an octopus is trying to get in at my window; but there it is. Unless I tell the truth to myself the whole point of keeping this journal is lost, and to continue it would be futile. As, too, I have never even seen the Thing itself, it must appear as if I am a pretty wet type to allow myself to be frightened by a shadow, however inexplicable its presence where no shadow should be, and however sinister its form and movements; but that is very far from being the worst part of the business.

The terrifying thing is, that the brute is not only haunting but hunting me. It moves up and down, up and down, in stealthy little runs, floundering from one window-sill to another and back again. And I know that in a blind, fumbling way it is trying to get in.

Yet even that is not the ultimate horror. It cannot possibly be a real octopus; a beast that one could slash at with a knife, and, if one were strong enough, blind and kill. It must be some intangible malefic force that has succeeded in materialising itself in hideous animal form.

Of that I am certain. For the sight of its shadow does not fill me with a normal, healthy fear; it makes my eyes start from my head and my limbs become weak as water. Its effect upon me is both different and worse than if I were brought face to face with a man-eating tiger. That is why I am positive that it can only be something unutterably Evil.

Once I wake and see that unholy weaving pattern of darkness, furtively moving to and fro across the silvery band of light, I simply cannot drag my eyes away from it. Sometimes I try to force myself to ignore it, but I never succeed for more than a moment. I long to put my head under the bedclothes; but I dare not. If I did the Thing might get in while I was not looking, and be upon me before I even had a chance to scream for help.

So I am compelled to lie there sweating with terror, my gaze riveted upon it and dreading every moment to hear one of the window-panes crack under its pressure; until at last the moon goes down and its foul shadow is blotted out. Only then can I relax. Sometimes, if I am lucky, towards morning I fall into the troubled sleep of mental exhaustion; at others my tired brain revolves round endless futile speculations, until the pale light of dawn creeps beneath the curtain.

But what is the Thing? Why does it come? Is it a Satanic entity that has battened and waxed strong upon thought-forms, thrown out at the time of some abominable crime committed long ago in the nearby ruin? If so, why is it not content to remain there haunting the scene of the crime? Why should it leave its lair and try to invade this modern house? Or can it be a monster that has been deliberately ordered up out of the Pit to attack me? If so, again why? And by whom?

Surely pretty well anyone would be more worthy of the Devil's attention than I am in my present state? Yet I know that it is I, and no-one else, that the brute is out to get. Sometimes its shadow blurs and quivers a little, and I know then, just as surely as I know that my name is Toby Jugg, that it is trembling with a kind of repulsive lust. Some chord deep in my subconscious vibrates to the waves it sends out, and my flesh creeps anew from the positive knowledge that it is activated by one single, all-absorbing thought – the urge to wrap itself about my body, suck out my soul and destroy me utterly. But why? Why? Why? Why me? Why me? Why me?

Later

Half an hour ago I had worked myself up into such a state that I could not go on. I am feeling a bit steadier now, and in the meantime I have reconsidered a few points.

Firstly; can the brute conceivably be an honest-to-God flesh-and-muscle octopus that lives in the lake? As the lake is very deep in places, and it apparently surfaces only at night, it might have inhabited a rocky cave on the lake-bottom for years without anyone being any the wiser. The Loch Ness monster is said to lead that sort of existence and is spotted coming up for air only once in a blue moon. And this creature may not be a true octopus, but another unknown species of primitive lake-dweller.

As against that, octopi are normally ocean-dwellers, and I have never heard of one being seen in a river or lake. Llanferdrack is in Radnor, and on the eastern slope of the Cambrian mountains – over forty miles from the sea – so how could it have got here? I don't know the age to which octopi live, but such low forms of creation often survive to great ages. If octopi do, this one might have been caught generations ago and brought here by one of the old Lords Llanferdrack. But captive octopi that are kept in aquariums have to be supplied with salt-water, and the lake is fresh. Moreover, it seems highly improbable that any species of octopi is capable of coming up out of the water and crawling any distance on land.

On balance, I suppose this theory is remotely possible, but only if the brute is some form of missing link; and I regard that as most unlikely.

My original idea, that the brute is a Satanic entity and owes its origin to some dark deed that took place long ago in the ruins, seems far more plausible. This hideous modern house was built only in the 1890s and it backs onto the southern side of the original Llanferdrack Castle. Some of the rooms in the Castle are still more or less habitable. In fact they are hardly less so than those of the house, as the latter has never been modernised and lacks most of the amenities – we still have to use oil lamps, and coal or wood for cooking as well as the fires, neither electricity or gas ever having been laid on.

But the part of the Castle that is still in fair preservation overlooks the lake, and abuts on the east wing of the house, in which Great-aunt Sarah has her quarters; whereas the west wing, where I am installed, backs onto the ruined Keep. The library is separated from it only by the courtyard, so it seems a fair bet that my enemy has his lair in one of the dark, rat-infested dungeons beneath it, where in ancient times unfortunate wretches were tortured to death.

My second new theory is based on the assumption that, although the Lord of Evil is said to be intelligent, it does not necessarily follow that his lesser minions are so too. Indeed, tradition has it that they are cunning and persistent but far from clever, and have often been tricked by the wit of man.

Thus, to the lower forms of Satanic energy one soul may appear as desirable meat as any other. If so, this foulness that comes by night is probably incapable of distinguishing between myself and a country bumpkin like my servant Taffy – or, for that matter, between my very ordinary personality and the heroic spirit of Mr Churchill. Perhaps it just gropes and gropes, patiently and tirelessly seeking for a suitable victim, and my present parlous state, together with the mental loneliness that afflicts me here, renders me peculiarly vulnerable to such an attack.

For the first time in my life I have real cause to regret that I was brought up as what the Church would term a heretic. If I had not broken away from the domination of Helmuth when I did I would still know next to nothing of religious matters; but during the two-

and-a-half years that I was free of his influence I read quite extensively to acquire information on what he would term 'the superstitions of the ignorant masses'.

It was a perfectly natural reaction that I should interest myself in the one and only subject which had previously been barred to me; and the fact that it was he who had inculcated in me the habit of serious reading gives a cynically humorous twist to the first use I made of my freedom to read what I wished.

Unfortunately, it is by no means easy to make up later for an almost complete lack of the type of knowledge that most children imbibe at their mother's knee, and all through a normal adolescence; so I find myself far from well-equipped to reason out these questions, the answers to which may mean for me the difference between having to admit to myself that I am going mad and finding a logical basis upon which to retain faith in my sanity. Nevertheless, I mean to stick to it; and I shall attempt to analyse the evidence supporting my belief that I saw a ghost when I was a small boy, first thing tomorrow.

Tomorrow! But first I have to get through tonight. So far this month I have had to face that ghastly ordeal four nights out of six. Last night I was blessed with a respite. Dare I hope to be granted one for two nights running?

No; I fear there is little chance of that. This month the attacks have been of much longer duration than they were on those first two nights early in April; and each time the Thing comes it seems more determined to get at me. During those early visits it came and went at intervals, so they seem to have been only in the nature of a reconnaissance. But now the attack is on in earnest. Although I cannot hear it I know, instinctively, that it keeps throwing its weight against the window-panes with ever-increasing violence. I would to God I could believe that its failure to appear last night could be taken as a sign that it has decided to abandon its efforts; but I cannot.

Last night, too, I managed to snatch that extra triple bromide from Deb, so perhaps the brute did come, but the double dose was sufficient to prevent its malefic influence from waking me. Deb will take good care that I get no chance to trick her tonight, though, so I had better try to resign myself to another night of hell.

I wonder whether I shall be awake or asleep when it comes? On four occasions my subconscious has registered the malefic force that the brute radiates, causing me to wake suddenly from a sound sleep and, on starting up, to find it there. On the other two I have been awake already.

I hardly know which is the worst. In the first case there is the appalling shock of being called on to face another ordeal unexpectedly, while in the second there is the added terror of anticipation that I suffer during those awful moments before I can bring myself to look round and actually see the shadow. I think the latter is really the more horrible of the two.

At such times I suddenly become conscious that a dank, raw chill is gradually pervading the room, and it becomes very silent – as silent as the grave. Then I get a definite physical reaction – just as definite as a whiff of rotting fish making one want to vomit. I know then, for certain, that my fears are justified – that this incredibly evil thing has clambered up onto the window-sill, and is once more searching for a way to get in. Instinctively my eyes turn towards the floor, and there is the big, black undulating shadow that it causes, sprawled across the band of moonlight.

I feel my heart beating like a sledge-hammer, and I have to bite my tongue to prevent myself from letting out an hysterical scream. I would give everything I possess to be free, if only for two minutes, from the physical bonds that hold me; but I know that, short of rousing the house, there is no alternative to my continuing to lie there suffering the agonies of the damned.

If, at the first warning touch of that awful cold, I could only spring from my bed and rush from the room! If I could only sit up, press a switch, and flood the room with light! If, even, I could only reach out and turn on my radio-gramophone! But such acts are all beyond my capabilities. Even in the daytime I am unable to rise unaided from my chair, and by night I am a prisoner in my bed!

What ill have I ever done to anyone, that I should be condemned to this now that my back is broken, and partial paralysis makes me a helpless cripple?

Thursday, 7th May

Nothing happened again last night, thank God; and Julia should be here today. Even if it means upsetting Helmuth, and a certain amount of inconvenience, I am sure she will have me moved when she hears what I have to say.

I shall try to persuade her to let me go back with her to Queens-clere. She'll oppose that because of the number of air-raids that they get down there in Kent; but, war or no war, it would be lovely to be living in the same house with her again.

Writing that reminds me that yesterday I had meant to go into the matter of the ghost that I saw when I was a small boy, but put off doing so because I suddenly decided that I felt up to setting down on paper a description of the Thing that is haunting me here. That affair took place not very long after I first went to live with Julia, and her knowing all about it is one of the things which will enable me to talk to her of my present plight, without giving her the idea that I've gone nuts.

I always think of this ghost as 'my burglar', because that is what I believed it to be at the time; and no doubt I should have continued to believe that up to this very day had it not been for a quite unexpected encounter several years later; but I will record that in its proper place.

At the age of eight years and four months I lost both my father and grandfather. They were killed together in October 1929, having gone up in the prototype of a new airliner to inspect her performance for themselves; but something went wrong with the wretched kite and she crashed.

I never knew my mother, as she died in giving me birth. From her picture and all accounts she must have been very lovely, and she was a rising film star when my father first met her in Hollywood, but she gave up her career when she married him. She was an American of Norwegian extraction and I evidently take after her. My hair and moustache are a shade darker than the red-gold curl of hers that we found in a locket among father's things; but I have her large grey eyes and straight features. Like her, I am tall and strongly built, and her Norwegian blood must have come through very strongly, as my friends in the R.A.F. nicknamed me 'The Viking'.

Anyway, my father's death left me an orphan. Whether I have any living relatives on my mother's side I have no idea. I have never heard of any, so she may have been an orphan too. On my father's side, my grandmother had been dead for years and grandfather had only one sister, my Great-aunt Sarah. She never married, as her fiancé, young Llanferdrack, who owned this place, was drowned just before the happy day; and she has lived here mourning him in seclusion most of her life. But the poor old thing's romance going wrong unhinged her mind and she is a harmless half-wit, so there was never any question of my being placed in her charge.

Apart from Great-aunt Sarah my only living relative is my father's younger brother, Uncle Paul; so the Trustees decided that I should go to live with him. I have since gathered that there was quite a bit of argument about it, because Uncle Paul was regarded as the black sheep of the family, and neither my grandfather nor father approved of him at all; but, naturally, I knew nothing of that at the time, and he offered to have me. I think the thing that really decided the Trustees to accept his offer was that about a year earlier he had married and at last appeared to be settling down.

All this seems quite irrelevant to the affair I started out to write about; but having begun this journal I find it rather soothing just to ramble on, setting down any thoughts and memories that come into my head, and, after all, it is only for my own edification, so why shouldn't I write anything I damn well choose?

To continue, then. After the double funeral Uncle Paul took me down to his house at Kew and presented me to Julia. Of course, as his wife she was my aunt by marriage, but I never called her aunt, because she said that first evening she would rather that I didn't. She said that when I was grown up there wouldn't really be much difference in our ages and that she felt much too young to be an aunt to anybody; so she would much prefer that I thought of her as a big sister.

I found that a bit surprising, as she seemed very grown-up to me; but it made things rather cosy, and she was quite the loveliest person I had ever seen. When she tucked me up in bed that night she kissed me, and having no female relatives I was not accustomed to that sort of thing.

Father used to go abroad a great deal on business trips and even when he was at home I didn't see much of him. I was still too young for him to have me downstairs when he was entertaining and on most days when he got back from the city he just dashed upstairs to my nursery for a few minutes, then changed and went out; so my world practically consisted of dear old Nanny Trotter and other nannies and their children that we met in the park.

Of course there was Miss Stiggins too, a dry old spinster who came to give me lessons every morning, but she never kissed me and I don't suppose that it would have registered if she had; whereas that first kiss from Julia remained an unforgettable landmark in my young life. Her lips were as soft as swansdown against my cheek and she smelled of some delicious perfume; from that moment I absolutely worshipped her.

Julia was then twenty and had been married nearly a year. Uncle Paul met her in Rome, and although she was an Italian she already spoke English so well that she did not seem like a foreigner, and her faint accent made her speech only more fascinating to listen to. She was medium tall and very slim. Her eyes were black with long lashes and she had the warm, rich colouring of the south. Her face was a long oval, her lips full and very red. She wore her dark hair parted in the middle and it fell smoothly to her shoulders, curling at the ends.

That first night, I remember, she was wearing a dress of oyster satin with a long, full skirt that swayed gently as she walked; as did also her pendant diamond earrings, which were the only jewels she had on. All her movements were smooth and graceful, and when she laughed it was lazily, her red lips opening to show two rows of strong little white teeth. I was still as innocent as a new-born babe and to me she seemed like an angel – a dark angel – come to life out of a story-book.

But I must get back to the matter of my 'burglar'. I had been living with Uncle Paul and Julia for about two months when the affair occurred. Their house at Kew seemed very strange to me at first, because it was so different from those in which I had been brought up; but Julia had a flair for decoration and I found her bright, modern rooms exciting after the much bigger but rather sombre ones to which I was accustomed.

The Willows was a suburban villa of the type that was built by the thousand during Queen Victoria's reign; a square three-storied building standing in its own small garden and one of a row of similar middle-class homes. Its front door opened onto a narrow hall with two rooms on each side of it, then continued on the left as a passage to the kitchen and on the right as a staircase leading straight up to the floors above. From the hall you could see the little half-landing where the stairs made a hairpin bend, then disappeared from sight. On the first floor there were four bedrooms and a bathroom, and another flight of stairs immediately above the lower ones led up to the servants' rooms and box-room at the top of the house.

Two months is a long time when one is only eight, so to me the tragedy that had deprived me of my father and grandfather was already ancient history. As I have said, I saw very little of my father, and of my grandfather I saw even less. They were to me Olympian figures who, apart from brief routine visits, impinged upon my consciousness only when they descended from their grown-up heaven either to admonish me if I had been naughty or give me lovely presents.

Nanny Trotter told me that they had both gone to live with my beautiful mother in Jerusalem-the-Golden, which I took to be a still more remote paradise than that they had presumably enjoyed down here. She made it quite clear that they would never return and it did not take me very long to get accustomed to the idea that I should not see either of them again. Grandfather's beard had rather a nice smell, which I think was due to lavender-water, and father had a jolly laugh; but I cannot honestly say that I missed either of them very much.

Besides, there were a thousand new interests to fill my small mind – and, above all, Julia. She did not seem to have any friends in the neighbourhood – although people often came down from London to spend the evening with her and Uncle Paul – so she let me be with her for a large part of every day. Nanny Trotter had been installed at Kew to look after me, of course, but Miss Stiggins had been sacked, as it had been decided that I should go to a prep school after Christmas and that until then I need not do any lessons.

Julia took me shopping with her – which was very exciting, as I had hardly ever been in a shop before – and to the cinema, and several times up to London, where we lunched in restaurants and afterwards went to look at all sorts of lovely things in Bond Street. So with all these thrilling new experiences I had not a moment left to brood.

I record all this simply to show that when I saw the burglar I was not grieving for my father and full of morbid thoughts about death. I was a normal, healthy small boy having the time of his life and without a care in the world.

It happened about a fortnight before Christmas on one of Nanny Trotter's nights out. Julia had let me stay up a little later than usual and it was nearly seven o'clock before she packed me off to my bath with a promise that, as a treat, she would bring me up some orange jelly with my milk and biscuits.

I went up the first flight of stairs as usual, at a run, then turned the hairpin bend and took the next flight two at a time. I had the banisters on my left but was heading half right, as my room was the first on that side of the landing. As this was in December it was, of course, already dark; but the light on the landing in front of me had not yet been switched on, so it was lit only by the faint glow coming up from the hall below. I was still two steps from the top of the flight when something made me glance to my left.

As I was then only a little chap my head was not much above the level of the nearest banister rail and below the further one which served the flight of stairs running up to the second floor. What I saw stopped me dead in my tracks. For a moment I remained there, paralysed by sheer terror.

There was the figure of a man just opposite me on the upper stairs.

He was crouching down as though attempting to hide; but he had one white hand on the further banister rail. That gave the impression that he was poised there ready to make an instant dash up the stairs if discovered.

The horrifying thing about it was that as he crouched there his head was below his hand and on a level with my own. He was peering at me from between the banisters and his face was less than twelve inches from mine. The light was too dim for me to see his features clearly but his face was large, round and flabby with small dark pits for eyes. He made not the slightest sound or movement but just remained there staring at me with the sort of bestial ferocity that one might have expected to see on the face of Jack the Ripper.

What broke the tension after that awful, age-long moment I have no idea. Perhaps he moved first; or it may be that my heart, having temporarily stopped, started again, so that in an automatic reaction I let out a terrified yell. As I screamed and jerked myself away I caught just a glimpse of him, still crouched almost double, gliding swiftly up the stairs.

I use the word 'gliding' because when I was questioned afterwards I could not recall having heard his footsteps, or, indeed, any noise at all. Had I been older that would certainly have struck me as queer, since the dark outline of the figure had been squat but bulky, and, even if he was wearing rubber-soled shoes, a heavy man could hardly take a flight of stairs at the run without his footfalls being audible. At the time, and for long afterwards, I simply assumed that any noise he made must have been drowned by the sounds of my own wild flight.

Scared out of my wits, I bounded towards the half-landing, swerved round the bend of the stairs and literally flung myself down the lower flight to arrive sprawling in the hall, still gasping and yelling.

Almost simultaneously, like a scene in a French farce, three of the doors opened. Julia came running from her sitting-room, Uncle Paul from his study with a friend of his who happened to be with him, and Florrie, the little housemaid, from the dining-room, where she was laying the table for dinner. To complete the party, Cook arrived a second later from the kitchen still clutching a saucepan.

As they picked me up I shouted: 'There's a man upstairs! A burglar! A burglar!'

Then, trembling with shock and excitement, I burst into tears and flung myself into Julia's arms.

The two men armed themselves with golf clubs and went upstairs.

The women remained clustered about me in the hall anxiously listening for sounds of strife, but the only ones that reached us were the faint opening and shutting of doors.

Uncle Paul and his friend seemed to be away a long time, but at last they rejoined us. They said that they had searched every room, looked under all the beds and in all the cupboards, but they had not found the burglar, and as far as they could judge nothing had been taken or disturbed; so I must have imagined him.

'But I saw him!' I cried, repudiating the suggestion with indignation. 'He's a horrid, bald old man! He glared at me through the banisters and I thought he was going to spring at me. If he's not there now he must have got out onto the roof.'

Their attempts to reassure me were in vain. I flatly refused to go to bed until further search had been made. The burglar could not have come down the back stairs because there weren't any, so I feared that he must be lurking somewhere and might come creeping into my room while the grown-ups were having dinner.

To quiet my fears the attics and roof were searched; but without result. The moon had risen and in its light there was no place on the sloping tiles of that small, square house where a man could have remained hidden. As the gaps between the roof of The Willows and those of the houses on either side of it were far too wide for any man to jump, the only other possibility was that the burglar had got out of one of the second-floor windows and shinned down a drainpipe. I insisted that he must have done so and was, perhaps, hiding outside, waiting to return when we were all asleep.

Julia made the two men go out into the garden with torches. There were flower-beds all round the house and anyone coming down a drainpipe must have landed on one, but there was not a footmark to be seen on any of them.

My tears had long since dried, but I was still very excited and nothing could shake my conviction that I had seen a murderous-looking thug crouching on the stairs. However, nothing more could be done about it, so I allowed myself to be taken up to bed while Florrie got a special supper that Julia ate with me; then she read me to sleep.

Next morning, of course, the whole affair was gone into again, but no fresh light was thrown upon it, and with the approach of Christmas I ceased to think about it any more. It was not until nearly eleven years later that there came a sequel to this strange affair.

One day just as I was leaving the mess at Biggin Hill, after lunch, a trim-looking W.A.A.F. came up to me and said: 'Hello, Master Toby! Don't you remember me?'

She was rather a pert-looking blonde of about thirty, and her face was vaguely familiar, but I couldn't place her.

'I'm Florrie Meddows,' she said. 'I was housemaid at The Willows when you were a little boy. My, sir; how you've grown! But I would have known you anywhere. How's Mr and Mrs Jugg; in the pink, I hope?'

Of course, I recalled her then and we talked for a bit of old times. After a while she asked: 'Did you ever see any more spooks at The Willows?'

'Spooks!' I echoed. 'What on earth do you mean?'

'Why, ghosts, of course. Surely you remember the night when you scared us all stiff by insisting that you had seen a ghost?'

'You're mixing me up with someone else,' I laughed. 'I've never seen a ghost in my life.'

She shook her head. 'No, it was you all right. You came yelling downstairs fit to wake the dead. But I remember now, you thought it was a burglar; and I suppose your aunt, not wanting to frighten you, never told you different.'

At that the whole episode came back to my mind as clearly as though it had happened only the day before. 'I've certainly always thought it was a burglar,' I agreed in great surprise. 'Whatever makes you think it was a ghost?'

'Well, a human being couldn't have flown out of the window,' Florrie countered, 'or disappeared like that without leaving a single trace, could he? Besides, your uncle and aunt may not have let on to you about it, but they were nuts about Spiritualism. There was hardly a night when they had friends down from London that they didn't go in for table-turning, wall-rapping, and all that. It wasn't none of my business, and Cook and me just used to laugh about it, thinking them a bit cranky, till the night you gave us all such a fright. That made us think very different, knowing what we did; and we were both so scared that we gave notice first thing next morning. We'd have sacrificed our money and left there and then if it hadn't been for letting Mrs Jugg down over Christmas, and her promising not to hold any more séances while we were in the house. If it was a burglar you saw, Master Toby, then I'm a policeman and Hitler's my Aunt Fanny. No good ever comes of calling on the spirits, and it was through them doing that some horrid thing started to haunt the house.'

Friday, 8th May

Another quiet night, although rather a restless one, owing to Julia never having turned up yesterday evening, as I hoped she would. Perhaps she decided to put off her visit till today and then stay over the weekend.

Fortunately, I became so interested in writing the account of my 'burglar' that I continued at it after dinner, and that occupied my mind enough to prevent my fretting over her non-appearance until Deb settled me down for the night.

I had better finish it off now. Actually, there is little more to tell; and I find it difficult to doubt that Florrie Meddows' explanation of the vanishing without trace of the figure that I saw must be the true one.

People do not tell children ghost stories or give them books about ghouls and vampires to read. Tales of witches who turn princes into frogs and of giants who carry off princesses – yes; but anything to do with the after-life or the supernatural is taboo. Therefore, at the age of eight-and-a-half I can scarcely have known what the word 'ghost' implied, hence my immediate assumption that the thing I saw was a man.

It is this, I think, that gives the occurrence peculiar and outstanding weight as proof that astral bodies are at times visible to humans. Everyone else in that house knew what was going on there, so, if any of them had seen what I did, one might fairly argue that thinking about the séances had played Old Harry with their nerves, and that they had imagined it. But I could not possibly have done so, because before one can make a mental concept of anything it is essential to have some basic knowledge of it, and in my case this was entirely lacking.

The next time I saw Julia I tackled her about it. At first she hedged and pretended to have forgotten the whole affair; but when I told her about my meeting with Florrie she shrugged and said with her lazy smile: 'Of course it was an astral, darling. It's quite true that when you first came to us at The Willows we used to hold séances now and then. But only for fun; and after you saw your "burglar" we were much too frightened ever to hold one again. When Paul had searched the house we knew that it couldn't have been a man who had scared you, and the only possible explanation was that one of our controls must be hovering about in visual form. Naturally, as you were only a child, we concealed the truth from you and tried to make you forget the fright you'd had as quickly as we could. I don't mind admitting now that we were pretty scared ourselves, and I was thankful that we had already arranged to move from The Willows soon after Christmas.'

I tried to get her to tell me about the séances they had held, but she insisted that there was really nothing to tell, as she hadn't proved a very good medium and, apart from the totally unexpected appearance of my burglar, the results had been disappointing; so I did not press her. The important point is that she fully confirmed all that Florrie had said.

I'm glad that I took the trouble to write all this out, as recalling the affair in detail makes me as nearly certain as anyone can be that I did see a supernatural manifestation when I was a healthy, innocent child; and that gives real, solid support to my belief that I am not imagining things now.

However, the fact that I have good grounds for supposing that apparitions do appear to humans raises again the question of Good and Evil; and I would like to clear my mind a bit on that. It is an axiom that nothing happens without a cause; so who pulls the wires behind the scenes? Is it always the Devil, or sometimes God? What is the object of such operations? And can humans really command spirits to do their will?

If the manifestation occurs without our seeking it, is some power beyond earth attempting to influence us, or could it have been sent by some evilly disposed human? Again, if through a medium, or the exercise of our own will employed in some ancient mystery, we provoke the supernatural occurrence, is it, in the first place, really a response from some loved one who has passed over and, in the second, a minor entity compelled to obey us; or, in both cases, have the forces of Evil accepted our rash invitation to emerge from some dark and hideous cavern of the underworld?

All these questions seethe in my tired brain when I cannot sleep at night, and fear that at any moment instinct may again make my flesh begin to creep at the approach of the Thing in the courtyard.

At least, as a starting point, I feel justified in assuming that the Otherworld must be another dimension of this one, and that its denizens have the power, given suitable conditions, to impinge upon our consciousness.

There seems, too, no reason to suppose that the will of a spirit in a physical body is necessarily weaker than that of a spirit in limbo. So the former may prove equal to forcing the latter to do its bidding; and that, no doubt, is the secret of the supernormal powers with which all the great occultists have been credited. From the same premises, though, should the disembodied entity prove stronger than the will of the living person who has conjured it up, woe betide the occultist; for it would then be he who would find himself the slave of some strange, potent, and almost certainly malignant force.

By worldly and academic standards Florrie Meddows is a person of the lower orders and mean intelligence; yet surely she voiced the sound sense and clear vision so often inherited through many generations of humble folk when she said to me: 'No good ever comes of calling on the spirits.'

However cautious and intelligent a seeker after occult power may be, or one who endeavours to gain information by consulting a professional psychic, it does not seem to me that they possess any yardstick with which to measure the results that they obtain. How can they possibly tell if the entities they contact are good or evil, or be certain that they are not being deceived by malicious spirits and led on to their ultimate ruin?

In my own case, God knows, I have not deliberately tempted Providence by seeking to probe these dark secrets, but

Later

I had to stop writing this morning because Deb came in. She doesn't often do so between eleven and one on a wet day, but as it had stopped raining by a quarter to twelve she wanted me to take my daily turn round the garden before lunch; so that she would be free this afternoon to have tea with the village schoolmaster, who is a friend of hers.

Her unexpected appearance gave me furiously to think. I am most anxious that no-one should learn about this journal – in case they get the idea that I've got a screw loose – and Deb, Taffy and Helmuth are all liable to barge in here without warning from time to time. I have been writing in an old exercise-book, and if they notice that I've taken to scribbling as a habit one of them is bound to ask what I am writing about. Then if I said that I was trying my hand at a short story, or something like that, they would be certain to want to read it.

While I was being wheeled round the garden I decided that I would tear out the sheets that I have covered so far and hide them between the leaves of my stamp albums. In future I shall write on single sheets, using one of the albums as a writing block, and as each is finished conceal it with the others. Then, if anyone comes in while

I am on the job they will think that I am making notes of the stamps I want to complete some of my sets.

This plan also provides a means of hiding the script when I am out. Nobody has any excuse for opening the albums, so it is extremely unlikely that anyone will come upon these sheets there – unless, of course, something happens to me.

That brings me to another point. I started this journal simply with the idea of putting down my recent strange experiences in black and white, so that I could consider them more objectively. At least, that is what I thought; but I believe that, all the time, I also had it in the back of my mind that since I am menaced by some intangible form of danger, should I fall victim to it I would like to leave behind a record of all that has occurred.

My stamp collection is of considerable value, so if anything did happen to me these notes are certain to be found; and the odds are that they would be found by Julia, which is what I want.

Of course it is absurd, really, even to suggest that I might be taken away from here in a strait-jacket, or die in a fit one night. Still, if fate has decreed some such horror for me I would like Julia to know that I did not succumb to it tamely; but fought it with all my might.

On the face of it the simplest way of achieving my object would be to keep these papers in a packet addressed to her, but if I did that it might be tampered with, or deliberately destroyed. Why should I fear that? I'm darned if I know. Such groundless suspicions are said to be a sign of madness. Perhaps I am going mad. Oh, God, I wish I knew!

Saturday, 9th May

Still no sign of Julia! It really is extraordinary! Even if she were ill I feel sure that, on receiving my last letter, she would send me some kind of message. The only possible explanation for her failure either to come here or write to me is that she must have been away from Queensclere for some days, and that my letter has not yet caught up with her – or that she is an air-raid casualty, which God forbid; but that is hardly likely as, were it so, Uncle Paul or one of the servants would have let us know of it by telegram.

If she had been coming yesterday it was a fair bet that she would have arrived in time for dinner; so when she didn't, instead of writing any more of this I wrote to her again, in the hope that if my earlier letter is still chasing her round the country this last one will catch her on her return to Queensclere. In it I did not mince matters, but spilled the whole story.

I had an untroubled night again – the fourth in succession – and I am now beginning to hope that I may remain immune from further attack until the end of the month. That proved to be the case in April, and it looks as if the Thing's activity is in some way dependent on the moon being either at, or near, full. During the dark quarter there is, naturally, no moonlight to throw the shadow; but I have never seen it while the moon was in her first or third quarters; neither have I felt the brute's presence at such times. So, now that the moon is on the wane, I am crossing thumbs that I'll be free of my accursed visitor for a bit. At present, though, the above is still only a theory, so I am certainly not going to start counting my chickens as yet.

Last night I thought a lot more about ways of ensuring that this record should reach Julia in the event of my apparently crazy forebodings taking concrete form. After all, some reason that I know nothing of may prevent her coming this week, or next; and tonight, or any night, the Thing may come again and – and succeed in forcing its way in. So I mean to keep at this journal until she does come or . . . And, in the last case, I am now convinced that using the stamp album offers a better prospect of achieving my end than any other means at my disposal.

If anything did happen to me, all my personal effects would become the property of Uncle Paul, as my next of kin; so it would be Julia who, sooner or later, would go through them, and all the odds are against anyone examining the albums before they came into her hands.

It would fall to Taffy's lot to pack up my things. He is the head gardener's son, and promoted to an indoor post as my body-servant only because of the present shortage of manpower, and the fact that his slightly deformed feet make him ineligible for National Service.

Taffy's strength lies in his muscles, not in his head; but the small, dark eyes set in his moon-like face suggest a certain slyness, and I wouldn't put it past him to pinch my cuff-links if he thought he could get away with it. But I doubt if it would even occur to him to monkey with my stamps. He wouldn't know which ones were worth taking, and he would be frightened at the risk involved to anyone who knows nothing about such things trying to turn them into money. Even if curiosity led him to glance through the albums and he came upon these pages I very much doubt if he would bother to read them.

If he did, though, I believe he is the one person here who would really sympathise with me. The farm people round about in these Welsh hills are still pretty primitive. Taffy must have heard plenty of tales of hobgoblins, and of old women putting a murrin on their neighbour's cattle. More 'sophisticated' people might laugh at me for being frightened of a shadow, but Taffy Morgan wouldn't.

Deb would certainly laugh; or, more probably, regard my 'ravings' with cynical disdain. I have to have massage for my back every day, and Helmuth says that, with the war on, we are lucky to have got a professional nurse who is also a highly skilled masseuse to come and live down here in the back of beyond. All the same, I would gladly have put up with a little less skill from someone a bit more human and cheerful. She is a good-looking girl, or, rather, woman, but one of those thin-faced, brainy Jewesses who are not given to laughter and consider that 'Life is real, life is earnest'.

There is no race further removed from the mystic than the Jews of these days; and those whom education has lifted out of bondage to the Mammon of Unrighteousness give their minds to art or politics. Sister Deborah Kain is the latter type. She is, not unnaturally, a fanatical anti-Nazi and, I suspect, holds most advanced views on political reform.

She is so reticent by nature that I really know very little about her, except that her father was a University professor. I feel sure that she is much too respectable to be dishonest; and as she has already looked through my stamps several times with me, there could be no reason other than an impulse to steal which might cause her to open the albums after – well, after the sort of thing that I prefer not to contemplate.

As for Helmuth, it is most unlikely that he would even give a thought to my stamps. By the Grace of God he despises stamp collecting. He admitted on one occasion, with a superior air, that as a hobby for young people it has the merit of teaching them a modicum of geography without tears; but more than once when I have had my albums out he has said: 'Hello! Wasting your time again with those silly little bits of coloured paper?'

I find it strange that such an intelligent man should be so intolerant of any pursuit requiring a certain amount of knowledge, discrimination and exactitude; but Helmuth has other queer gaps in his, generally speaking, quite remarkable mentality. As it happens now, this one is particularly fortunate for me, as he is the last person whom I would wish to see these pages. In fact, I might as well be honest with myself and admit that the real reason why I am so anxious to prevent Deb or Taffy finding them is because they might tell Helmuth what I am up to.

If I were asked to explain why I am so averse to Helmuth knowing what is going on in my mind, I couldn't give a reason – other than my natural anxiety that neither he nor anyone else should have grounds for suspecting that I may be going mad. Yet several times recently it has seemed to me that he looks at me now with a queer, searching expression, as if he already knows that something is wrong, and is trying to read my thoughts.

My feeling may be a genuine instinct, or it may be due to the fact that half a lifetime in his company has bred in me a spontaneous urge to protect myself from the uncanny knack he has of ferreting out my secrets; but, whatever its cause, an inner voice insistently warns me to keep from him even an inkling of my present mental state.

Anyway, the chance of his coming upon the script – whether I am here or not – is now extremely remote; and I am inclined to think that it was his contempt for philately which led me subconsciously to choose the albums as a hiding-place for it. Even in an idle moment he would find something more congenial to him with which to occupy his mind than my stamps, so he will never glance at them casually; and he certainly would not stoop to petty pilfering.

There is nothing petty about Helmuth. His mind is extremely subtle and his motives for doing or saying things are often so elusive that it is very difficult to form an accurate estimate of his real beliefs and character. Sometimes he gives the impression of having the most lofty ideals, at others his cynicism appears positively brutal; but he always 'thinks big'. In all the years we have been together I have never known him do otherwise, and if he wanted to rob the family he would devise some scheme which, by comparison, would make the proceeds from stealing my stamps look like robbing the poor-box.

All this about preventing anyone here tumbling to it that I am writing a journal has put me right off my stroke again; but, on looking back, I see that I got so far as recording my youthful experience with the 'burglar'.

I cannot state definitely that he was an 'evil' manifestation. He certainly looked horrid enough. However, I certainly did not feel what one might term 'the presence of evil' at the time. My reaction was simply that of a small boy who suddenly comes face to face with a brutal criminal and, fearing physical violence, flees in panic to the protection of friendly grown-ups.

In considering the matter it is worth remembering that, because certain human beings have the misfortune to be incredibly ugly or hideously deformed, it does not in the least follow that they are evil. Again, the apparition seen by Lord Dufferin had most repulsive features, yet it saved his life; and so, to him, it played the part of a guardian angel. Therefore I think one must keep an open mind about my burglar.

There was really nothing to suggest that he was an emissary from the Devil. Yet I have good grounds for believing that forces of a definitely Satanic nature do, at times, impinge upon man's consciousness. The Thing that comes to my window arouses in me a fear and nausea of such a special kind that they alone seem enough to indicate that it can have its origin only in Hell; but I have been leading the abnormal life of a sick man for so many weary months that I am now tortued by doubts about the soundness of my judgement; and it was not the thing that makes the shadow that I had in mind. I was thinking of the only other experience of the occult with which I met while still in full health and unquestionably sane.

On that occasion I did not see anything at all. I only felt it; so the bigoted sceptic would be more inclined than ever to assert that my imagination was playing me tricks. I can only vouch for my belief that quite suddenly and inexplicably I found myself in the immediate vicinity of what I can but describe as disembodied evil.

It is a commonplace for people to speak of houses having a good or bad 'atmosphere'; and every house agent knows that this intangible factor plays a very large part in determining whether empty properties are snapped up quickly or remain on his books for many months. In the majority of cases it seems reasonable to suppose that such atmospheres are created by the happiness or unhappiness of the previous tenants; and that they have left something of their healthy, cheerful mentalities or mean, base natures behind. But in exceptionally bad cases such atmospheres are openly termed 'hauntings', and are attributed to suicides, murders and other evil acts which have taken place, sometimes centuries ago.

Both explanations are, of course, further evidence for the existence of the supernatural in our midst; since it is really no more inexplicable that the spirit of a murderer should haunt the scene of his crime than that a happy, carefree family of still living people should leave behind them a feeling of sunshine and laughter. Neither can be explained by any human attribute that the psychologists have yet succeeded in codefying for insertion in medical text-books; so they

can be only manifestions of that something we all possess which is
quite independent of the physical body.

Recalling in detail this other psychic experience of my youth will, I
am sure, further strengthen my hold on the belief that I am still as
sane now as I was then.

It happened soon after the beginning of the first summer term that
I spent in the senior house at Weylands. That was in 1937, so I was
very nearly sixteen at the time.

Later

Most people have heard of Weylands Abbey and it is only natural
that opinion should be very sharply divided on the methods of education in practice there. Elderly people who have a bigoted prejudice
in favour of the old Public School system, with its birchings, daily
chapel and enforced games, go purple in the face at the very
mention of the place. Others, with ultra-modern views, maintain
that Weylands represents a new system of enlightened education
which must, eventually, become universal, if future generations
of children are to be brought up free of all the complexes and
inhibitions that are the secret impetus behind most kinds of unhappiness and crime.

Weylands is in Cumberland, and the school takes its name from the
ruins of the ancient Abbey that stands nearly in the centre of its vast
private park. The school itself is about a mile from the Abbey and
consists of a big, ugly mansion erected in Victorian times by a wealthy
Lancashire cotton-goods manufacturer; but it has since been completely modernised and considerably added to. In the stone of the
pseudo-Gothic arch over its front porch are carved the words DO WHAT
THOU WILT SHALL BE THE WHOLE OF THE LAW, and that gives the clue to
the theory on which the system of education at Weylands was based.

There were no classes or teaching in the accepted sense, but a large
part of each day was given to study hours. Every pupil could take
whichever subjects he or she liked best – for of course it was co-
educational – and they were given books suitable to their age to read
about it, then, when they felt inclined, they discussed what they had
read with the masters and mistresses.

In the recreation hours there were no organised games, as that
would have entailed captains of sides and obedience to them. Instead
there was tennis, golf, swimming, squash and other sports for those
who liked them; those who didn't could go for a walk, laze about or
even go to bed if they preferred to do so.

The only penalty for not getting up at the usual hour in the morning was that, when you did, you had to make your own bed; and the only penalty for being late for meals was that you missed them, or anyhow the first course. When newcomers got the hang of the thing they sometimes decided to live on their tuck for a bit and not get up at all; but they soon got bored with doing nothing and fell into the normal routine of their own free will.

In the junior house there were separate dormitories for girls and boys; but in the senior house the sexes were not segregated and everyone had separate cubicles. We were encouraged to express our own individualities by their furnishing and decoration, and there was no bar to a chap visiting a girl's cubicle or vice versa.

Whether all the parents were fully aware of the sort of thing that went on I rather doubt; but they may have been as, logically, it was simply part of the same system. We were taught that sex was a normal, healthy appetite, similar to a desire for food; and that the indulgences of it were only anti-social when jealousy entered into a sex relationship; so we must never give way to that emotion, or strive to prevent those who had given us pleasure giving pleasure to others if they felt so inclined.

Even in the lower house sex had no secrets from us, and we read the books on social hygiene that were put in our way with as much, but no more, interest than we read Kipling's *Jungle Tales*. The elder girls all willingly submitted themselves to a special routine whereby Matron and the resident Doctor took steps to ensure against their getting themselves into trouble, so there was never any bother of that kind.

We were really amoral rather than immoral and cases of excess were very rare. The fact that we could have a romp for the asking at any time we felt like one reduced the thing to a matter of no more importance than going for a swim, so most of us often went quite long periods without indulging ourselves at all. Anyhow, I must admit that, at the time, I accepted everything to do with our sex-life at Weylands as perfectly normal.

Sundays there were marked by a choice of going for a picnic, or attending a private cinema show in the afternoons, and in the evenings a dance in what had been the chapel of the original house. No religious ceremony was ever held and Scripture was the one subject in which there were no facilities for learning. We were taught that all religion was a product of the Dark Ages, when the development of the individual was retarded by a multitude of absurd taboos and superstitions.

Newcomers who had already received a certain amount of religious instruction were referred to pityingly as 'poor little savages' and soon laughed out of their beliefs. In order to encourage them in developing a contempt for the symbol before which the ignorant masses still bowed down all the doormats had a crucifix woven into them, so that we all trod on it every time we went in or out.

I need scarcely add that there was no prohibition on our swearing and blaspheming to our hearts' content, and the obscenities which used to issue from the mouths of some of the smaller children were, at times, remarkable; but most of them soon grew out of that, and I don't think the older pupils were any more foul-mouthed than their contemporaries at other schools.

Naturally there were no exams or end-of-term reports at Weylands, as the theory was that we were there to develop our individualities, not our brains. Nevertheless, the staff had its own methods of interesting us in all the essential subjects and it was rare for anyone to leave without having absorbed the rudiments of a fair, general education.

Moreover, in those who possessed an instinctive thirst for knowledge the theory of non-compulsion and a free choice of subjects worked wonders. Many of them left equipped far in advance of their age on their special lines, and have since become noted intellectuals.

Looking back on the way we were allowed to behave – shouting, blaspheming, throwing things about, teaching the girls tricks or being taught by them, lazing away mornings in bed and taking afternoons off to go birds'-nesting – it now seems almost incredible that an English school should have been conducted on such lines. But it was; and such is the adaptability of children that, after we had been there a few weeks, none of us thought it the least strange.

On the contrary, we thanked our Stars – not God – that our parents were sufficiently enlightened to choose such a school for us. We took pride in the fact that we were not like the miserable, ignorant, backward children that we met in the holidays, but a race apart, who had sloughed off all silly superstitions, were troubled by no stupid inhibitions about sex and, while still in our teens, were the masters of our fate, like grown-up men and women.

I see now that I have rambled on over several sheets about Weylands, which was certainly not my intention. I really started out only to make it clear that at a school run on those lines there was nothing

at all to prevent my spending a night out if I wished. The chaps and
girls often used to go out on moonlight picnics and not return till the
small hours of the morning; so I did not even think twice about it
when it occurred to me that it would be rather fun to spend the night
with Uncle Paul and Julia.

I see that it's later than I thought. I must leave it till tomorrow to
record the damnably unnerving experience I met with on my way
over to them.

Sunday, 10th May

We do not go in for Sunday services here at Llanferdrack, any more
than they did at Weylands; and for the first time in my life I am
inclined to wish that we did. The fact that I was brought up to
despise all organised religion has never before caused me any regret;
but, in view of my recent nightmares – the term will serve although
I'd give a packet to be able to think they are really only that – I
believe I should derive quite a lot of comfort from hearing the swell
of a church organ and the murmur of voices joined in prayer.

The Church has lost nearly all her temporal power and most of her
ancient wisdom, yet she still remains the only avowed champion in
arms against the Devil. Probably her loss of vitality can be accounted
for by the fact that comparatively few of her ministers seem to
believe in the Devil these days, so they don't give their energies to
fighting him any more. But the principles she represents remain
unaltered, so anyone who seeks protection through her from the
things that menace the spirit should be safe – at least, that is, if they
have faith.

Any attempt to secure Divine protection which was made half-
heartedly would obviously be futile; and I am by no means certain
that I could bring myself to pronounce the Creed – or whatever it is
that people do when they are confirmed – with genuine belief in
what I was saying. One does not have to be educated at Weylands to
have honest doubts about some bits of Christian dogma.

In any case it is a waste of time for me even to think about the
matter. If I sent for the local vicar, and asked him to prepare me for
confirmation, Helmuth would immediately conclude that my mind
had become unhinged; and giving him that impression is the one
thing I mean to avoid at all costs.

I don't think I have mentioned that Helmuth was the German
master at Weylands. He is not, of course, a German himself, but a
Czech, and his full name is Doctor Helmuth Lisický.

That brings us back to Weylands, and I must explain now how it was that Uncle Paul and Julia happened to be in the vicinity on the night that I was scared out of my wits.

The school is situated in one of the most desolate parts of Cumberland. It is lovely country, but there isn't an hotel, or even a comfortable inn, within twenty miles; and when the place first started that made it awkward for parents who wanted to come down in term time to see their young.

In consequence, the school authorities built a sort of bungalow village at the southern end of the park. It consists of about a dozen comfortable cottages, having from four to six rooms apiece, and a Club-house with rooms at the back for visiting chauffeurs and a permanent staff. Parents can write to the bursar and book one of the cottages for a night or two if they wish, and meals are provided for them in the Club-house during their stay.

Old boys were also accommodated there, as Weylands was very keen about keeping in touch with her ex-scholars, and some of them came down quite frequently. As a matter of fact the ramifications of Weylands resulted in a much closer community than is the case with most schools; perhaps because the new system of education practised there formed almost a cult.

Pupils were never accepted after the age of ten, in case they had already formed old-fashioned prejudices to a degree that might make them a disruptive influence; and each one had to be personally recommended by parents who had had a child at the school themselves for at least a year. So it was rather like a club; and sometimes parents who knew one another used to arrange to come down together and share one of the larger bungalows.

Anyhow, Uncle Paul and Julia had arranged to come down for a couple of nights right at the beginning of the summer term, because I had not seen them for some months owing to their having been abroad; and I knew that they had been allotted one of the smaller bungalows, where they would be alone. Naturally I had been looking forward to seeing them, but they did not expect to arrive until just in time for dinner, so in the normal course of events I should not have done so till the following day.

Actually it was not until I was just about to go to bed that I suddenly had the bright idea of paying them a surprise visit. It had been raining, but the rain had stopped and it was a warm night with the moon showing now and then between scudding clouds, so the idea of a walk seemed rather pleasant. Still, the bungalows were right at the far end of the great park, over two miles away from the school, and I didn't much relish the thought of the long tramp back after midnight, particularly as it might come on to rain again. The solution to that was easy: I could pop a pair of pyjamas and a tooth-brush into my attaché-case and, after a lovely long chin-wag with my visitors, spend the rest of the night in the spare room of their bungalow.

I didn't hurry myself about setting out, as I thought that after dinner they would probably remain in the Club-house talking to some of the other visitors till about half-past ten, so it was getting on for that when I put on my mac and let myself out of the school by one of its side doors.

Long winding drives led off from the house to the three gates of the park and the one I took passed fairly near to the ruins of the old Abbey, which was situated about halfway between the school and the bungalows. I was as fit and cheerful as any carefree youngster of nearly sixteen could be, and as I stepped out at a brisk pace I distinctly remember that I was humming jazz tunes to myself.

The drive approached the Abbey to within about four hundred yards, then curved away in a wide bend that made nearly a half-circle round it. By taking a short cut across the bend one passed within a hundred yards of the Abbey and saved quite a considerable distance. The only thing against it was that the ground was rather rough and scored every few yards with little ditches; but I had often taken the short cut in the daytime and, as the moon gave enough light to see by, I did so now.

I must have covered nearly a quarter of a mile and had the Abbey on my immediate right when I happened to glance in that direction. If I hadn't been so occupied in watching my step I should probably have noticed it before, but I suddenly saw the glow of a misty, reddish light in the middle of the ruins.

I was not so much surprised as intrigued, because it was common knowledge at Weylands that, soon after the place was started, the school authorities had converted the crypt of the Abbey into a Masonic Temple.

It was the one and only place that was out of bounds to us, and none of the masters would ever tell us anything about it, with the result that there was quite a lot of casual speculation as to what it was like inside, and what went on there.

All I had been able to gather from some of the older chaps was that it had no connection with British Masonry, but was a Lodge of the

Grand Orient, as Continental Masonry is called, and that Fellowship of it gave one lots of pull in the political and financial worlds. The masters were all believed to be Fellows, and pupils who had proved satisfactory were given a special course during their last term to prepare them for initiation before they left.

These initiation ceremonies always took place the night after the end of term, so the rest of us, having already gone down, had no opportunity immediately afterwards to try to get out of the initiates what it was all about; and when they came back on visits as old boys they proved as cagey as the masters. No doubt I should have been initiated myself in due course if I hadn't run away from Weylands before the end of my last term – but that is another story.

In view of all this, the sight of the red glow in the middle of the ruins naturally aroused my curiosity, but I hesitated at the thought of trying to find out what it was on account of the risk I should be running if I went much nearer. There were no punishments of any kind at Weylands but, of course, one could be expelled, and it had been made quite clear that such a fate would overtake any of us if we were caugh snooping round the Abbey. Still, the very fact that it held the one and only secret that we were 'not considered old enough to know' made it all the more tantalising.

I knew that I could not get right into the Abbey, even if I had been prepared to expose myself to almost certain discovery, as a six-foot-high wire-mesh fence had been erected all round it; but I thought that if I went as far as the fence I should be able to get a peep at the place from which the light was coming and find out what was going on there. For a minute or two I stood there undecided, staring at the red mist. Then the moon went behind a big bank of cloud, plunging the park in darkness, and feeling that there was very little chance of my being spotted for the next ten minutes, I began to walk cautiously forward.

As I advanced the light waxed and waned at irregular intervals, almost disappearing for a time, then suddenly flaring up again. At first I thought that it must be caused by a bonfire; but I could not be certain, as one of the great masses of masonry which formed the roofless shell of the church stood between the centre of the glow and my line of advance.

In order to get a better view I altered my course a little, until I came opposite a big gap in the ruin, and could see through a broken archway into the body of the church. I saw then that an imposing portico had been erected in the middle of the nave, presumably over a stairway leading down to the crypt. In it were framed a big pair of wrought-iron gates. They were backed with some opaque substance which might have been frosted glass. The dull red glow was coming through them; and its intermittent flare-ups were caused by dark figures that emerged out of the shadows every few moments, pushing one side of the gates open to pass through into the brightly lit interior of the portico.

I was still too far off to identify any of the figures, but the silhouettes of two out of the five I saw looked as if they were those of women. This intrigued me greatly, as I had once heard a rumour that the mistresses attended certain of the ceremonies, and that the pick of the girls were made associates on leaving, at the same time as eldest chaps received their initiation; so with the idea of settling the point I decided to advance as far as the wire-mesh fence. It stood only about twenty yards from the broken wall of the ruin, and on the far side of the ancient cemetery of the Abbey, which I had already entered.

The ground there was very rough, being broken with grassy mounds and, here and there, old grave-stones half-buried in the coarse grass; but having been brought up to despise all superstition it never even occurred to me that it was the sort of place in which I might meet a ghost. I was about halfway across it when I suddenly noticed that the moon looked like coming out again from behind the bank of cloud. That threw me into a bit of a flap, as I realised that if one of the people passing through the church happened to glance in my direction I was near enough now for them to spot me by its light; so I hastily looked round for cover.

Some thirty feet away I saw an old, box-like stone tomb, considerably bigger than most of the others, and I hurriedly made in that direction with the idea of crouching down behind it. Unnoticed by me my shoelace must have come undone, for I stepped on it just as I reached the tomb, tripped and lurched forward.

Instinctively I threw out my hands to save myself. They landed with all my weight behind them on the bevelled edge of the slab of stone that formed the flat top of the tomb. It was centuries old and may have been cracked already, or countless winters may have weakened it where there was a flaw in the centre of the stone. It gave under the sudden pressure and several large fragments collapsed inwards, leaving nearly half the tomb gaping open.

For a second my heart was in my mouth. But the bits of stone had not far to fall and their subsidence made only a faint slither, followed by a thump so gentle that it could not possibly have attracted the attention of anyone inside the Abbey. Thanking my stars that my mishap had had no worse results, I turned about and knelt down to retie my shoelace.

Suddenly – without rhyme or reason – I had the feeling that somebody was standing just behind me. The warning came to my brain as sharply, as unexpectedly and as imperatively, as the sudden shrilling of a telephone bell in an empty house.

In a flash I swivelled round, expecting to find myself face to face with – I don't really know who or what; certainly not a master, but someone or something that was regarding me with a fixed, hostile stare. With a gasp of relief I realised that I had been mistaken. There was nobody there; not a thing.

The moon had just come out from behind the cloud-bank, and now lit the scene with a dear, cold radiance. The shadows that it cast were sharp and black upon the ground. By it I could distinctly see the jagged edge of the broken lid of the tomb behind which I had been kneeling and, fifteen yards away, the stout wire-mesh fence that had been put up round the ruins as an additional precaution against unauthorised persons getting into them. The body of the church had become a pool of darkness splashed with insular patches of silver light. The red glow still showed faintly from the double gates, but the figures I had seen must have been those of late-comers to the meeting, as there was now neither sight nor sound to show that there was a living thing within a mile of me.

Inclined to laugh now at the fright I had given myself, I knelt down again to do up my shoe. I had hardly twisted the ends into a bow before the same horrid feeling assailed me. I could have sworn that someone was overlooking me from behind; that a pair of eyes were boring right through my back.

A swift glance over my shoulder confirmed my previous scrutiny of the place. There was nothing there. Absolutely nothing but the gravestones glinting whitely in the moonlight.

My fumbling fingers sought to tie the knot, but they trembled so much that they could not hold the laces in position. I tried to steady them, telling myself again and again that there was nothing of which to be afraid. If there was, I argued desperately, I could not possibly have failed to see it, because the full moon made the place almost as light as if it had been day.

Yet, fight as I would, I could not throw off the feeling. Instead, every second it grew worse. Shivers ran through me. The hair on the back of my neck began to prickle and rise like the hackles of a dog. A still, small voice somewhere in my mind now kept on insisting that the unseen presence behind me was something monstrous – something that meant to strike me down and do me deadly harm.

Being in such eerie surroundings within an hour or so of midnight would have been enough to lay most boys of my age open to a fit of the jitters, but the scepticism I had imbibed at Weylands had toughened me against such superstitious fears. I swore to myself that I would not give way to this childish, idiotic attack of funk, for which there was not the faintest base or cause, and that I would retie my shoelace before I looked round again – if it was the last thing I ever did.

How long that silent, weaponless battle lasted, I have no idea. Probably no more than a few seconds, although it seemed an age. I only know that I failed to tie the shoelace.

My eyes were starting from their sockets, the palms of my hands were damp, and I could feel my heart pounding against my ribs. It was suddenly borne in upon me that not for all the money in the world would I turn round again, from fear now of what I might see there. I knew, with a certainty that brooks no argument, that in another second it would be too late to escape. Something outside all human experience – something beyond belief, unholy, loathsome, terrifying – was in the very act of launching itself upon me where I knelt. My will broke. I sprang to my feet and fled.

Stark fear lent wings to my feet. Lurching, bounding, tripping over old grave mounds, stumbling in ditches, I raced away from the ruins as though all the devils in Hell were after me. Somehow I got back onto the drive, but I did not pause there. I only blessed its even surface that enabled me to run the faster. Panting, gasping, sobbing for breath, I pelted along it as fast as my legs would carry me, and I did not even notice in which direction I was going until, with unutterable relief, I glimpsed the friendly lights of the bungalows shining through the trees. With a last spurt I dashed straight for the cottage where I expected to find Julia and Uncle Paul, hurled myself at its front door, which was only on the latch, and flung myself inside. There was no answer to my choking cry, and the whole place was in darkness.

Monday, 11th May
I got so worked up writing this account yesterday that I forgot the time until Helmuth came in on his daily visit. He always spends an

hour or two with me between tea and dinner, when we talk of this and that and discuss the war news.

Yesterday evening I took special pains to study him closely and tried to regard him as if he were someone whom I had never met before.

He is a fine-looking man and must be very nearly as tall as I am, which is six feet three in my socks. His shoulders are a good bit broader than mine and his whole frame is more powerful. I think, too, that if one were called on to describe Helmuth's out-standing quality by a single adjective, 'powerful' is the word one would choose.

He cannot be more than thirty-eight or -nine, although his hair having gone prematurely white makes him look a good bit older. It is very thick, and he wears it rather long and brushed straight back, which gives his head a massive, leonine appearance. But even if he were bald the breadth of his forehead would still give him a commanding look, and it would take a brave man to challenge those strange light-coloured eyes of his. To say that they were yellow would give a false impression of them, as that makes one think of biliousness, from which he certainly does not suffer. Actually, I suppose they are pale tawny.

His nose is a formidable hook; rather fleshy but more Roman than Jewish; although the fact that his ears are set low on his skull suggests that he may have a dash of Jewish blood acquired two or three generations back. His mouth is his only bad feature. It is too thin and in repose would be taken as a certain sign that he has a cruel nature; but his smile is so quick and friendly that it immediately cancels out any such idea.

His vitality is so great that he rarely keeps still for long, and as he strode up and down in front of the big open fireplace, shooting out ideas on all sorts of subjects, I found it exceedingly difficult to form any definite impression of what really lies behind that constantly animated, lion-like mask. The interest that he never fails to show in everything that concerns me personally, as well as the running of the estate, is perfectly natural; and, whenever he is with me, the idea that he would lend himself to anything that would cause me harm seems perfectly absurd.

Nevertheless, after he had gone I was very thankful that I have taken to writing this on loose sheets inside the cover of one of my stamp albums. The dodge worked perfectly. Although his entrance came as a surprise I was able to complete the sentence I was writing, then calmly shut the album up and put it aside; while, to my secret amusement, he remarked: 'Ha! Ha! I see you have started playing with some of your old kindergarten toys again.'

In recounting my horrible experience at Weylands, I see that I had got to the point where I burst into the cottage that Uncle Paul and Julia had been allotted, to find that they were not there and that the whole place was in darkness; so there is still quite a bit to tell about that unforgettable night.

I was still panting like a grampus and sweating like a pig; quite as much from the awful fright I had had as from the fact that I had just run a mile. Finding the place dark, silent and untenanted unnerved me afresh – although that is hardly an accurate description of what I felt, as my nerve had completely gone already.

For a moment I was near bursting into tears, but I choked them back and then a particle of sense seeped through into my fright-befuddled brain. Grabbing at the switches I snapped on the lights in the hall and sitting-room. After I had done that I began to feel a trifle less scared, but I was still very far from being my own man. I was trembling from head to foot and a succession of shudders ran through my whole body. On stumbling into the sitting-room I caught sight of myself in the mirror over the mantelpiece. The pupils of my eyes looked twice their normal size, my lips were grey, my face as white as a sheet and dripping with perspiration.

It was quite a time before I succeeded in pulling myself together. The sight of some of Julia's belongings scattered about the room showed that my visitors had arrived as arranged, earlier that evening, so I could only assume that they must still be over at the Club-house, yarning with some of the other people there, or taking part in a game of cards. The Club was only a couple of hundred yards down the road but, much as I craved human companionship, nothing would have induced me to go out into the dark again. As soon as I got a bit of a grip on myself I made up the fire and settled down by it in an armchair to await their return.

I tried not to think of the abominable thing from which I had had such a narrow escape; but the thought of it kept coming back and filling me with waves of nausea. Then, as I couldn't get it out of my mind, I endeavoured to face it squarely and see if there wasn't some possible explanation to the affair that my panic had caused me to overlook.

When I had come into the bungalow I had felt terribly cold, in spite of my long run, but as the fire warmed me up I began to feel physically better and my brain started to tick over again.

It occurred to me that the school authorities might know about whatever it was that lurked in the vicinity of the Abbey, and it was for that reason they had put the place out of bounds to us. But I dismissed the idea almost immediately. I was no longer a child, but a well-grown youth of nearly sixteen, and I felt that if entering the territory of the horror could have such an utterly devastating effect on me, its effect on a fully fledged adult could be little less shattering. Yet, as I had verified for myself less than an hour before, the masters did go to the ruins at night to attend their Masonic meetings, and so too, I now believed, did some of the mistresses. It seemed incredible that they should deliberately expose themselves to the sort of experience that I had had; so the theory that they had put the place out of bounds on that account was not tenable.

It seemed certain, too, that the unseen presence could have no connection with anything that took place at the meetings in the crypt. I mean, I have little doubt now that my having seen the 'burglar' at the Willows was the result of the séances that were held there. Of course I was not aware of that explanation when I was at Weylands, because I had not yet run into Florrie Meddows. But by the time I was sixteen I had read quite a few ghost-stories, and heard tell of séances at which spirits were said to blow trumpets and that sort of thing. So it did cross my mind for a moment that the Masonic meetings might have something to do with the occult; but only for a moment. It was so obviously absurd to think of the masters at Weylands dabbling in spiritualism.

They were all dried-in-the-wool materialists, and if one does not believe in God one cannot believe in the Devil, or the existence of any supernatural beings; so the last thing they would have done was to meet for the purpose of calling on the spirits. They would have laughed at the very idea; and, anyhow, I had heard enough about the Fellowship to know that it was a very down-to-earth affair. It was no secret that its object was to ensure mutual co-operation in worldly matters, so that by assisting one another all its members could achieve wealth and position; and, of course, it was owing to its activities that Weylands was such an immensely rich institution.

Then, as I sat warming myself in front of the fire, a new thought struck me. I recalled that tripping on my shoelace had caused me to fall forward and clutch at the top of the tomb, and that under the sudden pressure it had given way. Perhaps my having opened the grave had enabled something to escape from it.

The more I thought about it, the more certain I felt that I had hit upon the right solution. A year or so earlier I had read *Dracula* and, at the time, I had taken all the stuff about vampires and the undead as pure invention; now I thought of it again in a very different light.

The gaping tomb had been behind me as I knelt; and when I swivelled round I had looked across it and all round it, but not down into it. About half the stone lid had remained intact and the open portion of the grave, into which the rest of the lid had fallen, had been obscured by deep shadow. It seemed possible that I had aroused some horrid, corpse-like thing that had been lying there in a state of suspended animation. Or perhaps, by some ancient mystery, the soul of an evil abbot had been imprisoned with his body in the grave – just as in the *Arabian Nights* the powerful Djinn had been sealed up in a bottle – and I had released a diabolical force that had been straining to get free for centuries, so that it could exact vengeance on humanity.

Such bizarre ideas were a world away from the atheism which we were taught to regard as enlightenment at Weylands. But human instincts and old traditions die hard; and most of us, while ready enough to sneer at religion, still retained a sneaking feeling that there might be something in the tales of ghosts and haunted houses we had heard. In any case, after what I had been through myself that night, no explanation of it sounded too fantastic. I was still vaguely speculating upon what sort of horror it could have been that had come up at me out of the grave when, mentally and physically exhausted as I was, I fell asleep.

Tuesday, 12th May
Last night I had the horrors again. I saw the shadow, but it was mixed up with all sorts of other beastliness in a nightmare. I do not mean that I actually had another visitation of the sort that I first had early in April, and almost persuaded myself were nightmares until their recurrence at the beginning of this month. I mean a genuine bad dream.

It must have been due to the vividness of the recollections that I conjured up yesterday, while writing an account of my terrifying experience at Weylands. Anyhow I dreamed that I was there again among the graves of the long-dead monks, and that the Thing that has recently been haunting me was chasing me towards the red glow that came from the wrought-iron gates.

Although the beast was behind me as I ran, I seemed to have eyes in the back of my head, for I could see it as it leapt from mound to mound in my tracks. Its body was the big, round, multi-limbed patch of blackness that I always see, but it had the caricature of a human face – and the face was Helmuth's, with his eyes multiplied to ten times their normal size and his fleshy nose changed into a great curved beak.

Julia was there too. She was standing by the glowing gates calmly watching the brute hunt me, and she made not the slightest move to come to my assistance when I screamed to her for help.

I suppose her appearance in my dream, and the callous attitude she displayed, are to be accounted for by a subconscious projection of the black fits of depression that I get from the thought that she seems to have abandoned me in my present plight. Why she did not arrive over the weekend, or at least answer my letter, I simply cannot think.

Of course, the only possible explanation is that she is no longer at Queensclere and has not had my letters yet. I know that she would come here on the very first train if she was aware of what I am up against. So it seems futile to write to her again. I can only thank God that we are now entering the dark quarter of the moon, which means I'll be safe for a bit, and pray that one of my letters catches up with her in the next few days, as it surely must.

Yesterday the village barber came to cut my hair. I am afraid I have always been a bit casual about my appearance, and I often got ticked off for letting my hair grow too long when I was in the ranks of the R.A.F., and later too, during my year's training as a Pilot-Officer. Once I became operational no-one bothered me about it any more, as we Fighter boys still had a bit of a halo round our heads – even those of us who had come in only for the tail-end of the Battle of Britain – and we rather prided ourselves in going about dressed any-old-how, our caps on the backs of our heads and the top buttons of our tunics undone. It was all rather childish, I suppose, but in an inverse way it had the same sort of effect that super-smartness has on the Brigade of Guards, and added quite a bit to our morale.

Still, as my hair is unusually silky for its reddish colour and dead straight, it is apt to fall forward over my forehead and bother me when it gets too long; so every few weeks I kick myself into sending for the local clipper-wielder, and submit myself to his inartistic ministrations.

It is raining today, so as I have a clear morning in front of me I'll polish off my account of that affair at Weylands. I see that I had got to the point where I had fallen asleep in the cottage while waiting for Julia and Uncle Paul to return.

I was woken by the sound of the sitting-room door opening with a rattle, then being swiftly shut again. The lights were still on but the fire had gone out, so I must have been asleep for a considerable time.

I felt very cold, and shivered as I stood up. The memory of the night's earlier events was just flooding back to me when I heard voices outside in the hall. Someone was muttering something, then Julia's voice came to me quite distinctly as she said: 'So that's why the lights were on! What on earth can Toby be doing here? Thank goodness he's asleep and didn't see me like this. Quick, pull yourself together, now! It's up to you to hold the fort, while I do something to my face.'

Instinctively I had moved towards the door, and she had scarcely finished speaking when I pulled it open. Out of the corner of my eye I caught a glimpse of her back as she hurried into her bedroom, but I found myself looking straight at Uncle Paul.

He was leaning against the wall on the other side of the narrow hallway; and it was clear that Julia's admonition, to pull himself together, had not been given without good reason. He was as drunk as an owl.

Uncle Paul must have been about thirty-seven then. He is a big-gish man with red hair and a 'Guards' moustache, brushed stiffly up. He has a ruddy face and pale, rather poppy, blue eyes. Brains have never been his long suit, and he is a weak rather than a bad man. The 'Demon Drink', alas, has always been his failing, and it was the cause of most of the scrapes that he got himself into with my grandfather, when he was younger.

After he married Julia he took a pull on himself. At least, as she is the dominant partner I suppose she made him toe the line. But he continued to have lapses now and then, and it was by no means the first time that I had seen him when he had had one over the eight. Fortunately he is the friendly type of drunk; and as he had always been kind to me in a casual sort of way it made no difference to the mild affection I felt for him.

Bringing himself upright with a shove of his broad shoulders, he grinned at me and said: "Lo, old man! How – how are you?'

'I'm all right, thanks, Uncle,' I replied, 'but you're looking a bit part-worn. You seem to have been making a night of it.'

'That's it,' he hiccupped. 'Li'le party.'

'It must have been a pretty rough one,' I smiled, as I took in the details of his dishevelled appearance. There were grease-stains down one of the lapels of his dinner-jacket, his collar was a crumpled rag, his bow-tie had disappeared, and there were obvious marks of lipstick all round his mouth. I had never seen him in such a state when tight before.

'Tha's it; li'le party,' he repeated. 'Was bit rough. Played kiss-in-the-ring.'

I had no idea that the parents who were up for a visit indulged in either high jinks or childish games at the Club-house in the evenings; but when one is in the middle teens one is still constantly learning unexpected things about the behaviour of grown-ups, so I made no comment.

For a moment we remained silent, just smiling inanely at one another, then he said: 'Lesh go into th' sitting-room – have a drink.'

He had obviously had far more than he could carry already, but it was not my place to tell him so. Accordingly I stood aside and he lurched through the doorway. There were whisky glasses and a syphon on a small side-table. Swaying slightly, he walked over to it and, with a deliberation that did not prevent him spilling some of the stuff, mixed himself a stiff peg.

Having gulped half of it, he muttered: 'Tha's better,' then relapsed into another longish silence, during which he stared at the carpet.

At length he looked up and asked: 'What you doin' here thish time-o'-night? Wash game, old man?'

I had no intention of discussing the matter uppermost in my mind with Uncle Paul while he was in that condition; so I simply said: 'I knew you and Julia were arriving this evening, so I thought I would slip over and see you. While I was waiting for you to come in I fell asleep in front of the fire.'

'I she,' he nodded ponderously. 'I she. Well, here's all th' besht,' and he swallowed the rest of his drink.

A moment later Julia came hurrying in. She had changed into a dressing-gown, and evidently done her best to put her face to rights; but I was much more shocked by her appearance than I had been by that of Uncle Paul.

Her dark eyes looked bigger than I had ever seen them, and her face was dead-white, so that the patches of fresh rouge stood out on her cheeks like the dabs of paint on those of a Dutch doll. Her full red lips were swollen excessively and broken in places, as though they had been savagely bitten, and a heavy coating of powder failed to hide an ugly scratch that ran from beneath her left ear right down across her throat.

'Good Lord! What on earth has been happening to you?' I exclaimed in alarm.

She did not kiss me, but bent her head and laid her icy cheek against mine for a second; then she said: 'Toby, darling; don't be upset. I'm quite all right, but we've had a frightful time tonight. Has Paul told you about it?'

'Only that you had been hitting it up at a party,' I muttered, 'and that you played kiss-in-the-ring.'

'Paul!' she said sharply, turning to her husband. 'Get up at once, and go to bed.'

My uncle had lowered himself into an armchair and closed his eyes; he was already half asleep. At the sound of her voice he blinked, lumbered to his feet, and with a vague wave of his hand by way of good-night, walked unsteadily out of the room.

'I've never seen him as tight as that before,' I said, as he jerked the door to behind him.

'No, thank goodness,' Julia agreed, with a sigh. 'He doesn't often get really stinking. It's a mercy, though, that he didn't kill the two of us tonight. If I'd realised how far gone he was, I would never have let him drive the car.'

'You had a smash, then?'

'Of course! How else do you think I came to get my face in such a mess?'

'I thought you had been down at the Club all this time.'

'If Paul gave you that impression you must have misunderstood him. He is in no state to know what he is saying. We had a few drinks at the Club before we started, and by now he's probably forgotten most of what happened after that.'

'Oh, you poor darling!' I cried, taking her hand. 'Are you quite sure that you're not badly hurt?'

She shook her head. 'No. I'm all right. He drove us into a ditch, and when I was thrown sideways I hit my mouth against something. I've got a few bruises, but nothing to worry about.' Drawing me down onto the settee beside her, she went on: 'As we were coming up here, Paul thought that he would like to see some old friends of his who live about twenty miles away. We wrote and proposed ourselves for dinner. They wrote back and said they would love to have us if we didn't mind a scratch meal at the end of a children's party, as it was their eldest girl's birthday. When we arrived the party was still in full swing. There were quite a number of other grown-ups there and we must have stood about drinking cocktails for a couple of hours at least.

'It was ten o'clock by the time the children packed up, and close on eleven before we sat down to supper. Afterwards, somebody suggested that we should play the children's games. What with our steady cocktail-drinking and the champagne at supper, we were all a bit lit-up by then, and just ripe to let ourselves go at any sort of nonsense. We played kiss-in-the-ring, blind-man's-buff, postman's knock, and all the rest of it.

'You know how time flies when one is fooling like that, and I didn't notice the amount that Paul was putting away. It wasn't until we were in the car that I realised that he was carrying such a skinful, and, of course, he insisted that he was quite all right until he ran off the road and nearly turned the car over. We had a most frightful job getting it out of the ditch, and I'm feeling an absolute wreck; so be a dear and don't keep me up longer than you can help. Just tell me why you came here tonight; then I must get to bed.'

Obviously it was no time to tell her about the thing that I had released from the tomb, and, anyhow, I did not feel much like a long heart-to-heart by then, as the room seemed to have got colder than ever since they had come in. I just told her I had only come over for a lark, then we went to see if the bed in the spare room was made up.

The curtains there had not been drawn, and to my surprise I saw that it was already morning. The sun was shining and the trees were casting long shadows in the early light. By it, poor Julia looked more haggard than ever; but she smiled at me and said something about it being a perfect May Day morn, then she left me.

By the greatest of luck I had instinctively grabbed up my attaché-case when I fled – as I should have been terrified of going back for it, even in broad daylight, yet afraid to leave it there in case someone found it, and that led to my being expelled – so I was able to put on my pyjamas and get some proper sleep.

I woke a little after ten, and on going into the sitting-room found one of the Club servants there, tidying up. There was a kitchenette in each bungalow and it was part of their job to cook breakfast on the premises for visitors; so I asked the woman to get me some. Then I telephoned the school to let them know where I was, in case they thought I had met with an accident, and had a bath.

Julia came in just as I was finishing my breakfast. She was looking slightly better, although she could not have had blacker shadows under her eyes if she had been out on the binge for a week, and it was evident that the car having run off the road had shaken her really badly. While she drank two larger cups of tea in quick succession she gave me further details of the awful time they had had getting it out of the ditch. Apparently it had rained again in the middle of the night and the mud had absolutely ruined her evening clothes.

Uncle Paul was still sleeping it off, and she said that she did not mean to wake him until it was time to dress for lunch. That meant we had a good hour before us, and the sitting-room was now warm and cosy, so I launched out on an account of my own ordeal the previous night.

When I had done, Julia could offer no explanation. At first she made a half-hearted attempt to persuade me that I must have imagined it; but, in the face of my positive conviction to the contrary, she was far too sympathetic a person to insist on that; and, eventually, she agreed with me that I must have released some horrible supernatural force by breaking open the grave.

We discussed if we ought not to try to do something about it; but the idea of getting a priest to exorcise the place would have been received at Weylands about as frostily as a tart at one of Queen Victoria's tea parties; and even to mention the matter would have meant disclosing the fact that I had broken the one and only rule in the place; so we decided that we had better not say anything about it to anybody.

Unlike the affair of the burglar, there is no sequel to throw further light on the matter. Unlike that, too, it made a lasting impression on me. The first I had accepted as a natural fright, and the eager interests of childhood soon blanketed it in my mind; but that was far from being the case after my midnight fit of terror near the Abbey. For weeks afterwards I dreamed of it every few nights. I used to wake up moaning, struggling and bathed in a cold sweat. It was not till end of term came, bringing the excitements of the holidays, that those beastly dreams grew more infrequent and finally ceased altogether.

Yet I never forgot the feeling that contact with unseen evil gave me; and my reason for describing my experience at Weylands so fully is to make it quite clear that I cannot be mistaken now. In spite of the passing of the years I recognised it again instantly that first night, now just on six weeks ago, when I woke to find the full moon streaming in under the curtain and saw upon the band of light that abominable, undulating shadow.

Five times since then I have known the same awful sensation; a second time early in April, and four times early this month. Soon after the cessation of both bouts, when my nerves have had a chance to settle down again, I have debated with myself endlessly whether it can be some form of nightmare that afflicts me, or a type of periodic lunacy. If it were not for that earlier contact of mine with disembodied evil in the Abbey cemetery, I might still be hesitant about definitely rejecting both those theories. But I am now fully convinced that it can be neither. I am not suffering from nightmares, and I am not going mad. But I may yet be driven mad – if I am forced to remain here during another full moon and these Satanic attacks upon me develop again with renewed force.

Evening

Helmuth has just left me. The mystery of Julia's silence is now explained, but in a manner that fills me with new distress and apprehension. He asked me if I had heard from her lately, and on my saying that I hadn't, he said: 'I don't suppose you are likely to for a bit. I had a letter from your Uncle Paul today, in which he says that she was near having a breakdown from war-strain and her doctor has ordered her complete rest. So he got special permission from the security people for them to reside in the banned area on the west coast of Scotland, and a week ago he took her up to the house on Mull. Even if she feels up to writing, all letters coming out of the area are held up for ten days or more in the censor's office; so don't be surprised if you don't hear from her for another two or three weeks.'

Three weeks! A new moon is due on the 17th, and on the 25th she will enter the quarter in which she becomes such a menace to me. I had counted on Julia arranging for me to be moved from here long before that. What am I to do? How can I save myself? If only I could get back the full use of my legs for a single hour!

Wednesday, 13th May

I spent a restless night, worrying quite a bit about Julia; but, I'll confess, as charity begins at home, that I was worrying a darn sight more about myself, and racking my brains for some possible means of getting away from Llanferdrack, now that there is no hope of her intervention.

I considered writing to Uncle Paul and my other Trustees, but if I don't tell them the truth they are bound to reply that while the war is on I could not possibly be better situated than I am, with Helmuth to look after me and so well out of it all, down here; whereas if I do they are certain to think that the injury to my spine has now begun to affect my brain.

Of course that isn't so; but Julia is the only person who would take my word for it. If I had had a nasty blow on the head at the time of the crash, I might be tempted to think that was the root of the trouble myself; but I didn't. I never even lost consciousness.

I had just put paid to my Jerry – I can see the whisp of smoke now that suddenly issued from his aircraft – when I got old Steve's warning that there was another of them on my tail. But it came too late. Next second I felt a frightful blow in the back, as though someone had coshed me with a rifle-butt low down on the spine. I tried to take evasive action, but for a reason that I didn't even guess then my rudder-bar refused to function. Before I could grasp that my feet were no longer responding to the orders of my brain, the aircraft had got into a spin and was hurtling earthwards.

When I found that I couldn't pull her out of it I decided that the time had come to bale out. The usual motions failed to produce the desired results, but it is not easy to coordinate one's actions when one is being spun round like a pea in a top; so even then I did not realise the truth, and thought that it was some of my gear having got hitched up that prevented me from heaving myself free.

The last moments, while the earth seemed to be rushing up to smash me, were pretty ghastly, and I felt certain I was for it. I remember the words of the song 'so they scraped him off the tarmac like a pound of strawberry jam' flashing grimly through my mind; but, by a miracle, the old kite plunged straight into the only big tree within a mile. Her engine broke away and crashed through the branches to the ground, but I was left up there with my lower half imprisoned in the buckled shell of her body. Some farm labourers had seen me crash and were already running to my rescue. They fetched a ladder and hauled me out from among the wreckage. I was still perfectly *compos mentis* and told them that I could climb down out of the oak on my own; but the moment they let me take my own weight my feet slithered along the branch and my legs folded up under me.

They only just managed to catch me as I fell, so that was really the nearest I came that day to breaking my neck. There are times now when I almost wish that I had, as my broken back has put an end for me to most of the things that are worth doing in life.

It was on the 10th of July that I crashed, and after that I spent eight months in various hospitals; but the doctors all reached the same conclusion in the long run. It seems that the Jerry's bullet snipped a bit out of me that it is still beyond the art of medical science to replace. In the end the specialists broke it to me as gently as they could that there was nothing else they could do for me, and that there was little hope of my ever regaining the full use of my legs.

But there has never been the least suggestion that either the injury or the shock had in any way affected my brain. Personally, I am convinced that they did not, and that I am still perfectly sane. At least, I was when they brought me here in March and, apart from the events which caused me to start this journal, there has been nothing whatever since in my quiet invalid's routine to upset my mind.

Of course I have suffered, and do still suffer, a lot of pain; but that has had no more effect on me mentally than it has on the vast majority of poor fellows who are now suffering from agonising wounds owing to this bloody war. My hand is as steady, and my sight is as clear, as ever they were. I haven't become hesitant in my speech and I don't jump out of my skin if somebody bangs a door. My reasoning powers are unimpaired and I can justly claim that I am now far better at keeping my emotions under control than I was before the crash.

In fact, my own experience is that being a chronic invalid is about the best inducement one can have to practise self-discipline. Anyone in my position is entirely dependent on others, and therefore faced with two alternatives. Either they can allow their disability to become the centre of their thoughts, and on that account make life hell for themselves and everyone in frequent contact with them, or they can school themselves to ignore their misfortune as far as possible, and, by the exercise of endurance, patience and tact, at least secure the willing and cheerful service of those who are looking after them.

To adopt the latter course is just plain common sense, so I take no particular credit for having done so; but it needed a certain amount of will-power and is, I think, a further proof that there has been no deterioration in my mental faculties.

But what chance is there of the Trustees believing that? I mean, if I write and tell them that I want to be moved from Llanferdrack because whenever the moon is near-full an octopus tries to get in at my window? Naturally they will think I am gaga; and who could blame them?

They would send a bunch of brain specialists and psychoanalysts down here to examine me; and before I could say Jack Robinson I should find myself popped in a mental home to be kept under observation. For airing fancies far less lurid than that of being hunted over dry land by an octopus plenty of people have been carted off to those sort of places; and once in it is not so easy to get out again. No, thank you. I am not going to risk that. Not while I have a kick left in me.

(Laughter!) *Hollow* laughter – as they say in Parliamentary reports – caused by the simile I used inadvertently. Its in appropriateness must be an all-time high, in view of the fact that for the past ten months I have not been able to so much as waggle my big toe.

Later

An extraordinary thing has happened. This morning I decided that I would go fishing. It is the only sport in which I can still indulge, but I haven't had much luck so far. I have caught only a few bream and perch, and what I am after is one of the big pike; so today I thought I would try the far end of the lake, and I made Deb wheel me round there.

Deb is hardly what one would call an 'outdoor' girl, and she always looks awkward sitting on the grass reading one of her highbrow books. So, when she had settled me and wedged stones under the wheels of my chair so that it couldn't move, I said to her: 'There's no need to stay here if you don't want to. Why not walk back to the garden and sit in the summer-house? You'll be much more comfortable there, till it's time for you to come and fetch me in for lunch.'

She thought that a good idea, so off she went. The drive approaches the Castle at that end of the lake and crosses a small stone bridge from which I was fishing. Deb had been gone only about ten minutes when I spotted the postman coming up from the village. I called to the old chap and asked him if he had any letters for me. He had one, and gave it to me as he passed. It was from Julia.

It was written from Queensclere and dated the 10th of May – yet Helmuth told me only last night that Uncle Paul had taken her up to Scotland a week ago!

More extraordinary still, it said not a word about any plan for going there, or that she was feeling done in from war-strain; and it made no reference whatever to any of my recent letters to her. In fact, while acknowledging that she was hopelessly erratic about letter-writing herself and excusing her slackness on the plea that she had so much to do, she reproached me with having all the time in the world on my hands yet leaving it for so long without letting her hear from me.

For the rest, there were several pages in her firm, round hand recounting the excitements of the last local air-raid, a battle with the War Agricultural Committee owing to her refusal to have the lawns ploughed up, and an unauthorised visit to Dover, with one of the officers billeted at Queensclere, to get a peep through a telescope at the activities on the nearest bit of Hitler's Europe.

After skimming through all this light-hearted chatter I only pretended to go on fishing, and sat there with my brain revving round like a dynamo, right up till lunch-time.

It was by the merest fluke that I intercepted the postman this morning. I have never even seen him before, and it is the first time since my arrival that I have been down to the far end of the lake. Had I not been there when I was I think it extremely unlikely that Julia's letter would ever have been delivered to me; and that belief is supported by the fact that in it she mentions another letter of hers, written about April the 25th, which I have never received.

One thing is now beyond dispute. Somebody has prevented all the letters that I have written to Julia in the past six weeks from being posted; and evidently whoever it is fears that if I receive one from her it might give away the fact that she is not getting mine; so, in order to prevent my suspicions being aroused, my inward as well as my outward correspondence with her is being deliberately held up.

But why? And by whom?

Either Taffy or Deb take such few letters as I have for the post, and bring me the few that I receive. But neither of them has any reason to interfere with my private affairs, of which they know next to nothing; and both of them have well-paid jobs with which they seem fully contented, so why should either risk the sack for a thing like monkeying with my mail?

It must be Helmuth's doing. That is borne out by the fact that he lied to me last night. Why, otherwise, should he have spun me that yarn about Julia having had a breakdown and Uncle Paul taking her to Scotland? It can only have been because he knew the contents of the letters I had written to her, and felt that the time had come when I must be provided with a reason for her failure to respond to my urgent appeals, so that I should not yet get the idea that someone was preventing them from reaching her.

In all the years that I have spent in Helmuth's charge I have never before had the least cause to suspect him of tampering with my correspondence; yet it seems impossible to doubt that he has been doing so for the past month.

It did occur to me that Julia might have used Queensclere note-paper, although actually writing from Mull, but the envelope bears the Queensclere postmark of the 11th; so it was written on Sunday and posted there on Monday. Obviously, then, Julia must have still been there last weekend; yet Helmuth distinctly said last night: 'I had a letter from your Uncle Paul today', and 'a week ago he took her (Julia) up to Mull'. The only possible explanation for such a lie is that he is double-crossing me for some purpose of his own which he wishes to keep secret.

What can that purpose be? There is only one theory which would account for his secretly sabotaging my communications with Julia. He knows from my letters to her that I have implored her to come down and make arrangements for me to be moved from Llanferdrack, and he wants to prevent that.

Yet he must also know from my letters the reason why I want to be moved. He knows that I am being haunted, or rather – as his cold, materialistic mind would assess my outpourings – that I imagine myself to be haunted. But his putting it down to my imagination does not detract in the least from the agony of fear that it arouses in me, and I told Julia that, in no uncertain terms. Yet, instead of taking such steps as he could for my relief, Helmuth is doing the very opposite, and deliberately preventing Julia from coming to my assistance.

Why, in God's name, should he wish to add to, and prolong, my sufferings? I can only suppose that it is because he derives some strange, sadistic pleasure from them. That would account for the queer, searching, speculative look with which I have often caught him regarding me during his evening visits, this last month or so. I can hardly believe it possible – yet what other explanation for his extraordinary conduct can there be?

These horrible suspicions about a man for whom, even if he has failed to inspire in me any deep affection, I have always thought of with respect, and regarded as a friend, are enough to make anyone think that I am suffering from persecution mania. But I am sure that I am not. Now that this business of the letters has opened my eyes, I am beginning to see clearly for the first time. There are so many little things for which I have accepted Helmuth's glib explanations, that, looked at now from the new angle, go to show that he not only knows what it is I fear, but is getting some horrible, unnatural kick out of doing all he can to deprive me of protection from it.

To start with, there is the question of the blackout curtain. It was little enough to ask that it should be lengthened by six inches, but he first postponed the issue, then vetoed it entirely.

Then there is my reading-lamp. When Deb settles me down for the night she always moves it onto the centre table. After I had the horrors on April the 30th, I asked her to leave it by my bedside, so that I could light it again and read if I felt restless; although, of course, what I really wanted it there for was to light and drown the moonlight if the Thing came again. But she refused. She said that she had had strict instructions from Helmuth that in no circumstances was the Aladdin ever to be left within my reach; because if I read late at nights I might drop asleep while reading, then if I flung out an arm in my sleep I might knock it over, the flaming oil would set the place alight, and I should probably be burnt alive in my bed before anyone could reach me.

That sounds reasonable enough, but, all the same, I tackled him about it. He said he was sorry, but while he was responsible for me he really could not allow me to run such a risk. I asked him, then, to get me an electric torch. He said he would; but next day he volunteered the information that there were none to be had in the village, as all available supplies were now being sent to London and the other big cities, where the need for them was more urgent owing to air-raids.

That sounds plausible too; but all these things add up, if one starts with the assumption that Helmuth's object is to ensure that at night I should remain a prisoner in the dark – apart from that infernal strip of light thrown by the moon – and to keep me isolated here. Which reminds me about the telephone.

The main line goes to Helmuth's office, and there are extensions to a few of the bedrooms, up to which, of course, I cannot get. The only other is here, in the library, and I thought that another point in favour of its having been turned into a bed-sit for me. But a few days before I had my first 'nightmare' it went wrong. I asked Helmuth to get it put right, and he said he would; but nothing was done about it. When I spoke to him again he said that he was awfully sorry, but he had heard from the Post Office engineers, and they were so terribly busy installing lines to camps and airfields that they could not possibly find the time to repair extensions in private houses.

He went on to point out that in the three weeks I had been here I hadn't used it more than half a dozen times, so I should hardly miss it; and that if I did want to telephone I could always do so in the daytime by being wheeled along in my chair to his office.

That is all very well, but when Helmuth is not in his office he always keeps it locked. The tacit assumption is, of course, that I have no secrets from him, so there is nothing that I should want to telephone about which it would cause me embarrassment to mention in his presence. But with him at my elbow how can I telephone Julia, as I've wanted to a score of times in the past ten days? I mean, I couldn't possibly tell her in front of him the reason why I want her to cancel all her engagements and fag down here to Wales.

Another pointer concerns the radiogram. Mine is a big cabinet affair, that also plays eight gramophone records off without being touched, and it lives on the far side of the fireplace. When things started to happen again at the beginning of this month I asked to have it moved up close to my bed, so that if I was subject to any more of these damnable visitations it would be within easy reach, and I could turn it on. I had small hope that the sound of martial music would scare the Thing off, but I thought it might fortify me and at least make the room seem a little less like a morgue.

Deb objected at once because the cabinet is so heavy that it takes two people to shift it, and would mean an awful performance each night and morning moving it to and from my bedside; or else it would have to remain there permanently, in which case, whichever side I had it, its bulk would prevent her from getting at me from all angles to give me my massage.

I was so set on having it by me that I appealed to Helmuth; but he supported her. He said that it was unreasonable of me to want to put people to so much bother for a sudden whim; and that, in any case, for the sake of my health I needed all the sleep I could get at nights, so he was averse to any innovation which would enable me to lie awake listening to music.

I suppose most people would consider me a pretty wet sort of type for allowing myself to be dictated to like that; but then they don't know Helmuth. He tackles every problem that arises with such cheerful briskness, and his views are always so clear-cut and logical, that it is almost impossible to argue with him. At least, I find it so; but that may be because he became the dominant influence in my life from the time I was thirteen, and years of unquestioning submission to whatever he considered best for me formed a habit of mind that I now find it almost impossible to break.

That is why I kow-towed to his decision that he could not agree to my shifting my quarters; although I am sure that it would not have made the slightest difference if I had gone off the deep end. He would have told me to 'be my age' and have walked out of the room; and he knows perfectly well that it is impossible for me to get myself moved without his consent. His attitude in this, more than in anything else, now convinces me that he is deliberately keeping me a prisoner here, because he knows it to be the focal point of my fears, and is deriving a brutal, cynical amusement from watching them develop.

After these two consecutive nights in early April I already had the wind up pretty badly, so I told him that I wasn't sleeping well, and would like to be moved to another room. There are plenty of others in this great barrack of a place, but he brushed the idea aside with reasons against which it seemed childish to argue.

Obviously, for me to be anywhere but on the ground floor would mean that all my meals would have to be brought up to me, and that I should have to be carried up and down stairs every day to go out for my airing – and that would be placing much too great a burden on our very limited staff. The rooms in the old part of the Castle have been long untenanted, and are damp and cheerless. That left only the east wing, which contained the suite of reception-rooms in which my Great-aunt Sarah vegetates, and I could not possibly turn her out after all these years. Here I have a fine big room that gets all the sun and has easy access to the garden; and if I wasn't sleeping well in it there was no reason whatever to suppose that I should sleep better elsewhere. What could I reply to that? And, as my 'nightmares' did not recur for over three weeks, it was not until the end of the month that I had cause really to worry about the matter further.

But on May the 2nd, after two more visitations, I was in a real flap, and I tackled him again. I said that I had come to the conclusion that Wales did not suit me, and I felt sure that a change of surroundings would do me good.

He dismissed that one as too silly for serious consideration; and I must admit that so long as Britain remains at death-grips with Germany we could hardly be better situated than we are down here. It is a far cry from Whitehall to this lonely valley in the heart of the Welsh mountains, and things like rations, Home Guards, A.R.P. and Flag days, seem to belong to a different world. In fact, if it weren't for the blackout, and the odd German bomber that has got off her course passing over us at night once in a while, we might regard the war as though it was taking place on Mars.

As I did not give Helmuth my real reason for wanting to leave Llanferdrack, I thought that his refusal to consider moving me might be due in part to a feeling that if I went elsewhere, he would be under a moral obligation to accompany. It seemed only natural that he should be averse to leaving such comfortable quarters for some place where we should probably suffer all the inconveniences of the war – not to mention air-raids.

That just shows how preconceived ideas of a person's character can give one a false conception of their motives. But it is clear now that he was perfectly well aware what lay behind my anxiety to be moved. He must have been, because he had intercepted my letters to Julia. Yet, instead of seeking a good pretext to cover my departure which would also have freed him from any obligation to leave with me, he chose to allow me to continue to suffer the torture of the damned, and even took measures to aggravate my situation, so that he could gloat in secret over the signs that my experiences were turning me into a nervous wreck.

Wait, though! It goes deeper than that. Why did he start to intercept my mail? He has never done so in the past. I have been assuming that he could have found out about my 'nightmares' only by reading my letters, and that he then took steps to isolate me for his sadistic amusement. But that is not it. I have been putting the cart before the horse. It must be so; because some of his measures to render me vulnerable to the attacks were taken before I wrote about them to Julia.

Then he is not simply making a callous study of me in the belief that I am a victim of hallucinations. He knows that the Thing in the courtyard exists. Since he did not learn of it through me, he must either have seen it himself or been told about it by someone here who has done so. This is the final proof that I am not mad; for, if someone else has also seen the brute, it must be something more than a figment of my imagination.

Later
This discovery, that Helmuth must have been aware of the Thing's existence before myself, opens up the most appalling abyss of treachery, and possibilities which it is horrible to contemplate.

It infers that he put me in this room next to the courtyard, and had the blackout curtains made six inches shorter, on purpose; that in a dozen different ways he is wilfully facilitating the attacks; that he cannot be a sceptic, as I always believed, but accepts the existence of evil occult forces and is gloating over the terror that they inspire in me.

Perhaps, even, he has great knowledge of them, as he has of so many queer subjects? Perhaps he has some control over this evil entity? Perhaps – yes, perhaps it is he who has conjured it up?

This is ghastly! It has become suddenly and appallingly clear that he must be deliberately plotting my destruction.

Thursday, 14th May

In view of the mental earthquake that I sustained yesterday, it is somewhat surprising to be able to record that I had an excellent night. Perhaps that was due to my brain having become addled with fatigue from straining to find answers to so many new conundrums; but usually that kind of mental tiredness leads only to restless, unrefreshing sleep. I think it more likely that I owe my good night to subconscious relief at the knowledge that I am up against a human enemy.

Perhaps I am being a bit premature in relegating the Thing to second place; and I certainly do not mean to imply that I would rank it lower than the most evil man ever born of woman, when it is actually present.

What I am getting at is that I now know Helmuth to be at the back of this horrible business. Whether he just found out about the Thing haunting the courtyard – as it may have done for centuries – and decided to place me in its vicinity, or whether he is in some way responsible for its appearance, I have no idea. But I do know that he is deliberately detaining me here and exposing me to its attacks. Therefore it is him that I have to fight; and he is only a man like myself – except that he has the advantage of having two sound legs and a far better brain.

In a human conflict there is always a sporting chance that the weaker party may come out on top; although the fact that he has succeeded in isolating me makes me terribly aware that the odds are now pretty heavy against my being able to save myself from – well, something that even to think of makes me break out into a sweat.

Why Helmuth should wish to expose me to such a diabolical fate is entirely beyond my comprehension. I have never done him the least ill; on the contrary, his association with myself and my family has brought him comparative affluence, and he must have had the best possible reasons for believing that his position was as secure as anything could be in these uncertain times.

If I ever get a say in the matter it will be so no longer. Even if he was in complete ignorance of the Thing, he would still be guilty of the most brutal callousness in refusing my requests – to be moved to another room, to have the blackout curtain lengthened, to let me have a lamp or my radiogram beside my bed, to get me a torch or have my telephone mended. What the hell is he here for, anyway?

Of course, since quite early in the war he has had the job of managing the Llanferdrack estate; but from the time I was brought here his first duty was to look after me, and see that I was made as comfortable as possible.

He seems to have forgotten that he is only an employee, and still liable to be sacked. But is he? After all, he was placed in charge here by the Trustees, and it is quite certain that I could not sack him myself – or get him sacked. At least, not unless I could put up such a hell of a strong case that it would completely destroy the faith that Julia and Uncle Paul have in him – and even that might not be enough, since he managed to get appointed as one of the Trustees himself, after old Wellard died in 1939.

Why, I wonder, am I now considering him in relation to the post he fills – which is virtually that of my Guardian – and realising for the first time since I arrived here how lamentably he has carried out its functions? It can only be because my eyes have suddenly been opened and I am thinking of him in an entirely new light.

I feel quite ashamed of myself when I think of my normal un-questioning subservience to him, and I still don't fully understand its continuance now that I am grown up. The habit of years is mainly responsible, I know, but looking back on some recent episodes, and regarding them dispassionately, I believe there is something more to it than that. The unwinking stare of those queer, tawny eyes of his, when he announces a decision, may have something to do with it. I am sure that he uses them as a vehicle for transmitting his will. Perhaps the answer is that he has secured my acquiescence to his wishes for all these years by holding me under a mild form of hypnosis.

If that is so, it is a game that two can play. Squadron-Leader Cooper, the R.A.F. doctor at Nether Wallop, told me that I had hypnotic eyes; and just for the fun of it he tried me out in the Mess one night. He had been a psychiatrist before the war, so knew the drill, and some of the successes he achieved were quite remarkable. I did not get very far, but in two instances I succeeded in putting chaps into a light sleep and got them to do simple things; and afterwards they swore that they had not known what they were up to.

This is worth thinking about. I don't suppose for a moment that I could challenge and defeat Helmuth's will; but practice might strengthen my powers of resistance; and with so much at stake I should be crazy not to try out any conceivable weapon that I may have in my sadly limited armory.

But I have been getting off the track a bit. Whether Helmuth has performed his *in loco parentis* function as my Guardian well or ill is now entirely beside the point. For some reason that I do not pretend to understand, he has suffered a 'sea change' from my aloof and cynical mentor to my secret, implacable enemy.

I am not quite certain that I am not mad, but it seems on the cards that he may be. No-one who knows him would question the brilliance of his mind, and it is said that only a hair-line separates genius from madness. Perhaps two-and-a-half years of seclusion here, with no-one of his own kind to talk to, have led to his indulging in the sort of long periods of morbid introspection that sometimes drive people over the edge.

Anyhow, whether he is mad or sane, I have got to get out of his clutches somehow. If I could get a letter to Uncle Paul I could make an official request that he and the other Trustees should come here to see me on business, then when they arrived have a show-down. That would be the hell of a risk to take, as I have not a shred of evidence against Helmuth, and unless I could trick him into making some stupid admission I should be laying myself open to their deciding that I ought to be put in a nut-house. Anyway, it is not worth even considering fot the moment, as he would be just as certain to intercept any letter I wrote to Uncle Paul as he would another to Julia.

If only I had a doctor visiting me regularly I could try getting at him to pull a fast one over Helmuth, by ordering my removal to a local nursing home. But I haven't. Apart from the injury to my spine, my health is excellent; so there has been no occasion since I arrived here to call the local sawbones in, and I don't even know his name. The specialists in London declared that nothing further could be done for me, except to continue the massage, so Helmuth said it seemed waste of time and money to drag some country G.P. up here to look at me once a week; and, little realising how glad I might be later to have someone like that on tap, I agreed.

Reconsidering the matter, I am inclined to wonder if the present arrangement, by which I am to be re-vetted by a specialist two or three times a year, really is enough; and if I ought not to have a local man keep a watching brief over my case. It looks as if the present set-up is another item in Helmuth's plan to isolate me; anyway I am certain that he would not agree to any alteration of it now.

Of course I could say that I had ear-ache, or something, and insist that the local man be called in. But if I did Helmuth would make a point of being on hand in the role of 'anxious Guardian' during the doctor's visit; so I would have no chance to talk to him in private and beg him to get me away from here.

It now seems all too damnably clear that I cannot hope to bring any influence to bear on Helmuth from outside which will force him to accept my removal; so the only remaining possibility is to take the law into my own hands and get away one night without his knowledge.

But that is utterly impossible without assistance, and the devil of it is that there is no-one here of whom I can make a confidant, or trust to help me. Both Deb and Taffy are obviously scared stiff of Helmuth, and I rarely see any of the other servants. Great-aunt Sarah's establishment is run separately from ours and she has her own dining-room, so I have scarcely exchanged a word with that gawky old stick Miss Nettelfold, who acts as her housekeeper-companion. My few friends are all up to their necks in the war, so none of them are able to come all the way down here to Wales to see me; and I know nobody locally, so I never have any visitors. Even if I could get hold of one of the servants I am sure they would not dare to aid in my escape. They would be much too scared of Helmuth and the certainty that they would lose their jobs afterwards.

Of course, if I were in a position to make it really worth some-body's while to get me into a car, or even wheel me down to the station in the small hours so that I could catch the early-morning train, that would put a very different light on my chances. If I had fifty pounds with which to tempt Taffy I'm pretty sure that I could get him to play. But Helmuth pays all my bills for me and, as he pointed out when we arranged about that soon after I arrived here, an invalid has no use for ready money; so I haven't even fifty pence.

How absurdly ironical that is, seeing that I am one of the richest men in England. At least, I shall be if I am still alive and sane on the 20th of June next – when I reach the age of twenty-one.

Saturday, 16th May

I wrote nothing yesterday, as I spent a good part of the day reading over what I have so far written. It seems an awful woffal, without any proper sequence, and practically nothing about who I am or how I came to be associated with Helmuth.

Of course, I started these notes solely with the idea of trying to get certain things clear in my own mind; but, on finding that scribbling down my thoughts just as they arose helped to keep them off the 'horror', I began to let myself ramble on about this and that. Then I began to think of this script as a sort of personal testament that I hoped would reach Julia if anything happened to me. But I see that I have covered pages and pages with stuff that she already knows about – which seems a pointless thing to have done. Still, I am not sorry about that now, as a new theory to account for what is happening here occurred to me last night; and, in view of that, this journal may yet serve a different and more practical purpose. If it does, most of what I have so far written will not, after all, have been a waste of time.

My new line of thought inclines me to believe that Helmuth is not mad, but either on his own account or in association with others has hatched a diabolical plot – the object of which is to drive me insane.

I have not a title of evidence to support this new theory, but it is, I believe, an axiom that the basis of all crime is motive and opportunity and both are present in my case.

It was re-reading the last paragraph I wrote on Thursday that gave me this idea. There is more than a grain of truth in the old saying 'Money is the root of all Evil', and in my life and sanity are vested a great fortune.

Should anything prevent my coming into my inheritance, at the end of next month, there are quite a number of people who would benefit. Not directly, perhaps, but by continuing to enjoy the control of my grandfather's wealth, and all the opportunities that gives for amassing riches themselves. Therefore it is by no means inconceivable that one, or more, of them would like to ensure that I shall never assume the reins of power in the vast commercial Empire that old Albert Abel Jugg built up.

I do not fear murder, because scientific crime investigation has made it extremely difficult to get away with murder in these days. The sudden death of anyone so potentially rich as myself would be certain to arouse widespread comment in the press. A flock of reporters would arrive to get the story. Each of them would question everybody here in the hope of picking up some 'human interest' line that their colleagues had missed; and they are a bright lot of boys. If one of them tumbled on the least suspicious circumstance it would result in Scotland Yard being tipped off to look into matters. Besides, Julia would call the police in at once if there were the smallest thing to suggest that my death had been due to foul play. So I do not believe that any secret enemies I may have would dare to risk it.

An even stronger argument against it is that my death would result in the dissolution of the estate. Great sums would pass to the nation and to various charities; some individuals would benefit, of course, but Helmuth is not among them; and most of the other Trustees would lose on balance, because once the estate was wound up they would cease to enjoy their present lucrative and powerful stewardships.

On the other hand, should I become insane, those who are now responsible for handling the Jugg millions will firstly escape being called upon in a few weeks' time to give an account of the uses to which those millions have been put during my minority and, secondly, continue in indisputed control of them for as long as I remain a candidate for a strait-jacket.

Once I was certified it would mean a life-sentence. It is said to be difficult to get a chit from the Board of Lunacy, but it must be a darn sight more difficult to get the chit rescinded. If I am right, and there is a conspiracy to put me in a loony-bin, one can be quite certain that, in the event of its coming off, the conspirators will find it an easy wicket to prevent my getting out again.

Well, there is the motive. As for opportunity: here I am, a semi-paralysed hulk, cut off from communication with the outside world, and completely in the power of an ambitious man who has succeeded in getting himself made one of the controllers of the Jugg millions.

Perhaps my imagination really has run away with me now; but, all the same, I have decided to make this journal a very different document from anything that might have resulted from my earlier intentions. I mean to tell the whole story from the beginning; then, even if these sheets of paper never reach Julia, but fall into the hands of any honest person, they may yet be produced as evidence of my fundamental sanity, and perhaps assist in bringing my enemies to justice.

I shall not start on this new departure today, though. In fact I should not have made any entry at all, had I not been anxious to get down my latest ideas on what lies behind Helmuth's secret moves against me. Yesterday, after tea, I succeeded in finding a book on Hypnotism in the library, here, and I am already deep in it, so I may not have much time for writing during the next few days.

Sunday, 17th May
I find some of the technical stuff in the book on Hypnotism pretty heavy going, and it is no good fuddling my brain by sticking to it for too long at a time; so I shall write a page or two of this between whiles.

Here goes, then, on the facts about myself:

I am Flight-Lieutenant Sir Albert Abel Jugg, Bart., D.F.C., R.A.F.V.R. (Ret.). The title, of course, came to me from my grand-father; the Royal Air Force rank and decoration I got for myself.

My father insisted on my being christened Albert Abel after his father and himself; but my mother must have had a sense of humour, as before I was born she vowed that, whatever I might be christened, she meant to call me Toby. She died giving me birth, but my father carried out her wish, so Toby I have been to my family and friends all my life.

I know nothing at all of my forebears on my mother's side, and on my father's I can go back only two generations; although I do know that he came of Yorkshire stock and that the family were poor farm people just outside Sheffield; and that it was in the office of one of the smaller iron-founders there that my grandfather began his meteoric career.

He was a money-spinner – one of those amazing Victorians who started life as an office-boy at the age of eight and by the time they were thirty emerged as great industrialists. In those happy days British goods were the most sought-after in the world's markets, and handsome profits could be put back into a growing business to make it more prosperous still – instead of being swallowed up by the crippling demands of a fantastically high income-tax – so it is easy to understand how a clever, energetic man could soon convert a modest capital into considerable riches. But the transition from poverty to even moderate affluence is the part in such stories which always mystifies me. How did the little thirty-bob-a-week clerk without influence or backing ever manage to make his first five thousand pounds?

One thing is quite certain: no ambitious young man, however brainy and hard-working, would be able to do so now. Socialist economics have chained the masses and are relentlessly pressing them into a pattern so that in another generation they will be no more than human robots.

The Trade Unions already decree that no man must work longer hours or receive a bigger pay packet than the laziest and most incompetent of his companions employed on the same type of job – and soon they will make it illegal for him to attempt to better himself by leaving the job he is in for another. It is almost as hopeless for non-union men and black-coated workers to try to build up a little capital, or for people who already have small businesses to increase theirs; because, as soon as any of them begin to make a bit more than a living wage, the Government takes away the best part of anything they might save, in taxes largely levied to support a vast bureaucracy which is entirely non-productive.

But things were very different in Queen Victoria's day. My grandfather was only one of thousands who started from nothing and ended up a man of property. It was, I suppose, a blend of luck, thrift, scope for initiative, payment by results, and the freedom to work eighteen hours a day if they wanted to, that enabled them to make those first little sacks of golden sovereigns; then the untaxed profits on bold, imaginative business ventures did the rest.

Albert Abel Jugg was, therefore, a typical product of his times. He differed only from most of his successful contemporaries in being one of the first to realise that far greater profits could be made by operating a chain of companies, which between them produced a raw material and converted it to its final purpose, than from any one link in it. Thus, having started in an iron-foundry, he persuaded the partners to buy a small iron-mine; then a coal-mine so that they made a profit on the fuel they used. The firm went in for making steel plate for shipping, and his next move was to buy up a shipbuilding company that had got into low water.

A few years later they decided that they would sell no more ships, but run a shipping line themselves. He did not go in for luxury liners, but stout little tramps and soon he had scores of them ploughing the seas with mixed cargoes from port to port all over the world. Later he went in for building commercial motor vehicles and, lastly, aircraft. By that time he had his own rubber plantations, timber forests, tanneries, chrome, bauxite, nickel and tungsten mines. At the time of his death he held a controlling interest in more than sixty companies, and he left over fourteen million pounds.

He had a flair for picking his subordinates and oceans of hard, sound common sense; but I never heard of him pulling off any spectacular financial coups, or, indeed, doing anything remarkable. He was blessed with excellent health, so he never retired, and remained till the end entirely wrapped up in his business. His tastes were simple and his appreciation of beauty, art, culture and grace apparently non-existent; he never went out of his way to acquire the appurtenances of great wealth; they seemed rather to collect haphazard about him.

The big mansion in Kensington Palace Gardens, where I spent most of my early childhood, was not his deliberate choice for a London home; he moved into it only because he had taken it over in settlement for a debt that a peer, who was a director of one of his companies, could not pay. Queensclere he bought, not for the lovely old house, but because the eastern part of the estate lay adjacent to the Kentish coal mines, and he was advised that some two hundred acres of it had valuable deposits beneath them.

Rather than go to the trouble of furnishing either house himself he bought the bulk of their contents with them. Queensclere had belonged for many generations to a family of moderate fortune and excellent taste, whereas the Kensington mansion had been acquired by the nouveau riche peer only a decade earlier; so when in the country we lived in an atmosphere of dignity and grace, and when in London surrounded by Victorian horrors; but I doubt if he noticed the difference.

Llanferdrack Castle was bought by him on account of my Great-aunt Sarah. Since the poor lady refused to leave the vicinity of the tragedy that had robbed her of her fiancé, he said that she had better have the Castle to live in. Here, too, he bought most of the contents for an all-in price; but in the library there was quite a number of rare books, and when he saw the valuation he refused to include it in the deal. In consequence the library was sold separately and the room was left bleak and denuded, with rows and rows of empty shelves. That offended his sense of the fitness of things and the way he dealt with the matter was typical of his mentality.

On Friday, when I searched the shelves for a book on Hypnotism, I already knew that they held one of the most astounding collections of junk that any room calling itself a library could ever have contained, but quite how astounding I did not realise until I started to go through them systematically. The explanation is that when my grandfather wanted to refill the shelves he contracted with a book-seller in the Charing Cross Road to do the job at a flat rate and, irrespective of size, he refused to pay more than ten shillings a foot!

Naturally, the bulk of it consists of out-of-date encylopedias, the colected sermons of long-dead divines, books of dreary personal reminiscences that their garrulous authors must have paid to have printed, fifty-year-old novels of incredible dullness, and pub-lishers' remainders of all kinds. But, by a piece of exceptional good fortune, I found a bulky volume called *Hypnotism, its History, Practice and Theory*, by J. Mime Bramwell, which, for this array of mainly nineteenth-century trash, bears the comparatively recent date of 1903.

It could not have been out long when it was condemned to make one among the seven or eight hundred feet of books that cover the walls of this room; so no doubt its presence here is due to the fact that its title page is missing and its cover loose; but, luckily, its 470-odd pages of text are intact and they contain a wealth of information, so, thanks to Dr Bramwell, I am gradually getting a grip on the theory of this fascinating subject.

Reverting to my grandfather. It was not unnatural that a man so entirely absorbed in the great commercial structure that he had created should wish to found a dynasty, and many years before his death laid plans to ensure that his heir should enjoy the same undisputed authority over his Empire as he had himself.

So that his heir should not be compelled to part with the con-trolling interest in any of the companies at his death, in order to raise the vast sum necessary to pay death duties, he devoted a considerable part of his income to insurances which would cover them; and as soon as my father showed that he had inherited his father's talent for business he was given one directorship after another, so that long before he died he was openly recognised as the heir-apparent.

That my father should have turned out to have all the makings of a worthy successor must have been a great joy to the old man; he was far from being so fortunate in his second son. Father entered the business on leaving Cambridge, and was already an important executive in it by the time the First World War broke out, so he was considered too much of a key man to be allowed to volunteer for one of the services; but Uncle Paul was nearly ten years younger, and went straight into the war at the age of eighteen.

It may have been that which unsettled him and made him later unfitted for a business career. But I don't think he would ever have been capable of controlling a big organisation. He is much too lazy and pleasure-loving, and no amount of training can give a man a first-class brain if he hasn't got the right type of grey matter to start with.

Anyway, grandfather evidently decided that he was a hopeless bet, and preferred to take a gamble on me to carry on the dynasty should anything happen to my father. As I was only a few years old when his last will was drawn up, he went to considerable pains to protect my interests in the event of both my father and himself dying while I was still a minor; and the arrangement he decided on was that a Board of seven Trustees should be formed, which would have the following powers:

(1) To appoint such of its members as it considered most suitable to directorships of the Jugg companies, for the purpose of representing the interests of the Trust.

(2) Elect new Trustees to fill any vacancies which might occur on the Board through death or retirement, and to create additional Trustees should this be considered desirable.

(3) To invest all profits accruing to the Trust during my minority, either in taking up further shares in the Jugg companies, or in acquiring holdings in other concerns which it was planned ultimately to bring within the Jugg organisation.

(4) To appoint one of their number as my Guardian, who would undertake to give me the personal care of a parent, and be responsible to them that my education should be designed to fit me for taking my place as the head of the Jugg Empire in due course.

It will be seen that the old man's scheme, while sound enough in its broad principles, did give the Trustees certain opportunities to feather their own nests at my expense if, at any time, the Board included two or three dishonest members who got together and were clever enough to pull the wool over the eyes of the others. The Trustees were, no doubt, purposely given no direct remunerations, as the old man felt that they would be more than adequately paid for their trouble by the fees they would get from sharing out the sixty-odd directorships between them. That is fair enough; but the Clause empowering them to invest profits in concerns which it is planned 'ultimately to bring within the Jugg organisation' opens the way for all sorts of double-dealing.

The Jugg interests are now so varied that an unscrupulous Trustee might buy up the shares of pretty well any business that looked like going on the rocks, and, after nursing it for a year or two, make a very handsome profit – if he had enough backing on the Board to be sure of selling it to the Trust.

I have wondered, more than once, if that is how Harry Iswick has succeeded in making so much money during the past ten years. He owes his place on the Board to the fact that he was my grandfather's confidential secretary; and so, apart from my father, knew more than anyone else about the old man's affairs. I remember Julia telling me that, in those days, he used to live in a little semi-detached house out at Acton, but now he has a flat in Grosvenor House, a big place at Maidenhead, and just before the war he had bought himself a villa in the South of France. He has not yet been nominated by the Board as their representative director on any of the larger companies, so I should not think he collects more than two thousand five hundred a year in fees, and he certainly could not live in the way he does on that.

Of course he is a clever little devil, and his position on the Board gives him access to all sorts of information out of which he could make money more or less legitimately: so he may be reasonably honest. In any case grandfather must have thought him so, as, in selecting the original Trustees, the old man would naturally have picked only men he believed that he could trust.

The others he chose were: Lord Embleton, Sir Stanley Wellard and Mr C. J. Rootham – all men who had been closely associated with him in business for many years; two partners of the firm of Bartorship, Brown and Roberts and one partner from the firm of Smith & Co. The former were his Chartered Accountants and the latter his Solicitors. In both cases the Trusteeships were really vested in the firms rather than individuals, so as to ensure that they would retain permanent representation on the Board. The accountants nominated Mr Alec Bartorship and Mr Charles Roberts; the solicitors, Mr Angus Smith.

Since the inception of the Board there have been several changes. Mr Rootham retired in 1934, after having persuaded his colleagues to accept his son, Guy Rootham, as his successor. Mr Bartorship retired in 1935, and his firm nominated his nephew, Claud Bartorship, to take his place. Sir Stanley Wellard died suddenly in September 1939, and as, in the excitement of those first few weeks of war, the more likely candidates for this desirable vacancy appear to have been too occupied to press their claims, Helmuth succeeded in getting himself appointed; mainly, I believe, owing to the influence exerted on his behalf by Harry Iswick and Uncle Paul.

I should have mentioned that Uncle Paul was co-opted as an additional Trustee, soon after the first meeting of the Board. This was partly because everybody felt very sorry for him. The will had been drawn up four years earlier, in 1925, just after he had had to be pulled out of a most hopeless financial mess for the fourth time in six years; so the only mention of him in it was as beneficiary under a small, separate Trust, which was to administer a capital that would bring him in about fifteen hundred a year.

That really was pretty hard on the only surviving son of a multi-millionaire; and the Trustees all thought that had my grandfather made a fresh will, just before he died, he would have treated him much more generously, now that he seemed to have turned over a new leaf and looked like settling down with Julia.

Perhaps, though, their sympathy might not have gone further than to give him another chance to make good with one of the companies, had it not been for the question of myself. But it so happened that, while every member of the Board was prepared to give me a home, none of them really wanted the bother and responsibility of bringing me up.

Before Uncle Paul knew anything about the contents of the will he had announced that he considered it up to his wife and himself to take care of the orphan, and immediately after the funeral he had installed me at Kew; so he seemed to be the obvious person to act as my Guardian. As, under the will, my Guardian had to be one of the Trustees, to make him one, which would at the same time enable the Board to compensate him a little for the raw deal he had had under his father's will by giving him a few minor directorships, was clearly the solution.

At present, therefore, the Board consists of:

Lord Embledon, who is now over eighty, and rarely attends meetings; although he still retains the office of Chairman, which he has held from the beginning.

Harry Iswick, a very active, but, to my mind, not altogether trustworthy type; who, on Sir Stanley Wellard's death in 1939, got himself elected as Deputy Chairman and, owing to Embledon's withdrawal from affairs since the war started, now more or less runs the Party.

Guy Rootham, a good, sound chap; but, unfortunately for me, one with such an expert knowledge of medium-sized shipbuilding that he is now disguised as a Brigadier and on permanent loan to the United States to help them design improved types of Landing Craft.

Charles Roberts, an elderly and very staid accountant, who, on the few occasions I have met him, appeared incapable of taking an interest in anything except figures.

Claud Bartorship, of the same firm; a nice fellow, but now a

Captain in the Pay Corps stationed, when I last heard of him, in Cairo.

Angus Smith, the solicitor, who, like Embledon, is now in the neighbourhood of eighty, and won't give up because he doesn't want to loose the fees his directorships bring him; but has retired to his native Scotland, and comes down only to clock-in at the minimum number of board meetings requisite to prevent his co-Trustees being able legally to demand his resignation.

Uncle Paul, who, I am sure, is very well disposed towards me, but is weak as water, and could be swayed, either by Julia in my interests, or by Helmuth against them.

Dr Helmuth Lisický, who, I am convinced, is the nigger in the wood-pile – if there is a wood-pile?

So what it boils down to is that two out of my grandfather's three remaining contemporaries, Embledon and Smith, now so rarely attend the meetings of the Board that they can know little of what goes on at it, and the third, Roberts, is so lacking in personality that he can never have exerted any great influence over its decisions; Rootham and Bartorship, the two men upon whom I could best rely to safeguard my interests, are both abroad on war-service, and Uncle Paul, who knows nothing of finance, would accept without question any proposal put up by the others. That leaves Iswick and Helmuth as the only strong men remaining in the party; and, as four out of the other six have been more or less out of the game for most of the war, they have had only old Roberts and my dull-witted uncle to deal with; so it seems pretty clear that for the past few years Messrs. I. and H. have virtually controlled the Trust between them.

Perhaps my suspicions of Iswick are entirely unfounded, but there can be no getting away from it that, if he is in collusion with Helmuth, the war has given the two of them a unique opportunity to do the Trust down. If they have, one can quite understand their now being prepared to go to pretty well any lengths rather than risk exposure by handing over the accounts.

On my coming of age, were it not for the war, I suppose there would have been gigantic celebrations; every factory and office in the combine closed for the day; beanfeasts for all the workers followed by dances and fireworks at night; a huge reception in London for all directorates and senior staffs, at which the eight Trustees would formally hand me my sceptre to the accompaniment of loud cheers and the drinking of much champagne.

As things are, all I can do is to arrange that everyone in the organisation should receive a handsome bonus. There certainly won't be much celebrating so far as I am concerned; just a birthday lunch, which the Trustees will come down from London to attend before giving me an account of their stewardship; and for that the two old crocks will drag themselves out of their retirement to make a special appearance – so six out of eight of them will be here.

What an opportunity for a showdown with Helmuth! I had forgotten that, although he can prevent me from writing to ask them to come here, they will be coming anyhow on my birthday.

But June the 20th is still over a month away; and I've another full-moon period to get through before that. Somehow I've got to find a way to outwit Helmuth. Unless I can, I've a horrible conviction that by the time the big day does arrive he will have reduced me to such a state that I shall be judged incapable of taking over anything.

Monday, 18th May
I have finished Dr Bramwell's book on Hypnotism and re-read some parts of it several times, so I have now got a pretty good grasp on the theory of the business. It remains to be seen whether I can apply it in practice. The fact that I succeeded with those two chaps in the Mess at Nether Wallop cannot be taken as an indication, since they lent themselves willingly to the experiment, whereas here I must attempt it without the cooperation of my subject.

Dr Bramwell says that although it is not impossible to hypnotise a person against his will, it is very difficult to do so. Unfortunately he gives no information about the relative difficulty of hypnotising a person without their knowledge; and the two are obviously very different matters. In the first case, the subject having refused to play naturally sets up a strong mental resistance if he is seized, his eyes held open, and the experiment proceeded with; in the second, it seems to me that if the subject can be caught unawares, and proves susceptible, he might be got under with comparative ease – and provided, of course, that the operator could catch the subject's glance and hold it for long enough to do the trick without him suspecting what was being attempted.

Normally such a problem does not arise, as doctors who treat patients under hypnosis naturally never do so without first having obtained their consent, except sometimes in the case of lunatics, and then to have their eyes held open is presumably the usual method. But for me, success or failure depends entirely on whether I catch my subject napping.

As Taffy is far slower-witted than Deb I shall start on him, and I have decided that the best time to make the attempt is when he is giving me my before-dinner bath. He has to lift me in and out of it, but I am still capable of washing myself except for my lower limbs. While he is waiting to do my feet and ankles he always stands at the foot of the bath. If I say something to him he looks straight at me, but otherwise he just remains there with a vacant look on his round face; and it certainly provides the best opportunity for a prolonged attempt without risk of interruption, as no-one will butt in on us and I have never known Taffy move from his habitual position until our routine is completed.

In glancing over the pages I wrote yesterday, I see that I omitted to mention what provision my grandfather had made in his will for the possibility that both my father and I might pre-decease him, or that both of us might die before I reached the age of twenty-one.

Here again, in the main, the old gentleman displayed his dominating desire that, even if there was no Jugg at the head of it, the Empire he had created should survive and prosper. As a gesture to Charity he left a million to the Benevolent Fund for his employees that he had already founded in his lifetime, and a further half-million to the Seamen's Homes; but the great bulk of his fortune was willed back to the Companies out of which it had come, to be divided amongst them in proportion to the value of the holding that he had in each and the sums concerned added to their reserves, thus enormously strengthening them against the hazards of slumps, strikes, and periods of restricted trading.

The effect of my death, therefore, would be to send up the value of the shares in all the Jugg controlled companies by several points. That would make big stockholders like Embledon, Rootham and a number of others potentially richer by several thousand pounds; but in view of their long association with the combine, it is most unlikely that they would cash in on their holdings on that account. So there is no-one who would derive an immediate and really worthwhile benefit from knocking me off.

Before leaving the subject of the Will and the Trust I should like to put it on record that, up to the outbreak of the war, I never had the least reason to suppose that any of the Trustees were neglecting their duties, and that I recall with gratitude the personal interest they all showed in me.

From time to time in the holidays each of them asked me to their houses, or took me out to lunch, and put me through a friendly catechism designed to satisfy themselves that I was happy, healthy and making reasonable progress with my studies. Of course, it was part of their responsibility to make sure that I was being groomed for industrial stardom, but they did it very nicely.

As I adored Julia, regarded Uncle Paul as a good-natured stooge, and enjoyed ample opportunity for self-expression at Weylands, the only complaints I ever made were that I was seldom given the chance to be with other young people in the holidays, and was expected to continue my studies under Helmuth with as much enthusiasm as I did in term-time.

In various fashions peculiar to each they laughed that off; the gist of their refrain being that I must think of myself as a young royalty, whose duty it was to fit himself for the great power he would wield when he grew up, and that since it was necessary for me to acquire a working knowledge of a far wider range of subjects than the average boy, I must grin and bear it, if some of them had to be taken in the holidays, with the result that the time I could spend just idling about with other youngsters was heavily curtailed.

As a matter of fact Julia had already sold me that one as soon as I settled down with her at Kew; and I give her full marks for the way she handled me. Her line was that the better educated I became the more enjoyment I should get out of my great wealth when I grew up; so I must not look on lessons as a bore but as a necessary preparation to the appreciation of a thousand delights to come.

She, too, encouraged me to look upon myself as different from other children, and no doubt it was in order to prevent me from realising that I was not that she kept me away from them; but, on the other hand, she checked any tendency in me to become swollen-headed by decreeing that, until I was seventeen, I should always be known in the household as 'Master' Toby, instead of the servants addressing me by the title I had inherited, that I should never give orders to any of them without her permission, and that my pocket money should not exceed the average amount given to boys of my age.

I do not think that my brain is in any way out of the ordinary, but Julia and Helmuth between them certainly induced me to make the best of it, as I found when I went into the R.A.F. that my general knowledge far exceeded that of the great majority of the junior officers with whom I mixed. The secret of this is, I am sure, that I was never forced to continue at any subject until I got stale and tired of it.

At Weylands, of course, one was allowed a free choice of work, but the fault of the system is that, despite the cleverness of the masters in inducing the pupils to acquire at least a smattering of the subjects that attract them least, most of them do leave with some pretty thin patches in their education, and Helmuth was taken on especially to thicken up the more faulty parts of mind, during the holidays. Even so he managed to do it without arousing in me a permanent prejudice against work, by sandwiching short spells at the uncongenial tasks between much longer ones on such fascinating matters as early voyages of discovery, Chinese art, the transmutation of metals, the causes of revolutions, the strange fish that live at great depths, and so on.

It strikes me only now, as a point of interest, that by the time I was fifteen I was already able to talk quite intelligently with all my Trustees – except that old human calculating machine, Roberts – on their hobbies and favourite recreations. Obviously Helmuth must have found out what those were and deliberately coached me in them – although that never occurred to me at the time – but it is no wonder that they were all so well satisfied with him as a tutor for me; and no doubt it was his use of me, over a period of years, to convey to them something of his own wide knowledge and varied interests, that made it easy for Iswick and Uncle Paul to persuade the others that he would be a good man to replace Sir Stanley Wellard on the Board.

But I owe just as much to Julia as to Helmuth, since he did not become the dominant influence in my life until I was thirteen.

My sojourn at Kew lasted only a little over three months, and with it ended that happy, exciting period of exploring a new world of restaurants, cinemas and shops instead of doing lessons. The Trustees agreed that Uncle Paul must be furnished with the means to bring me up in the sort of surroundings that I should have enjoyed had not my father died. After he became a widower, he had returned to live in Kensington Palace Gardens, and at Queensclere, with my grandfather; so it was in these two big houses that I had spent my childhood and would, presumably, have continued to live had my father survived the accident. In consequence, soon after Christmas, the contents of the little suburban villa were packed up and we transferred outselves to Millionaire's Row. Then, a fortnight or so later, I was sent as a day-boy to the nearby prep school in Orme Square.

So far as I can judge, the teaching there was excellent but limited, of course, to a normal curriculum; and, as Julia remained my guiding-star, I am sure that I picked up more useful miscellaneous knowledge in my evenings, outings, weekends and holidays with her than I did in my hours spent at lessons. But I attended the school in Orme Square only for a year. In the autumn of 1930 Julia told me about Weylands.

At the time she could not have known very much about the place herself, but some friends of hers had two boys there. After giving me a rough idea of the system, she said that it did seem to offer special opportunities for anyone who really liked learning things, as she was sure I did; so, if she sent me there, would I promise to work reasonably hard and not let her down with the Trustees by lazing about the whole time.

Like any other boy of nine-and-a-half I was most averse to the idea of leaving home; but I knew there was no escaping a move in the near future to a prep school in the country, to get me used to being a boarder before I was sent to a public school. It seemed that my guardian angel had found a way of saving me from the worst, as she assured me that at this new-fangled place there were no prefects, no bullying and no enforced games. So I duly promised not to let her down, and off to Weylands I went in January 1931.

Looking back from my present standpoint I do not think one can possibly defend Weylands as an institution. It is a terrible thing to bring children up as atheists – just how terrible no-one can fully appreciate until, like myself, they find themselves pursued by some creature of the Devil.

Then the tacit encouragement of the young to indulge in immorality must be a bad thing. Their freedom to experiment in sex without reproach may save a few of them from later developing secret complexes and abnormalities, but I believe that for every one it saves it robs a hundred – who, if subject to the usual prohibitions, would turn out quite normal – of their illusions.

It certainly did me; and that goes, too, for every other senior pupil, male or female, that I knew at all well there. We had all eaten too greedily of the tree of knowledge, and although appetite remained there was no longer any mystery surrounding the fruit. Both sexes had discovered too early that the other, like itself, had feet of clay; so when we went out into the world nothing was left to us but a cold, cynical seeking after partners in pleasure. Never could any of us hope to be carried away with the sort of mad, self-sacrificing, glorious intoxication of which we had read in books. All too late we were conscious that for us, in connection with a member of the opposite sex, three great words must for ever remain meaningless – glamour, romance, love.

Again, the whole conception of teaching people that they should develop their own, ego, irrespective of every other consideration, is all wrong. It makes them hard, selfish, greedy, aggressive and incapable of cooperation in a time of crisis. When I went into the R.A.F. I knew nothing of the team spirit, except that at Weylands it had been sneeringly defined as 'a conception typical of the human-herd mentality, as it excuses the timorous from emerging from the mass and accepting personal responsibility'. What utter tripe!

In view of the opinions I aired during my early days in uniform I must have appeared to my companions the most bumptious, self-centred young cad; and I marvel now that they were so good-natured as to do no more than laugh at me. But I was always a pretty quick learner and it did not take me long to find out the worthlessness of the Weylands definition of the 'team-spirit'. In a Fighter Squadron your life and the lives of your friends depended on it. If we had started to play for our own hands instead of for our side, when opposed to a superior enemy formation, the lot of us would have been hurtling down in flames within a matter of minutes.

Had there been no war, I would probably still believe that the Weylands creed embodied the highest achievement in logical human thinking; but I know now that much, if not all, of it is false. Nevertheless, I believe that I acquired far more academic knowledge there than I would have at any school where it was forced upon me, to be learned parrot fashion as an alternative to receiving punishment; and I can look back on my school-days as happy ones – which is more than a lot of chaps can say.

All that I owe to Julia; and I certainly do not hold her responsible for anything I may have missed through the bad elements of the Weylands system, for I am convinced that of those she cannot have known enough to appreciate their possible results.

Helmuth was not at Weylands when I first went there. He did not arrive until the summer of 1933, and during his first year I had little to do with him. It was my backwardness in languages that brought about our special association. Naturally, for my future it was considered important that I should be able to speak French, German and Spanish fluently; but I was much more interested in chemistry, engineering, history and geography, so gave hardly any time to the uncongenial business of trying to master foreign tongues.

My Spanish was not too bad, as it resembles Italian, and Julia had taught me from the age of eight to speak her own soft brand of that; but she was worried by my lack of progress in the other two, and decided that the best way to get me on was to have someone who would talk them to me in the holidays. In consequence it was arranged that Helmuth should spend the August of 1934 with us at Queensclere.

Looking back, I can see now that he took great pains to make himself agreeable to us all. He was about thirty-seven then, and his strong personality was already fully developed. There was no trace in his manner of the retiring diffidence often displayed by private tutors; but the ideas he threw out were always well calculated to appeal to Uncle Paul and Julia.

My uncle's main interest has always been horses. Helmuth, as I have learnt since, dislikes all animals and considers horses stupid brutes; but he threw himself into helping Uncle Paul arrange the local horse show at Queensclere that summer, as though they were his ruling passion.

With Julia he had a more congenial row to hoe, as he really likes and understands period furniture and she was then busy planning a new *décor* for some of the rooms at Kensington Palace Gardens. He not only helped her find many of the pieces but got them for her much cheaper than she could have done herself; and that was a big feather in his cap with Uncle Paul as well as Julia, since the Trustees gave them a good allowance to keep the two houses up, but were always a bit sticky about weighing out additional sums for such things as antique furniture.

So far as I was concerned Helmuth played his cards most skilfully. He announced at once that we would have no set lessons and would not bother with books – at least, not grammars and dreary set-pieces of translation – but he would like me to read one or two that I should find amusing, with the aid of a dictionary.

One, I remember, was Dr Madrus's unexpurgated translation of the *Arabian Nights* in French, and another an edition of Casanova's *Memoirs* in German. Both gave vivid pictures of life in an age totally different from our own, as well as being spiced with a wealth of bawdy stories, so they held my interest and induced me to acquire extensive vocabularies in a very short time. For the rest, Helmuth always talked to me when we were alone in French or German, repeating in English any bits I didn't get, so without any great effort on my part I was soon able to gabble my thoughts in both languages.

It is hardly surprising that he was asked to stay on through

September, and to come to us again for the Christmas holidays. By the time we were due to go back to Weylands at the end of January I could speak colloquial French and German with considerable fluency, so Helmuth thought of another way in which he could make himself useful. He said he thought that, now I was rising fourteen, it would be a good thing for me to go over some of the factories that I was one day to control; so it was arranged that part of his Easter holidays should be spent taking me on a tour round the most important ones.

On our return from it, Julia broke the news to me that she and Uncle Paul were anxious to make a long tour through the United States that summer, so they had asked Helmuth to look after me. Naturally I was disappointed at first that I should not be spending my holidays with them; but the pill was gilded by the news that they had taken a little house on Mull that had excellent shooting, for Helmuth and myself; and the present of a brace of Purdys, which enabled me to have visions of doing terrific execution among the grouse.

That outlines the first of the five years that I spent with Helmuth 'as my guide, philosopher and friend'; and the others differed from it only in detail. With each year this viper, that the unsuspecting Julia has nurtured in her bosom, became more deeply entrenched in her regard and in my uncle's confidence, so that latterly they did nothing without consulting him; while I tamely accepted his authority, partly from habit and partly because he was clever enough to refrain from attempting to make me do anything he knew that I would really have hated. Nevertheless, our wills did clash eventually.

By the spring of 1939 Helmuth had established himself so firmly as the arbiter of my fate that no-one even thought of contesting his opinion when he announced that, instead of my going up to Cambridge, as my father had done, at the beginning of 1940, he felt that I would derive much more benefit from being taken by a suitable mentor on a two-year tour of Europe, which would include a stay of a few weeks in the Rhur, the Saar, Hamburg, Turin and each of the other great industrial centres.

The last point was especially calculated to appeal to the Trustees; and when it emerged that Helmuth was willing to resign his mastership at Weylands to act as my cicerone, they not only jumped at the idea but urged that the tour should be extended to two-and-a-half-years, so that the last six months of my minority might be spent visiting the industrial zones of the United States. It was even urged that we should make an earlier start, and, as my eighteenth birthday was in June, set out on our travels soon after the ending of the summer term. However, the authorities at Weylands were unwilling to release Helmuth before the end of the year, and many Weyland pupils stayed up till they were nearly nineteen, so it was agreed that we should put in a final autumn term there.

But things did not turn out according to plan. We were still up on Mull in the first week of September when the war broke out. I told Helmuth that Sunday night that in the morning I proposed to take the first train south from Oban, and, on reaching London, volunteer for the R.A.F.

There was the hell of a row. Apparently it had never occurred to him that I might react to the news like that. But he soon got his bearings and, once he had recovered his temper, he began to produce all sorts of well-reasoned arguments in favour of my holding my hand for a bit.

His first line was that it would be silly to rush into the ranks when, just as in the last war, every well-educated youngster would, in due course, be needed as a junior officer. Then he said that this time the Government was better prepared, and did not need volunteers, as they had already arranged to call up such men as they required by classes. Finally he urged that so much had gone into fitting me to hold great responsibilities that my life was not my own to throw away; the least I could do was to submit the matter to my Trustees and hear what they had to say, before jeopardising all the hopes that they had placed in me.

Thinking things over a few weeks later I came to the conclusion that none of these arguments had weighed with me in the least. I was a strong, healthy young man of eighteen and a bit, with a very fair knowledge of aircraft design and engineering. I knew perfectly well what I ought to do, and what I wanted to do. Yet I did not do it.

Helmuth's will proved stronger than mine. The battle between us went on for over a week. Again and again I tried to screw my courage up to the point of defying him and walking out. Several times I was on the verge of slipping out at night and making off in the motor-boat to the mainland. Yet I could never quite bring myself to do either.

I feel certain now that it was neither his reasoning nor my in-grained respect for his authority which was the paramount factor in keeping me there against my will. It was the silent, compelling power that at times lies behind the steady regard of his tawny eyes. He used a form of hypnotism to bind me like a spell.

I wonder what luck I'll have when I try that out on Taffy this evening. If I succeed I'll be out of here by the end of the week. I have got to be; the new moon rises on Thursday.

Tuesday, 19th May
It was no good. I have never before realised how difficult it is to catch a person's glance and hold it for any length of time. Taffy was engaged for his strength – not his brain. He is only about five feet ten, but broad and long-armed, like a gorilla. His hair is dark and curly, and his eyes are small; but his face is as round as a full moon, and he has a curiously feminine quality. He stood there, docile as usual, at the foot of the bath, for a full ten minutes while I was soaping myself, but every time I said something to him to attract his attention he just looked at me for a second, then looked quickly away again.

At last, in desperation, I said to him: 'Taffy, have you ever tried staring anyone out?'

'No, indeed, Sir Toby,' he replied. 'What would I want to be doing a thing like that?'

'For fun,' I said. 'Come on; look straight at me and let's see which of us can make the other blink first.'

'Fun it is, is it?' he repeated with a sheepish grin; and for a moment his round brown eyes peeped at me from beneath the dark, curling lashes that many a girl would envy. But almost at once he dropped his glance, gave an embarrassed laugh, and muttered: 'A strange game it is, and I no good at it.'

I felt that it might arouse the oaf's suspicions and a permanent resistance if I persisted further, at the time; so I chucked up the attempt and ate my dinner in a very bad humour. But I am hoping that I'll catch him napping some time today. A good chance is bound to present itself sooner or later; the trouble is that I have no time to waste.

After dinner last night, to take my mind off my failure with Taffy, instead of switching my radio off at the end of the nine o'clock news I listened to a broadcast on the war. I must confess that I haven't been taking very much interest in the war of late, owing to preoccupation with my own troubles; but hearing this commentator quite cheered me up, as it seems that in this past week or so things haven't been going too badly for us.

The best bit of news is that General Alexander has succeeded in extricating all that was left of our army from Burma. It must have been hell for them all these months, fighting desperate rearguard actions in that ghastly country against enormously superior forces, and it is a miracle that they were not surrounded and cut to pieces.

It was Alexander, I remember, who assumed command in the last phase at Dunkirk, after Gort had gone home, and was himself the last man to leave the beach there. I think he must be a really great General, as any fool can make a breakthrough if the odds are in his favour and he has plenty of supplies, but it requires military genius of the first order to conduct a successful retreat with war-weary troops who are short of everything. Now that he is back across the Chindwin, on the Indo-Burmese frontier, it should be easier to get supplies and reinforcements up to him; so let's hope that he will be able to hang on there and prevent those filthy little Japs from swarming down into India.

The Ruskies are still getting the worst of it in the south, and the Germans claim to have driven them from their last foothold in the Crimea; but the success of Marshal Timoshenko's counter-offensive against Kharkov more than makes up for that. Those Russian battles are on a scale that make our little set-tos in Libya look like backyard brawls, and they must be costing the Nazis tens of thousands of casualties a week. If only the Russians can keep it up they will yet bleed Hitler's Reich to death.

This morning's bulletin was cheering, too. Yesterday Coastal Command put on another good show. Our bombers caught the Prinz Eugen off Norway, slammed several torpedoes into her, and raked the decks of her escorting destroyers with cannon fire. God, what wouldn't I give to be able to fly again!

As must be obvious to anyone who, knowing nothing of me, comes upon this journal and has read so far, I got the better of Helmuth in the end. During those last three weeks on Mull, as he was constantly with me, his influence proved so strong that all my efforts to throw it off were in vain; and I was still in the same state when, on September the 24th, we returned to Weylands.

For the first week of the term I continued to be a bit befuddled and half-persuaded by his arguments; but about a fortnight earlier old Wellard had died, and I imagine that Helmuth was already hard at it, intriguing with Uncle Paul and Iswick to get himself appointed to the vacant Trusteeship. Anyhow, on October 1st he was summoned to a meeting of the Trustees in London. After I had spent twenty-four hours without seeing him my mind began to clear, and the next night I decided to make a bolt for it.

Getting away presented no difficulties. I packed into one small suitcase some spare underclothes and a few personal belongings; then, having read a book till about half past three in the morning, I quietly carried the case downstairs and strapped it onto the back of the first bicycle that I came upon in the staff bike-shed. As it was seven miles to the station I had to take an unauthorised loan of the bike; but I knew that it would be returned in due course, since I meant to leave it in the station cloak-room and post the ticket for it to the school bursar.

At the station I slipped the ticket into an envelope that I had all ready for it, and at the same time posted a note that I had written to Julia, asking her to do her best to stop Helmuth trying to find me, and telling her that she was not to worry about me, as I should be very well looked after at the place to which I was going, and that I would write to her within the course of the next few weeks. Then, twenty minutes later, the milk train came in and took me to Carlisle.

As I was still technically a schoolboy I thought it possible that when my absence was discovered a hue-and-cry would start after me, and I was uncertain what powers the authorities might have to send me back, so I had already decided to take evasive action. London was the place they would naturally expect me to head for, so, instead, I took the train from Carlisle up to Glasgow. That afternoon I went to the City Recruiting Office there and volunteered for the R.A.F.

My age was then eighteen and three months, but I could have passed for a year older had I wished, as I was both tall and well-built; also I was, as the police descriptions term it, 'A person of good address', so I had little fear of being rejected. But I did not mean to sign on in my own name, as it was quite on the cards that in another few hours the police would be looking for me, and the thought that I might be caught out in that part of the business made me go pretty hot under the collar.

I knew that I would have to show my identity card and there was no disguising the Weylands address, as it had been issued to me there the previous May; but my name had been inserted simply as Jugg, Albert, A., with no 'Sir' or 'Bart.' in a bracket behind it to give away my title, and the previous evening I had added the letters Ler to both the block-letter surname and my scrawled signature. It was a bit of a risk to take, as the card informs one that any alteration of it is punishable by a fine or imprisonment or both; but I felt that if I could get away with it the odds would be all against anyone up in Glasgow associating the missing heir to millions, Sir Toby Jugg, with Aircraftsman Albert Juggler – and get away with it I did.

I found those first few weeks in the R.A.F. extraordinarily exciting. A high proportion of my fellow recruits were Glasgow mechanics, but there were also clerks, salesmen, colonials, farmers, small tradesmen and other types, most of whom had previously been entirely outside my ken.

The life, too, was utterly different from anything I had ever known; although I did not find it as hard as I had expected, for we were excellently fed and very well looked after. No doubt the routine and restrictions inseparable from communal life under discipline would have palled after a bit, but to start with, for me, everything held the glamour of strangeness, and every new face I encountered held a thrilling real-life story of effort and achievement – or failure, which could usually be heard over a can of beer.

During the ten weeks that I was in the ranks I had no chance to get bored with any one set of companions, as in less than two months the grading system caused me to be transferred from one hutted camp to another four times. It takes a lot of people to keep an aircraft in the air, so out of the many who offered themselves comparatively few possessed the qualifications and had the luck to be graded for operational training; the others had to be content to serve as ground-crews, signallers, clerks, tradesmen and in all the scores of jobs without the conscientious performance of which the operational people could not have functioned. But my youth, health, keenness and high standard of education led to my being picked as one of the lucky ones; and it was that which resulted in the discovery of my true identity.

My one object when I volunteered had been to become a fighter-pilot; and constant application coupled with the O.K. from half-a-dozen medical boards and selection committees had got me as far as this fourth station. When I had been there about ten days it came to my turn to be summoned for a personal interview with the Station Commander.

He asked me a few questions, glanced through my papers, and said: 'I see, Juggler, that you have made a pretty good showing, so far; and that your Flight Commander considers your possibilities to be above the average. I think he is right; so I propose to recommend you for a commission. You may not get it, but at all events you will be given your chance on transfer as a Cadet to Receiving Wing.'

I suppose the good man expected me to blush, stammer my thanks, salute smartly and float out as though my elation was so great as to render me airborne already. But my surprise was only equalled by my consternation, as I knew that if I let him have his way the next step was that somebody would be demanding a copy of my birth certificate. In consequence, I blurted out, a little awkwardly, that I did not want a commission; I wanted to become a Sergeant Pilot.

He went a shade redder in the face and said a trifle huffily: 'I cannot compel you, of course; but, presumably, you joined the Royal Air Force with the object of serving your country to the best of your ability. If, in the opinion of officers such as myself, who are practised in forming judgements of this kind, you are considered to have the fundamental qualities required for commissioned rank, you must surely see that it is your duty to accept our decision and do your best to obtain it.'

Before I could reply, another officer, a Flight-Lieutenant who was sitting at a side table, stood up and said: 'D'you mind if I handle this, sir? I think I know the answer.'

The Group-Captain looked a bit puzzled, but nodded his assent, and the Flight-Lieutenant beckoned to me to follow him into the next room.

As soon as the door was closed behind us he motioned me to a chair and offered me a cigarette. He was a lean, bronzed-faced, tough-looking little man of about thirty, with very blue eyes. When we had lit up, he grinned at me and said: 'I take it the birth certificate is the snag, isn't it – Sir Toby?'

What the hell could I say? I knew I was caught out. It transpired that until the outbreak of war he had been a test-pilot at Juggernauts – the Jugg combine's biggest aircraft plant; and that he had recognised me from having met me on a visit that I paid to the factory with Helmuth in 1938.

I had watched the papers carefully, and no report of my disappearance had so far been published in them; so I took it that Julia had shown my letter to the Trustees and they thought it wiser to wait for me to reappear in my own time than to start a scandal by having me publicly hunted. But somebody on the Board must have talked, as Flight-Lieutenant Roper had heard that I had run away from school, in a letter he had had from a friend in his old firm.

He put it to me that I was in a jam. Sooner or later I was bound to be rumbled, and it might happen in circumstances where my C.O. had no alternative but to send me for court-martial on a charge of having made a false declaration to the recruiting authorities; and following that there might be a civil prosecution for having faked my identity card. He said that, as my motive had clearly been a patriotic one, he did not think either court would take a very serious view of the matter; but one could not be certain of that, as they could not afford to give the press a chance to publish the fact that anyone had been caught out breaking war-time security measures and allowed to get away with it – and, I being who I was, it was certain the press would make it a headline story. So he thought that instead of going on as I was and risking anything like that I should be much wiser to let him try to sort matters out.

I was still afraid that once the Trustees found out where I was they would endeavour to regain control of me; but Roper said that since I had managed to get into the R.A.F., and was over eighteen, it was quite certain that the Air Ministry would never agree to release me for the purpose of being sent back to school; so I accepted his very kind offer. We agreed that he should tell the Group-Captain that I had asked for a fortnight to think over the question of the commission and, in the meantime, he would put my case in confidence to an Air Marshal who was a personal friend of his.

Between them they did the trick. On the 11th of December I received orders to proceed to London and report at Adastral House. On the 12th I signed a lot of papers there, with the result that Aircraftsman Juggler was released from the service and for about five minutes I became a civilian; after which I was sworn in again under my proper name and left the building with orders to get into a civilian suit, post my uniform and kit to the R.A.F. Depot in Hallham Street, and go on leave till further notice.

Down at Queensclere Julia and Uncle Paul killed the fatted calf for me; and when Helmuth came south just before Christmas he showed not the slightest trace of ill-will at my having got the better of him. In fact he said that, while he had felt it to be his duty to keep me out of harm's way if he possibly could till I was called up, he thought the initiative I had shown did me great credit; so we quite naturally fell into our old friendly relationship.

As he had resigned his position at Weylands and there could now be no question of his taking me abroad, his co-Trustees asked him if he would like to take over the Llanferdrack estates, since it was felt that with an able man to administer them the farms, villages and forests here could make a much bigger contribution to the war. The idea of having his own small kingdom evidently appealed to him, and by a curious coincidence he left Queensclere to start his new job the same day as I left on Air Ministry orders to report at Reception Wing as one of the new intake of Cadets.

That was the beginning of months of arduous training; first at the I.T.W.; scores of lectures, hundreds of tests, then the E.F.T.S.; more lectures, more tests, solo flying, formation flying, night flying, all through the spring of the phoney war, then all through that desperate summer while Hitler smashed his way to Calais and the Loire, and on into the autumn while the Battle of Britain raged overhead.

Sometimes we saw bits of the battle fought out in the distant skies. The crowd I was training with were pretty good by then; again and again we begged to be transferred to 10 Group, or even a fighter station outside it where there might be some chance of our joining in; but the authorities were adamant.

How we raved against the old boys at the Air Ministry, with their rows of ribbons and scrambled eggs, when we learned how exhausted our first-line pilots were becoming, and were not allowed to go to their relief.

But those veterans of the last great war were right. They must have been just as worried as we were, but they knew from experience that a pilot's chance of survival in combat is in exact relation to the perfection, or otherwise, of his training; and they had the guts to reject the temptation even at a time of crisis to reduce by a single day the schedules of training that had been laid down in peacetime. Had they allowed us to go in three-parts trained half of us would have been massacred, and it was their refusal to be panicked into doing so that gave the R.A.F. dominance over the Luftwaffe in the following year.

So we had to go on with our lessons and pretend to ignore the fact that any night the invasion might come and find us still not on the operational list.

But at last the great day came, and I was one of the lucky ones, as I was posted to Biggin Hill, right in the thick of it. My third time up I got my first Heinkel III. Her escort had been dispersed and she was trying to sneak home alone. I was on my way in, and hadn't much juice left, but just enough to turn and go after her. It was touch and go. I opened up at 300 yards and gave her two bursts, but nothing seemed to happen. As I circled and came in again some bullets from her spattered through my aircraft. I wasn't hit, but my engine began to stutter. I let her have all I'd got, but a moment later I began to lose height rapidly. I was mad with rage at the thought that I would have to make a forced landing and let her get away; but just as I was coming down in a field outside Maidstone I caught sight of her again. I had got her after all and she was a swirl of flame and smoke just about to crash among some trees half a mile away.

Then two days later I got an Me. 109. But there is no point in writing all this. It's a good thing to sit and think of, though.

Wednesday, 20th May

I have had no luck with Taffy yet; and am beginning to fear that, short of giving him a direct order to stand dead still and stare at me, I never shall. I don't want to do that, but I have got to get a letter past Helmuth somehow and can think of no way to do so other than by making Taffy act as my unconscious agent. Unfortunately I am up against the time factor, so if I fail to pull it off today I'll have to risk an all-or-nothing attempt on him tomorrow.

According to Dr Bramwell, however difficult persons are to hypnotise, once they have been got under it is always much easier to get them under a second time. So I had hoped to try Taffy out once or twice with simple tests before actually giving him a letter; but there is not now a sufficient margin of time left to take any chances. If I can get him under I shall have to make the most of the opportunity.

In consequence, most of the time I have spent indoors today has gone in writing a letter to have ready to give Taffy should my efforts to put him under control prove successful. I have given Julia full particulars about the haunting to which I have been subject, and have implored her to come to my rescue at once; but I have said nothing about Helmuth being at the bottom of it. She has shown such faith in his abilities and his apparent devotion to me, for such a long time past, that I feel it would be unwise to make any accusation against him in a letter.

When she recalls my 'burglar' and my horrible experience of the broken tomb at Weylands, I am sure she will not think that I am appealing to her without real cause now; and knowing Helmuth's apparent scepticism about such matters she will take that as my reason for asking her to arrange for my removal; but if I told her in addition that I believe he is deliberately attempting to drive me insane, I fear she would begin to wonder if I were not so already.

It will be time enough to tell her the sickening truth about him when she gets here. However, I've made it clear that I have already sounded him about my being moved, and that he is very averse to

it, so she must come prepared to meet with, and overrule, his opposition. I even went so far as to suggest that she should bring with
her a chit from Uncle Paul, authorising her to take me away.

That line will prove a bit of a bombshell to her, as on no previous
occasion has it ever been necessary even to consider giving Helmuth
a direct order concerning me. She may put it down to my being
terribly overwrought, or read into it that I have told Helmuth about
my 'spooks', and since he does not (?) believe in such things, we have
quarrelled violently. Whichever way she takes it will be all to the
good, as in the first sense it would stress the gravity of my condition,
and, in the second, prepare her for ructions between Helmuth and
myself on her arrival.

I doubt very much if she will bring a chit from Uncle Paul, as it is
a hundred to one that she will think it a fantastic idea, and quite
unnecessary. All the same, I hope she does, as Helmuth seems determined to keep me here and may take a high-handed line with her.
But Uncle Paul is still my Guardian and I believe that even Helmuth
would think twice about refusing to accept his written order.

I urged it on Julia that, even if she did not bring a chit from Uncle
Paul with her, she must speak to him about my letter and at least
secure his verbal consent to my immediate removal, as then Helmuth
would not be able to postpone the issue by saying that he must
consult Uncle Paul before the matter could be finally decided.

To stress the vital importance of quashing any proposal on Helmuth's part about postponement, I pointed out to her that the full
moon is due again on the 30th, so, judging by the previous bouts, I
shall be in acute danger again from about the 27th on, although there
is no guarantee at all that these damnable attacks may not start
even earlier.

It is already the 20th, and I have yet to get this letter off; so I said
that when she does get it she must act without a moment's delay, tell
Uncle Paul any damn thing she liked, and come down here with his
authority to take me away, if possible before the 25th.

Thursday, 21st May
Last night proved a milestone in my silent battle against Helmuth.
While I was in my bath I had another crack at Taffy, but, as on
the two previous occasions, without result; until I suddenly thought
of a new line of attack. I pretended that I had got something
in my eye and, holding it open, asked him to fish the offending
body out.

As there was nothing there he naturally could not find it, but he had to keep peering down into my eyes and I stared up at his. After we had had our glances locked like that for a few moments, with only about nine inches between our faces, I said softly: 'Taffy, you're looking very tired. You are tired, Taffy, aren't you – very tired?'

As he did not reply, I went on: 'I think you had better go to sleep, Taffy. A sleep would do you good. Go to sleep, Taffy. Close your eyes.'

Imagine my elation when his eyelids drooped and those lovely dark eyelashes of his fell like two little fans upon his cheeks. I took his hands and stroked them gently, as, according to Bramwell, a lot of hypnotists have found that touch helps the thought waves to flow into the subject.

My wheeled chair was standing beside the bath, so I made him sit down in it and relax. Then I asked him a few simple questions, such as where he had been born, if he had had a nickname when he was at school, if he would have liked to be a gardener like his father or preferred being with me, and so on; all of which he answered between half-closed lips in a toneless voice, but without hesitation.

Next, I told him to stretch his right arm straight out from the shoulder, and hold it there. In a normal state the average person can hold their arm out at right angles to their body without showing fatigue for about three minutes, then their hand begins to droop. They can keep lifting it, but each time they do so it starts to sag again almost at once; and after about five minutes the pain of keeping their arm extended becomes too much for them.

Under hypnosis the muscles hardly seem to tire at all, and Bramwell's book cites instances where subjects have remained with their arms outstretched for long periods, even when heavy weights have been attached to their wrists trebling the normal strain. I sat in the bath watching Taffy while I slowly counted five hundred. That must have been a good eight minutes, and his arm was still as rigid as when he had first stretched it out in obedience to my order. I needed no further proof that I had him properly under.

Then, to my fury, I suddenly remembered that I had not got the letter to Julia with me; it was still in the top drawer of my bedside table.

Yet, having at last succeeded with Taffy, I simply could not bring myself to abandon the opportunity of using him, so long as there was the least chance of my being able to do so.

When I have had my evening bath I am not dressed again, but put to bed; Deb gives my back a quarter of an hour's massage while Taffy gets me a cocktail; then my dinner is brought to me there. Sometimes Deb is ready, waiting for me, when I get back from the bathroom, but at others she is a few minutes late.

It is certain that both she and Taffy have instructions to take any letters I may give them for the post to Helmuth, so if I gave one to Taffy in front of her the odds are she would mention it to Helmuth and it would be taken from Taffy before he had a chance to get down to the village with it. Moreover, I am exceedingly anxious to keep secret the fact that I can hypnotise people, and Deb might have guessed the reason why Taffy's face was looking so wooden and expressionless if she had seen him as he was when with me in the bathroom last night.

So it came to a race against time. The second after I realised my blunder in leaving the letter behind, I saw that if I could get back to my room before Deb came in to massage me, I should still be able to pull the cat out of the bag; but if she got there first I would have to abandon my plan for the time being.

One of the most maddening things about being semi-paralysed is its effect when one wants to do something in a frantic hurry. Had I had the use of my lower limbs I would have been out of that bath in a jiffy, given myself ten seconds' rub with the towel, pulled on my dressing-gown and been back in my room under the minute. As it was I had to submit to the infuriatingly slow ministrations of Taffy; and the fact that he was still under my hypnotic control did not help matters; on the contrary, it seemed to slow him up.

At last he had me back in my chair and began to wheel me along the corridor. He was still acting like an automaton, and I did not want to wake him while there was a chance that things might be all right; because I knew that, at best, I would have only a few minutes to work in, and that might not be enough to get him under again. But I was worried stiff what construction Deb would put upon it if she saw him like that. Halfway down the passage a sudden inspiration came to me, and I said: 'If Sister Kain is in my room when we enter it, Taffy, you are to wake up. Directly you see Sister Kain you are to wake up, d'you understand; and you are to forget all that has happened in the past twenty minutes.'

'Yes, Sir Toby,' he murmured obediently, and at that moment we reached my door.

I suppose if I had been accustomed to hypnotising people I should have said that to him earlier. Anyhow, thank goodness I did say it before we entered my room, as Deb was there.

It was a bitter disappointment. Afterwards, on glancing at the clock, I realised that it was not Deb being unusually early that had caused me to miss the boat, but our being unusually late. In the excitement of trying to beat her to it I had quite forgotten the time I had spent in putting Taffy through the tests, and including the eight or nine minutes for which I made him hold out his arm, they must have taken up the best part of a quarter of an hour.

Still, although I was stalemated last night, I am immensely heartened by this success. Now I have had Taffy under I feel confident that I can get him under again. Moreover it means a lot to know that he reacts to post-hypnotic suggestion. It was an anxious moment as he wheeled me across to my bed and I screwed my neck round to get a glimpse of his face as soon as I could. He was wide awake, and went about his duties quite normally, without indicating by a word or look that he had just passed through an unusual experience. I feel confident now that, provided no entirely unforeseen piece of misfortune upsets my plans, I shall be able to get my letter away by him tonight.

Now I will set down the little more there is to tell of my personal history, and so be finished with it.

I continued to be a fully operational G.D. officer in the R.A.F. up to July the 10th, 1941, the date on which I was shot down for good. I had, of course, been shot down several times before, as was the case with nearly everyone who flew consistently for any length of time in the early years of the war. Once a Jerry followed me in and shot me up when I was flying too low to dare to bale out, so I had to crash-land on a reservoir. That was not funny, as I darn nearly drowned; but, if I had to make a choice, I'd rather go through that again than repeat my only experience of baling out over the North Sea. Fortunately that was in mid-May, as it was seven hours before they found me, and had it been earlier in the year I should have died of cold; I was blue when I was pulled out of the drink, and if my strength had not enabled me to go on flailing my limbs for the last hour or two, I would have died of it anyhow.

My bag was 14 Jerrys and 7 probables, more than half of them being scored during my first ten weeks as an operational pilot. After that it got more difficult, as we had given the Luftwaffe a bloody nose, and they went over to the defensive. My D.F.C. came through in May, and I was promoted to Flight-Lieutenant just before I got my packet.

As I did not hold the rank for six months I am no longer officially entitled to it. In all such cases if an officer 'goes sick' – which covers everything from appendicitis to having his eyes shot out or being burnt to a living skeleton – and is unable to perform his duties for more than three weeks, he is automatically deprived of the rank he has held and reduced by one ring.

Of course, the idea is to save money on their pensions. I am one of the fortunate ones to whom it does not matter, but by now there must be thousands of poor fellows to whom those extra few pounds a month would make an enormous difference. As the ruling applies to all three Services it is pretty obvious that it was inspired by the Treasury; and, if only I had the use of my legs again, nothing would give me greater pleasure than to have five minutes behind a haystack with the mean-minded little Whitehall rat who thought that one up.

After the excitement of flying and the fun of sing-songs in the Mess, and sometimes going with a crowd of good fellows for an evening's bust to the towns near the various airfields at which I was stationed, I got awfully browned-off in hospital; but once it had been broken to me that there was very little chance of my ever walking again I did my best to resign myself to my fate.

I was operated on five times and, within the limits they set themselves, the surgeons were successful, as they managed to repair a certain amount of the damage. In fact I owe it to them that I can sit up for two or three hours at a stretch without discomfort instead of having to be wheeled about on my back the whole time; but to get me on my feet again proved beyond them. A long-term policy of rest and massage was, in the end, all that they had left to suggest; so, after nine months of living in an atmosphere of iodoform, I was, at my own request, boarded and invalided from the Service.

The problem of what was to happen to me had already been settled. I should greatly have preferred to go to Queensclere, but Kent is constantly the scene of enemy ops; and, although I was quite prepared to stay put during air-raids, Julia and Uncle Paul would have thought it imperative to get me down to a shelter every time a siren sounded, so I could not decently make myself such a burden to them. The same applied to London. Helmuth had been running Llanferdrack for over two years then, and he had had the care of me all through my teens. One could have searched Britain and not found a place more suitable for anyone in my condition; and Helmuth as good as said he would be deeply hurt if I did not allow him to look after me.

I wonder, now, if he had already hatched this devilish plot to drive me insane once he succeeded in getting me down here?

Anyhow, on March the 14th last I arrived at Llanferdrack, and was duly installed with all the honours of a war-scarred hero. For the first fortnight I enjoyed the change of scene and the freedom from hospital routine enormously; then things began to happen. But I have already gone into that.

Perhaps I should add for the sake of anyone who, never having known me, may one day find and read this journal, that my hair and moustache – I still retain one of those fluffy affairs that many of us grew in the R.A.F. – are red. My face is freckled, my eyes are grey, my teeth are a bit uneven but white and strong. My shoulders continued to develop even while I was in hospital, and I swing a pair of Indian clubs for ten minutes every morning, so the upper part of my body is that of a minor Hercules; and if I couldn't wring a python's neck I could guarantee to give it one hell of a pain there for the rest of its life. I will eat and drink pretty well anything, but I am allergic to oysters, cauliflower, almond icing and pink gin. I was always keen on outdoor sports, but I now thank God that I have always loved reading too. My sex-life started early but, in all other respects, was, up to the time of the crash, perfectly normal – unless it can be considered abnormal that I have never been in love. I am white – inside as well as out, I hope – but I am not free, and I am not yet twenty-one.

That, then, is all about me; and also all the speculations regarding the plot of which I believe myself to be the victim, that I have to make for the present. So, for the future, the entries in this journal will consist of little more than day-to-day jottings, recording the development of the battle I am waging to retain my sanity and regain my freedom.

Later

This evening I put Taffy into a trance again without difficulty. I gave him my letter and told him that after dinner he was to go down to the village on his push-bike and post it; and that he was not to mention the matter either before or afterwards to anyone.

Friday, 22nd May

I am furious. That oaf Taffy bogged it. But I suppose it was partly my fault, as I ought to have realised that the letter needed a stamp and that the village post-office would have already shut for the night when I gave Taffy my letter.

Naturally I was anxious to get confirmation as soon as possible that he had actually sent it off, so as soon as Deb had left us this morning and he started to dress me, I said: 'Look at me, Taffy,' and in a moment I had him under. It is as simple as that now, and I have only to point the two first fingers of my right hand at his eyes, then lower them slightly, for his eyes to shut.

To my amazement he immediately burst into tears. Of course, in his normal state he does not remember my having given him the letter, but directly I put him into a trance his subconscious again made him fully aware of that, and the fact that he had been unable to carry out my instructions.

Apparently, what happened was as follows: He had his supper with the other servants as usual, then, although he had no memory of my handing him a letter, it suddenly came into his mind that he had one, with orders to go down to the village and post it, and, when he looked in his pocket, it was there.

But it was not stamped, and realising that he would not be able to buy a stamp in the village at that time of night, he asked the other members of the staff if any of them could lend him one. Unfortunately none of them were able to do so, but Helmuth's man, Konrad, said at once: 'There are always plenty in the office, and I am going up there now to take the Doctor his evening coffee, so I will get you one.'

A few minutes later he came downstairs again and told Taffy that the Doctor wanted to see him about something, and at the same time would give him the stamp for his letter.

Taffy went up all unsuspecting, but as soon as he reached Helmuth's room, Helmuth said: 'I hear you have a letter you wish to post. Is it one of your own or one of Sir Toby's?'

That put the wretched Taffy in a first-class fix. His subconscious mind reiterated the instructions I had given him, that he was to tell no-one about my letter, while in his conscious mind he knew quite well that he had standing orders that he was to bring every letter I gave him to post to Helmuth.

Apparently he stood there in miserable indecision saying nothing for a few moments. Helmuth then got up from his desk, glared at poor Taffy, seized him by the shoulders, shook him violently, took my letter from his pocket, and threw him out of the room with the warning that if he was caught in any further attempt to smuggle letters out for me it would result in his instant dismissal.

Angry as I was, I could not help feeling sorry for Taffy as he stood there with the tears running down his fat face; so I told him that it was not his fault that things had gone wrong, and woke him up.

Later

I think the fates must have decided that I was due for a little something to cheer me up, after the rotten setback I suffered this morning. Anyhow, just before Deb came to fetch me in for tea I caught one of the pike. He is not a very big chap, as they go, only a ten-pounder; but I sent a message to Cook asking her to stuff and bake him for dinner, and I've told Taffy to get me up half-a-bottle of Moselle.

As a matter of fact, I darn nearly missed him, as when he took the bait my mind was on very different matters. I had been trying to work out the implications of this Taffy business and decide on my next move.

I wish I knew for certain the role that Konrad played. Did he inadvertently arouse Helmuth's suspicions by specifically naming Taffy, instead of just saying: 'Please may I borrow a stamp for one of the servants?' Or was he deliberately responsible for what followed? Perhaps, though, even the unusualness of the request would be enough to set that quick brain of Helmuth's ticking over.

I don't know what the arrangements are about the staff's outgoing mail here, but presumably it goes down to the village in the carrier's cart each morning with that from upstairs, and if the servants are short of stamps they give the carrier the money to get them at the same time as they give him their letters.

Anyhow, as the servants in this part of the world live at such a slow tempo, it would be quite exceptional for any of them to have correspondence that they felt to be of such urgency that it could not wait until morning. That may have occurred to Helmuth, and caused him to ask which of them was in such a hurry to get a letter in the post overnight. Then when Konrad replied 'Taffy Morgan' Helmuth guessed the rest.

On the other hand Konrad is Helmuth's man, body and soul. He looked after him for all those years at Weylands; in fact, he came over from Czechoslovakia with him in 1933 and has been in his service ever since. So it is quite probable that he is in Helmuth's confidence about what is going on here, anyhow to some extent. If so, he probably smelt a rat directly Taffy asked for the loan of a stamp; especially if Taffy gave it away – as he very likely did – that he meant to go down to the village with the letter there and then.

Konrad would certainly have thought that worth reporting if he is acting as Helmuth's spy, and it was easy as winking for him to do so without Taffy suspecting his intention.

I wouldn't mind betting that is what happened; and that Helmuth is using Konrad to keep him informed of any gossip that may go on below-stairs which might jeopardise his secret intentions regarding myself. He would then be in a position to think up an excuse to sack anyone who seemed to be getting too inquisitive, before they found out enough to become dangerous to him. The way that servants get to know things is amazing, and Helmuth is too shrewd to neglect taking precautions against the truth leaking out through them.

Konrad would be just the man for such a job. He comes from Ruthenia, the eastern tip of Czechoslovakia that reaches out towards the Ukraine, and he is a typical Slav; big, fair and boisterous, with a hearty laugh that deceives people, until they come to know him well and find out how cunning he is below the surface. He is cruel, too, and there has never been any love lost between him and myself since the day I caught him torturing Julia's pet monkey, at Queensclere.

Helmuth tried to laugh the matter off, and said that I was exaggerating, but Julia was so mad about it that she barred Konrad the house for the rest of that holiday, and instead of continuing to live like a fighting cock with the rest of the servants he had to do the best he could for himself in the village.

One thing emerges from this catastrophe over my letter last night; it will be useless to attempt to get Taffy to take another. Helmuth scared him out of his wits, and as that was due to his having sought to evade the censorship of my mail that Helmuth has set up, his fright will crystallise a definite centre of resistance in his mind.

A hypnotist can make his subjects perform any physical feat that their bodies are capable of enduring and many mental feats which are far beyond their normal capabilities, provided he has their full – and by full I mean their subconscious as well as their conscious – cooperation. He can also make them do most things to which they are indifferent – or even mildly antagonistic – according to the depth of trance state in which he is able to plunge them. But if they are strongly opposed to doing something, either on moral grounds or through fear of the consequences, that resistance remains permanently active in their subconscious, and it is next to impossible for the hypnotist to overcome it.

So there we are. Having got Taffy just where I wanted him, it is a sad blow that I should no longer be able to make him perform the one service that is of such paramount importance to me. I may be able to use him in some other way; but I have got to think again about a means of establishing some form of lifeline by which I might haul myself to safety from the menace that, Devil-impelled like the Gadarene swine of old, is now rushing upon me.

Saturday, 23rd May
I have had a showdown with Helmuth. Ever since I came to Llan-ferdrack in the middle of March he has devoted an hour or so to visiting me between tea and dinner, except on the few occasions when he has been away on business.

Now and then we see one another at other times of the day, should we chance to meet in the gardens or the hall; but I am allowed to be up and about in my wheeled chair only between ten- and twelve-thirty, and between three and five o'clock, and those are the busiest hours of his day; so, should we meet during them, we rarely exchange more than a greeting.

On his evening visits he tells me of the latest problems that have arisen regarding the estate and any news he has had from mutual friends of ours; and we discuss the progress of the war and such books as either of us happen to be reading. His mind is so active and his comments so provocative of new ideas that I have always looked forward to his visits as a mental tonic – even when I have felt at times that he was secretly trying to probe my reactions to things about which he would not ask me openly. That is, I looked forward to them up till a week ago; but since I became convinced of the hideous treachery that he is practising towards me I have found it difficult to tolerate his presence in my room.

To let him know what I know – or at least suspect him of on a basis of sound reasoning – prematurely seemed to me both point-less and stupid; so I have done my damnedest to conceal the change of my mental attitude towards him, and to continue to show the same animated interest in his sparkling discourse as I have done in the past.

But yesterday evening some devil got into me and I was seized with a sudden feeling of recklessness. He was standing in the south bay window with his back towards me, his legs apart, his broad shoulders squared and his hands thrust deep in the pockets of his plus-fours. He was wearing a suit of ginger tweed, and I don't know why but country clothes always seem to accentuate his foreignness. In evening dress he looks tremendously distinguished and might easily be taken for the 13th Earl of something, but the dash of Jewish blood that he got from somewhere always comes out when he is wearing country things, and he never looks quite right in them.

As he looked out over the vista of garden, woods and mountains, which seemed more beautiful than ever softened by the evening light, he remarked with a cynical humour which showed that he was not thinking of the view: 'From the past week's communiqués about the fighting on the Kerch peninsular it is quite impossible to say who holds it now, or even to form an estimate whether the Germans or the Russians are the biggest liars.'

Instead of replying I suddenly flung at him: 'Helmuth! What the blazes d'you mean by interfering with my mail?'

For a second he remained absolutely motionless, then he whipped round with a broad grin on his face. 'So Taffy told you about last night, eh?'

I had given vent to my accumulated rancour, and it had not even occurred to me that he would assume that I could have known about his stopping my letters only through Taffy having blown the gaff to me that morning. I saw now that that was all to the good, as I could have it out with him on this single issue. I need make no mention of the secret stranglehold that I knew him to have been working to secure on me for the past two months, unless it suited my book. So I snapped: 'Of course Taffy told me! He is my servant and it was his duty to do so. And you'll kindly desist from further threats to sack him, or I'll know the reason why!'

The sardonic grin remained on Helmuth's face, and his tawny eyes flickered with amusement. 'If you addressed defaulters in that tone when you were a Flight-Lieutenant you must have been the terror of your Station.'

His gibe added to my wrath, and I retorted angrily: 'I'll not have you bully my servants!'

The grin suddenly disappeared, and he said in the harsh voice that now alone makes his Czech accent perceptible: 'They are not *your* servants. Except for your Great-aunt Sarah's people, everyone here has been engaged by me. I pay them and I allocate their duties to them. If they do not give satisfaction I shall dismiss them, with or without a character, as I see fit. Also, I bully no-one. I simply give my orders and take whatever steps appear necessary to ensure their being carried out.'

'The staff here are paid by the Trust,' I countered, 'and you are only its agent.'

'Why seek to split straws? At Llanferdrack, for all practical purposes, I *am* the Trust; and you know it.'

'On the contrary, you are no more than its representative,' I said firmly. 'The Board put you in charge here, but it can equally well remove you.'

He smiled again, and his glance held open mockery as he enquired: 'Are you thinking of asking them to do so?'

I knew that he had me there, for the time being anyway; so I reverted to my original attack. 'Even if you do regard yourself as answerable to no-one here, that still does not give you the right to intercept my private correspondence.'

'I disagree about that.' With surprising suddenness his tone became quite reasonable. 'You have at least admitted yourself that I represent the interests of the Board. In my view it is against their interests, and yours, for them to see such letters as you have taken to writing lately.'

This was an admission that he had intercepted more than one; but I hedged a bit, hoping that he would commit himself further, and said: 'I have not written to the Board since I came here, and my letter last night was to Julia.'

He shrugged his broad shoulders. 'I know it. But what is the difference? If Julia received these letters of yours she would show them to Paul and he would tell the other Trustees about their contents. Besides, I do not wish Julia to be worried either. Your friends have quite enough anxieties these days without being burdened with additional ones concerning you.'

'For how long have you been stopping my letters?' I demanded.

'Since the beginning of April,' he admitted blandly.

'And what possible reason can you give as an excuse for ever having begun to do so?'

'My dear Toby!' He looked away from me for a moment, then an expression of hypocritical pity came over his face, and he went on: 'Surely you must realise that for the past six weeks your conduct has been, well – to say the least of it – queer.'

'In what way?' I cut in.

'It would be distressing to go into that,' he parried. 'In any case, soon after you came here it was quite apparent to me that your injury had affected your mind.'

'Such a thing was never even hinted at by the doctors.'

'Ah, but none of them knew you as intimately as I do, Toby. Besides, the symptoms were only just beginning to show when you arrived here in March. I decided at once that if you became worse the best course I could pursue was to conceal it for as long as possible. That is why I started to open your letters; and later, to account for your not getting any replies from Julia, I invented a story about her having been ill and gone up to Mull.'

I stared at him, almost taken in by his glib explanation, as he continued: 'I have been most terribly concerned for you; but, as I had accepted the responsibility of having you under my care, I felt that it would be cowardly to offshoulder that responsibility on to others so long as there seemed any chance of your getting better. And to have let your letters reach their destination would have amounted to the same thing.'

It sounded terribly plausible but I knew damn well that he was lying. All the same I felt that there was nothing to be gained by telling him so. That he had been holding up my mail was bound to come out sooner or later; in fact he must have known that there was a good chance of Taffy's confessing to me his failure to post my letter the previous night, giving the reason, and at the same time blurting it out that for weeks past he had been under orders to take all my letters to the office; and if I had just learned about that it would have been unnatural for me to refrain from making a protest. But to let Helmuth know yet that I believe his interference with my mail to be a move in a criminal plot of the most revolting baseness would have been to give valuable information to the enemy. So, instead, I endeavoured to get him in a cleft stick by saying: 'Since you were already under the impression that I was becoming unbalanced before you read my letters to Julia, I take it that their contents fully convinced you of it?'

He nodded.

'Then why the hell didn't you do all you could to save me from suffering those terrors that I described to her?'

'What could I do?' He spread out his thick, powerful hands in a gesture of helplessness. 'There is no way in which I can prevent your being subject to these hallucinations.'

The time was not ripe to challenge his assertion that my attacks are hallucinations; so I let that pass and cracked in on the target at which I had been aiming: 'You admit that you were fully aware of the circumstances that caused this queerness that you say you noticed in me, yet you ask what you could have done about it. You could have had me put in another room; you could have got me an electric torch; you could have had that damn blackout curtain lengthened; you could have got me a night-nurse or stayed up with me yourself; you could have made arrangements to have me moved from here!'

Then I added, with a guile that matched his own: 'I cannot understand your refusal of my requests at all, Helmuth. If I did not know so well how devoted you are to me, I should almost be tempted to think that you have become so occupied with running the estate that you have no time left to give a thought to me once you are outside this room.'

'Toby, Toby!' He shook his leonine head and looked at me reproachfully. 'Those are just the sort of ideas which first convinced me that you are no longer your old self, and suffering from a type of persecution mania. But surely you see that my hands are tied. If I agreed to any of these things that you suggest it would mean a departure from the normal routine that we arranged when you first came here, and that would be fatal.'

'Why?' I asked.

'Because it would draw the attention of the staff to the fact that, at times, your mind becomes unhinged. Don't you understand yet what it is from which I have been endeavouring to protect you? If anyone but myself is given cause to think that you have become mental the matter will be taken out of my hands. Your own letters were positively damning, and you know how servants talk. If by any channel it leaks through to the Board that you have become abnormal, and are "seeing things", they will send brain specialists down here to examine you. In your present state that could have only one result – you would be put into a mental home. Even a short period in such a place might affect you for the rest of your life; and as it could not possibly be kept secret, it would have the most disastrous results on the confidence that all your future business associates would otherwise place in you.'

For a moment I found myself completely bewildered. Could he possibly be speaking the truth? Was I, after all, going out of my mind? Were the attacks really no more than figments of my imagination? Had he noticed the early symptoms of madness in me and ever since been loyally striving to prevent anyone else guessing my condition? Had I shamefully misjudged him?

I have not an atom of proof that he is really plotting against me. My whole theory was based on his interference with my mail and his refusal of all my requests which, in my belief, would have enabled me either to evade or lessen the effect of the attacks. And he had now explained his conduct in both matters.

A little feebly I said: 'Surely you could find an excuse to have me moved to another room without arousing Deb's suspicions that I have gone crackers?'

He passed a hand wearily over his mane of prematurely white hair. 'I'm afraid not, Toby. If only there were another room that was equally suitable I would do so gladly, but as we agreed when we talked of it before, there isn't.'

'At least you could get me a torch,' I hazarded desperately.

'There are none to be had.' His voice took on an impatient note.

'Then get the blackout curtain lengthened. Please, Helmuth, please.' All the snap had gone out of me now and I found that I was pleading with him.

'No,' he said firmly. 'Deb is a shrewd young woman. If that curtain is lengthened now she will realise that you must have insisted on it, and attribute your insistence to the moon having an upsetting effect on you. After that she would need only to pick up another hint or two from your behaviour to guess the truth. Besides, the length of the curtain makes no real difference. What you think you see is nothing but the product of your own imagination, so you would believe you saw it just the same if you occupied a bedroom at the Ritz in London or a mud hut in Timbuctoo. All I can do is to prevent others from suspecting your affliction for a time, and in that way give you a chance to recover from it before rumours of your condition reach the Board and bring about a danger of your being certified.'

So, on the face of it, he and I seemed to be dreading that the same grim fate might overtake me; and, if he was to be believed, he was doing his best to save me from it. For a minute or two he went on to reproach me, with what I felt to be commendable forbearance, for having written to Julia so fully about my fears, yet not having said one word of them to him.

I could only reply that, knowing how busy he was, I had not wanted to worry him. The discussion ended by his urging me to do my utmost to keep my imagination under control; and my promising that I would not write any more letters which would cause my friends grave anxiety and endanger my own freedom, by giving grounds for the belief that I am going mad.

Later

I am not going to keep my promise to Helmuth. Last night, after he left me, I was fully convinced that my suspicions of him were unfounded, that I have been the victim of hallucinations, and that he was doing his best to prevent anyone knowing about my mental state so that if it proved no more than a phase I might have a chance to snap out of it without anyone being the wiser. This morning, when I wrote the last entry here, my mind was not quite clear and still partially under the strong influence that he exerts. Now, I am sure that all he said was a pack of clever lies, and am more certain than ever that he is plotting against me.

In order to excuse himself for having held up my letters, he stated his belief that my injury has affected my brain. I did not prompt him to any such theory; he produced it spontaneously, entirely off his own bat. That shows which way his mind is working. He knows from my letters that I fear I may be driven insane. He would like to see me insane. So, as a further step towards his object, he tells me that he believes me to be insane already. That, so far, is his sole contribution towards *helping* me to preserve my sanity.

Let us assume that I *have* shown signs of mental derangement. What would a true friend, who noticed this and was responsible for me, do? As soon as he was certain that I really was becoming abnormal he would call in the best doctor he could get to advise about my treatment; and, in the meantime, if he realised that any special circumstances were connected with my queerness and tended to increase it, he would at once do all he could to counteract those circumstances. Helmuth has done neither of these things, but *the exact contrary*.

If he *does* believe me mad he is guilty, not only of denying me such help as he has it in his own power to give, but also of deliberately preventing me from sending out letters which would have led to my receiving proper medical attention. If he does *not* believe me mad his stopping of my letters is inexcusable, and his suggestion that I am mad a deliberate attempt to make me think that is so. Therefore, whichever way one looks at it, there can be no doubt that he is acting in accordance with a secret design flagrantly contrary to my interests.

The amazing thing is that it has taken me the best part of twenty-four hours to throw off his influence and fully re-convince myself of his enmity. Before, I was going almost entirely on suspicion, but now that I realise the true implications of our showdown I feel that he has convicted himself out of his own mouth. It is an advance of sorts, as it stresses my danger; but, now that time is so precious, those twenty-four hours were a high price to pay merely for a clearing of the mist through which I had already seen the red light glowing.

Sunday, 24th May
A good break this morning. Quite unexpected and very cheering indeed, now that any further possibility of using Taffy to post a letter for me has been ruled out.

I settled that point quite definitely while I was having my bath last night. Without the least difficulty I put Taffy under, but a moment later he began to blubber and. plead with me not to make him do anything contrary to 'the Doctor's' orders. It was just as I feared; Helmuth's treatment of him on Thursday evening has set up such a strong resistance complex in his mind that it would need powers far greater than mine to overcome it; so if I forced the issue his fears would prove stronger than my influence and send him scuttling to Helmuth the moment he was out of my sight.

If I could have got him into a really deep trance I might, perhaps, have overcome his resistance, as I could then have worked on a level of his consciousness so far down as to be still unaffected by Helmuth's prohibitions. But, for one thing, I am still only an amateur hypnotist and, for another, in some types – particularly in simple ones, I gather from Bramwell – it is often very difficult to get down to the deep levels. Anyway my efforts to get down to Taffy's failed entirely.

In such a case the only means of overcoming the resistance is to talk to the subject when he is fully conscious, explain the whole matter and endeavour to argue him round. If one succeeds, that is the end of the opposition, and, in my case, it would then be unnecessary to hypnotise Taffy further, as he would do as I wish without.

The snag is that Taffy is far too frightened of Helmuth, and the prospect of losing his job, for me to be able to persuade him to help me with his eyes open. He would, I think, take the risk if I could offer him a good fat wad of cash as a bonus if he is lucky, or compensation if he got the sack; but it would have to be the equivalent of several months' wages, and I have not even a fiver – or the means of getting one.

Still, my failure with him last night was more than compensated for by my surprising success this morning. As soon as Deb had settled me in the garden I told her that I had got a fly in my eye, and asked her to fish it out. I had intended only a tentative attempt to test her susceptibility; but the trick worked both more swiftly and more effectively than it did with Taffy. The moment I widened my eyes and projected my will through them – that her mind should empty itself and that she should become drowsy – her dark eyes became quite limpid, as though they had suddenly gone sightless, and her eyelids drooped languorously.

I have never thought of her as physically attractive before. She is certainly a handsome piece, but perhaps it was the hardness of her expression, and the intense, serious manner in which she takes everything, which have put me off. But to see her strong features softened and relaxed into a sort of dreamy, yearning look came as quite a shock to me, and I suddenly realised that if only she let herself go she could be a passionate and seductive young woman.

I doubt if my mind was occupied with that thought for more than a couple of seconds, but even that was enough for her to make a partial recovery and almost snap out of it. The change in her expression gave me an instant's warning, so I swiftly concentrated again with all the power of my will; then I had only to touch her forehead lightly with my fingers and murmur 'Sleep, Deb' to have her right under.

It was only then that I recalled a passage in Dr Bramwell's book where he states that, generally speaking, intellectual types prove much easier subjects than the less complex minds usually found among manual workers. He offers no explanation for this, but adds that he has known many cases in which people with a high standard of education have scoffed at hypnotism, yet, on agreeing to a trial, have gone into a trance almost immediately.

The relative lack of resistance in Deb compared with Taffy certainly proved his point, and I rated myself for having not taken more notice of it at the time; but Deb's surface hardness had naturally led me to assume that she would prove difficult. As it was, the unexpected success of the test caught me unprepared, as I had no letter ready to give her.

Unfortunately, too, as it is Sunday afternoon she has gone down to have tea with her friend the schoolmaster in the village. There was no chance to get a letter written, put her in a trance again after lunch and give it to her to post before she left; and I shall not see her again until she comes in to settle me down for the night. I could put her under and send her off to the village with a letter then, but I fear it is too big a risk to take, as if Helmuth spotted her going out at that late hour he would think it strange and be almost certain to question her. So, anxious as I am to get the letter off, I feel that I must curb my impatience till tomorrow morning. If I do the trick directly we get out into the garden she can hop on her bike right away with practically no risk at all of being intercepted.

All I could do this morning was to take measures which should ensure her ready submission to me in the future. While she was still under I said: 'From now on, Deb, whenever I look straight in your face you are to meet my glance and keep your eyes fixed on mine. When I raise my right hand and point my two first fingers at your eyes you will close them, and fall asleep. In your waking state you will not remember that I have hypnotised you. Now, when you wake you will remember only that you have just removed a small fly from my right eye. Wake up.'

It worked like a charm. After thirty seconds she opened her eyes; said: 'Your eye may continue to smart for a little, but don't rub it,' and she even wiped the handkerchief that she had got out to fish with for the fly, before putting it back in her pocket.

Later

I have written my letter, but this one is not to Julia. Time is getting short, and after careful thought I decided that I should do better to attempt to secure more direct action than she is really in a position to take.

If Julia were my Guardian and could give a positive order to Helmuth, I would not have hesitated for a second. But she is not, and Helmuth might take the line with her that 'in my present state' he cannot accept the responsibility for allowing her to remove me from his care.

Uncle Paul, on the other hand, *is* my legal Guardian, and if *he* says that he is going to take me away Helmuth cannot possibly refuse to let him.

The snag about this change in my plan, by which I have decided to rely on my uncle, is twofold. Firstly, I cannot discuss the whole matter with him as I could have with Julia; secondly, he is a much weaker character than she, and so, normally, more liable to be browbeaten by Helmuth. But he *has* got the authority, and I think I know a way by which I can force him to use it.

Unfortunately, the way I mean to play it precludes me from asking him to bring Julia with him; so that I could, as it were, 'have the best of both worlds'. As he is certain to show her my letter, she may come with him anyhow, and in some ways I shall be very glad if she does;

but I should find it a bit embarrassing to say in her presence what I mean to say to him, and it would be a bit awkward for him too; so with that in view I didn't feel that I could decently ask him to make it a family party.

In my letter I said nothing at all of the Horror, about my correspondence with Julia having been suppressed, of my suspicions of Helmuth, or of wanting to leave Llanferdrack. I simply told Uncle Paul that I had recently been considering certain financial arrangements that I intend to make immediately on attaining my majority, and that as time was now short I proposed to send instructions for the drafting of the necessary documents to the lawyers in the course of the next few days.

I added that I really ought to have thought the matter out much earlier, and apologised for the fact that my not having done so now compelled me to ask him to come to see me at such short notice. Lastly I said I thought it important that he should come down and let me have his comments on my proposals before I actually sent them off, as they would materially effect his own income.

If that does not bring him rattling down to Wales within twenty-four hours of receiving my letter, nothing will.

Monday, 25th May

It is 'all Sir Garnet now', as the Victorians used to say. At least, I think so; as after I had done the trick Deb went off on her mission like a lamb.

At about a quarter past ten this morning I put the 'fluence on her and gave her my letter to Uncle Paul, with instructions that she was to set off with it on her bike at once, and that if she met anyone she knew on the way she was not to stop and talk to them, but to confine herself to a friendly greeting, and push on as if she were in a hurry. That ought to ensure that she is not deflected from her purpose, even if she happens to run into Helmuth.

I also made certain that there should be no breakdown this time owing to her hunting for a stamp for the letter before she set off. That risk gave me a nasty moment when I thought about it last night, but the solution proved simple. I took an unused twopenny-halfpenny out of my own collection and stuck it on the envelope. It temporarily spoils the set, but who cares! If that little stamp gets me out of this jam I'll be able to replace it with a twopenny blue Mauritius this time next month, if I want to. How queer the old Queen's head would look in the middle of a set of modern British! But by jove, I'll do that, even it costs me a couple of thousand pounds, as a permanent memento of having got the better of my enemy.

Later.

I am worried, and don't know what to think. Can Deb possibly have been fooling me, both today and yesterday? I should be tempted to think so if it were not for the fact that she almost entirely lacks a sense of humour.

The joke would certainly be on me if she realised yesterday that I was attempting to hypnotise her without her knowing it, and let me think that I had succeeded for the fun of quietly watching me make an idiot of myself. But Deb is not that sort of girl; she is a very serious minded German Jewess and she simply has not got it in her. What is more, she is no actress, and I would bet my last cent that on both occasions I put her into a trance.

All the same, her behaviour is a puzzle, and I wish to goodness that I knew more about the workings of the brain of a person who has received an order while under hypnosis; but I wasn't able to gather very much from Dr Bramwell on that.

It seemed to me that all sorts of complications might arise if I had sent either Taffy or Deb down to the village while still in a trance, so, in both cases, after having given them their instructions I woke them up. Taffy said nothing, but on my waking Deb this morning she remarked: 'You won't need anything for the next hour or so, will you? as I have a job to do.'

From that I could only infer that, as a result of my order given while she was under not to tell anyone what she was about to do, her reaction on waking was that she must keep it secret even from me.

She was back by midday, as I caught a glimpse of her at her window; but I did not see her again until she came to fetch me in to wash before lunch, and I thought it a bit risky to delay our usual programme then by putting her under for a direct check on whether she had done her stuff. Naturally I was on tenterhooks to find out, but, as I was so uncertain about the drill, I thought it wiser not to ask her direct; so I said: 'Did you see anyone you knew in the village?'

'Only Mrs Evans of the Lodge,' she replied, 'but I did not stop to speak to her.'

That sounded pretty good, so I went on cautiously: 'I suppose the little post-office shop was as crowded as usual?'

'Yes,' she nodded; then she quickly contradicted herself. 'No. I'm sorry. I was thinking of something else. I really don't know, as I didn't go there.'

At that, I had to leave matters for the moment; but it is certainly very puzzling. Since I woke her out of her trance before she left here one would assume that she must have been fully conscious while in the village and that on her return she would know that she had posted a letter for me; but evidently that is not the case. Perhaps the hypnosis has the effect of isolating everything connected with certain ideas imposed on the subconscious, in an otherwise normally; functioning brain. On the other hand, it is possible that as Deb was not in a trance while she was in the village the initial reason for her going there never emerged into her conscious mind, and she still has my letter in her pocket.

I shall soon know now, as my rest hour is nearly up, and at three o'clock Deb will be coming in to take me out to the garden again.

Evening
All is well. Deb posted the letter and, what is more, although she has seen Helmuth since, she said nothing to him about it.

I put her under directly she came to collect me this afternoon, and it now seems clear that an order given to anyone under hypnosis does create a kind of blank spot in their conscious mind. Unless circumstances over which they have no control prevent them, they carry out the order at the appropriate time without knowing why they are doing so and as soon as the thing is done they forget it. At least, that is what appears to have happened in this case.

While I had Deb under it occurred to me that it would be interesting, and perhaps useful, to find out a bit more about her. So I made her wheel me out to the summer-house, where I knew that we should be safe from interruption, then told her to sit down, relax and tell me about herself.

There ensued the most extraordinary conversation in which I have ever participated. Deb did most of the talking, while I just put in a question now and then or helped her with a few words when she seemed to find difficulty in expressing her thoughts. I told her to talk in German, as I thought that would be easier for her, and for the best part of two hours she spoke in a monotonous, toneless voice, revealing her inmost thoughts and beliefs.

I must confess that I felt rather a cad in prying into her secrets by such unscrupulous means; but this taking to pieces of a human being proved absolutely fascinating, and in my present situation I feel fully justified in taking any steps that may strengthen my hand against Helmuth.

The first thing that emerged is that she is in love with him. Apparently he made a play for her soon after she arrived here and she fell for him right away. She is thirty, and has never cared much for young men. Helmuth is forty-five and a fine specimen of manhood; besides which his outsize brain gives him an additional attraction for any woman as intellectually inclined as Deb.

She was seduced when she was seventeen by a medical student who was a lodger in her father's house, and has had a number of affairs since; she is by no means the prude that her thin-lipped, hard little face led me to believe. In fact, the glimpse that I caught of this other side to her when I asked her to fish the fly out of my eye was truly revealing. I did not go into the details of the matter, but I am sure that Helmuth met with little trouble in making her his mistress.

However, for the past few weeks the *affaire* has not been going at all well. Helmuth has been neglecting her, and it is for that reason she has been encouraging Owen Gruffydd, the village schoolmaster. It struck me as pathetic that she should attempt to make Helmuth jealous, and particularly of anyone like that.

Helmuth's sex-life is in the true Weylands tradition, and if she told him outright that she was thinking of going to bed with Gruffydd he would probably say: 'Why not, I hope you enjoy yourself.' As it is I doubt if her poor little ruse has even registered with him. If it has I can imagine him chuckling to himself at the thought of anyone attempting to set up a small-time teacher as his rival. Helmuth evidently felt like a little amusement, but is now tired of her, and nothing she can do will get him back – unless he feels the urge again, and then he is capable of taking her off a better man than Gruffydd, whether she likes it or not.

Gruffydd seems to be a respectable type, and he wants her to marry him. I can understand that, as although Deb might look pretty small game in Bond Street she must appear quite a glamour-girl to anyone who lives down here in the back of beyond. She does not love him, but they have tastes in common and the marriage would give her security; so she is toying with the idea. The trouble is that she is still in love with Helmuth and determined to get him back if she can – although she knows that the odds are all against it leading to anything permanent – but, meanwhile, Gruffydd is pressing her for an answer; and, as his 'old Mum' is fighting tooth and nail against his marrying a Jewess, Deb may lose him altogether unless she grabs him while he is all steamed up about her. So she is in a bit of a jam at the moment.

I learned quite a lot about her early life and it turns out that she is really a Russian, although she was born in Germany. Her family were Russian Jews living in Kiev until 1905. That was the year of the abortive revolution, and as many of the nihilists who staged it were Jews it was followed by an exceptionally fierce pogrom.

In those days it was quite an ordinary occurrence for a *sotnia* of Cossacks to gallop their ponies into a ghetto, apply their knouts lustily to the backs of anyone who came in their way, and loot a few of the richer houses. It was done by order and just the simple Czarist way of keeping the Children of Israel from getting above themselves. But this time the authorities had got really angry and were marching hundreds of these wretched people off to Siberia; so Deb's family decided to get out while the going was good, and the whole issue migrated to Leipzig. She was born seven years later.

In the first great war most of her uncles and cousins fought for Germany; but when the real Russian revolution came in 1917 they all deserted, or got themselves out of the army, as soon as they could, and went back to Russia to join the Bolsheviks. Deb's father seems to have been both cleverer and better educated than the rest of his clan. In the dozen years he had lived in Germany he had taken several degrees, and by the outbreak of the 1914 war he was already a junior professor at Leipzig University. So he and his wife decided to remain and bring up their children as good Germans.

Despite Germany's defeat, and the chaos and hunger that succeeded it, between 1918 and 1933 the Kain family prospered. When Hitler came to power the old boy was a leading light on his subject and much revered by his colleagues; his eldest son was a doctor, his second son reading for the law, two daughters were married, while Deb, who was then twenty-one, was getting on well with her training as a professional nurse, and engaged to a bright young journalist.

From 1930 on, while the Nazi boys were getting control of first one thing, then another, the Kains suffered a certain amount of unpleasantness, although nothing compared with what the old folks had known during their youth in Russia. But after Hitler became Chancellor things began to happen.

It was the usual sordid and horrifying story, beginning with ostracisation and ending with violence. The old professor died of a heart attack, after having had his trousers pulled off and being chased ignominiously down the street by a pack of young hooligans. A Nazi truncheon smashed the nose and *pince-nez* of the doctor brother, blinding him in one eye; but all the same he was frog-marched along the gutters for a quarter of a mile before they flung him into a prison van, and he finally disappeared, presumably to a concentration camp.

Within a few months the whole family were dead, in prison or in hiding. Deb appears to have been the only lucky one, if you can call it lucky to survive seeing your fiancé caught in a *bierhalle*, hustled into a corner and used as a target for several hundred bottles, while your own arms are held behind you and you are forced to look on. Anyway, she got away to England.

I asked her how she managed it and she replied: 'The Party got me out.'

At that I was a little mystified, as we had been talking of the Germany of 1933, and in that connection, to me, 'The Party' signified the Nazis. But a brief question to her soon cleared the mystery up. Her two brothers and her fiancé were all members of the 'Communist' Party, and it was the Moscow-run Communist Underground that got her by devious means across the German frontier.

She had been provided with a letter to a Miss Smith, who runs a private nursing-home, and a nursing service for out-patients, at Hampstead. On reaching London she presented her letter and was taken on. For the first two years she worked in the home, until she had completed her training; then she was put on the regular roster for small outside jobs alternating with periods of duty in the home. Now she is one of the senior Sisters and either has charge of a floor in the home when in London or goes out to jobs such as this, where the pay and responsibility are high.

I remarked that while the pay might be good here my case was a routine one involving no danger to life, so there was little responsibility attached to it; and added that, since she had such cause to hate the Nazis, I found it surprising that she had not seized the opportunity to help in the fight against them, by volunteering for active service with one of the military organisations on the outbreak of war.

Her reply came as tonelessly as everything else she had said, but it positively made me blink. She said: 'I could not do that because if I had I should have been making a contribution to the British war-effort.'

I pondered that one for a moment, then I recalled the fact that, although she was a Jewess and an anti-Nazi, she had been brought up as a German, so I hazarded: 'I suppose you still have pleasant memories of your childhood in Germany, and so have a sentimental reluctance to see the Germans defeated?'

'No,' came the answer. 'I have long outgrown all such stupid sentimentality, and I am an Internationalist. I feel no obligation to either country.'

Again I remained silent for a bit, to think that one over. In the early years of this war I had seen enough to know that among her race her attitude could not be uncommon. The coast-resorts in southwestern England and towns like Maidenhead were packed with Jews. No doubt some of them are doing valuable war-work, but how is it there is always such a high proportion of Jews in the 'safe' places where there is still good food and soft living to be had?

I met a few Jews in the R.A.F., and they weren't a bit like that; so I think there is good reason to believe that the British Jews are pulling their weight; but I am sure that does not go for the majority of the Jewish refugees to whom we have given asylum. After all, we are fighting their battle, so one would have thought that they would be only too willing to accept a full share of our dangers, privations and discomforts; but many of them are not.

I said to Deb: 'If you had remained in Germany I suppose it is a hundred to one that you would have died like your sisters from ill-treatment and starvation in a Nazi concentration camp. As it was you succeeded in getting to England, where for the best part of ten years you have had the full protection of British justice, and been free to live where you chose and earn your living in any way you like, with absolute security from any form of discrimination, oppression or persecution. Don't you really feel that you owe this country something for that; and that instead of taking cushy jobs like this you ought to have offered your services when the first call went out for nurses for the forces?'

'I could not,' she said. 'I was under orders not to do so.'

'Whose orders?'

'The orders of the Party. The Soviet Union had entered into an alliance with Germany. It was not for me to question the wisdom of Comrade Stalin and the Politbureau. The order came to us all that we must do nothing to aid Britain in her war against Germany.'

I stared at the expressionless face in front of me. I suppose I should have realised a few minutes earlier that, if Deb's brothers and fiancé had been active Communists and 'the Party' had smuggled her out of Germany, the odds were that she was a member of it, too. But I hadn't; and, as far as I knew, I had never met a real dyed-in-the-wool Red who owned a Party ticket before.

'I see,' I said slowly. 'But how about your own feelings? I can understand your having felt a certain loyalty to the Comrades who saved you from the Nazis, but doesn't the ten years of security that we gave you mean anything to you at all?'

'I had to live somewhere,' she replied. 'I would have gone to Russia if I had been allowed to, but I was ordered to come here. The British Government is Capitalist and Imperialist; it is the keystone of resistance to world-rule by the Proletariat, and more Comrades were needed to work for its overthrow.'

At that, I began to wonder if I ought not to do something about Comrade Deborah Kain, and try to find a way to tip off our security people that she is one of the secret enemies in our midst. But on second thoughts I realised that it would be futile. The British Union, as the Fascist Party calls itself, has been banned, and its leaders live on such fat as is left in the land on the Isle of Man; but not the Communists. They are our gallant allies and are still permitted to share our dangers and ferment strikes, when and where they like. This is a free country – even if the Home Office is run by a collection of lunatics who are incapable of understanding that Fascism and Communism differ only in being two sides of the same penny – and Deb is legally just as much entitled to her opinion as I am, even if she would like to kill the King and have Churchill thrown into a concentration camp.

Still, on the offchance that some day somebody at the top may see the red light, and the information then prove useful, I asked her: 'From whom do you receive your orders?'

'From Miss Smith,' came the reply.

'Who gives her hers?'

'I don't know.'

As I expected, they are still working on the old cell system. But what a clever racket. An expensive nursing organisation must get lots of calls from important people who have had operations or gone sick. Bright girls like Deb can be sent out to look after them. No-one suspects a trained nurse; papers are left about and telephone calls made in their presence. The Reds must pick up quite a lot of useful information on the way the war is going, and the industrial situation, like that.

'Are all the nurses in your organisation Party Comrades?' I enquired.

'Oh, no; at least I don't think so. Owing to the war there is a great shortage of private nurses, so in these days Miss Smith takes on anyone she can get.'

From that it appears that I have been honoured. No doubt Miss 'Smith' decided that as I am potentially a great industrial magnate it would be worth sending one of her ewe-lambs to look after me; but if she hopes to pick up anything worth while about the Jugg aircraft plants I fear she is going to be disappointed.

However, as a matter of interest I asked Deb if she had learned anything worth reporting since she had been in Wales.

'Only about Owen Gruffydd,' she said. 'He is Labour and wants to stand for Parliament after the war. He is very Left and has the right ideas already. If I marry him I am sure that I could make something of him. The fact that he had joined the Party would be kept secret; and it is part of the plan that we should get as many Comrades as possible elected under the Labour ticket. Besides, if he got in I should meet a lot of his fellow members. I took out naturalisation papers in 1938, so I am already a British subject, and I could work on them to get me nominated by the Labour Central Office as their candidate for another constituency. I am quite as intelligent as most of the men I have met, and I am sure I could get myself elected, if only I were given a chance as the official Labour candidate in a good industrial area.'

That was the end of our conversation. I had always thought Deb to be a hard, capable, superficially intelligent little go-getter, but I was far from realising the height of her ambitions or the depths of her perfidy. This last revelation took me so aback that I could think of nothing else to ask her, so after a few moments I told her to forget all she had said, and woke her from her trance.

Then I closed my own eyes, in order to avoid looking at her, and said I felt like a nap. But I didn't go to sleep. I sat there feeling shattered and sick – just as though I had found a toad in my bed.

Tuesday, 26th May
I had a fright last night – a very nasty fright. For the past few days the weather has been patchy, with mostly bright, sunny mornings, then getting overcast in the afternoons; and on both Sunday and Monday evenings we had showers of rain. In consequence, although there was

a new moon on Saturday, cloudy skies saved me from seeing its light – until last night.

I would not have seen it then but for the fact that I had lobster for dinner. I was not, thank God, woken by my subconscious shrilling a warning to me that the Horror was approaching, but by an attack of indigestion, which roused me into sudden wakefulness about one o'clock.

In the old days I used to be able to eat anything with impunity, but since my crash ruled out all exercise – except the little I get from swinging a pair of Indian clubs for a quarter of an hour every morning – my digestion is not what it was. I suppose I ought to be more careful what I eat, but I never seem to think about it till the damage is done. Anyhow, the lobster woke me and there was that damnable band of moonlight on the floor.

It is three weeks now since I have seen it, and it gave me a frightful shock. It has been said truly enough that 'time is the great healer', and this long immunity from attack had certainly healed, or at least dulled, the awful impression that the visitations of the Thing made on my mind. Seeing that broad strip of moonlight again, with the two sinister black bars across it made by the shadow of the piers between the windows, had the same effect upon me as if someone had suddenly ripped the bandages from a hideous wound I had received some time ago, exposing it again all raw and bleeding.

But I am glad now that lobster chanced to be the main dish last night and that I ate too much of it. In spite of my having told myself repeatedly that time was slipping away, and that I must not let myself be lulled into a false sense of security during the dark period of the moon, that is just what I have done. Not altogether, perhaps, as the fate that menaces me has never been far from my thoughts, but I feel now that I ought to have made more strenuous efforts either to secure help or to escape from Llanferdrack. What other line I could have tried that I have not yet attempted I still cannot think; but there it is. I cannot help cursing myself now for the time I have given to fruitless speculations on this and that, instead of concentrating entirely on the all-important problem of saving myself.

Last night was a blessed warning, arousing me anew to my danger as sharply as the sounding of an air-raid siren, and I am wondering now if the lobster for dinner with my resulting indigestion was, after all, pure chance. Providence is said to work in strange ways, and, although I haven't mentioned it in this journal, since early this month I have been praying for protection.

Until then I hadn't said a prayer since old Nanny Trotter left, when I went to Weylands. She taught me my prayers and always made me say them, however tired I was; but I don't think that any child prays from choice, and I was as pleased to stop praying as I was to cease from washing my neck, when other boys at Weylands told me that the first was 'not done' and the second optional.

Even when I was a fighter-pilot I never called on God to help me. In those days I was fully convinced that it was a calm head, a clear eye and a steady hand that did the trick. It was you or the Jerry and the best man won, with no darn nonsense about Divine intervention. At least, that was how I saw it then.

But, once I had argued it out with myself to the conclusion that the Thing in the courtyard is, and can only be, a creature of the Devil, it seemed logical to fall back on God. In view of my past neglect of Him I didn't feel that I was entitled to hope for very much, but the Christian teaching is that His mercy is infinite; so night and morning, and sometimes at odd periods of the day, I began to pray.

At first I felt very self-conscious and awkward about it; particularly as I could not go down on my knees, and to pray sitting in my chair or lying on my back in bed seemed disrespectful; but after a bit I decided that if God was taking any notice of me at all He wouldn't let that make any difference, seeing how things are with me. So, although it may sound a bit far-fetched, it isn't really at all improbable that Cook may have been guided to her choice of giving us lobster for dinner last night in response to my prayers for guidance and protection.

I don't quite know why, but I am inclined to believe that God may grant us guidance and warnings but expects us to fight our own battles and protect ourselves; except, perhaps, in dire extremity when the dice are weighted too heavily against us. Anyhow, having seen the red light, whether it was a Heaven-sent one or not, I made up my mind early this morning that I must take immediate action.

My letter to Uncle Paul was posted only yesterday. It should be in London this morning, but there is no afternoon delivery at Queensclere, so even if it is now on its way down into Kent he won't get it till tomorrow. When he does get it I think he will come here as soon as he can, but Thursday is the earliest that I can reasonably expect him; and, if he has engagements that he feels he cannot break he may not arrive till the weekend. Looking at the matter from his point of view, he would be quite justified in feeling that I could hardly be in such an almighty hurry to get the new financial schemes I mentioned off to the lawyers without giving him a few days' grace.

On the other side of the picture the moon will be full again on Saturday the 30th; but my danger period starts well before that. Last time the attacks occurred nightly from the 30th of April to the 4th of May, with a blank only on the 2nd, when the moon was actually full; but that was because it was a night of heavy cloud and the moon never came through. So, judging by the previous bout, I'll be in danger from Thursday night on. But if the nights remain clear the attacks may start before that – perhaps on Wednesday, or even tonight.

I ought to have worked all this out before, or anyway yesterday when I was so cock-a-hoop at having got my letter off to Uncle Paul. Then, I more or less counted on his jumping into a train on Wednesday; or, anyhow, getting here on Thursday. But I feel sure now that there must be some subtle influence at work which has obscured my judgement in such matters and made me over-sanguine about the success of my plans.

My fright last night has entirely dissipated the feeling of temporary security that seems to have accumulated like fleecy clouds of cotton wool round my brain. I realise now that it would be crazy to count on Uncle Paul turning up before the trouble starts again. He may or he may not; but I am not going to stay and chance it. I am going to get out tonight, or at least have a damn good try.

If I can hypnotise Deb to a degree at which she will post a letter for me and remember nothing about it afterwards, and send her into a trance deep enough for her to reveal her dirty little schemes against poor old Britain, I see no reason why I should not make her come and fetch me in my chair in the middle of the night and wheel me out of the house.

Once outside, Comrade Kain can damn well keep on wheeling me along the King's highway; and if round about dawn she drops with fatigue it won't cause me any pain and grief at all. In fact I rather like the idea that this earnest little disciple of Papa Marx and Uncle Lenin should have to go to bed for a week, to recover from the effort of saving Flight-Lieutenant Sir Toby Jugg, D.F.C., R.A.F.V.R., from the Devil.

Later

This journal has been a good friend to me. When I made the first entries in an old exercise book my nerves were stretched to breaking-point, and forcing myself to make a logical analysis of my thoughts did a lot to keep me sane. Since then, writing it, besides providing what may yet prove a valuable record of events here, has whiled away many an hour of my dreary invalid existence. But I hope that this will be my last entry in it.

All is set fair for tonight. Deb has her 'Sealed Orders' (not to be opened until 00.45 hours 27.5.42). That is actually what it comes to, as my instructions, verbally issued this afternoon, are sealed up in her subconscious, which will not release them to her conscious mind until a quarter-to-one in the morning.

Even Helmuth keeps fairly early hours here in the country. He usually goes up to bed about eleven o'clock, so by one I can count on the coast being clear. As Deb will have to get up and dress it is unlikely that she will come for me till a bit after one, and it will take another twenty minutes or so for her to get me dressed. Usually Taffy does that, but with my help Deb will manage some-how. Although I cannot stand, even for a moment, the strength of my arms is fortunately so great that I can support my dead weight by clinging to one of the posts of this big four-poster bed, and if Deb holds my chair steady I'll be able to heave myself off the bed into it. So I plan to make my break-out about half-past one in the morning, which should give me six-and-a-half hours clear before my escape is discovered.

With my fright last night still vivid in my mind, it occurred to me that I would ordinarily have to lie here in the dark between ten o'clock and one, and that if there was a moon again the Thing might seize this last chance to attack me; so I put my blessed gift to good use again when Deb came in to settle me down. Having completed the usual ritual, she was just about to pick up my Aladdin lamp and carry it off with her, but I caught her eye, put her under, and said: 'Leave the lamp where it is, Deb. You may go now, and you will not wake until you have turned the angle of the corridor. When you wake you will have forgotten that you have left the lamp burning here.'

As she reached the door I called her back, on the sudden thought that it might be as well to do a final check-up. I made her repeat the instructions about tonight and she had the whole thing clear; so it is now only a matter of killing time until one o'clock.

That is why I am making this final entry. I am in much more of a flap than I ever was before going out on an operational sortie, and this is the best means I can think of to occupy my mind. My idea of making her leave the lamp is therefore now proving a double blessing, as I have never before been able to read or write after ten o'clock.

After Deb had gone I said prayers for the success of my venture, but one can't keep on praying for very long; at least, I can't, as I find that I start to repeat myself, which begins to make it monotonous and seems rather pointless. However, I had a new line tonight, in additional supplications that all should go well with my escape.

It suddenly struck me that it was soon after I first started to pray that I remembered Squadron-Leader Cooper telling me that I had hypnotic eyes; and it was that which led to my present prospect of getting the better of Helmuth. I think now that memory must have come to me as a direct answer to prayer, and that, seeing my utter helplessness, God has granted me the swift development of this strange power for my defence against the machinations of the Devil.

It is certainly little short of miraculous that within a few days I should have acquired such an ascendancy over Deb as to make her reveal to me her most jealously guarded secrets. She has never disguised the fact that her sympathies are with the Left, but that is a very different matter from admitting that she is a Communist agent actively working against Britain.

The idea that a foreigner like Deb is eligible to become a Member of Parliament, and actually laying long-term plans to do so, positively horrifies me. Can we do nothing to prevent such a monstrous perversion in the representation of the British people? Is Party backing, superficial intelligence and a glib tongue really all that are required, irrespective of race or creed, to gain a place in that august assembly where Walpole and Chatham, the younger Pitt, Wellington, Joe Chamberlain, and now Churchill have thundered forth the tale of Britain's defiance, courage and integrity?

I suppose it is. If Deb's husband was already a Labour member, and the people who run the Labour Party Office were unaware that she was secretly a Communist, they might well agree to her nomination as a Labour candidate.

Gruffydd won't stand much chance of getting in if the country sends back the Conservatives at the next election with a large majority; but it would not surprise me at all if, after the war, there is a big landslide towards Labour. In any case, now that Liberal representation is so small, Labour is H.M.'s Opposition, and the swing of the pendulum is bound to bring them in within the next ten years; so Deb might easily get a seat by the time she is forty-five. And by then how many other Communists will there be who have infiltrated into the House on a Labour ticket?

What is the answer to that sort of thing? One cannot prevent British Communists from using the Labour Party as a stalking-horse, and we don't want to close the doors against foreigners settling here. Neither, shades of Disraeli, do we want to discriminate against our own Jews. Incidentally, his family had been resident in London for nearly a hundred years before he first went to sit at Westminster. But the laws governing the qualifications for election to Parliament were made in a different age, and I think they need bringing up to date. At least we could check this infiltration of foreigners into the House by passing a law that no man or woman whose parents were not British *born* should be eligible to become an M.P. And – perhaps even more important – to prevent their being appointed to high executive posts under the Government, make a minimum residence of twenty-five years in Great Britain an essential requirement to secure nationalisation.

Is that reactionary? I don't think so. 'Reactionary' is just the parrot-cry howled at anyone these days who has the courage to think and act as did our forefathers who made the Empire.

Of course, if such a law was passed the joke would be on me, because my mother was born an American, so I should not be eligible for Parliament myself. But I would willingly surrender my present right to stand if it helped to ensure that Britain should continue to be ruled by the British.

Thank God it is just on one o'clock. Letting off all this hot air has filled in the time nicely. Deb should be here any minute now.

Later

It is two o'clock and Deb has not come. What the hell can have gone wrong? Perhaps an order given to a subject under hypnosis is not enough to rouse them from a natural sleep. I ought to have thought of that and ordered her to remain awake. She may come yet, but I doubt it, Anyhow, thank God I've got the lamp. I've turned it down a bit to economise the oil, so with luck it should last me till the moon has set.

Wednesday, 27th May

Deb never turned up, and there was a bit of a *contretemps* this morning. When she came into my room she was naturally not in a trance state and she saw the lamp still on my bedside table. I imagine Helmuth must have more or less threatened to flay her alive if he ever found out that she had failed to remove it, as she went into a frightful flap.

I managed to laugh the matter off and she thinks that she forgot it through a normal lapse of memory; but she remarked rather sinisterly: 'I can't think what came over me last night.'

Later, in the garden, I put her under, and got the low-down on why she had failed to carry out my orders.

It appears that after she had tucked me up she decided that the time had come for her to have a show-down with Helmuth, so she went along to his study. With the idea of making him jealous she told him that she didn't care for him any more and was going to get engaged to Owen Gruffydd.

Helmuth's reaction to that was just what I could have told her it would be. After half an hour's talk over a couple of glasses of port he took her along to her room and seduced her afresh. She, poor mutt, imagines that she has pulled off her big trick and won him back to her because he could not bear the thought of losing her to another man. But I'd bet my bottom dollar that the real set-up is that Helmuth does not really give a damn for her; it simply provided him with a little cynical amusement, and flattered his sense of power, to dispose of Gruffydd with a snap of his fingers, and make her his mistress again in spite of the fact that she had told him that she now loved someone else.

It would be interesting to see what happens during the next few weeks, if I were going to remain here – but I hope to Heaven that I'm not. My forecast would be that Helmuth would derive a lot of fun from proceeding to neglect her again until she went back to Gruffydd; perhaps he would even let her get engaged, then he would seduce her once more, and so on, until the wretched woman became half crazy with misery and despair. As it is I hope to make my exit tonight, and so break up the whole party.

To continue about last night. At a quarter to one Deb's mind clicked over and she suddenly realised that she had to come and get me out of the house, so she got out of bed and started to dress. Unfortunately Helmuth was still there, and at first he could not make out what the devil had got into her, as she flatly refused either to answer his questions or obey him when he told her to come back to bed, but simply went on dressing without uttering a word. Then he jumped to the conclusion that she must have dropped off to sleep and was sleepwalking.

As far as I can make out he took her by the shoulders, imposed his will upon her and, his hypnotic powers being stronger than mine, woke her up. Luckily for me she accepted the explanation that she had been sleep-walking, although she has never known herself do such a thing before, and immediately he brought her out of her trance she naturally lost all memory of the orders I had given her. So things might have turned out worse, as it seems that neither of them suspect the real reason for her apparently strange behaviour.

Unless I am entirely wrong in my assessment of Helmuth's psychology, I don't think that he will spend the night with her again until he can get a fresh kick out of once more believing himself to have brought her to heel against her will. I don't think, either, that she is such a fool as to betray her own weakness by asking him to do so as early as tonight, and, even if she does, I can see him beginning the process of twisting her tail by making some excuse to refuse her.

So I think the odds are all against my being held up by the same sort of hitch two nights running, and while I had Deb under I laid on the operation again for 00.45 hours on the 28th May, 1942.

Thursday, 28th May

A bitter disappointment. Everything went according to plan. Deb arrived and got me dressed. With her help I struggled into my chair. She wheeled me down the passage and across the hall to the front door; then she left me sitting there for a moment while she went forward to unlock it. As the door swung open Helmuth's voice came from the stairs behind me: 'Good-evening, Toby. Or should I say good-morning?'

My heart missed a beat. There came the sound of his footfalls on the parquet, and he went on in a sneering tone: 'You must love the moon a great deal not to be able to resist the temptation of going out into the garden to see her. But it is not good for you to be up at this time of night. Perhaps, though, I can arrange to have your blackout curtain *shortened*, so that you can see a little more moonlight from your bed.'

There was nothing to say. I sat there dumb with misery; but the threat made me break out in a slight sweat.

Meanwhile, Deb had propped open the front door and turned back towards me. It was clear from her wide eyes and blank expression that she had neither seen nor heard Helmuth, and she stepped up to my chair with the obvious intention of wheeling me out of the house.

He was beside me by that time, and I saw that his eyes were cold with fury. Suddenly he raised his open hand and struck her with it hard across the face.

'Stop that!' I yelled. 'The shock may kill her! She's in a trance!'

Deb gave a whimpering cry; her eyes seemed to start from her head and she staggered back. For a moment she stood with one hand on her heart, gasping and swaying drunkenly, then she sagged at the knees and fell full length on the floor.

Ignoring her, Helmuth swung on me. 'So that's the game you've been playing, you young fiend!'

'Never mind me!' I snapped. 'You look after your girlfriend, or you'll have a corpse on your hands.'

He continued to mouth at me furiously. 'I suspected as much last night; but I simply could not believe it. Who the hell taught you how to hypnotise people? '

'Is it likely that I'd tell you?'

'I will make you !' He grabbed my shoulder and began to shake me.

But in that he made a stupid blunder. I am much stronger in the arms than he is. I grabbed his wrist, pulled it down against my stomach and twisted, at the same time throwing my weight forward onto it. He was jerked round and forced right over sideways. His mouth fell open and there was a gleam of fear in his tawny eyes as I said: 'I'll tell you nothing.' Then I flung him from me, adding: 'Now, for God's sake, try to revive that woman.'

Almost snarling with rage, he turned, grasped Deb under the armpits, heaved her into a nearby chair, and forced her head down between her knees. After a minute or so, she began to groan. Then she gave a shudder, looked up at us, and muttered with a puzzled frown: '*Was machen wirhier?*'

'You little fool!' Helmuth rasped at her in German. 'You allowed him to hypnotise you; and with your help he nearly got away. Get along to your room. I'll come and talk to you presently.'

Deb stared at me, her black eyes distended with surprise and anger. She was about to say something, but Helmuth cut her short. Grabbing her by the arm, he pulled her to her feet and gave her a swift push in the direction of our corridor. Suddenly bursting into a passion of tears, she staggered away across the hall.

He waited until she had disappeared, then slammed the front door and turned on me. 'Now, Toby; I've had enough of your nonsense for one night. I'm going to wheel you back to your room and put you to bed.'

'Oh, no, you don't,' I said, as a vision of the Horror doing its devil-dance on the band of moonlight flashed into my mind. 'I prefer to spend the night here.'

'You can't do that,' he replied, and I felt my will weaken as his glance held mine.

With an effort I pulled my eyes away from his, concentrated on looking at my own knees and muttered: 'I'm damn well going to. If you lay a hand on me I swear I'll strangle you.'

The threat gave him pause. For over a minute there continued an absolute and highly pregnant silence, while our wills fought without our glances meeting. Then he broke off the engagement, turned abruptly, and marched angrily away from me.

As the sound of his footsteps receded I sighed with relief. I thought I had won that round, and that he had gone off to blackguard the wretched Deb. But he hadn't. He had gone to rouse Konrad, his Ruthenian manservant.

Bitter disappointment at my failure to escape, and excitement over my scene with Helmuth, did not make me feel a bit like sleep at the moment. But he had left all the lights on in the hall, and twenty minutes or so after he had taken himself off I was vaguely wondering if I would be able to get any sleep at all in their glare, when I heard footsteps returning.

Evidently Helmuth had given his man instructions beforehand; neither of them said a word, and they ran at me simultaneously. The attack came from my immediate rear, so I could make no pre-parations to meet it. They seized the chair rail behind my shoulders, swung me round, and rushed me across the hall. I tried to grab, first a table, next a door-knob, then some window curtains. But they were too quick for me. Before I could get a firm grasp on anything they had raced me down the corridor back to my room.

There, a prolonged scuffle took place, while I hampered their efforts to undress me by every means in my power. But the two of them, together, were able to break every hold that I could get on them or my clothes, and at last they succeeded in getting me into bed. By then all three of us were scratched, bruised, weary and breathless with cursing. Still panting from his exertions, Heimuth picked up the lamp and, without another word, they left me.

However, my fight for time was not in vain. It had been just after half-past one when Helmuth caught Deb and me in the hall. His angry exchanges with me, getting her out of her faint, going to find Konrad, waiting until he had pulled on some clothes and then returning with him, had occupied half an hour; and the struggle I put up when they undressed me had accounted for a further three-quarters. So by the time they slammed the door behind them and left me in the dark it was getting on for three in the morning; and the moon had gone down behind the ruins of the old Castle.

I was still much too excited to think of going to sleep; and, disappointed as I was at the failure of my plan, I knew worrying about that was futile, so I tried to concentrate on the future and figure out what chances remained of making any new moves.

Tonight the moon will be within two nights of full; so, unless the sky is overcast, I shall be really up against it. Think as I would I could find only three lines of thought which shed faint rays of light in the blackness of the general picture.

Firstly, Uncle Paul should have had my letter yesterday, Wednesday, morning; so it seemed a possibility that he might arrive here this afternoon. But I knew it was more likely that he would not come down until the weekend, so, fortunately, as it has turned out, I did not put too much hope in that.

Secondly, there was Deb. I realised that since she now knew I had been hypnotising her, that was bound to set up a strong resistance in the future. But I had gained such a much greater degree of dominance over her subconscious than I ever did over Taffy's that I hoped I might still be able to put her into a trance and make some use of her. I counted it a certainty that Helmuth would take adequate precautions against her helping me in another attempt to escape – probably by locking my door each night and keeping the key himself – but I thought that I might get her to send off telegrams to Julia and Uncle Paul, saying that I was ill and urging them to come at once; and also to get hold of a torch for me somehow, or smuggle me in some candles, so that I could counter the moonlight tonight.

Thirdly, I decided that as a second string it would be well worth while to have another go at Taffy. I regarded it as unlikely that I should be able to overcome his resistance to taking messages, and that even if I could he would probably be subject to some form of subconscious reaction which would result in his giving my telegrams to Helmuth; so it would be better not to attempt that. But it seemed possible that I might succeed in using him to procure me a torch or candles.

I was still turning over such projects in my mind when I dropped off to sleep; but, alas, nearly all those hopes have since been disappointed.

Taffy called me as usual and began the morning routine, but Deb did not put in an appearance; so, after a bit, I asked him as casually as I could what had become of her.

His fat face flushed and he looked sheepishly away from me as he replied: 'She'll not be coming to you any more, Sir Toby. It is packing her trunk she is, now. For the Doctor has sacked her this very day, whatever.'

That was bad news and, in view of it, I thought I had better get to work on Taffy without delay, so I told him to look at me; but he shook his head and muttered: 'Come you, Sir Toby, don't ask me that. It is the evil eye you have, as the Doctor was telling me, himself, but ten minutes since.'

'What nonsense!' I exclaimed, and I managed to raise a laugh of sorts. 'You must have misunderstood him; or more probably he was pulling your leg.'

'No indeed, Sir Toby,' he replied resentfully. 'It is the truth he was telling; and myself has been a victim to your wickedness. It was not right in you to give me that letter and me knowing nothing of it. The look in your eyes is uncanny, right enough, and the Doctor has warned me not to look at you. I would be glad if I could now go from here to my brother Davey's in Cardiff. Indeed, go I would this very day, if I were skilled in the engineering, as he is. But the fees at the technical school are high for poor people; so it is stay here I must till I have more money put by.'

I think that was the longest speech I have ever heard Taffy make; and after I had got over my first feeling of anger I was glad that he had blown off steam, as it told me where I stood. Helmuth had sacked Deb, and aroused Taffy's superstitious fears as an impregnable barrier against my hypnotising him. That put paid to any hope of getting telegrams despatched, or securing a light for tonight, through either of them.

Controlling my annoyance as well as I could, I told Taffy that the Doctor got queer ideas at times, and that no doubt his strange assertions about me this morning were to be attributed to the fact that we had had a disagreement the previous night. I added that he had no cause whatever to be frightened of me, and that in the long run he would find it paid much better to carry out my wishes than the Doctor's, particularly if he wanted to be an engineer, as I could easily get him free training in one of the Jugg factories.

His expression became a little less stolid at that, and he could not resist stealing a quick glance at me to see if I meant it; but he is still as nervous as a cat and it would obviously be futile to try to tempt him with any definite proposition on those lines at the moment.

Having brought me my breakfast tray, Taffy left me; and soon afterwards Helmuth came in. I gave him no greeting and throughout the interview did nothing to disguise the feelings of distrust and aversion with which I have now come to regard him. I said very little, so he did most of the talking and, somewhat to my surprise after last night, he continues to maintain the attitude of a fond Guardian who is doing his best for a troublesome ward in very difficult circumstances. How he reconciles that with his actions, and some of the remarks he made, I can't think, but that is certainly the impression he endeavoured to give.

He opened up by saying that he really could not allow me any opportunity to repeat the disgraceful scene that I had made the previous night, and had been forced to take certain precautions against my doing so.

In the first place he had sacked Deb, which was most inconvenient; but it was clear that I had 'got at her', to a degree in which she had come so much under my influence that she could no longer be trusted with the care of me in my 'unbalanced state'.

Secondly, he knew that to a lesser degree I had 'got at' Taffy, so it had been necessary that morning to put certain ideas into his head which would prevent me from 'corrupting' him further. This had resulted in his giving notice, and only with some difficulty had he been persuaded to stay on. His replacement in due course was now desirable and would be a simple matter; but with Deb gone it would have been extremely inconvenient if Taffy had insisted on walking out on us that morning.

I could not help being amused at the thought that Helmuth had nearly over-reached himself to the point of having me left on his hands without trained assistance of any kind; but I pulled my thoughts back to what he was saying.

He continued to the effect that, in spite of the *picure* he had administered to Taffy, he could not regard him as a strong enough personality to be entirely relied on. Therefore he was not prepared to let him take me out into the garden, or even to dress me and lift me into my wheeled chair. So, until fresh arrangements can be made, I must remain in bed.

That was a nasty one; as, while Taffy had been holding the bowl for me to shave, half an hour earlier, it had occurred to me that when he took me outside for my airing I could send him back into the house for something, and set off down the drive on my own. I probably would not have got far before I was overtaken, but there was just a chance that I might have escaped that way; and now I cannot even attempt it.

'How long do you intend to hold me a prisoner in my bed?' I asked gruffly.

He shrugged. 'It all depends whether a suitable new nurse is available, and if so how long she takes to get here. I have already wired the Home that supplied Deb to send someone to replace her, so you may not have to remain cooped up here for more than a few days.'

His strong teeth showed in a sudden grin as he went on: 'As a matter of fact I am not altogether sorry about Deb's departure, as I was getting very bored with her. The Matron of the Home from which she came is an old friend of mine and knows my requirements. She will, I am sure, pick me out a young woman who is not only reliable but also a good-looker. In this dreary hole it will be fun to have someone fresh to sleep with.'

I said stonily that when he started his tricks I hoped she would stick a knife into him, but he only laughed and replied: 'These girls aren't that type. But I wouldn't mind if they were; it would add to my amusement to reduce anyone who tried that to abject submission afterwards,' and he walked out of the room.

So here I am, still in bed, although it is now past midday, and I am feeling far from good. Last night's catastrophe was the most damnable luck, and Helmuth's new measures this morning have deprived me of practically all my remaining chances of my escaping having to spend another night here.

In the whole pack there is now only one card left which, if it turned up, might yet save me from that ordeal. It is Uncle Paul. I dare not pin my faith on his arriving this afternoon, yet I dare not think of what awaits me if he doesn't. I must not think of that. I must not give way to morbid anticipation. I *must* keep my whole mind concentrated on seeking ways by which I may yet defeat Helmuth.

Later

Helmuth has just been in again. He flung two letters on the bed and said: 'There's your post.'

A glance was enough to show that one was an official communication from some Government department, as it had O.H.M.S. on it; and that the other envelope was in Uncle Paul's writing. The first was unopened, the second had been slit across the top.

With a sinking feeling in the pit of my stomach I picked up Uncle Paul's letter. As he writes to me only once in a blue moon I felt sure that it must be an answer to mine, and for it to have got here so quickly showed that he must have replied by return of post; but the fact that he had written could only mean that he was not coming down today, at all events; and Helmuth having brought it to me was an even more certain indication that it could not contain news I should be pleased to have.

I took the letter from its envelope, but before I had a chance to read it Helmuth said: 'From this it is clear that you hypnotised that weak-minded slut, Deborah Kain, into posting a letter for you, although you promised me last week that you would make no further attempts to get in touch with your relatives. It is most distressing that you should recently have displayed such dislike and distrust of me, Toby, but I have been appointed to look after you while you are here; and you may as well understand once and for all that I intend to continue to deal with your malady in the way I think best, whether you like it or not. And I shall not allow this proposed visit by your uncle to make the least difference to my plans.'

With an angry shake of his mane of white hair he turned and marched out of the room, leaving me a prey to the most mixed sensations.

For a moment I almost believed again that he was honestly concerned for me; that he has no hand in this devilry but really thinks me to be the victim of hallucinations and is doing his best to protect me from being publicly branded as insane. His conduct is explicable on those grounds. Yet my instinct flatly rejects such an explanation. I feel positive that he is developing a plot to drive me mad. And in the midst of these conflicting thoughts was that of my immense relief when Helmuth had spoken of my uncle's 'proposed visit'.

Swiftly I opened the letter out and skimmed through it. Uncle Paul said how much he appreciated my thought of wishing to consult him before I finally settled my new financial arrangements. He would be delighted to come down and discuss them with me. But lawyers always took months over the completion of such matters, anyway; so he felt sure I would agree that a day or two either way would make no material difference. He could not come down at the weekend because they had old Archie Althwaite and his wife coming to stay; and on Tuesday and Wednesday he had to attend an important sale of bloodstock, at which he was disposing of a few of his own brood mares. So the earliest he could make it was Thursday, June the 4th. Julia was down with a nasty go of summer 'flu, which had driven her to bed; but she sent her fondest love, etc.

Once more I had that empty feeling under the solar plexus. To me, next Thursday is not a week, but *a whole lifetime*, away. These next five days, while the moon glares down with her maximum intensity, may mean to me all the difference between sanity and madness; between life – as a cripple it is true, but one still able to enjoy the things of the spirit – and a living death, in which the mind is the wretched plaything of distorted emotions and terrifying visions.

What shall I do? Where can I turn for help? Yesterday, or the day before, when I was out in the garden I could have forced Deb to set off with me down the road, or to wheel me through the woods until we came to a farmhouse. But I didn't. I must have been crazy! Perhaps Helmuth is right, and I have softening of the brain.

Friday, 29th May

What a night! At the time I thought it the worst so far; but, viewing the whole series in retrospect this afternoon, I am sure that the attack was not as intense as that on April the 30th, or as prolonged as on at least two other occasions. Yet in some ways it was more terrifying, as there were certain new developments which now make me frightened not only for, but also of, myself.

At a few minutes to ten Taffy came in to settle me down for the night. As he has always assisted Deb to do the job in the past he knows the drill, and that I am allowed one triple bromide if my back is paining me. I had planned to snatch the bottle from him, but when I asked him for it he said in his sing-song voice: 'A sleeping-tablet, is it? See you, Sir Toby, the Doctor said you would not be needing one of those things tonight. And that naught is to be done here now without himself giving the word for it.'

I knew then that Helmuth had been at him again, and that it would be no good arguing. All the same I did, because I was so desperate at the thought of what the next few hours might bring. I even pleaded with him; but it was useless. He said he had orders not to talk to me apart from answering simple questions, and he kept his glance averted from my face the whole time, so obviously he still fears that I may ill-wish him.

An impulse came to me to cling on to him when he picked up the lamp; but had I done so the odds were that it would have upset or got smashed in the resulting struggle, and we both would have been burned to death. With an effort I checked the impulse and, in a strangled voice, answered his good-night.

The moon was already up, and the radiance from the band of it on the floor lit the room with a faint misty twilight. It was not enough to see anything distinctly, but as my eyes got accustomed to the greyness I could make out darker patches which I knew to be pieces of furniture. Having nothing else to occupy my mind, I kept staring at them, trying to make out their proper outline, but after a time, instead of solidifying, the black patches seemed to waver, grow larger and assume strange shapes.

That was simply the effect of eye-strain, and I knew that I must be imagining things, which was a bad thing to do at the very beginning of my ordeal. So I took myself to task, shut my eyes, prayed very earnestly for several minutes, then did my damnedest to get to sleep.

Of course, I couldn't. It was utterly hopeless, and how long I continued the attempt, I don't know. Anyhow, at length I gave it up, opened my eyes again and lay staring at the ceiling.

It seemed that I remained doing that for an interminable time. At first I could now and then hear distant noises, but gradually they became more infrequent until the house was very quiet. Then, I suppose because I was no longer trying to go to sleep, I dropped off; but only into a light doze.

I was roused from it by a quickening of my heart. I suddenly became conscious that it was hammering in my chest, and that the blood was pulsing more swiftly through my body. Yet my face had gone cold. It was almost as though, while I had been dozing, the temperature of the room had dropped to zero, and that the icy air was congealing into a thin rim of frost on my cheeks, nose and forehead.

Very slowly, knowing yet dreading what I should see, I turned my head and squinted at the floor below the blackout curtain. There was the shadow of the Thing, in the centre panel of the broad moonlit strip.

It was not moving but quite still, as if the beast had pressed itself up against the window and was peering in. I have never seen it still before, and was able to get a better idea of its shape than I had previously. As I see only its shadow – simply a black outline without depth – it is extremely difficult to visualise the beast itself. I have no means of telling if it has eyes, a beak, a snout, or is a faceless thing like a starfish, only, instead of being flat, having a big round body from which its tentacles project.

I don't think now, though, that this evil entity can have the form of an octopus, as they have eight tentacles, whereas it has only six. Moreover, an octopus's tentacles come out from under its body, and those of the Thing seem to be joined to it about two-thirds of the way up. Then again, an octopus's tentacles are smooth, apart from the suckers on the undersides, whereas the shadow outline of these is always a little blurred, as though they might be covered with hair.

For several minutes the Thing remained as I had first seen it, and might have been a gargoyle carved out of stone, except for the fact that the ball-like body undulated slightly, showing that it was really pulsing with horrid life. I, too, remained dead still, instinctively fearing that if I made the least movement it might provoke it into some form of terrifying activity.

Suddenly my heart seemed to leap up into my throat. Without a flicker of warning it had sprung to life and, with incredible fury, was flailing its limbs against the window, trying to smash its way in.

I clenched my hands until the nails dug into my palms – the red marks are still there this afternoon – and gritted my teeth. The attack must have lasted well over a quarter of an hour, and every moment I feared that the window-pane would give way under the brute's weight.

At last it stopped its violent thrashing and, instead, began its devil-dance to and fro, to and fro, from one window-sill to another, blindly, persistently, seeking some crack or weakness in, the barrier which might give it a better chance to break through.

In spite of the intense cold the sweat was pouring off me, and once I caught myself groaning aloud with terror. I prayed and prayed, frantically begging God to intervene and put an end to my torment, but my prayers met with no response.

I forced myself to close my eyes, first while I counted ten, then while I counted twenty; but every second while I had them shut I was terrified that when I opened them I would find that the Horror had got into the room.

Still, I kept at it, as a test of my own will-power, and I managed to get up to thirty-five. Then, when I let out my breath with a gasp and looked again, I saw that the brute had ceased its dancing and was crouching once more in the corner of the centre window. For a while nothing happened, yet I was vaguely conscious that I was becoming subject to a new form of apprehension, although I could not determine what the basis of the fresh fear could be.

Suddenly I *knew*. The Thing had a will and it was pitting it against mine. It was trying to hypnotise me.

I have never known any sound to come from it before, and it may be that I imagined this. All I can say is that it seemed to me as if it was making a faint tapping on the window – the sort of tapping that the beak of a bird might make against thick plate-glass. But the tapping was in a persistent rhythm – long, long, short, short, short – long, long, short, short, short; and those dashes and dots *translated themselves in my brain* as 'You must let-me-in. You must let-me-in.'

I shivered anew with stark horror, but there was no escaping the sounds; or, rather, the refrain that trilled like a clear little silvery voice in my mind. I stuffed my fingers in my ears, but it still came through.

Then the tapping changed to a new morse rhythm, and the silvery voice said to me gently but firmly: 'Tomorrow night, you will tell Taffy to leave the window open. Tomorrow night, you will tell Taffy to leave the window open.'

It was exactly the same technique as I had used with Deb, when I had said to her: 'You will wake up at a quarter-to-one, dress yourself and come to me' over and over again, to impress it firmly in her subconscious.

Once more the rhythm changed, this time to 'Go to sleep. Go to sleep. Go to sleep.' And the thing that terrifies me most of all is that I *did* go to sleep.

Later

My new nurse arrived this afternoon. Her name is Cardew. She seems a pleasant, friendly sort of girl, but I shouldn't call her a real good-looker. In fact she does not seem at all the type that Helmuth was expecting his Matron friend to send him. She is a hefty wench with a freckled face, blue eyes and a broad nose that inclines to turn up a trifle.

As Helmuth was out when she got here, Taffy brought her straight in to me, without even giving her a chance to tidy herself; so she was still wearing a suit of old tweeds and the heavy brogues in which she had travelled down. Her light brown hair is naturally fluffy and had got a bit windswept; so her general turn-out put the thought into my mind that she ought to be swinging a hockey stick. I doubt if she is any older than I am, so my first impression of her is that she is a nice, healthy English hoyden, not overburdened with brains but the sort that has been brought up to believe in God and the King, and marries respectably to build bonnie babies for the Empire.

Anyhow, she shows promise of being a more cheerful companion than Deb, and I am glad that she arrived when Helmuth was out. As soon as he gets hold of her it is certain that he will put all sorts of ideas about me into her head; but, at least, she saw me for the first time without prejudice.

Later

I have been worrying myself stiff all day about this new development of the Horror attempting to hypnotise me. I don't think it can possibly have succeeded in doing so – yet, for two reasons. Firstly, I am certain that I did not go into a trance while it was urging me to tell Taffy to leave the window open; secondly, I can remember the attempt perfectly clearly, which, presumably, I should not be able to do if the brute had managed to dominate my subconscious. On the other hand, I *did* fall asleep at its order, and while it was still at the window – which I should not previously have believed to be even remotely possible. So, in a way, it must have succeeded in getting some sort of control over my mind.

The only precaution I can think of against my giving way to a sudden impulse to obey its order tonight is to tie a handkerchief round my wrist. The sight of that should, I trust, be enough to pull me up with a jerk if I find myself apparently talking at random. But it is damnably unnerving.

I have found out why my new nurse is not the hard-faced, good-looking type of bitch that Helmuth expected his friend to send here for his amusement. Apparently the Matron had no hand in her selection. She got his telegram yesterday afternoon and nominated a Nurse Jollef for the job, then went off for a long weekend in the country. This morning Jollef fell downstairs and sprained her ankle, so the deputy Matron picked Cardew to come here instead.

All I hope is that Helmuth does not decide to send her back to London and ask for a substitute more to his taste, as she is young and friendly. If Helmuth does not poison her mind too much against me there seems a chance that I may be able to make her my secret ally. In any case she should be much easier to get round than Deb.

I have pulled a fast one on her already by telling her that I always take one sleeping tablet, and that the bottle is left beside my bed in case I wake in pain during the night and need another; so she put the bottle in the top drawer of my bedside table. As soon as she had left the room to get my hot-water bottle I slipped four more tablets out of it; so even if she meets Helmuth on the way back and he tells her to collect it, I'll be able to cheat the Horror tonight at all events – that is, provided that I don't suddenly get a blackout and tell Taffy to open the window.

Here they come to settle me down.

Saturday, 30th May

It is mid-afternoon, and I am still feeling like death. Five sleeping tablets proved an overdose. It did the trick all right, as within twenty minutes of my lamp being taken away I was 'out', and I remained in complete oblivion for the best part of twelve hours. This morning they had the hell of a job to get me round, and it seems that if I hadn't the constitution of an ox I should probably have kicked the bucket.

Nurse Cardew may be young, but she can be tough enough when she likes. Naturally such an episode occurring immediately on her arrival was a bit hard on her, as it reflects on her professional competence, and she gave me a terrific raspberry.

Perhaps it was bad strategy on my part to put her in a position where, through no fault of her own, she appears to have stepped off on the wrong foot. It will certainly make it far more difficult now for me to win her sympathy and possible help. But what the devil was I to do? So long as the moon remains near-full, every night means for me a new crisis in a most hideous battle. I simply *cannot* afford to think of long-term policies; I just *have* to seize on any means that offer to escape immediate danger.

Later

At tea-time I managed to get myself partially back into Nurse Cardew's good graces. Apparently the name 'Jugg' is not quite such a bell-ringer as I have always imagined; she had never heard of it before she was sent down here, and knew nothing about me at all. She asked in what sort of accident I had broken my back, and when I told her that I had been shot down she became much more matey. Her only brother – a Lieutenant in the Fleet Air Arm – was shot down too; but that happened nearly a year ago in the Eastern Mediterranean; and as he was reported 'missing, presumed dead' it's a hundred to one against the poor girl ever seeing him again.

Like myself, she is an orphan and, now that her brother has gone, she has no close relatives. Her father was a Naval Officer. He and her mother were both drowned in a yachting fatality when she was three, and she and her brother were brought up by an aunt who lives at Dawlish, in Devonshire. I gather they have very little money, but she doesn't seem to mind that, as she says that up to the time Johnny – that is her brother – got his packet, she found life enormous fun; and she is beginning to again, now that she doesn't think quite so often about his never coming home.

I have always been distinctly allergic to this hearty attitude to life, and I still cannot believe that I should find it 'tremendous fun' to go up to London with half-a-dozen other young people on an excursion ticket, for the sake of an afternoon's shop-window gazing, a 'Club' dance of some sort at one of the lesser hotels and supper in the small hours at Lyons Corner House. Still, on the debit side I must admit that, apart from my time in the R.A.F., my own youth was extraordinarily barren of hilarity; so perhaps being surrounded by riches really has very little bearing on the amount of enjoyment that one can get, and that it depends much more on an attitude of mind.

Owing to the Naval influence in Sally's – that is, Nurse Cardew's – family, she went into the W.R.N.S. at the beginning of the war. Incidentally, she *is* older than I am, by just over a year, although I would never have thought it from either her appearance or conversation. But she was blown up by a land-mine in the Plymouth blitz and, in consequence, invalided from the Service.

She is quite all right again now, unless she hears something go off with a loud bang. Apparently a bursting motor-tyre, or even a child popping a paper bag, is enough to do it; but any noise resembling an explosion still shatters her completely. She dives for the nearest cover – which, as she told me with a loud guffaw, usually means under the table, then bursts into a flood of tears and makes a general nuisance of herself for the next two hours. That is why, since the Wrens decided that she was no longer 100 per cent reliable for any regular duty, she had herself trained as a private nurse and has been taking jobs in country areas where bombs rarely fall.

Her nursing qualifications are pretty slender; she makes no secret of that. She went in for nursing only because she felt that she could not remain idle after she was boarded out of the Wrens, and she didn't much like the idea of going into a factory.

As she cannot do shorthand she could not have got anything but a stooge-job in an office, whereas she did know a bit about massage from having been taught by a half-Swedish cousin of hers, who used to come and stay at Dawlish. So she did a course in first-aid, swatted up a few books on this and that concerning the most general types of ailments, and got taken on by Miss Smith for sending to patients in the country where massage was the principal requirement. Her last case was an old Colonel with a game leg, up in Shropshire, and two days after her return to London a new throw of the dice sent her here.

It is nice to have someone fresh to talk to, however mediocre their mentality, and over tea we got on like a house on fire; but, unfortunately, later this evening I blotted it again.

Helmuth has spared me his evening visits since we had our show-down; so when Sally came in, about six o'clock, to ask if she might borrow a book from the library, I let her browse for a few moments, while concluding a paragraph of this, then opened up our conversation again.

Most regrettably, as it turned out, I chose the subject of Helmuth as a lead in. I asked her what she thought of him.

While still searching the shelves for something readable, she said: 'He's terribly distinguished-looking, isn't he?'

'The roebuck probably thinks of the lion that way till he takes a big jump and fixes his claws in her back,' I remarked acidly.

'Am I supposed to be the roebuck in this analogy?' she enquired.

'You might be,' I murmured, 'and while Dr Lisický's eyes and hair give him some resemblance to the King of Beasts, you can take it from me that there is nothing kingly about his mind; it is as low as that of any reptile.'

She straightened herself a little, but continued to keep her back turned, as she replied: 'I gathered from Dr Lisický this morning that you have recently taken an acute dislike to him. That sort of twist in the mentality of a permanent invalid against the person who is looking after them does sometimes occur; but you should do your best to fight it. Personally, from what little I have so far seen of the Doctor, I think him a most intelligent and charming man; and I am not going to encourage your morbid ideas by letting you say such horrid things to me about him.'

Like an idiot, I did not see the red light, but plunged in further with a sneer: 'Since you think him "distinguished-looking, intelligent and charming" it's pretty clear that he is well on the way to getting you where he wants you already. But I warn you that he has the morals of a sewer-rat. He made your predecessor his mistress, drove her half-crazy with neglect, then, when a respectable fellow wanted to marry her, he started to sleep with her again for the fun of busting up her engagement.'

Suddenly Nurse Cardew swung round on me; her blue eyes were hard and her freckled face flushed.

'Listen to me, Toby Jugg!' she exclaimed angrily. 'At tea-time this afternoon I thought I was going to like you, and I'm still prepared to do so; but we had better get matters straight before we go any further. When I took on this job I was not told that you were a mental case, and I don't believe that, strictly speaking, you are one. But Dr Lisický warned me last night that you've got a mind like a cesspool, and that your letters have to be censored because of the obscenities you put in them. What you have just said of him is obviously a wicked and disgusting lie. I'm not narrow-minded but I don't like filth and I don't like slander; so for the future you will kindly refrain from both in my presence, or I'll chuck up the case and go back to London.'

'Okay!' I snapped. 'I won't sully your shell-like ears again. But if you prefer to believe Dr Helmuth Lisický rather than me, it will be your own fault if you get yourself seduced.'

At that she flounced out of the room, and a few minutes later I was regretting that I had put her back up. Personally I don't give a damn if Helmuth makes her his mistress, but it seemed only fair to warn her of the sort of man he is. Where I was stupid was in putting it so bluntly, and in losing my temper with her because she wouldn't believe me.

In normal circumstances I should have handled the business much more tactfully; but the truth is that my nerves are in absolute shreds, so that I am hardly responsible for what I am saying, and my temper is as liable to snap as the over-taut string of a violin. But how could it be otherwise, seeing what I may have to face tonight?

Sunday, 31st May

I don't think I can stand much more of this. If Helmuth's object is to drive me mad, as I am convinced it is, he is well on the way to succeeding. What is more, he is starting now to collect the evidence which will later be put before the Lunacy Board in support of an application to have me certified.

He already had my letters to Julia, describing my 'hallucinations', and the fact that I attempted to escape from his 'loving care' in the middle of the night, with Deb; and now, after last night, he will be able to produce visual evidence that I was seen raving. I suppose that was largely my fault; but it was bound to happen sooner or later, and I expect he has been counting on an occurrence of that kind giving him a solid basis for his case.

As a matter of fact I very nearly broke down when Nurse Cardew and Taffy were about to leave me last night. I implored her not to take away my lamp; but she said that the danger of fire from my knocking it over was too great for it to be left at my bedside. So I retorted: 'All right, then, put it out of my reach if you like, but at least leave it somewhere in the room.'

She was still a bit shirty from my having rubbed her up the wrong way before dinner, but I think it was more the influence Helmuth has already gained over her that decided her to refuse me. With a shake of her head, she replied: 'If I did you couldn't put it out; and if you had to take five sleepers to get off last night you would never get off at all with a light burning in your room. Anyhow, after the way you made a fool of me over that I am certainly not going against Dr Lisický's instructions to please you.'

So that was that; and in utter misery I had to watch them go.

It was the night of the full moon and the day had been fine with hardly a cloud in the sky, so I knew that I must anticipate a maximum attack. For what seemed an age I alternatively prayed and lay there with my brain whirling round in sick apprehension, then my heart began to hammer and the cold sweat broke out on my face. I turned my head, and there was the shadow of the Thing on the band of moonlight. It was crouching on the sill in the left-hand corner of the middle window, its round body pulsing horribly. The malefic force it radiated made my flesh creep, and the back of my neck began to prickle.

I found myself counting my heartbeats, and I had got up to eighty-nine when I suddenly caught the tapping noise that I first heard the beast make two nights before. I tried to go on counting, so as to shut out from my mind the rhythm of this tapping, but I couldn't.

Again that infernal morse code translated itself in my brain into the small, clear silvery voice, and it kept on reiterating: 'You've got to give way. You've got to give way.'

Then the rhythm changed to that of the gently swinging pendulum of an old clock, which said: 'Forget . . . Remember. Forget . . . Remember. Forget . . . Remember.' And I knew as certainly as if the Brute had explained its intention that it was endeavouring to mesmerise me, so that I should accept some instruction into my subconscious, forget it, and then at a stated time remember and act upon it. I knew, too, that when the instruction came it would be on the lines that I must tell Taffy to open one of the windows looking onto the courtyard, before leaving me the following night.

In a moment of time all sorts of thoughts jostled for place in my terrified brain: Could the Horror hypnotise me against my will? Why had it left out this all-important middle stage of the process two nights before? Was it, perhaps, as much mentally blind and fumbling as it seems to be physically? How could I best attempt to thwart its evil purpose? What means could I employ to stop that sinister little silvery voice from impinging on my mind?

Of all those questions the last was that which called most urgently for an immediate answer. While the sweat trickled in icy rivulets down my face and I wrung my hands together in an agony of fear, I strove to concentrate upon it.

Suddenly, in the very midst of a groan that broke from me at my impotence, the answer came. It is difficult to catch any remark addressed to one in a room where a person is singing, and next to impossible to do so if one is singing oneself. By roaring out a song I could drown that small, insidious, evil voice that uttered its phrases over and over again in my own mind.

I suppose it was the fact that I had been praying so hard which instinctively led me to launch out with a hymn. I started with 'Rock of Ages', but the tempo seemed so slow and dirge-like that I quickly switched to 'Onward, Christian Soldiers'.

The effect was instantaneous. The voice was smothered and the Thing out in the courtyard knew it. From having remained quite still it suddenly leapt into its devil-dance. Quivering with rage, hate and fury, it sprang up and down, and hurled its heavy body against the window-panes.

But my triumph was short-lived. The only Church services that I have attended since I was a child were the compulsory parades to which I was detailed during my early months in the R.A.F., so I could remember only the first verse and chorus of 'Onward, Christian Soldiers'. I sang them over three times while I frantically searched my mind for another hymn, but I could think of nothing. Then, as I began to falter, the tapping came through again.

'Stop that! Stop that! Stop that!' it commanded angrily.

In desperation, rather than fall silent, I changed from the sacred to the profane, and began to roar out 'There is a Tavern in the Town'. From that I ran through half-a-dozen old favourites that had always figured in our repertoire when, in those now far-off days, we had shouted ourselves hoarse grouped round a piano after guest-night dinners in the Mess. With one thought only in my mind – to keep on singing – I made no attempt to pick the songs, but sang them one after another as they came into my head; so it is hardly surprising that such pieces as 'Roll Out the Barrel' and 'We'll Hang Out the Washing on the Siegfried Line' became interspersed with bawdy choruses like 'A German Officer Crossed the Rhine', and 'She was Poor but she was Honest'.

I was bawling out 'The Harlot of Jerusalem' at the top of my voice, when the door was suddenly flung open. There stood Helmuth, holding a lamp aloft in his right hand, and beside him Nurse Cardew. Both of them were in their dressing-gowns.

No doubt from fear, strain and effort I was as near off my rocker as makes no difference at the time. Anyhow, the sheer impetus of the song and the paramount necessity of continuing to drown that evil voice caused me to carry on for a couple of lines. It was only when Helmuth shouted at me: 'Toby! Stop singing that filthy song – instantly!' that I realised the significance of the chorus I had been yelling.

At that second I caught Nurse Cardew's glance and, goodness knows why, but a quick flush of shame ran through me. In this day and age it takes more than a few bawdy words to shock most girls, and as a trained nurse she must have heard plenty. All the same, just for a second, I felt as though I had been caught out doing something quite frightful.

But the feeling had passed in an instant, submerged by the far more powerful causes for agitation which were still making me sweat and tremble. With my head craned up to stare at my visitors over the foot of the bed I thrust out my arm and pointed to the strip of moonlight: 'Look! Look!' I cried. 'D'you call that an hallucination?'

Then I swivelled my glance to follow my own pointing finger.

With a groan I let my head fall back onto my pillow. The shadow was no longer there.

Helmuth's voice came, with the false sadness of crocodile's tears in it. 'This is a tragic business, Nurse. It was lucky that I heard the poor boy and fetched you. I'm afraid he has been suffering from something worse than a bad dream, and that we have real grounds to fear for his sanity.'

At that I went off the deep end. I called him a dirty, lying, hypocritical bastard, and every other name that I could think of. For a good two minutes or more I raved and shouted at him, and their efforts to check me were in vain.

People with red hair are said to have violent tempers, and mine can be a pretty hot one if I once let myself go. When Helmuth set down the lamp and came near the bed I grabbed his arm and tried to pull him to me. If I could have got my hands on his throat I really believe that I would have killed him. But Nurse Cardew came up on my other side and gave me a sharp slap in the face.

I was so astonished that I let go of Helmuth, stopped shouting, and turned to stare at her.

'That's better,' she said quietly. 'You ought to be ashamed of yourself, making such a scene, and attacking Dr Lisický. You don't want to be put into a strait-jacket, do you?'

'Oh come, Nurse! Please don't suggest such a terrible thing,' Helmuth protested. Then, after a second, he added: 'But, loath as I am to do so, I fear I shall have to call a mental specialist in if he goes on like this.'

Her remark, and his right on top of it, sobered me up completely. I cannot believe that she is a party to Helmuth's plot – as yet, at all events – so her mention of a strait-jacket could only have been made spontaneously as a direct result of seeing me, as she evidently thought, behaving like a madman. It flashed on me then that Helmuth must have been waiting for something like this to happen, and had deliberately brought her along so that later he would be able to call her as an eye-witness. By letting fly at him I had played right into his hands.

With an effort I collected my scattered wits and did the little that could be done to repair the position. I said: 'I'm sorry, Nurse. I shouldn't have used such language in front of you; but, believe it or not, I have very good grounds for losing my temper with Dr Lisický. For weeks past I have been sleeping abominably badly in this room, and again and again I have asked him to move me to another. Since he flatly refuses to do so I hold him responsible for my nightmares.'

'There is nothing wrong with this room,' she replied coldly, as she began to remake my pillows. 'It's large and light and airy, and most invalids would consider themselves lucky to have such a beautiful apartment to live in. Since you suffer from nightmares you would have them just as badly anywhere else; and it is very wicked to get such horrible ideas about people who are doing their best for you. Now, if I give you two triple bromides, will you promise to behave yourself and try to get off to sleep again?'

As further argument seemed futile, I said 'Yes'; then, as soon as I had drunk the draught, Helmuth picked up the lamp and, having wished me better sleep for the rest of the night, they left me.

But the night's battle was not over. Within five minutes of their having gone, the cold came again, and I had a sudden empty feeling in the pit of my stomach. One glance at the band of moonlight was enough. There was the shadow back where it had been before, and the horrid, insistent tapping started once more.

After that I am not quite clear what really happened. I can recall praying again, sweating anew with funk, and saying choruses and nursery rhymes over to myself in an effort to shut out the silvery voice. The struggle seemed to last for an eternity, and the frightful tiling is that I have no idea how far the Horror succeeded in dominating my subconscious before the bromides took effect, and I drifted off into a sort of coma – or rather a nightmarish, hag-ridden sleep.

This morning I feel, and look, like a piece of chewed string. Nurse Cardew seemed quite shocked at my appearance, but she puts it down to my having over-excited myself last night; and when I started to tell her about Helmuth's refusal to have the blackout curtain lengthened, and to let me have my radio beside my bed, she wouldn't listen to me. It is clear that he has already completely won her over, and she thinks that my requests are inspired solely with a view to making trouble.

What will happen tonight, God alone knows; and I can now place my hope only in Him. If the Devil in the courtyard did succeed in hypnotising me, the odds are that I shall become subject to a blackout sometime this evening, and ask either Taffy or Nurse Cardew to open that window after the curtain has been drawn, then come out of my trance without realising what I have done.

If that happens I have no illusions about my fate. The Horror will slither in and across the floor, one swift spring and it will be on the bed, wrapping its filthy tentacles round me in a ghastly embrace. By the time my screams bring help it will be too late. They really will find me a raving lunatic.

Later

I believe my desperate prayers for help have been answered in the nick of time. I cannot tell for certain because, being Sunday, Taffy has the afternoon off, so I have not yet had a chance to tackle him. But an entirely unforeseen event has brought me new hope, and I have been hard put to it to conceal the intense excitement I am feeling from Nurse Cardew.

Indirectly I owe this lifeline which seems almost within my grasp to the great raid on Cologne. Last night Bomber Command went out in force – in far greater force than most people would believe possible. They sent a thousand aircraft against one objective, and at a guess I would not have thought that we could have put half that number in the sky. It makes a landmark in the war, and its effect on the city must have been too frightful to contemplate.

All the same, I would rather have been there, and taken my chance as the bombs rained down, than as I was, lying on my back here sweating with terror under the baleful influence of the Evil that is hunting me.

But that is beside the point. It was thinking about this giant R.A.F. raid that recalled to my mind the official letter Helmuth gave me when he brought me the one from Uncle Paul on Thursday. I was so put out by Uncle Paul's reply that I did not even open the other; I just pushed it into a drawer of my bedside table and forgot all about it. But this morning I remembered it, and on opening the envelope I found that it was from the Air Ministry and contained various papers, including a cheque for £147 10s. 5d.

The money is the final settlement – exclusive of pension – on my being invalided out. Most of it was due to me months ago, but as I could not account for some of the items of flying-kit with which I had been issued, the usual generous procedure was followed. They hung onto the whole lot, while numerous dreary little men made quite certain that the total could not be further reduced by docking me for some other article of war-equipment graciously lent to me by the nation as an aid to fighting our enemies.

However, in this case, praises be for the dilatoriness of those chair-born warriors whose lot is cast among ledgers. If the bulk of this cash had been paid to me last March it would long since have joined the rest of my private money in the bank, where I can't get at it without Helmuth knowing; whereas it has now arrived like manna from Heaven, providing me with the means for an attempt to bribe Taffy.

It is still a toss-up whether he will be prepared to risk Helmuth's wrath, but I think he will for close on £150. That is a lot to a young Welsh country bumpkin who, but for my arrival here, would still be doing odd jobs in the garden at about £2 a week. Besides, there is this laudable ambition of his to become an engineer, like his brother Davey in Cardiff. A wad like this would easily cover his fees at a technical school for the elementary course, which is all he is capable of mastering to begin with, and keep him while he is on it into the bargain.

The thing that I fear is most likely to put him off is the idea of taking a cheque – particularly one made out to someone else and crossed account payee. But I hope to get over that by also giving him a letter to my bank, instructing them to credit the cheque to my account and to pay the bearer out its value in cash. That would amount to giving him an open cheque in exchange for paying in the other, really; although he won't realise it. Still, it should help to allay any apprehensions he may have that when he presents the cheque the cashier will think he has stolen it and send for the police.

Of course, if only I can get to London I'll be able to see to it myself that he gets his money; but my bank being there presents another snag. Naturally, if he does his stuff and gets me out, his instinct would be to grab the cheque and make a bolt for Cardiff. But I can think of no way of enabling him to cash the cheque except by taking it to my London bank.

In one way that is an advantage as, although I could have myself put in the guard's van in my wheel-chair and make the journey on my own, it would make everything much easier, particularly at the other end, if I had him with me. But it means that I'll have the additional fence to cross of persuading him that, instead of disappearing into the blue, he must accompany me to London.

Lastly there is the question of our fares. As I have no ready he will have to ante-up for both of us. I don't doubt that he has a bit tucked away somewhere, but it may be in the Post Office; and for me it is tonight or never. If it is there he will have no time to draw it out, and God forbid that he should attempt to borrow from the other servants. Still, if the worst comes to the worst we can use whatever cash he has on tickets to carry us part of the way, and I can offer my gold cigarette-case to the collector as security for later paying the surplus on the remainder of the journey.

Taffy always gets back in time to give me my bath, and there could be no better opportunity for tackling him. He can't make any excuse to get away and leave me there, so he will have to listen to all I have to say. I shall offer him the full amount of the cheque in any case, as an assurance against failure and the loss of his job; and double the amount in addition, payable at the end of next month, in the event of his getting me safely to London.

To offer him more might make him suspicious that I mean to rat on him; but a round £500 – and that's what I'll make it – won't sound to him too high a price for the successor of his family's feudal Lords to pay for freedom. On the other hand, he'll know without telling that it is only once in a lifetime that a poor gardener's son has the chance to earn such a sum for a single night's work.

If he agrees, I mean to get him to come back as soon as Nurse Cardew has gone to her room, dress me, get me into my chair and wheel me along to the bathroom. It was the old flower-room, and was specially fitted up with a bath for me so that I wouldn't have to be carried upstairs; but it has no window, only a blacked-out skylight, so I'll be safe there from the Horror while the household is settling down for the night.

I daren't leave my get-away later than midnight, in case Taffy should drop off to sleep; but by twelve o'clock everyone should be in bed, and he can come and get me.

On second thoughts, though, I think I'll keep him with me; that will eliminate the risk of his giving the game away inadvertently to any of the other servants, or anyone thinking it strange if he is seen loitering about instead of going to bed.

That is certainly an improvement in my plan, as it means that we won't have to leave the house till it is a safe bet that everyone is sound asleep.

It is four miles to the station, but downhill most of the way; so, making due allowance for Taffy's deformed foot, which has saved him from being called up, he ought to be able to push me that far in well under three hours. So if we leave at two o'clock we should reach the station by five, easily; and I doubt if the earliest train leaves much before six.

So that is what is cooking. I pray God that it comes to the boil.

Later

Taffy fell for it; and tonight's the night. I fancy my grandfather must be turning in his grave, though, as the avaricious little bounder stuck out for £1,000 and a job in the Juggernaut factory, if he succeeds in getting me to London. But who cares! I would give him the Castle and make him the Lord of Llanferdrack just for getting me out of this room until tomorrow morning.

Tuesday, 2nd June

I am still here. I could not bring myself to write anything yesterday, I was too utterly depressed and mentally exhausted. My only remaining hope is that I may manage to hang out somehow till Uncle Paul arrives on Thursday.

On Sunday night everything went according to plan; but my luck was too good to last. Taffy came for me, dressed me, took me along to the bathroom, waited there with me for nearly three hours, then got me out of the house with no more noise than a first-class burglar would have made getting in. The moon was still up and for the first time in many weeks I was glad to see it, as it lit the way for us through the grounds and for the first mile or more down the road. We reached the station by a quarter to five, and had to wait outside it for three-quarters of an hour, as it was not open; but soon after 5.30 the staff of three made their appearance and began the day's routine. Taffy is a bit suspicious of the Post Office, and he keeps his savings in an old cigarette tin concealed somewhere in his room, so we were able to buy two tickets to London, and went onto the platform.

At 5.55 a milk train came through. Why, oh why, didn't we take it? I must have been crazy not to. But everything was going so perfectly that it seemed much more sensible to wait for the 6.20, that does not dither round the loop line but goes direct to the junction.

We were the only people on the platform, and the whistling of the solitary porter was the only sound that broke the stillness of the post-dawn hour. Suddenly I caught the hum of a car engine driven all out. Next moment it roared up to the station entrance. There was a brief commotion and the noise of running footsteps, then Helmuth and Nurse Cardew shot out of the booking-office and came dashing towards us.

At the sight of them I knew the game was up. The train was nearly due, but even if it had come in at that moment I could not have got Taffy to heave me into it. From fear of Helmuth, he had already taken to his heels.

All the same I meant to make a fight for it; and, anyway, it seemed a bit hard that his panic should cost him the compensation I had promised him for the loss of his job; so I shouted after him: 'Come back, Taffy! Come back, you fool! Don't go without your cheque!'

That halted him, and he came ambling back with a hang-dog look on his face, just as Helmuth and Nurse Cardew reached me.

She was in her nurse's uniform but had evidently dressed in a hurry, as her fluffy brown hair was sticking out untidily from under her cap and she had odd stockings on her long legs. Probably it was knowing about that which made her young face so flushed and angry. Without a word she grasped the back-rail of my chair, and swivelling it round made to wheel me off the station. But I was too quick for her. Stretching out a hand, I grabbed the iron railing at the back of the platform and brought her up with a jerk.

'Now Toby!' said Helmuth a bit breathlessly. 'Please don't make a scene. You've already given us an awful fright. Don't add to our distress by making an exhibition of yourself.'

'If there is any scene it will be your fault,' I retorted. 'I am about to take the train to London; and you have no right to stop me.'

Although the platform had been empty a few minutes earlier, a little crowd began to gather with mysterious suddenness. The porter, two soldiers, a land-girl, a leading aircraftsman and a little group of children had all appeared from nowhere and were eyeing us with speculative interest.

'You are in no fit state to travel,' Helmuth said sharply.

Striving to keep as calm as I could, I denied that, and a wordy battle ensued in which both of us rapidly became more heated. We were still arguing when the train came clanking in.

The little crowd had increased to over a dozen people and it was now further swollen by others getting out of the train. Seeing it there actually in the station made me desperate. If I could have only covered those few yards and heaved myself into a carriage it meant safety, freedom and sanity; whereas to let Helmuth take me back to Llanferdrack threatened imprisonment, terror and madness. He caught the gleam in my eye and endeavoured to bring matters to a swift conclusion. Grabbing my wrist, he strove to break my grasp of the railing, while Nurse Cardew pushed on my chair from behind with all her weight.

'Help! Help!' I shouted to the crowd. 'I want to get on the train to London, and these people have no right to stop me.'

An elderly Major, who had arrived on the train, stepped forward and said rather hesitantly to Helmuth: 'Look here! This is none of my business, but I really don't think you ought to use violence towards a cripple.'

Helmuth let go my wrist and turned to him; but I got in first. 'I appeal to you, sir,' I cried. 'I am an ex-officer wounded in the war; but I am perfectly fit to travel, and these people are endeavouring to detain me against my will.'

'That is only partially true!' Helmuth said quickly. 'This poor young man was shot down nearly a year ago. But the injury to his spine has affected his brain. I am a Doctor and – '

'A Doctor of Philosophy!' I cut in, but he ignored the sneer, and went on: 'He is in my care, and escaped from Llanferdrack Castle last night. I assure you that he is not fit to travel, and that I am only doing my duty in restraining him from doing so. It would be dangerous both for himself and others, as he is subject to fits of insanity.'

'That's a lie!' I declared, and Taffy came unexpectedly to my assistance by adding: 'Right you. The young gentleman's as sane as myself, is it. And it is a good master he is, too.'

As the Major looked from one to another of us doubtfully, Helmuth brought up his reserves. With a gesture towards Nurse Cardew he said: 'This lady is a professional nurse. Since you appear to doubt me, she will tell you that she has seen the patient in such a violent state that she had to threaten to have him put into a strait-jacket.'

She confirmed his statement at once, and added: 'Two nights ago he was screaming obscenities and attacked the Doctor.'

All these exchanges had taken place in less than a couple of minutes; but the train was overdue to leave, and the guard, who was standing on the fringe of the crowd, blew his whistle.

The Major gave me a pitying look and said: 'I'm very sorry, but I really don't think I can interfere.' Then he saluted politely and turned away.

I thrust my hand in my pocket, pulled out the cheque and the letter for my bank manager, held them out to Taffy and cried: 'Here you are! Quick, man! Jump on the train!'

As Taffy snatched them Helmuth grasped him by the arm and snapped: 'Give that to me!'

I don't know if he realised that it was a cheque or thought that it was a letter that I was trying to get off to somebody without his knowing its contents, but his act was the last straw that made me lose my temper completely.

'Damn you!' I yelled. 'Let him go. That's my money to do as I like with. He's earned it by doing his best to get me out of your filthy clutches. If you take that cheque from him I'll call the police in and have you arrested for theft.'

But Taffy had already wrenched himself away and jumped on the moving train.

To give him the papers I had had to let go the railing and Nurse Cardew seized the opportunity to start pushing me along the platform. Further resistance now that the train had gone was pointless; but, having finally lost my temper, I continued to shout abuse at Helmuth all the way to the car.

Only when they had got me into it, and were tying my wheelchair onto the grid behind, did it suddenly dawn upon me that, by my outburst, I had provided Helmuth with invaluable fresh evidence that he could use in seeking to prove me insane, as a score of people must have heard me raving at him.

That thought, coming on top of my bitter disappointment, was more than I could bear. I broke down and wept.

Later

I had to stop writing a quarter of an hour ago, as the memory of the ignominious manner in which I was brought back here, after my attempted flight, made me start crying again.

Really it is too absurd that a grown man like myself should give way to tears, but I suppose it is because my nerves have been reduced to shreds, and the appalling strain of knowing that my situation is going from bad to worse.

The worst factor is the way in which Helmuth is steadily gaining ground towards his secret objective, of collecting enough evidence about my disturbed mental state to get me certified as a lunatic. But, in addition, there are the various changes that have resulted in the past week from my two attempts to escape.

Taffy was a great stupid oaf with a streak of low cunning and greed in his make-up; but on the whole he wasn't a bad sort, and, normally, he was willing, cheerful and friendly. His departure was admittedly my own fault, but I am paying for it now pretty heavily, as his place has been taken by Helmuth's man Konrad. There has never been any love lost between us at the best of times and, quite apart from the fact that I dislike him touching me anyhow, whenever Nurse Cardew is not with us he takes an obvious delight in handling me roughly.

Deb, too, was very far from being a gay and lovable companion, and my new nurse is no better. I am sure she could be, but the trouble is that I set off on the wrong foot with her the very night she arrived, by taking that overdose of sleeping tablets; and since then she has seen little but the worst side of me. Unfortunately, I find it practically impossible to conceal any longer my hatred for Helmuth, and she has already developed a strong admiration for him; so she regards me as an ungrateful young brute, and whenever his name crops up we snap at one another.

She obviously does not like it here; which is quite understandable, seeing that she expected a quiet life looking after a simple spinal case, and now finds that she is in charge of someone whom she believes to be a dangerous lunatic. In addition, my latest escapade has made her work much more exacting, as she now has to come upstairs to me a dozen or more times every day.

When they got me back here, Helmuth again played the role of Uriah Heep and pretended to be greatly distressed about me. But his concern took the form of actually and officially making me a prisoner.

Hating him as I do, I could not help feeling a sneaking admiration for the way he did it, as in achieving his secret object he killed two birds with one stone. On the drive back he declared that some means must be devised to prevent me from escaping again, in case I did myself an injury, and devilishly led Nurse Cardew into discussing with him how best this might be done.

As I have twice succeeded in securing aid for an intended get-away and might, perhaps, corrupt another of the servants to help me in a third attempt, their problem really amounted to – what arrangements could be made so that I would need more than one person's assistance to get out of the house without their knowing?

Helmuth was driving and Nurse Cardew sitting in the back with me. By that time I had more or less recovered from my weeping fit and I cut in sarcastically: 'Why don't you take me down to one of the dungeons and chain me to the wall? That's what they used to do to the poor wretches in Bedlam, isn't it?'

That brought a shocked protest from them both, and assurances that they were only trying to protect me from the possibility of something awful happening to me as a result of my own folly.

Then Nurse Cardew said a piece of her own which left me undecided if I ought to curse or kiss her. The gist of her remarks were: (1) She thought the best thing would be for her to take away my chair at nights, as two people would be needed to carry me, and even then it would be difficult for them to get me very far without it. (2) That was, unless the Doctor would agree to moving me to an upstairs room; as in that case, even in my chair, no-one person would be able to get me down the stairs. (3) In any case, it was clear that I had a phobia about my present room, and she had always understood that in mental cases the cause of the phobia should never be referred to, and eliminated as far as possible. Therefore, she felt most strongly that I ought to be moved.

For the moment Helmuth did not reply, as he was just driving up to the front of the house. While they got me out of the car and into my chair, my brain was working furiously. The previous after-noon I had considered the possibility of hypnotising Nurse Cardew if Taffy failed me, and now, quite unconsciously, she was suggesting measures which would render any success in that direction futile, as well as actively co-operating with Helmuth in seeking means to make certain that I should not get away again. On the other hand, if she managed to persuade him to move me to another room it seemed that she would be rendering me an inestimable service.

I felt sure that he would refuse, and that if he did it would cost him a lot in her estimation; even, perhaps, convince her that he was deliberately persecuting me by keeping me there; in which case I might soon be able to win her over completely. So it looked as if whichever way things went I stood in to gain on the outcome.

But Helmuth wriggled out of the spot she had unconsciously put him on very neatly. When we were inside the hall he said: 'For your own protection, Toby, I shall adopt Nurse Cardew's suggestion. There is a room in the old part of the Castle on the first floor, abutting onto the chapel. It has a little terrace of its own, so if we put you there it will be unnecessary to carry you down to the garden for your airings; and tucked away in the east wing of the Castle you won't even see any of the servants, except my man Konrad, so you will not be under the temptation to try to bribe one of them.'

As he spoke I caught just the suggestion of a malicious gleam in his tawny eyes, and I knew then that to make me a real prisoner had been his aim the whole time. If he had bluntly suggested doing so that might have shocked and estranged Nurse Cardew, but he had skilfully led her into practically suggesting it herself, and had then made capital out of his willingness to pander to my phobia about being moved from my old room. So here I am.

After breakfast yesterday several of the staff were mobilised to move furniture, and by midday I was installed with all my belongings in my new quarters. It is a big square room with a vaulted ceiling, a large open fireplace and two arched doorways framing stout oak doors that have iron scrollwork and huge bolts on them. One of them leads to a spiral stone staircase, up which I was carried in my chair with considerable difficulty; the other leads to the terrace, which is about twenty-five feet across and shaped like the quarter segment of a circle. It lies in an angle of the Castle, its two straight sides being formed by the outer wall of this room and the wall of another, to which there is no entrance; the curved side is castellated, and this part of the battlements has a fine view over the lake, which lies about fifteen feet below it.

The room is not in bad condition; a little plaster has flaked off the ceiling and here and there the wainscoting that lines the walls has been stained by patches of damp, but the fire which is being lit daily to air it will soon dry them out; and now that it has been furnished with such pieces as they could get up the narrow, spiral stairs, it is quite comfortable. All the same, it gives one a somewhat eerie feeling to have been lifted out of a late-Victorian setting and dumped down in another overnight that is still redolent of the Middle Ages.

The thing about my old room that I miss most is the big south window. Here there is no window at all; at least, not in the modern sense. Instead, a large iron grating, about six feet long and three deep, let into the east wall, serves to provide the room with plenty of daylight and an ample supply of fresh air. As the grill is not fitted with glass, a blind, or even curtains, the wind whistling through it must make the place an ice-house in winter; but, fortunately, we are now in high summer, so that does not worry me at the moment. No blackout is needed, as the grill is not in an outer wall, but in that beyond which lies the partially ruined chapel. If I were able to stand I could look through it down into the chapel, but as its lower ledge is about five-feet-six from the floor I can see only on an upward angle some of the groined rafters of the decaying roof, and the tops of the upright baulks of timber which have been wedged under them to prevent it falling in.

Since I have been here I have been wondering a lot what Helmuth's motive can be in agreeing to my removal from the library. At first I was tremendously elated at the thought that, at last, I had escaped from the vicinity of the courtyard and that damnable band of moon-light; but, somehow, I cannot bring myself to feel any permanent sense of security on account of my move.

The courtyard is on the far side of the chapel from the lake, but that is no great distance; and the idea has begun to prey upon my mind that the Thing, having some horrible form of intelligence, may know of my move and follow me here – or Helmuth may have some way of telling it where I am.

If it does seek me out here, and climb up the chapel wall to the grating, I shall be forced to look on it for the first time face to face – that is, if there is moonlight filtering through the broken roof of the chapel. When Nurse Cardew and Konrad left me last night I had a bad half-hour fearing that might happen; but to my great relief the weather changed, it began to rain gently and the moon could not get through the clouds.

There is another thing that has been worrying me all day. Just as I was dropping off to sleep last night, at about eleven o'clock, I heard footsteps. They were light and clear, and sounded as if someone was descending a stone staircase behind the head of my bed.

At the time I thought nothing of it. But this morning, I suddenly realised that the wall behind my bed-head is an outer wall of the Castle, and I am certain that there is no staircase there.

Can those footsteps be the first indication of some fresh manifestation of Evil to which Helmuth is about to subject me? Is that why he put me in this room? They cannot have been made by any human agency, unless they are some curious echo. Perhaps that is the explanation. Pray God it is, for my nerves are strained to breaking-point already.

Wednesday, 3rd June
I slept badly last night, but, thank God, had no actual trouble. It was stormy again and the moonlight only showed fitfully now and then through the grating.

This morning I managed to get a look through it down into the chapel but, in doing so, I got myself into a bit of a mess, which ended with surprising and terrifically exciting results.

As I have mentioned before, my shoulders and arms are very strong. After I had had my airing on the battlements I wheeled myself up to the grating, sideways on, and stretched up my right hand as high as it would go. I was just able to get a firm grip on the ledge and, exerting all my strength, pulled myself up until I could grasp the iron grill with my left hand; then I shifted the right to a firmer hold and, hanging there, peered through.

The chapel is both long and lofty – in fact it is as big as the average country church. Its floor is a good twenty-five feet below me as, to give it additional height, the old builders sank it about twelve feet into the ground. Actually, I suppose they excavated the whole site for the Castle to that depth or more, and instead of making cellars and dungeons out of this bit, carried the walls and pillars of the chapel straight up from the foundations.

It must have been a damp and cheerless place to worship in, as its floor is well below the level of the lake, which runs parallel to its south wall and only about forty feet away, but our ancestors don't seem to have minded damp and cold as much as we do.

The roof is about fifteen feet above my head, and is not as badly damaged as I expected. There are a few big rents in it, but they are all this end. Looking down from the grill I was directly facing the altar, and the whole of the far half of the roof over the chancel and a good part of the nave is intact.

There are now no pews in the chapel, as it has not been used for many years; but there are a number of large, stone box-like graves with effigies of chaps in armour, and their ladies, on them, as the Lords of Llanferdrack were always buried here. Parts of four out of the six pillars, which were the main support of the roof, have crumbled away, and it has been shored up in places with wooden scaffolding. It looks, too, as if its disintegration has been arrested, as there is no debris littering the stone floor. In fact the whole place is as clean as if it had been swept out yesterday, which seems rather surprising. I was just wondering why anyone should bother to keep it in such good order when my chair slipped from under my feet, and I found myself stranded, like a fly on the wall, clinging to the grating.

It was a quarter of an hour before Nurse Cardew came in and found me like that. She promptly pushed my chair back and got me down into it, while scolding me for taking such a risk of injuring myself. I simply laughed at her and said that I could have hung on there for an hour or more without serious discomfort, had I wished.

She looked me straight in the eye and said; 'I don't believe it – unless you were taking some of the weight on your feet.'

I said I didn't think that I had been, not perceptibly, anyhow; upon which she told me to put my hands on her shoulders and try to stand up.

I tried, and I couldn't manage it. But she is amazingly strong for a girl, and she practically lifted me into an upright position. With one hand grasping the grating and the other round her neck we found that I could just remain erect for a moment or two.

Nurse Cardew says that is a sure sign that my back is mending; and that although we must go very carefully, if I practise standing like that for a short time every day, until I can take the whole of my own weight, there is a real chance that I may eventually be able to walk again. I gather that I should be doing well if I could walk from one room to another unaided by this time next year but, to me, even such a modest prospect is wildly exciting.

Besides, once I can manage a dozen steps they would let me have crutches. They daren't as things are, for if a crutch slipped I should go flat on my face, or on my back, and if my head struck something hard I might kill myself. But if I was strong enough to recover my balance there would be no danger of that, and with the aid of crutches I could get about all over the place.

This really is terrific, and Nurse Cardew seemed as pleased as I was. She has a nice smile that lights up her freckled face, and really makes her quite pretty while it lasts. But like a fool I spoilt the whole thing by asking her if she managed to keep Helmuth in his place last night; and got the tart answer to 'Mind your own business'.

I knew that she had had dinner with him because she told me she was going to yesterday afternoon. She asked me if I minded having my evening massage a little earlier than usual, so that she would have longer to change out of uniform. Naturally I agreed; I could hardly have done otherwise, and I forbore to make any comment.

However, a few minutes after having snapped me up this morning she resumed the subject of her own accord. She said: 'I do wish you would try to get these horrid ideas about Dr Lisický out of your head. It was kind of him to ask me to have dinner with him, and I hope he does again. He couldn't have been more charming, and the pre-war atmosphere of candlelight and wine made a nice change for me from the routine of having my meals served on a tray in the small library.'

There was nothing much I could say to that which would not have led to another row, so I let it pass. I wish, though, that she had been here as a fly on the wall when Helmuth was discussing the re-placement of Deb, and had heard him say that it would be 'fun to have someone fresh to sleep with', as I am quite sure that he would never bother to ask her to dine with him unless he had designs on her.

As she is so young Helmuth may have decided that the best policy is not to rush his fences. On the other hand it may be a case of 'still waters run deep'. No girl can be a nurse and remain ignorant of sex, and this one looks healthy enough to have the usual urges of her age. If she had been 'educated' at Weylands she would be a veteran by this time. Still, I don't believe, somehow, that she is that kind.

Those queer footsteps came again last night, and I heard them twice; first at eleven o'clock, as before, and, as I was wakeful, again about one o'clock. The second time they were going back up the stairs. Yet there cannot be any staircase there. It hardly seems possible that the Thing could make that sort of noise – yet it gave me a slight fit of the jitters. Thank God that tomorrow is Thursday. Unless Fate plays me some scurvy trick to prevent Uncle Paul turning up, within twenty-four hours now I'll be a free man again.

Thursday, 4th June

Last night it was calm with a clear sky, so for the first time I saw the full effect of a bright moon in this room. Praises be, there is no thick bar of it on the floor, as there was downstairs, for it does not shine in direct through the grating. It comes through the holes in the chapel roof, then filters through here filling the room with a soft radiance; but it was not strong enough to throw a shadow of the criss-cross bars of the grill.

As the appearance of the Horror is so tied up in my mind with moonlight, I was naturally in a pretty nervy state; and when the footsteps came again at eleven o'clock I broke out into a sweat. But nothing happened and after a bit I managed to get off to sleep.

This morning, while I was sitting in the sunshine on my terrace, I went over in my mind what I mean to say to Uncle Paul. As he has always been very decent to me I dislike the idea of being tough with him; but I am afraid that is the only way I can make certain of getting him to stand up to Helmuth.

I have always been rather sorry for my uncle, as in the natural course of events he should have come in for his share of the Jugg millions and be a rich man in his own right. But that he did not, and will be almost entirely dependent on me after I attain my majority, is largely his own fault. His early life, before he married Julia, was really rather a shocking record of weakness and stupidity.

When he came down from Cambridge in 1917, my grandfather secured him a commission in the Welsh Guards; but early in 1919 he got tight one night at the Berkeley, and struck a waiter, who was trying to persuade him to go home. Naturally that led to a pretty nasty stink and I gather that he narrowly escaped being cashiered; but they let him off with sending in his papers. The old man sent him to South Africa for a couple of years, to be out of the way while he sowed the rest of his wild oats, then brought him home in 1921, and put him into the offices of our Newcastle shipyards.

There he got involved with a typist and his father had to pay a tidy sum to prevent an action for breach of promise being brought. He was transferred to London after that, so that an eye could be kept on him, but that didn't do much good. He was always at the races instead of the office, and in the next few years my grandfather had to pay up his racing debts on three occasions.

Then he got into the hands of a real top-line card-sharper; one of the chaps who do things on the grand scale with a nice little house in Mayfair, run a perfectly straight game for a whole season and take just one mug for a ride in a big way at the end of it. In the season of 1925 Uncle Paul was the mug selected, and in an all-night session he was stung for seven thousand pounds.

It all appeared perfectly above-board, as there were scores of other gamblers who were prepared to swear to the honesty of the crook. My grandfather paid again, but that was the end. Uncle Paul was sent abroad with a thousand a year, payable monthly, and told that in the future he could go bankrupt or go to prison, but he would not get another cent.

In 1928 he married Julia. I have no doubt that he was in love with her on account of her bewitching beauty; but, in addition, she is connected with the noble Roman house of Colona, and I think he thought that a respectable marriage would put him right with his father. But it didn't. Albert Abel I would not even receive them; and Julia has no money of her own, so they took The Willows and settled down there in the hope that the old man would relent.

That is where Uncle Paul was unlucky. Before sufficient time had elapsed for his father really to appreciate that he had turned over a new leaf the air-crash put an end to his chances. So poor Uncle Paul's own income is still no more than it was when he had the little house at Kew.

Later

Uncle Paul has been and is now on his way back to London. He arrived in time to lunch with Helmuth and immediately afterwards Helmuth brought him up here.

Perhaps it is the result of having lived for three years in an area constantly subject to air-raids, but I thought Uncle Paul was looking a lot older. He can't be much more than forty-three, but his red hair has got a lot of grey in it now and the pouches under his eyes are heavier than ever, so he might easily be taken for fifty. All the same, his ruddy face does not look unhealthy, and he greeted me with his usual hearty manner.

'Hello, old boy! It's grand to see you again. Wish I could have come down before, but this cussed war keeps me so *feahf'lly* busy.

Never realised in the old days that serious farming took up so much time; still, we must all do what we can, eh?'

Helmuth was standing in the doorway, looking like a benevolent Bishop. I had feared that I might have considerable trouble getting rid of him; but not a bit of it. With a smile, he said: 'I'm sure you would like to have a talk with your uncle alone, so I will leave you now.' And off he went. I heard his footsteps echoing on the stone stairs, so I am quite sure that he did not linger to listen through the keyhole to what I had to say about him.

Meanwhile Uncle Paul was saying how Julia had sent me her fondest love, and that when he had shown her my letter she had wanted to come too; but that he hadn't let her because last week she was in bed for several days with a nasty go of summer 'flu and, although she is up again now, he didn't think she was really fit enough to make such a tiring journey.

In view of the way I meant to deal with my uncle, I was by no means sorry that she had not come; but I was a bit perturbed by the apparent indifference with which Helmuth had left us on our own, and debarred himself from the possibility of butting in on us at a critical juncture. It argued enormous self-confidence on his part, or else that he had already anticipated me and fixed Uncle Paul over lunch. So, after we had exchanged platitudes for a bit, I sought to test the situation by saying: 'I don't know if Helmuth has mentioned it to you, Uncle, but he and I haven't been on awfully good terms lately.'

'I say, old boy! I'm *feahf'lly* sorry to hear that.' Uncle Paul looked a shade uncomfortable, but he had not answered my question, so I persisted: 'He and I hold distinctly different views as to the state of my health; and I was wondering if by any chance he had suggested to you that the injury to my spine might now be having an unfortunate effect on my brain?'

Uncle Paul looked really uncomfortable at that, and began to shuffle his large feet about, as he replied: 'To tell you the truth, old man, he did say something to that effect. Nothing definite, you know; but just that recently you seemed to be getting some rather potty ideas into your head. If I'd taken what he said seriously I'd have been damn worried – *feahf'lly* upset. But I didn't; and anyone with half an eye can see that you're as fit as a two-year-old.'

'Thanks, Uncle,' I said quietly. 'I'm glad you feel that, because one of the reasons why I asked you to come down was to make a request which you may think rather unreasonable. I know it will sound to you like an invalid's whim, and one that is going to cause quite a lot of needless trouble; but I have given the matter very careful consideration and I am absolutely set on it. I don't like being here at Llanferdrack, and I want you to make immediate arrangements for my removal.'

Evidently Helmuth had briefed him on that one, as he produced all the arguments against it that Helmuth had used to me. I let him ramble on for a couple of minutes, then I said: 'All right, let's leave that for a minute, while I put up to you another idea. You will consider this one much more startling, but I have excellent reasons for making my request. I want you to sack Helmuth.'

His pale blue eyes fairly popped out of his head. 'Sack Helmuth!' he repeated. 'My dear old boy, you can't be serious. I mean, what's he done?'

'What he's done,' I said, 'is to make himself a sort of Himmler, so far as I am concerned. He has got this bee in his bonnet that I am going nuts, so he is now treating me as if I were an escaped Borstal boy of fifteen. And I won't bloody well have it! Do you know that during the past month or more he has had the impertinence to stop all my letters to Julia?'

He nodded. 'Yes, he told me that. He was afraid it would upset us if we knew that – well, you know what I mean. Got the idea that you were going gaga, or something.'

'Look, Uncle.' I caught his glance and held it. 'I am as sane as ever I was; but if I *were* going gaga who are the first people who ought to be informed of that?'

'Myself and Julia,' he admitted a bit sheepishly.

'Right, then,' I cracked in. 'Helmuth has exceeded his duties and abused his position. I am now making a formal request to you as my Guardian that you should sack him.'

'But I can't, old man. It just isn't on, you know. With the best will in the world I couldn't do that. You seem to forget that he is a Trustee.'

'What about it?' I retorted. 'In just over a fortnight I shall attain my majority. On June the twentieth the Board of Trustees will cease to have any further function. The whole outfit has to cash in to me, then it goes up in smoke. It is you, Uncle, who seem to have forgotten that.'

He gave me an unhappy glance from beneath his red eyebrows. 'Of course, Toby old boy, I quite see what you mean. But, all the same, after all these years we can't just kick Helmuth out. It wouldn't be playing the game.'

My tone was acid as I remarked: 'After nearly a year as a helpless cripple, I am no longer interested in games. Helmuth is endeavouring to keep me here against my will, and I am not going to stand for it. I want to leave Llanferdrack, and leave at the earliest possible moment.'

'But hang it, old chap! We've just been into that and you couldn't be better situated than you are here as long as there is a war on.'

Feeling that I had now got to make him face up to the issue, I said firmly: 'That is beside the point. I want to get out, and I'm going to get out. If you're afraid to sack Helmuth leave it to me, and I'll do it myself in a fortnight's time. But either he goes, or you take me with you when you leave. Now, what about it?'

For a moment he sat in miserable silence, then he muttered: 'Toby, this isn't like you. I'm really beginning to be afraid that there is something in what Helmuth said, and that you're no longer quite all right in the upper story.'

I hadn't wanted to discuss the implications of that idea with him, as if Helmuth does succeed in getting me into a loopy-bin I may never get out; but Helmuth may have already put that possibility into his head, so on second thoughts I decided that it would be best to put all the cards on the table, and bluff for all I was worth that I was completely confident that even if I was certified I would manage to regain my freedom later. I gave him a calm, steady smile, and threw the cat among the pigeons.

'You know perfectly well, Uncle, that you have never talked to a saner man that I am at this moment. Since Helmuth has given you the idea that I am going nuts, there is something else I've got to tell you. It is my considered opinion that for criminal ends he has been deliberately trying to create that impression.'

'Oh, come, old man! That's a frightful thing to say about a chap. After all, he is one of us – even if he is a Czech. And why in the world should he?'

'Because he wants to keep his hold over me. You know as well as I do that he and Iswick are virtually running the Board of Trustees at the moment. If it could be shown that I am unfitted to take over, they would go on running it. And that's what they want. That might benefit certain innocent parties too, Uncle; such as yourself – but only for a time.'

'What the hell are you driving at?' he protested.

I shrugged, and put up my big bluff. 'Simply this. If Helmuth could get me certified you, as well as he, would continue to enjoy the directors' fees and other perks that you get from being a Trustee. But, clever as Helmuth is, he could not succeed in stalling me out of my inheritance indefinitely. Sooner or later the doctors are going to agree that I am fit to handle my affairs. Once that happens the balloon goes up. I'll be Jugg of Juggernauts and all the rest of the caboodle. For those who have stood by me nothing will be too good, but God help anyone who has lent Helmuth a hand, either actively or passively, to play his dirty game.'

I felt the time had come to be really tough; so after a moment's pause I went on: 'One way and another you've been jolly decent to me, Uncle Paul, and I'm very grateful to you; but you haven't been ill-rewarded for giving me a home. The Trustees agreed that I should be brought up in the sort of surroundings I should have enjoyed if my father had still been alive. Queensclere and Kensington Palace Gardens were kept on, and you were allowed twenty thousand a year to maintain them as a suitable background for me. I couldn't have cost you much more than a twentieth of that, and the rest was yours to play around with as you liked.

'For thirteen years you have lived like a Prince on my money. You have had your hunters, your racing-stable, your shooting, and trips to Deauville and the South of France whenever you felt that way inclined. I don't grudge you one moment of the fun you've had. All I want to know this afternoon is if you wish it to go on?'

He stared at me, his mouth, under his brushed-up Guard's moustache, a little agape. Then he stammered: 'Is – is this what you meant when you asked me to come down to see you about – about future financial arrangements?'

'That's it, Uncle,' I said. 'Until quite recently I have always had it in mind that, when I come of age, I would make a settlement to ensure that you and Julia should have everything in reason that you wanted for the rest of your lives. I'd still like to do that; but I'm in a spot. You may think some of my present views a little eccentric, but you know darned well that I am not insane. If anyone has gone a bit haywire it is Helmuth. But you have got to side with either him or me. I am appealing to you now as my legal Guardian; and if you do as I wish you are going to be in clover; not for a few months only but for good and all.

'If you prefer to shelve your responsibility and leave me in his hands, one fine morning you are going to wake up to find yourself stark naked in the breeze. Because from the moment I *do* get control of the Jugg millions you are going to be right back where you were thirteen years ago; and, as God is my witness, you shall never see another penny of them.'

I suppose it was pretty brutal, and I could never have put it so bluntly if Julia had been with him. Afterwards, I felt an awful cad about it, but not at the time; and it had a most curious effect on him. He hunched his shoulders and almost cowered away from me, as though he was a dog that I had been giving a beating. Then, when I'd done, he gave a slight shudder, and sighed: 'You mean that, Toby, don't you? Perhaps old Albert Abel was right to leave you the Jugg Empire, lock, stock and barrel, although you were only a kid. Perhaps, even then, he sensed that you had something of himself in you and would make a go of it. I believe you will, too, if you're ever able to get about again. Anyway he was right about me. There was too much money for me to have gambled it all away; but cads like Iswick would have had the breeches off me within a couple of years. They won't off you, though. When you were speaking just now it might have been your grandfather browbeating some wretched competitor into selling out. I had no idea you could be so hard.'

'I'm not being hard,' I countered. 'I'm only being logical. I'm up against it, and I'm simply using such weapons as I possess; that's all. I know you're frightened of Helmuth; everybody is; that's why I have to go the limit to get you on my side; otherwise I would never have put it the way I did.'

He nodded, 'I see your point, old man. Lot in it, too. Mind, I don't believe for a minute that you're right about Helmuth. He honestly thinks you've gone a bit queer, and that the fewer people who get to know about it the better. As he has been stopping your letters, and you couldn't let us know how you felt about wanting to leave Llanferdrack, I suppose there's quite a case for your having tried to escape on your own. But that nice young nurse of yours tells me that you've created merry hell here more than once, and used the most *feahf'l* language.'

'True enough,' I admitted. 'And wouldn't you, if you were treated like a prisoner? I'm not even allowed in the garden now; and look at this room. Can you possibly imagine anything more like a cell in the Bastille?'

'I could get Helmuth to alter all that,' he offered, a little more cheerfully, 'but as you say yourself, he's a tough proposition. I'm afraid it would take a greater nerve than I've got to sack him. Even if that were justified, which I don't think it is. And as the Trustees placed you in his care, I don't at all like the idea of telling him that I've made other plans for you.'

'You are going to, though; aren't you?' I insisted, striving to keep the anxiety out of my voice. 'Getting him to ease up the prison routine is not enough. I am relying on you to get me out of his clutches at once, and for good.'

'Yes, old man. I quite see that.' He stood up and, thrusting his hands into his trouser pockets, began to pace agitatedly back and forth, evidently wondering how best he could set about the unpleasant task I had forced upon him. After a few turns, he stopped in his tracks and faced me: 'Look here, Toby, I can't tackle Helmuth alone. He's too fast for me. In any argument over you he'd win in a canter. You know that. You must give me a day or two to get a bit of help for the job.'

'What sort of help?' I asked suspiciously.

'Well, if I called a meeting of the Trustees, exclusive of Helmuth, and they – '

'No good,' I cut him short. 'It would take at least a week to get them together. I can't wait that long.'

'All right, old man, all right. But I could have a word with one or two of them and get their backing. Iswick and Roberts are both still in London. Besides, I simply must talk to Julia about it. She'll be *feahflly* upset, as she has always taken such a good view of Helmuth. But she's much cleverer than I am, and once she realises that you're dead set on being moved she'll think of some way of doing the trick neatly.'

I saw that if I forced him to act there and then he would only make a mess of things, so with considerable reluctance I said: 'Very well then. But the best I can do is to give you forty-eight hours. I hate to put it this way, Uncle, but I really did mean all I said a little while back. So, for your own sake as well as mine, don't let Iswick, or anyone, argue you round into doing nothing. I'm pretty well at the end of my tether, and if you haven't got me away from here by the weekend I shall consider that you have deliberately let me down. Is that clear?'

'Yes, old man.' Uncle Paul nodded vigorously. 'You've made it as plain as a pikestaff. Not giving me much time to work in, though, are you? I'd meant to stay here the night; but since you're in such a desperate hurry, perhaps I'd better travel back to London this evening.'

'I think that would be an excellent idea,' I agreed. 'As a matter of fact I meant to suggest it; because as things are I think it would be a very bad thing for you to spend the evening with Helmuth. Seeing that it's a fine afternoon, he is almost certain to be out at this hour; so if you telephone for a car at once you may be able to get away without even seeing him. Anyway, I'm sure you'd be well advised to avoid a long session with him tonight. He's a persuasive devil, and drinking a couple of bottles of Cockburns 12 with him after dinner might cost you a five-figure income.'

He laughed, a little weakly. 'By gad, Toby, you've got a darned unpleasant sense of humour; but it's just like your grandfather's.'

'I wasn't being funny,' I said quietly.

After that we said goodbye, and he hurried off to order a car, and get his things repacked while waiting for it.

An hour and a half later Helmuth came in. He gave me a searching look and said: 'What's happened to your uncle? Why did he rush off like that?'

'How would I know?' I replied with a bland smile. 'He said something about not being able to stay the night because he had urgent business in London.'

A cat-like grin spread over Helmuth's face and he gave a sudden sardonic laugh. 'If you think that your Uncle Paul is capable of removing you from my care, you are making a big mistake. Kill or cure, I mean to see this matter through; and you still have a lot to learn about my powers for asserting my will.' Then he turned on his heel and marched out of the room.

In spite of what he said, there was something in his manner which told me that he was both annoyed, and a little rattled, at Uncle Paul having side-stepped him. And I am pretty confident that I have really scared my uncle into taking action. So, although I'm very far from being out of the wood, I feel tonight that I can at least see a ray of daylight.

Friday, 5th June

I have solved the mystery of the footsteps. Doing so shook me to the core. I break out into a muck sweat when I recall the terror that engulfed me as a result of my curiosity overcoming my fears.

It was the knowledge that the odds are now on my being out of here before the weekend is over that had restored my nerve and tempted me into opening this Pandora's box. When I heard those steps on the stairs again last night at the usual hour, I plucked up all my courage and rapped with my knuckles sharply on the wainscoting behind the head of my bed.

The steps halted for a moment, then went on. I rapped again. They halted again; then there came a weird creaking sound.

It is now seven nights since the moon was full, so tomorrow she will be passing into her last quarter. The light she gives is already nowhere near as bright as it was. It does no more than make the grating stand out as a luminous patch in the middle of the wall, and dilute the darkness with a faint greyness. I could barely discern the outline of my bedside table and the wall beyond it was a solid patch of blackness until, as the creaking sounded, it was split by a long, thin ribbon of light.

I held my breath and my heart began to thump. I wished to God that I had let sleeping dogs lie, but by then it was too late to do anything except curse myself for a fool.

A bony hand suddenly emerged from the strip of light. I saw it plainly. I cowered back. My teeth clenched in an instinctive effort to check the scream that rose to my throat.

It was a small hand; but the fingers were very long and the knuckles very pronounced. It seemed to claw at the nearest edge of the lighted strip. The creaking recommenced. The strip of light widened. I realised then that a panel in the wainscoting was being forced back. I wondered frantically what frightful thing I had so wantonly summoned to me. Something, I knew, was about to emerge from behind the panel into the room. Was the hand human or the limb of some ghastly, satanic entity, that had its origin in the Pit?

I was so overcome with fear as to what I might see next that I shut my eyes. The creaking ceased and was followed by a rustling sound. Then there was a faint clatter and a shuffling on the floor, only a yard from my bed. My eyes started open and I saw a vague grey figure leaning forward to peer at me. I shrunk away; thrusting out my hands to protect myself and moaning with terror.

Suddenly the figure laughed – a high-pitched, unnatural, eerie cackle. The sound seemed to turn my blood to water. Then its voice came – brittle but human, with a child-like treble note: 'Why, it's Toby Jugg. What are you doing up here?'

With a gasp of ineffable relief, I realised that this midnight visitor was only my poor, old, half-witted Great-aunt Sarah; and that the outer wall of the Castle must contain a secret stairway that she uses for some purpose of her own each night.

'God, what a fright you gave me!' I exclaimed, with a semi-hysterical laugh. Then I levered myself up in the bed with my hands, till I was sitting propped against the pillows, to get a better look at her.

She had left her candle on the steps behind the opening of the panel through which she had come. By its light I could see now that she was wrapped in a long pale-blue dressing-gown, the skirts of which trailed on the floor. Her scant hair hung in grey wisps about her thin face, and her eyes gleamed with a bright, feverish light. As I took in the macabre figure that she cut I felt that I had no reason to be ashamed of the panic with which I had been seized at the first glimpse of her. Despite the fact that she entirely lacked the aura of Evil that had made my flesh creep with the coming of the Shadow, she was infinitely nearer to the ghost of tradition, and am sure that on coming face to face with such an apparition at dead of night plenty of people far braver than I am would have lost their nerve.

Picking up her candlestick and holding the light aloft, so that she could see me better, she repeated in her shrill treble: 'What are you doing up here, Toby Jugg?'

Since my arrival at Llanferdrack I had seen her only about half-a-dozen times with her companion, in the garden; and, although I had exchanged a few words with the latter, she had never spoken to me herself, so I was surprised that she even knew who I was. Evidently the old girl was not entirely gaga, and as I wanted to find out what she was up to, I said as gently as I could: 'Dr Lisický had me moved up here a few days ago, Aunt Sarah. I'm living here now. You don't mind that, do you? But what are you doing? Why do you go down those stairs every night at eleven o'clock?'

'To dig my tunnel,' she replied at once. Then a sudden look of fear came into her eyes and she clapped a skinny hand over her mouth, like a child who realises that it has inadvertently let out a secret.

'Why are you digging a tunnel?' I asked quietly.

'You won't tell – you won't tell! Please, Toby Jugg, please! Nettie must never know. She would stop me. He's waiting for me there. I am his only hope. You won't tell Nettie – please, please!' Her words came tumbling out in a spate of apprehension. By 'Nettie' I guessed that she meant her old sourpuss of a companion, Miss Nettelfold.

'I wouldn't dream of telling anyone,' I assured her. 'But now you've told me about the tunnel there is no reason why you shouldn't share the rest of your secret with me, is there? Where does your tunnel go to; and who is "he"?'

'Why, he is Lancelot, of course.' Her eyes widened with surprise at my ignorance. 'Surely you know that she is keeping him a prisoner there, at the bottom of the lake?'

Bit by bit I got the whole story of the strange fancies that for many years have obsessed the poor old madwoman's brain.

The bare facts I already knew. When she was a girl of twenty she fell in love with the last Lord Llanferdrack, and he with her. She was many years younger than her only brother – my grandfather – so although he was not then the multi-millionaire that he afterwards became, he had already amassed a considerable fortune. Nevertheless, the Llanferdracks were a proud old feudal family, and the young lord's mother was most averse to his marrying the sister of a jumped-up Yorkshire industrialist, so there was considerable opposition to the match.

All this happened well over forty years ago, and in Queen Victoria's time young people were kept on a pretty tight rein; so for a while the lovers had great difficulty in even meeting in secret, and every possible pressure was put on young Lancelot Llanferdrack to make him give Great-aunt Sarah up. Probably it was that opposition which made them madder than ever about one another. Anyhow, they wouldn't give in, and eventually Albert Abel took matters in hand. He came down here to see old Lady Llanferdrack and, somehow, succeeded in fixing matters for his sister. The engagement was formally announced, and little Sarah Jugg was asked down to meet her fiancé's family in the ancestral home.

She had been here only a few days when the most appalling tragedy occurred. They were out in a punt on the lake and Lancelot was fishing. He missed his footing and went in head down. It seems that he must have got caught in the weeds at the bottom of that first plunge, for he never came up. He simply disappeared before her eyes. The lake is very deep in parts and they never recovered his body.

The shock turned her brain. Against all reason she insisted that he would come up sooner or later, and that she must remain near the lake until he did. All efforts to persuade her to leave the district were in vain; and eventually Albert Abel bought the Castle from Lady Llanferdrack, so that poor Great-aunt Sarah could have her wish and live by the lake for the rest of her days.

That is where fact ends and the strange weaving of her own imagination begins. Perhaps her fiancé's name having been Lancelot is the basis of the fancies that years of brooding over her tragedy have built up in her mind; or it may be that local tradition has it that this lake in the Welsh mountains is the original one of the Arthurian legend.

In any case, she believes that the Lady of the Lake lives in it and, being jealous of her, snatched Lancelot from her arms. She is convinced that he is still alive, but a prisoner at the bottom of the lake, and that her mission is to rescue him. This apparently can be done only by digging a tunnel, over half a mile long, through the foundations of the Castle and right out to beneath the dead centre of the lake; then Lancelot will do a little digging on his own account, and having made a hole in its bottom over her tunnel, will escape through it to live with her happily ever after.

I asked her how far she still had to go, what the tunnel was like, and various other questions. It seems that it is only large enough to crawl through, and that she shores it up as she goes along with odd bits of floorboard and roofing that she collects from some of the rooms in the Castle that have been allowed to fall into ruin.

But progress is slow, and she does not get far enough to need a new roof-prop more than about once in six weeks. It was the wizard Merlin who put her on to this idea for rescuing her lover, and he told her that the whole thing would prove a flop if she used a tool of any kind, or even a bit of stick, to dig with, and that each night she must take every scrap of dirt she removes out under her clothes; so it is a kind of labour of Hercules, and the poor old thing is doing the whole job with her bare hands.

Merlin also put another snag in it. He said that she must not arouse the Lady of the Lake's suspicions by digging straight towards the centre of the lake; instead the tunnel must go the whole length of the chapel, then out as far as the bridge and, only there, turn in towards its final objective. On four occasions too, while burrowing alongside the chapel, she came up against impenetrable walls of stone in the foundations, and after years of wasted work had to start again practically from the beginning.

That has worried her a lot, as she is a bit uncertain now in which direction she really is going; but she thinks it is all right, as she can hear Lancelot's voice calling to her and encouraging her more clearly than she could a few years ago. He is being very good and patient about the long delay in getting him out, and he must certainly be a knight *sans peur et sans reproche*, as he still refuses even to kiss the hand of the black-haired Circe who has made her his captive – in spite of the fact that she comes and waggles herself at him nightly. At least, that's what he tells Great-aunt Sarah, and who am I to disbelieve him?

I should have thought that after the dark enchantress had put in her first twenty years attempting, every evening, to vamp Lancelot without success, she would have gone a bit stale on the type, and started looking around for a more responsive beau; but evidently she and my great-aunt are running about neck to neck in this terrific endurance contest.

After talking to the old girl for about half an hour I had got the whole pathetic business out of her. By then she was obviously anxious to get along down to her digging, so I once more promised that I wouldn't give her secret away and, closing the secret panel carefully behind her, she left me.

So far, today has been one of the pleasantest that I have had for a long time. My quadrant of private terrace faces south-south-east, so it gets full sunshine till well past midday, and all the morning I sat out there with Sally. I call Nurse Cardew Sally now, as she says she prefers it.

After we had been out there a little while she asked me if I thought it would be terribly unprofessional if she sunbathed; and I said 'Of course not'; so she went in and changed into a frightfully fetching bathing dress – white satin with no back and darned little front – which she said she had bought at Antibes the summer before the war. She is a Junoesque wench, and it would take a man of my size to pick her up and spank her, but she has one hell of a good figure.

Before I had had a chance to take in this eyeful properly she started in to get my upper things off, and she stripped me to the waist, so that I could sunbathe too. Then she lay down on a rug near my chair and we spent the next two hours talking all sorts of nonsense.

But, of course, the thing that has really made such a difference to my outlook is my talk with Uncle Paul yesterday. I am certain that I scared the pants off him, and convinced him that he will practically be selling matches in the gutter unless he gets me out of this before I am a couple of days older.

Saturday, 6th June

Another lovely morning and more sunbathing with Sally on the terrace. After we had been chatting for a while I asked her if I really and truly believed that I was nuts, and would be prepared to take her oath to that effect in a court of law.

She looked up at me from where she was lying on her rug, and her nice freckled face was intensely serious as she replied: 'I'd hate to do that, but I'm afraid I'd have to, Toby. Of course, you're not out of your mind at all frequently, but very few mental people are all the time. I wouldn't have believed that you were mental at all if I hadn't seen you as you were last week, and known about your quite unreasoned hatred of Dr Lisický.'

'Surely,' I said, controlling my voice as carefully as I could, 'the riots you saw me create downstairs in the library, and after my escape, could easily be accounted for as outbursts of temper, due to the frustration felt by an invalid who believes that an undue restraint is being put upon him?'

She pulled hard on her cigarette. 'But that's just the trouble, Toby. You *imagine* that an undue restraint is being put upon you; but it isn't really so.'

'Are you absolutely convinced of that?'

'Absolutely. There is nothing whatever about the arrangements here, or Dr Lisický's treatment of you, to suggest that you are being persecuted. Yet you think you are. So I'm afraid there is no escaping the fact that you are suffering from a form of persecution mania.'

'All right, then,' I said after a moment. 'Naturally, I don't agree about that; but we'll let it pass. Do you think that my state would justify putting me in an asylum?'

'Oh, please, let's not talk about it,' she begged. 'Tell me about some of the exciting times you had when you were in the R.A.F.'

'No, Sally. I want you to answer my question,' I insisted.

'Well then,' she said in rather a small voice, 'if you must know, I think it might. That is, if these bouts of yours continue. You see, nearly all lunacy is periodic, and yours seems to take the classic form, in which the subject is affected by the moon. Dr Lisický says that you are perfectly normal during the rest of the month, but suffer from these outbreaks whenever the moon is near full. This last time you raved, used the most filthy language – which I am sure you would never do in front of me when you are your real self – wept and became violent.'

'And that,' I cut in, bitterly, 'is just what mad people do, isn't it?'

She nodded. 'I'm afraid it is. So you see, if you go on getting these attacks every month, it may become necessary to put you under restraint while they last. But that would be only for a few days each time, of course. And *please* don't worry yourself about it, because that sort of mental trouble is perfectly curable, and I'm sure that you'll be quite all right again in a few months.'

'Thanks, Sally,' I said. 'I'm very grateful to you for being honest with me. Now we'll talk of shoes and ships and sealing-wax, of cabbages and kings – or of anything else that you like'; and we did for the rest of the morning.

All the same, I am damnably disturbed by what she said. She may admire Helmuth, but I am positive that she is not under his thumb to the extent of deliberately deceiving me on his instructions. She was speaking from her own convictions, and with considerable reluctance. I am certain of that, and it has given me furiously to think.

Of course she knows nothing of the huge financial interests that are involved in this question of my sanity or madness; and she knows nothing about the Horror – which is the prime cause of my outbursts. But did I *really* see that Shadow or did I only think I did, owing to my mind having become subject to the malefic influence of the moon?

I can't help wishing now that I had never raised the matter with Sally and forced her to answer my questions.

Monday, 8th June
This journal has served an admirable purpose. Keeping it has helped to distract my thoughts from my anxieties for many hours during the past five weeks, but to continue it further is now pointless; so I am making this last entry simply to round it off neatly.

Some day, when I am quite well again – mentally I mean – I may read it through with interest and, I think, astonishment at the extra-ordinary thoughts that have recently agitated my poor mind; so it is worth the trouble of giving it a proper ending.

During the past forty-eight hours a lot has happened. Just before tea-time on Saturday Uncle Paul returned, as he had promised, and he brought Julia with him. They had tea with me; over it they told me that they had already had a talk with Helmuth, and that he had said that he would not raise the slightest objection to their taking me away with them. He was sorry that I wished to remove myself from his care, and considered that I should be very ill-advised to do so, but if I decided to take that course I was perfectly free to go when and where I liked.

Naturally, at the time, I thought he was putting on a hypocritical act, to cover as best he could his inability to defy the Trustees openly. But I was greatly relieved to think that the matter was already settled and that I had in the end achieved my victory with so little trouble.

After tea Uncle Paul left Julia and I together, and we settled down to a real heart-to-heart.

She was looking as lovely as ever, and it seems impossible to believe that she is thirty-three. She has hardly changed at all since she reached the height of her beauty, and I don't think a stranger would take her for more than twenty-six, or -seven. When I was a little boy I never understood why the angels in the Scripture books that Nanny Trotter used to read to me were invariably portrayed as fair; and after I first saw Julia I always used to think of her as my dark angel.

Her big eyes and her hair – which she has always worn in her own style, smoothly curling to her shoulders – are as black as night, and her flawless skin has the matt whiteness of magnolia petals. She might well have sat as the model for a Madonna by one of the old masters, and perhaps one of her Colonna ancestresses did when the Italian school of painting was at its height. The only unsaintly thing about her is the exceptional fullness of her red lips. That makes her beauty rather startling, but even more subtly devastating, as it gives her a warm, human touch.

She began by reproaching me very gently for the way I had treated Uncle Paul. She said that I should have known that he would at once take all possible steps to safeguard my happiness, without my threatening to reduce him to penury. And that I must have known that would mean poverty for her too; so, after all we had been to one another, how could I even contemplate such a mean and ruthless act against two people who had given me their love?

I felt terribly guilty and embarrassed, but I tried to explain the dire necessity I had been under to get myself removed from Llanferdrack at all costs; and I began to tell her about the Horror.

After a bit she said: 'Please, darling, don't harass yourself further by reviving these horrid memories. I know all about it already. Helmuth gave me your letters – the ones he stopped because he didn't want me to have fits about you – before I came upstairs. I read them all, and I have them here.' Upon which she produced them from her bag.

'Then, if you know that part of the story,' I said quickly, 'you must understand how imperative I felt it to get away.'

She nodded, but a sad look came into her eyes. 'I do understand, darling. You must have been through a terrible time. But the thing that worries us all so much is that there has never been any suggestion before that this place is haunted; and we are afraid that you would have seen – or thought you saw – this terrifying apparition, during the periods of the full moon, if you had been with us at Queensclere, or anywhere else.'

'Then you don't believe that I really saw anything at all?' I challenged her.

'I wouldn't say that,' she replied thoughtfully. 'Helmuth does not believe in the Supernatural, but I do. I've never seen an apparition myself, but I am certain that the "burglar" that you saw when we were down at Kew was one. Perhaps you are more psychic than I am, and so more receptive to such influences.'

'I've never regarded myself as a psychic type,' I admitted. 'But you remember that business of the Abbot's grave at Weylands. After that horrible experience I described my sensations to you, and I had exactly the same feelings of cold, repulsion and stark terror down in the library here.'

'That could have been caused by a recurrence in your memory of the Weylands affair.' She took out a cigarette. I lit it for her, and she went on: 'I'll tell you what makes me doubt if you really did see anything. When Helmuth and your nurse were telling us all about it, before I came up, they described the night just a week ago when you started bawling barrack-room choruses at the top of your voice, and they ran into your room. You pointed wildly to the bottom of the blackout curtain and yelled: "Look! Look! Do you call that an hallucination?" But neither of them saw anything; and I should have thought one or other of them would have, had there been anything to see.'

'Perhaps neither of them is psychic,' I argued a little weakly.

'That might be the explanation,' she shrugged, 'but I don't think so. I have been at séances where trumpets and tambourines have floated in the air, and others where the medium has emitted large quantities of electoplasm; and it is not just one or two people who see such manifestations, but the whole audience – and sometimes some of them are convinced sceptics before the séance starts.'

For quite a time we argued round the matter. She pointed out that although Great-aunt Sarah and Miss Nettelfold had lived here for a lifetime, no complaint had ever been made by them to the Trustees that Llanferdrack had a family horror which periodically gave trouble; and that although servants were usually the first to get the wind up about such things, none of the staff here had ever given notice on the grounds that the place had a bad atmosphere.

So, eventually, I was forced to agree that such evidence as we had to go on all pointed to the Shadow having no existence outside my imagination.

About seven o'clock Julia left me to go and change; but she said that she would have her dinner sent up on a tray with mine, so that we could dine together.

I think most beautiful women look their best in evening-dress, and although Julia is a sight to gladden the heart in anything, she is certainly of the type whose proper setting is satin and pearls rather than tweeds. She looked absolutely ravishing.

We had a couple of cocktails apiece, split a bottle of Burgundy and rounded things off with some Kümmel. By the time we had finished I was feeling so good that I was almost resigned to the thought that I had gone a bit mental – provided I could get away from Llanferdrack, and there was a decent hope of my being cured pretty quickly. But I was still of the opinion that Helmuth's conduct needed a lot of explaining, and when Konrad had carried away our dinner trays I started in on the subject.

We went into the whole business piece by piece: the letters, the blackout curtains, my telephone extension; the refusal to leave me my lamp, or get me a torch, or move my radio; or let me have more than one sleeping tablet; Helmuth's arbitrary treatment of Taffy, his stopping me from getting into the train and, finally, his virtually making me a prisoner in this old part of the Castle.

Looked at in retrospect, I must honestly confess that there was really very little to it all, if one once accepts the following premiss:

(1) That shortly after my arrival here Helmuth began to suspect that my injury and eight months in hospital had, to some degree, affected the balance of my mind.

(2) That he at once began to keep me under observation and opened my mail as part of the process.

(3) That, on finding his fears confirmed, he considered it his duty to my relations to save them from worry, and his duty to myself to take all possible steps to prevent the knowledge leaking out and prejudicing my future.

(4) That he hoped the rest and a regular routine would put me right, and decided that nothing must be done which would encourage me to believe that I was suffering from anything worse than nightmares.

The above is the gist of how he had put it to Julia, and as she passed it on to me. After thrashing the matter out we fell silent for a bit; then she suddenly said: 'Besides, what possible motive could he have for adopting such an extraordinary attitude towards you? I mean, trying to make things worse for you instead of better, as you still seem to half-suspect?'

I was surprised that Uncle Paul had said noth... to her about my theory that there was a conspiracy to drive me insane; but perhaps he had thought it too far-fetched to mention. I told her my ideas on that and her eyes widened in amazement as she listened.

'But Toby!' she exclaimed at last. 'How *could* you think such base thoughts of a man who has given some of the best years of his life to developing your mind and character? This is the first time that I have ever been ashamed of you.'

'Oh, come!' I protested a bit uncomfortably. 'After all, he was damn well paid for what he did.'

She shook her head. 'One can't pay for care and affection with money, darling. Perhaps, though, I am being a little hard on you. To talk to, you are so perfectly normal that I forget about your not being quite well in your mind. It is only when you produce ideas like that of turning Paul and myself out into the street, or this one that Helmuth wants to lock you up and rob you, that I sudd... right he is about your no longer being your real self.'

'All the same,' I argued, 'you must admit that the Trustees would stand to gain if a Board of Lunacy ruled that I was unfitted to inherit.'

'Not sufficiently to provide a motive for them to enter into a criminal conspiracy,' she countered. 'You seem to forget that most of them are immensely rich already. Paul, of course, is an exception, but he knows as well as I do that if you come into your money you will make a most generous provision for him; and Smith and Roberts don't stand to lose anything, because they are professional advisers and would go on drawing their fees just the same, whatever happens.'

'That still leaves Iswick and Helmuth.'

She laughed. 'Really, Toby darling, you're being too silly. We may all look on Harry Iswick as an awful little bounder, but he is as clever as a cart-load of monkeys. In the past ten years he has made a fortune on his own account, and his interest in the Jugg combine is only a sideline with him now. I know that for a fact. As for Helmuth, surely you see that he has much more to lose than to gain from your being put in a home. Big business isn't really his line of country, so it is unlikely that he would be able to improve his position much by continuing as a Trustee. Whereas, with you in possession of your millions, he would have every right to expect you to find a suitable use for his abilities, at a handsome remuneration, in recognition of all he has done for you in the past. I give you my word, sweet, that this conspiracy idea is absolutely fantastic.'

There seemed no answer to her arguments, and reviewing them again, now that I no longer have her glowing presence before me, I still don't think there is. But accepting them brought me face to face with the question of Helmuth, and I asked her what she thought I ought to do about him.

'Sleep on it, darling,' she advised me, 'and see how you feel about it in the morning. If you find that you really cannot rid yourself of this awful prejudice that you have built up in your mind against him, I think it would be better to let sleeping dogs lie. Later, perhaps, you will feel differently; then you can let him know how sorry you are that you suspected him so unjustly. But he is terribly fond of you, and must be feeling very hurt at the moment.

'So if all that I have said has convinced you that you are in the wrong, the generous thing would be for you to let me bring him up to you tomorrow. You needn't eat humble pie, or be embarrassed about it; but just say that you realise now that you have not been quite yourself lately, and have given him a lot of unnecessary trouble. That's quite enough. He'll understand; and I am sure it would please him a lot to know that you bear him no ill-will before you leave here.'

It was late when she left me, but I lay awake thinking about it a long time after she had gone. I came to the conclusion that in many respects Helmuth had shown very poor psychology in his treatment of me, and that the arbitrary way in which he had handled matters was enough to make anyone who was slightly mental develop a persecution complex, but that my conspiracy idea was the wildest nonsense, and that there was not one atom of proof to show that he had not acted throughout in what he *believed to be* my best interests.

In consequence, on Sunday morning I told Julia that I would like to see Helmuth, and later we had a grand reconciliation on my sunny terrace.

For such entertaining as my grandfather had to do, he bought anything that was going cheap in the City, in big parcels of forty or fifty cases at a time; so the cellar he left was not distinguished for either its variety or quality. But in the past thirteen years Uncle Paul has spared no pains to make up for those deficiencies, and soon after the war broke out he had a large part of the Queensclere and London cellars moved down here as a precaution against their being blitzed. So for us to celebrate he was able to order up a magnum of Krug, Private Cuveé 1926, and I don't think I have ever tasted better champagne in my life.

Everything went off remarkably easily. I said my piece and Helmuth met me more than halfway. He admitted that many of his acts must have seemed high-handed and even tyrannical, but he had been dominated by the one thought of preventing it from leaking out that I had become mental.

As he explained, it is just like a man going bankrupt; however unlucky he may have been, and even if he pays up one pound in the pound afterwards and gets an honourable discharge, it always prejudices his future commercial undertakings. So with mental trouble, the effect would be little short of disastrous to me as the head of the Jugg enterprises if it ever became known that I had once suffered from hallucinations.

He went on to say that he had moved me from downstairs only with the greatest reluctance, because he was most loth to give the servants grounds for talk; but that after my attempts to get away he had felt that to do so was the lesser evil. And that when he had decided to move me he had chosen this room because it was one of those furthest removed from the servant's quarters, so they were less likely to hear me if further attacks led to a renewal of my singing and shouting. He added, too, that he found it a considerable inconvenience to be deprived of Konrad's services, but he knew that the fellow could be trusted not to blab, so he had willingly given him up to me, rather than risk letting a new man, who might later prove untrustworthy, into our secret.

We went on then to discuss what should be done with me. Julia said that she would willingly have me at Queensclere; but the difficulty about that is that the house is occupied by the Army, and she and Uncle Paul have been allowed to retain only what amounts to a flat of half-a-dozen rooms on the first floor. So, apart from the question of air-raids and the business of getting me down to a shelter – which they insisted would have to be done if I went there – in the event of my having further attacks it would be practically impossible to prevent the officers who are billeted in the house from learning about my condition.

Kensington Palace Gardens is out, because it has now been taken over to provide additional accommodation for the Soviet Embassy;

so, of my own properties, that left only the little house on Mull. And if I were put into a nursing-home it is a certainty that the secret of my affliction would get out.

I suggested that a small house should be bought for me in Devonshire or Cornwall, but they all seemed to think that it would be practically impossible to find anything suitable at the present time, as every available property in the 'safe' areas had been taken over to house evacuees; and even if we could find one it raises the problem of who is going to run it and look after me.

Of course, the same thing applies to Mull, but eventually Helmuth offered to throw up his work here and take me up there. That was very decent of him, and it seemed a possible solution for the next few months. But it would be far from attractive as a permanency, as to have to winter there would be incredibly depressing and grim; and even during the summer we would have none of the good things, such as the garden produce, that we enjoy down here. Still, it seemed the best thing we could think of when lunch-time came, so they left me to think it over.

When they joined me again about three o'clock, Julia put it to me that, since I was now reconciled to Helmuth, did I really still feel so strongly about leaving Llanferdrack? She pointed out that, so far, I had been subject to attacks only while down in the library, and that now I had been moved I might not be afflicted with them any more. The advantages of Llanferdrack over Mull needed no stressing, and my acceptance of Helmuth's offer would mean sabotaging much of the fine war-effort that he has built up here during the past two-and-a-half years. Therefore, didn't I think that I could bring myself to stay on here for a time at least – anyhow until the next full-moon period – and if it transpired that the attacks did recur, then I could always be removed at once.

Actually, while I had been eating my lunch, I had been thinking on much the same lines myself; so I agreed.

We then went into the question of my birthday and it was decided that, in present circumstances, it would not be a good thing to have the Trustees down here on the 20th. If Iswick, Roberts and the rest got the least suspicion that I was not quite normal they might consider it their duty to have me examined by a committee of brain specialists before agreeing to hand o

In consequence Uncle Paul is going to inform the others that I hope to be fit enough to make a short visit to London in the latter part of July; so I have suggested that the whole business – presents and everything – shall be put off for a month, as it will be much more convenient for them to meet me there.

It was agreed, too, that I should remain in this room; partly for the original reason that Helmuth put me here, and partly because there is no other – except the library, downstairs, which is at all suitable. Actually, this big chamber with its vaulted roof is not without its attractions. Even in summer it would ordinarily be a bit chilly, but every afternoon a fire is lit for me in the great open fireplace, and in the evenings its glow on the wainscoting and old stone makes the place rather cosy.

And I have come to love my little private terrace with its view over the lake. The only real snag is that it would require too much effort to get me to the nearest bathroom every evening; so I have to have my tub in an old-fashioned hip-bath, for which Konrad has to boil up large kettles of water on the open fire. But, after all, the types who occupied this room for hundreds of years managed quite well that way; and lots of our chaps in the Western Desert, and elsewhere, are not lucky enough to get a bath at all.

Julia and Uncle Paul returned to London this morning, and Helmuth went with them, just for the night, as he has to attend a Board Meeting of one of the Companies tomorrow. Before they left we had a final chat, and Helmuth promised that as soon as the moon begins to wax again he will come in to me every night, round about midnight, to see that I am all right. If I am not, he will make arrangements to take me up to Mull as soon as possible, and, in the meantime, he will help me to fight my trouble.

He is a tower of strength, and I have been terribly unjust to him. He was absolutely right to keep me here and showed his true fondness for me in doing so. Only here am I really safe from prying eyes and whispering tongues. Here we can keep the secret of my miserable affliction safely concealed until I am well again.

We all feel now, though, that the change of room may do the trick. Regaining confidence in Helmuth has helped me enormously to regain it in myself, and I do not believe that there is the least danger of my becoming a mental case permanently. Therefore I am able to end this journal on an optimistic note; and, now that I really do know where I stand, there is no point in continuing it further.

Wednesday, 10th June
Here I am again. The fact is that I have become so used to setting down my private thoughts that yesterday, during the time I usually

devote to these jottings, I felt quite at a loose end. I felt the same way this morning, until it occurred to me that it was the height of stupidity to stop doing anything that helped me to while away my time pleasantly, merely because the occupation in itself had ceased to have any serious purpose. Moreover, having got that far I realised that I have something of considerable interest to record.

Helmuth did not get back from his trip to London until just before dinner last night; soon afterwards he came in to see me. He is usually rather restless when making casual conversation, but on this occasion he settled himself down in a way that showed he had something serious to say; then, after a bit, he started off more or less as follows: 'Now that we are friends again, Toby, we can talk freely together, just as we used to in the past. I have been wanting to have a heart-to-heart with you ever since you arrived here; but at first I didn't want to rush matters, and later I was afraid you might not feel like discussing your future plans with me. I am naturally deeply interested to know what they are. When you come into your inheritance, do you intend to assume control of the Companies, as far as your health permits, or will you continue to let other people handle matters for you?'

'I shall assume control,' I replied with a smile. 'At least, I hope so. After all the time and trouble you have given to educating me for the job I'd be a pretty poor specimen if I let you down to the extent of not even attempting to tackle it.'

He nodded. 'I'm glad you feel like that. I was afraid that your time in the Air Force might have altered your outlook. Since you are still prepared to take on this enormous responsibility it is doubly tragic that your health is likely to prove such a heavy handicap.'

'This new trouble may,' I agreed. 'But before that started I saw no reason why the injury to my spine should prevent me using my brain; so I had been toying with the idea of having a special motor-ambulance-caravan fitted out, in which to tour the factories. It would probably take me the best part of a year to get a real grip of things, and I had no intention of throwing my weight about to start with; but after a tour like that I should have picked up enough of the practical side to argue the pros and cons of the broader issues with my co-directors.'

Helmuth nodded his white head again. 'That sounds an admirable scheme. You will have to continue to observe your rest hours, and be careful not to overdo it until your back is a bit stronger; but if all goes well in the other matter, I see no reason why you should not start on a tour of that kind in the autumn. It would certainly prove a most popular move with all your employees, and, as you say, give much more weight to your opinions when you do decide to give vent to them at Board Meetings. Yes, I congratulate you on that idea, Toby.'

'Thanks,' I said, and after a moment he went on: 'All the same, I wonder if you fully realise what you will be up against. However tactfully you set to work, most of these middle-aged and elderly industrialists who are running your Companies at the present time are not going to take at all kindly to a young man of twenty-one walking in and insisting on changes in old-established policies.'

'I hope that in most cases that will not be necessary.'

'My dear Toby; if it is not you will have put yourself to a great deal of trouble for nothing. The whole object of a new broom is to sweep clean. With your intelligence you are bound to spot all sorts of effort-wasting, obsolete practices, incompetent executives and unnecessary wastages to which the others have become blind through seeing them go on for years. If you do not initiate reforms to abolish these weaknesses you will be letting yourself down as well as your shareholders, and never become a great leader of industry.'

'I suppose you are right,' I said thoughtfully. 'If that does prove the case, I shall certainly introduce reforms and endeavour to overcome any opposition that I may meet with.'

'It will take a lot of overcoming. Most of these men have had to fight hard to attain their present positions, and they will have an instinctive prejudice against your youth and inexperience. Those who are uncertain of themselves will combine against you, from fear that you may think them not up to their jobs and get rid of them; while others, who are of stronger mettle, will do their utmost to dominate you and climb on your back to greater power.'

'You paint a gloomy picture,' I remarked. 'It looks as if instead of being able to devote most of my time to making my Companies more prosperous I shall have to spend it defending myself from the jealousy and intrigues of my co-directors.'

'I think you will – anyhow, to start with,' he said frankly. 'But, if you will let me, I can help you to overcome a great deal of such opposition.'

Naturally, I thought he was suggesting that I should make him my private adviser; and evidently he guessed what I was thinking, as he waved aside my murmur of thanks, and said quietly: 'If, later on, you find any use for my personal services I will give them gladly; but that was not what I had in mind. I expect you remember hearing about the Brotherhood when you were at Weylands?'

At that my ears fairly pricked with interest. 'Rather! It was the great mystery of the place, and we all used to speculate on what went on at those meetings in the crypt of the old Abbey. It was a Masonic Lodge of the Grand Orient, wasn't it?'

'No. A number of its members are also Freemasons who had been initiated on the Continent; so we use that Grand Orient story as cover; ours is a much older fellowship. The main reason why I tried to prevent you joining the R.A.F. was because I did not want you to miss initiation; but by running away you stymied me over that. However, it is not too late, and membership of the Brotherhood could be of immense value to you in your business life; so if you are agreeable, I propose to start preparing you for initiation now.'

'How thrilling!' I exclaimed. 'Do tell me about it. What is the object of the association, and what should I have to do?'

'It is a Brotherhood, based on the old principle that Union is Strength. Each member contributes to it according to his means and receives from it according to his needs.'

I laughed. 'That sounds rather like Socialism to me. As I am exceptionally rich it looks as if I should be expected to make a contribution out of all proportion to anything I was likely to get back.'

'It *is* Socialism, but on the highest plane. You need have no fears that your millions will be scattered to the masses.'

'My millions!' I echoed, raising an eyebrow at his joke.

He shrugged. 'Even if it cost you your whole fortune you would still be the gainer on balance. That may sound a tall statement, Toby; but in due course I believe you'll agree with me.'

'I'll be better able to form an opinion when I know more about it,' I said, with a grin. 'If the rumours which used to circulate at Weylands had any truth in them, the Brotherhood consists of a considerable number of people all of whom possess wealth, influence or brains; and are pledged to help one another. Is that a fact?'

As he nodded assent, I went on: 'I can fully appreciate that membership of such a fraternity must be extremely valuable; and I see now why you think it would prove a big asset to me in dealing with my fellow industrialists; but obviously there is a limit to what such secret assistance in one's dealings would be worth.'

'Why should there be?' he asked quite seriously. 'You are an immensely rich man. Your grandfather left in trust for you assets to the value of over fourteen million sterling. If that had happened half-a-century ago, by the re-investment of the bulk of the income at cumulative interest during your minority, by now you would be worth something like thirty millions.

'But time marches on; owing to your grandfather's death not having occurred till nineteen-twenty-nine, income- and super-tax had already risen to such heights that in the past thirteen years the Trustees have been able to add only a beggarly million-and-three-quarters to your original capital. Since the war the situation of people in the top income groups has deteriorated still further. By the time it ends you will be lucky if you are allowed to keep sixpence in the pound of what your money earns. So what will your fortune be worth to you then?'

I did a quick calculation. 'In Government stocks it would bring me in only about ten thousand a year, but in my own companies it should produce at least double that. And you forget the Directors' Fees that I should draw; they would easily amount to a further twenty thousand.'

It was Helmuth's turn to grin. 'My dear Toby, Directors' Fees are taxable, and twenty thousand sixpences comes to only five hundred pounds. On your own showing your net income would barely exceed twenty thousand a year, all told. You already allow your uncle that figure to keep up Queensclere and the London house, and I gather you have now promised that he shall lose nothing by your assuming control of your own money. Actually, of course, your tax-free allowances for business expenses will save you from having to give up cocktails and cigarettes; but the sooner you disabuse yourself of the idea that the possession of millions still endows their owner with almost limitless spending power, the better.'

'You have shaken me quite a bit,' I confessed. 'I have been out of touch with all this sort of thing for so long that I had no idea that the picture had become so black for the working rich. Still, however high they raise income- and super-tax, a fortune is always a fortune; and, although Grandpapa Jugg might turn in his grave, I could sell out capital to ante-up my income. Even if I live to be a hundred and spent twenty thousand a year from capital for the next eighty years, that would consume less than the million-and-three-quarters that has piled up during my minority. So I should still be able to leave my heirs the original fourteen million.'

Helmuth threw back his massive head and roared with laughter: 'Toby, Toby; did you think of nothing but Hurricanes and Heinkels while you were in the R.A.F. and in hospital? Time marches on, I tell you. If you do live to be a hundred, it is most unlikely that you will have fourteen thousand – let alone million – left to leave anybody; and if you have your heirs will be lucky if the Government of the day permits them to keep more than one thousand of it.'

I smiled a little ruefully. 'Of course I know that death duties have been going up for years; and that even now they would cut the Jugg millions in half. But do you really think that in another fifty years or so there will be practically nothing left of them?'

'Indeed I do. By that time all public services and every form of industry will be State-owned: and it is highly probable that private ownership of land, houses and investments will have been abolished. But you won't have to wait that long before the bulk of your fortune is taken from you.'

I said that I thought, myself, all the odds were on the Socialists coming to power soon after the war; but that most of their leaders were sensible enough to realise the danger of throwing the nation's economy out of gear by doing anything too drastic. Helmuth shrugged and replied: 'They will be moderate to start with, but as is always the case when the Left gets into the saddle, the masses expect a Silver Age – if not a Golden one – to dawn before very long. That gives the extremists a rod with which to beat the moderates. They will never be able to raise enough money by ordinary means to propitiate the Labour electorate, by carrying out all the Socialist conceptions; but it can be taken from those who have it.

'The wiser men will realise that it is suicidal to seize a large part of the wealth, which for generations has financed the nation's commerce and industry, and fritter it away in unproductive channels; but they will be forced to it. They will introduce some form of Capital Levy. And then, my dear Toby, what of your fine fortune?'

'That would be killing the Goose that lays the Golden Eggs,' I said, 'because if they do, it is inevitable that they will skim the top off the cream. Say they introduced legislation to collect a hundred million, the great bulk of that would come from people like myself who might be paying anything up to nineteen-and-sixpence in the pound in taxes already. That means that the following year there would be the equivalent number of nineteen-and-sixpences less to go into the exchequer. And not for one year only, but for good. It is far worse than anticipating taxes; it is destroying the source from which they come. We couldn't continue to pay on what we no longer had; so they would have to introduce new taxation affecting the lower-income groups to make up the deficit. It would be a crazy policy, even from their own point of view, because sooner or later the masses themselves would be left holding the baby.'

'Of course,' Helmuth agreed. 'But political extremists are never statesmen, otherwise they would not be extremist. Such people allow their hatred of the rich to dominate every other consideration. And it would be done in gradual stages. That is the insidious part about it. As you say, they will go for the big fish first; and if you are forced to realise only half your holdings to pay up, very few people are going to think that you have been hardly done by.

'No-one will squeal until some of their own savings are seized to pay the dole. You are right too about the drop in income and surtax receipts having to be made up from somewhere, but there is a limit to what can be got by normal means; so with each successive Budget the level at which the thrifty will be robbed of their savings will go down and down, until even the little man with his few hundreds tucked away in the Post Office will find himself caught.'

He paused for a moment, then went on: 'As for yourself, having paid the first time will not exonerate you from having to pay up the second, third and fourth. So, my poor friend, I fear you will find your rosy dream of being able to spend twenty thousand a year of your capital turning out to be moonshine, long before you are my age. It won't be there any longer for you to realise.'

It was a black future that he conjured up, but I had to admit to myself that his grim prognostications were based on a perfectly possible and logical sequence of events. For a bit we remained silent, then I said: 'Well, if you are right, I'll be in a pretty mess. But I suppose the State will take care of cripples?'

'Oh yes,' he smiled cynically. 'You'll get your keep in an institution and a pound a week. You might do quite a lot better, though, if you are prepared to follow my advice. All I have been endeavouring to show you is, that if you decide to play a lone hand your millions may be reduced to hundreds by the time you are forty.'

'Do you think, then, that by becoming one of the Brotherhood I could save them?'

'No, Toby; I don't think that. But I am confident that whatever loss of fortune may overtake anyone else – and even themselves, individually, as far as the possession of shares, property and bank-balances go – the members of the Brotherhood will continue to enjoy comparative affluence, and even luxury to such a degree as it is obtainable, in a world where all but a very few will live on a miserable pittance as little cogs in the machinery of a vast slave State.'

'How would they manage to do that?' I enquired.

'There must always be rulers,' he said quietly; 'and we shall be the rulers of the Britain of tomorrow. The bulk of the upper classes are bound to be submerged, because they have no unity. But we shall survive, because we are bound together by an indissoluble bond, pledged to help one another to the limit, and holding all our assets in common. We already have men in all sorts of key positions, both here and abroad. Our level of intelligence is far higher than that of any ordinary group of professional politicians, and we have resources that such people do not possess. The attainment of power in all its forms is the object of our association, and that having been our special study ever since our foundation you may rest assured that you will be shown how to attain it too – if you decide to join us.'

'I don't quite understand.' I said. 'One can study all sorts of sub-jects, a knowledge of which is valuable for attaining one's ends; but I shouldn't have thought that there could be any royal road to attaining power, as such.'

'Oh yes, there is,' he smiled, as he stood up, 'and at our next chat I will tell you something about it. But I must go now, as I have some letters to write. In the meantime, you might think over what I have said.'

I did think it over, and the whole thing's extremely intriguing; but I am far from certain that I would care to become involved in this Secret Society of his.

Of course, when he said that about my whole fortune not being too big a price to pay for membership, he could not have been speaking seriously. All the same it sounds as if from anyone as rich as myself they would expect the hell of a big cheque.

If Helmuth is right in his contention that when the Socialists do get in, after a time, the extremists will dominate the moderates, and introduce a series of Capital Levies which will eventually swallow up all private investments, great and small, it would certainly be worth my while to go into this thing as a form of insurance – even if they did stick me for a hundred thousand pounds. Plenty of people used to pay that much in my grandfather's day for a title, and I shouldn't miss it.

But the thing that I don't like about it is this pooling of interests business. That is all very well in its way, but they might want me to do all sorts of things that I should not care about. Helmuth more or less inferred that in exchange for their help one became subject to some form of control by them. If that is the case, I would rather stand on my own feet and keep my freedom.

As I have decided to continue this journal, I may as well record a rather revealing conversation that I had with Sally this morning.

Some reference had been made to my weekend visitors, and I asked her if she did not think Julia one of the loveliest people she had ever seen.

'I didn't think her all that,' she replied. 'I suppose when she was young she must have been rather a poppet. But that's the worst of these Mediterranean types; they always age early.'

'Oh, come!' I protested. 'You talk as though she was middle-aged already.'

She shrugged. 'Well, it all depends on what you call middle-aged. I bet she'll never see thirty again.'

'She won't,' I agreed. 'But that's just the point, she doesn't look it.'

'Not to a man perhaps. Any woman who has enough money to dress a shade eccentrically, and go to a first-class beauty specialist for regular treatments, can pull the wool over a man's eyes about her age; but she can't deceive her own sex.'

I resisted the temptation to tell Sally that, however much money she had, no beauty specialist would ever succeed in turning her into a real lovely, and that I very much doubted if she would ever acquire the clothes sense to become even tolerably smart. But as I was thinking on those lines, she added with a laugh: 'Anyone could see that you think your aunt is tops. I suppose she sold you the idea that she is in the Mona Lisa class when you were in your cradle, and you have never got over it.'

I feel sure that normally Sally is not given to making catty remarks; so it was easy to guess which way the wind is blowing. Julia and Helmuth are such very old friends, that the gallantry with which he always treats her is accepted as a habit by all who know them. But Sally would not realise that, and seeing them together has made her jealous.

I knew she admired Helmuth, but evidently the handsome doctor has made a deeper impression on her than I realised. She was probably hoping that he would ask her to dine with him again over the weekend; and Julia being here put her nose completely out of joint.

Actually it is over a week now since the only occasion on which Helmuth asked her to dine. As he has not repeated the invitation it looks as if he found her too unsophisticated for his taste, and is not going to bother with her further.

On the other hand, his having turned the battery of his charm on

her for just one evening and since treated her only with friendly
politeness is well calculated to keep her guessing, and so predispose
her to go halfway to meet him should he choose to make another
move. He is up to all those tricks, and that may be the game he is
playing.

I hope not, for if he does make a real set at her it is a sure thing that
she will get the raw end of the deal. Of course, now that Helmuth
and I are good friends again, I have nothing to lose if they do have an
affair and she falls completely under his spell; but I can't help having
a sort of protective feeling about her. God knows, I couldn't protect
anyone from anything, as things are, but Helmuth has never made
any secret to me of his attitude towards women, and I would hate to
think of Sally becoming the plaything of a cynical roué.

Thursday, 11th June
I am profoundly disturbed. That is putting it mildly. I had another
long talk with Helmuth yesterday evening and he told me a
lot more about the Weylands Brotherhood. In view of the importance of this conversation I shall strive for the utmost accuracy
in recording it.

As soon as he had settled himself comfortably in front of the fire,
I said: 'Last night you were saying that there is a royal road to
acquiring power. I'd be terribly interested to hear about it.'

'So you've thought things over and are inclined to regard my
proposition favourably, eh?'

As I was curious to learn more, I saw no point in denying that, so I
let it pass, and he went on: 'I am glad for both our sakes; and if what
I said last night intrigued you, I am sure that what I have to say now
will intrigue you to an infinitely greater degree. Power is the thing
that men have craved more than any other, all through the ages.
Now tell me, what would you say were the four most powerful forces
in the world?'

I thought for a moment, then said: 'Faith, Love, Hunger and
Money.'

'Wrong,' he declared. 'They are the Elements – Air, Earth, Fire
and Water. If you can control those you can do anything.'

I nodded. 'I suppose Science is gradually succeeding in that. Gas
and electricity are forms of fire; we harness rivers and the tides;
and the back-room boys of the R.A.F. are tackling the problem of
dispersing fog.'

'Oh, Science plods along'; his tone was faintly contemptuous, 'but all those types of control require elaborate machinery to operate them. I was referring to the control of the elements by the human will.'

He saw my puzzled look, and added: 'For example, Jesus Christ *walked* upon the water.'

Never before had I heard him mention Christ's name except in connection with some sneer; and I said in surprise: 'But I thought you didn't believe in Him?'

'As a God, I don't,' came the quick reply, 'but there is no reason to doubt that he was an historic Personage, and that he had "power". However, there are innumerable other examples of the sort of thing I mean. There are well-authenticated accounts of Indian Fakirs who have mastered the art of levitation; that is, defeating gravity by remaining suspended in mid-air. The witch-doctors of the North American Indians could walk on red-hot embers without burning the soles of their feet. The juju-men of Africa can bring rain when it suits their purpose.'

'Do you seriously mean that the members of the Brotherhood can perform such extraordinary feats?'

'Some of us can. But each feat requires long and exhausting training and, after all, what point is there in devoting years to learning such tricks? They are really rather childish, and have no practical value except to impress the vulgar; and we are not interested in attempting to attract the multitude. Most of us prefer to devote our energies to more subtle tasks, and use the special powers that we acquire in support of our worldly activities. If you think for a moment what that means, in conjunction with brains, wealth and influence, you will be able to appreciate, far better than you could yesterday, that not only will the Brotherhood survive the general destruction of the upper classes in this country, but eventually dominate it.'

'All this is so staggering,' I murmured, 'that you must forgive me if I haven't quite gripped it yet. Accepting what you say about the Brotherhood's powers to perform miracles, I still don't see how they can be applied to further your ends in modern political and commercial life.'

'Don't you!' he laughed. 'Then I'll give you a few examples. You have already stumbled on the fringe of the matter yourself by using hypnotism to impose your will on people. You didn't get far with Taffy, but for an amateur you were amazingly successful with Deb. Properly trained you could use it with considerable effect on many of your future business associates. The trained will can also read thoughts, and confer good or bad health on the operator's friends or enemies. It can – '

'Could both my mental state and the injury to my spine be cured?' I interrupted. 'That is, if I become a member of the Brotherhood?'

He nodded. 'The first would be simple. That was what I meant when I promised that if the attacks occurred again I would help you to fight them. You need have no further worries on that score. Your spine presents a more difficult problem, because it is a physical injury. If a man has a limb shot off no power, however great, can enable him to grow another in its place. But the will can perform incredible feats of healing; and I am reasonably confident that within a few months we could enable you to walk again.'

'I would give a lot to be able to do that,' I sighed. 'I have often wondered if anything could be done for me by faith-healing.'

'This is much more than that,' he smiled, 'and far more potent, as it brings into play certain ancient laws which are entirely unknown to the ordinary faith-healer. But I was telling you of some of the feats that the human will can perform when properly directed. Quite apart from the use of hypnotism it can put thoughts and impulses into other people's heads. It can attract women and dissipate their moral scruples, so that they surrender without even realising that they are acting entirely contrary to their original intentions. Given certain aids and great concentration of will one can foresee glimpses of the future.

'By similar means one can also see what is going on through walls or at a distance. That is how I found out that you were preparing to escape with Deb's help, and was able to come down to the hall just as you were leaving. I should have found out that you were about to escape with Taffy, too, if I had had my mental eye on you; but that night I was occupied with other matters. By projecting the will one can influence people through their dreams, and one can also ill-wish them. As a last resort one can even cause them to decline and die. Those are only some of the weapons possessed by the members of the Brotherhood; and it is prepared to use them all in order to overcome such opposition as it encounters.'

I was silent for a moment; my brain whirling with the appalling thoughts he had conjured up. At length I said: 'Hypnotism, faith-healing, thought-reading and other mental processes where the operator imposes his will face to face with the subject, are recognised by the medical world and explainable by the direct human contact that takes place. But to see what is happening at a distance, to influence people's dreams, to be able to ill-wish them and send them death, are surely powers which can be acquired only through God or the Devil.'

He shrugged. 'That is an old-fashioned way of putting it.'

'Perhaps it is,' I muttered. 'But you don't deny it; although you have always told me that you do not believe in either.'

'One may reject the teaching of the Bible, yet accept the fact that forces outside this world govern everything in it.'

Suddenly Helmuth stood up; his tawny eyes gleamed with a strange light and his foreign accent became more marked as he went on: 'The secret of willing down power, or, if you prefer it, setting great supernatural forces in motion on one's own behalf, has been known to the initiate from time immemorial. Generation by generation it has been handed down, and today this priceless knowledge is the greatest asset of the Brotherhood. To become an initiate one must take the oath of obedience, subscribe to certain tenets of faith and master various complicated rituals. Those rituals are the jealously guarded secret of the chosen few; but, once you have become adept at them, you can operate the forces which we term Supernatural, because they are beyond all normal experience; and, through them, achieve your ambitions and desires. Such power is infinitely greater than any that wealth alone can bring, and in the name of the Brotherhood I offer it to you.'

I collected my wits as quickly as I could, and said: 'To become one of such a gifted company would be a great honour; anybody could see that. But the whole thing is so astonishing – so extraordinary – so, well, so utterly fantastic by all ordinary standards, that I am still very much at sea.'

He grinned at me. 'Yes. It is hardly surprising that you should feel a bit bowled over on first learning the magnitude of the powers that the Brotherhood possesses. But now that you know the truth about it, if there are any questions you want to ask, fire away.'

Controlling my voice with an effort, I replied: 'You have already answered the one that interests me most: that about the possibilities of getting back my health. But there is one other thing I would like to know. To put it bluntly, what is it going to cost for me to become a member?'

'I thought I told you yesterday.' He raised the well-marked dark eyebrows that contrast so strangely with his mane of white hair. 'In that way it is the same as joining a Religious Order. You would make over to the Brotherhood everything you possess. But there the resemblance ends; because the fact that you had done so would always be kept secret, and you would not be required to take a vow of poverty; so for all practical purposes you would continue in the full enjoyment of your fortune.'

'Isn't that a bit too much to ask?' I protested rather meekly. 'I mean, there can't be many new initiates who have more than a few thousand to make over; so why should the Brotherhood require the whole of the Jugg millions to accept me?'

With a wave of his hand he brushed the question aside. 'My dear Toby! The amount that an initiate can contribute in worldly wealth does not enter into the matter. Some who have practically nothing of a cash value to offer are accepted on account of their intelligence, or the promise they show in some other direction. You cannot expect an exception to be made for you in the rules of a foundation that has existed unchanged for countless centuries. It could not be considered even if you were the King of England.'

'I see,' I said, still very humbly. 'I only enquired because of my grandfather.'

'What has he to do with it?' Helmuth frowned.

I endeavoured to look as worried as I could. 'He made all this money; and he went to extraordinary lengths to leave his fortune to me intact – even to spending a considerable portion of his income during the latter part of his life in insuring against death-duties. In view of that I am wondering if I really have the right to part with the control of it.'

Helmuth took the scruple I had raised quite seriously. 'I see your point,' he said. 'But I am sure that, on consideration, you will feel that he would approve your surrendering the lesser power that his wealth can give you for the greater power that has now been placed within your grasp. Anyhow, the last thing I would wish is to influence you into doing anything against your conscience. There is no immediate hurry. Think it over, and we'll talk about it again tomorrow.'

So I succeeded in stalling him without arousing his suspicions. To fight for a little time seemed the only possible line that I could take. Had I refused point blank I would not even have gained these few hours to prepare myself to face a renewal of his hostility. But at last the naked truth is out. Helmuth *is* a Satanist.

Friday, 12th June
Yesterday was, I think, the blackest of the many black days that have fallen to my wretched lot since I arrived at Llanferdrack. After I had

written out the conversation I had with Helmuth the previous night – as near word for word as I could remember it – I spent practically the whole of the rest of the day turning over in my mind the terrible implications of his admissions about the Brotherhood.

Actually, except for what little sleep I got, I had been doing that ever since he left me; but as the day wore on my speculations plumbed ever grimmer depths. However, to record them would be pointless, as I have since seen Helmuth again, and he has come out into the open.

He came up here soon after tea, and Sally was still with me; so for about ten minutes the conversation was general. She remarked that although there must be thousands of books in the library she could not find a thing worth reading there. Upon which he laughed, told her about how old Albert Abel I had bought them for so much the yard, then added: 'But I have plenty of good modern books in my study. You had better dine with me again one evening; we'll go through them afterwards and you can see which you would like to borrow. My evenings are rather fully occupied at present, as I am getting out some special figures in connection with the estate; but how about Sunday?'

Sally accepted with obvious pleasure. Shortly afterwards she left us, and while her high heels were still echoing on the stone stairs Helmuth grinned across at me.

'What a splendid specimen of the female *Homo sapiens*; and what an interesting contrast to Deborah Kain! Such a simple, healthy young animal is certain to possess all the normal urges, but it will be amusing to see how deeply they are overlaid by middle-class inhibitions.'

I did not reply. I've done my best to warn Sally, and if she still persists in sticking out her neck, that is her affair. I had far too much reason for acute anxiety on my own account to give it further thought at the moment; and, anyway, there was nothing I could do about it.

'Your mind is obviously on graver issues,' he remarked. 'What decision have you reached as a result of our talk yesterday?'

I took the only line I had been able to think of, and said as tactfully as I could that, while I greatly appreciated all he wished to do for me, I could not square it with my conscience to hand over my grandfather's fortune to anyone.

He stood up, thrust his hands in his pockets and began to pace up and down. Without inviting any comment from me he went on talking for a long time, and this is what he said:

'You are being very foolish, Toby; and I don't think that you can have yet fully appreciated your position.

'According to the last vetting by your doctors you are likely to remain a helpless cripple for a long time to come, if not for life. Added to which you have recently developed mental trouble, of which I will speak later. I have offered you a very good chance of being able to walk again within the next few months, and a definite cessation of what we will term your "hallucinations". Moreover, I have shown you that in ten or fifteen years at the most everything points to a Socialist Government depriving you of all but a fraction of your millions, and I have suggested a means by which, in spite of that, you may continue to enjoy all the benefits of wealth. Yet you pigheadedly refuse to accept my proposal.

'Now, I should like you to understand one thing clearly. No man can serve two masters; and I do not regard you as my master. My whole allegiance is given to the Brotherhood and all it stands for. I had hoped that while serving them I might also help you. But since you will not see reason I must proceed to carry out the project that I have in mind; even though it will result in what virtually amounts to your destruction.

'This project is no new idea conceived within the last few weeks. It was considered and approved by the Brotherhood many years ago while you were still a small boy; shortly after you came to Weylands. It was decided that, as soon as you came of age, the great fortune which is still being held in Trust for you must come under the Brotherhood's control; and I was selected to carry out the plan to secure it. That is why I have devoted so much of my life to you.

'By running away from Weylands and joining the R.A.F. you temporarily upset our calculations; because had you not done that you would have been initiated on leaving, at the end of nineteen-thirty-nine. Like all our other scholars, life at the school had prepared you to accept initiation without question. Your mind had been conditioned to do so by the elimination of all moral scruples and primitive taboos. You would have thought the ancient mysteries fascinating, the rituals exciting, and the whole conception a perfect outlet for your abilities and ambitions. Had things panned out according to our original plan you would have been a member of the Brotherhood for two-and-a-half years now; and on the twentieth of this month you would have handed over your fortune without the least hesitation or regret. But Fate decreed otherwise.

'If it had not been for your being shot down when you were we might have had some difficulty in getting you into our hands again; but, even if I had not succeeded in doing so, I think you may take it as certain that some of your old school friends would have appeared upon the scene, and sooner or later manœuvred you into a position from which you would have found no escape but to join us.

'As things are, your crash brought you back to me with three clear months in which to work upon you before you attained your majority; so it turns out in the end that not a day will be lost in the Brotherhood assuming control of your money.

'When you arrived here, it did not take me long to see that life in the R.A.F. had undone a great part of the work that had been put in upon you during your school years. Many of the petty little ideals and outworn shibboleths of your brother officers had proved contagious. It would have taken years to argue you out of all of them, even if that had proved possible at all now that your mind has attained maturity and no longer has the plastic quality of youth. So I had to adopt other measures.

'You have no doubt heard the expression "conditioning" as applied to the Gestapo's treatment of prisoners from whom they wish to extract confessions, and so on. I am told that they plunge them into baths of ice-cold water, and tap their muscles gently for an hour or two each day with rubber truncheons. Well, during April and May, although the methods I employed were not of a violent nature, I have been conditioning you.'

'You filthy bastard!' I burst out; but he ignored me and went on: 'The object of the "conditioning" was, of course, to create a situation, and to bring you to a frame of mind, in which you would agree to sign certain papers on your birthday, and accept initiation into the Brotherhood as soon as that can be arranged.'

My temper snapped, and I shouted: 'I'll do neither! I'll be damned if I'll make my money over to a lot of Devil-worshipping crooks!'

He smiled sardonically. 'You may beg to be allowed to before I am through with you. But by then it may be too late. Your state may be such that the Brotherhood would no longer consider it desirable to have you as a member.'

'Then you'd have cut off your nose to spite your face,' I retorted, 'for in that case they wouldn't get my money.'

'Oh yes, they would!' His smile broadened to a grin. 'At least, they would be able to control the use to which it is put; and that is really all they wish to do. It is to your *mental* state that I was referring, and if it had deteriorated to that degree you would be judged unfit to inherit. The Board of Trustees would then continue to administer your affairs; and it would not take me very long so to arrange matters that the Board's future decisions were in accordance with the wishes of the Brotherhood.'

Except that Helmuth would be acting as an agent, instead of on his own account, it was the very thing I had been fearing all through the latter half of May and early June. Yet, even so, it seemed as though a trap had suddenly snapped to behind me, when I heard it actually put into words. I swore at him again; but, once more, he ignored me, and launched out on another steady spate of words.

'You must not imagine that we abandoned our project just because you had run away to the Air Force; or that I remained idle about the matter all the time you were in it. Since I managed to get myself appointed as a Trustee in the autumn of nineteen-thirty-nine I have spent thousands of hours going into your affairs, and I now know more about them than any man living. It was important that I should acquire this knowledge, because it will be my role to advise the Brotherhood on the Jugg Companies; and, if you have the sense to abandon your present attitude, give you their instructions regarding the policy they wish you to pursue. But it has also enabled me to make a personal assessment of each of my co-Trustees, and prepare the way for disposing of those we do not wish to retain, so that the Board can be re-created with all its members our willing servants.

'Rootham and Bartorship are now in the Services, so we do not have to worry about them for the moment. Embledon and Smith are almost moribund, and no longer attend meetings. That leaves your uncle, Iswick, Roberts and myself.

'Your uncle will do what I tell him. Iswick is both ambitious and unscrupulous, but he is an extremely able financier, so I wish to retain his services. At the right moment he will be offered membership of the Brotherhood. Unless I am much mistaken he will jump at it. Should he not, I know enough about his financial dealings to put him in prison, so he will be compelled to play ball with me.

'Having secured him as my ally I shall tackle Roberts. It may surprise you to hear it, but that dried-up old stick of an accountant is keeping a young woman in a flat in Maida Vale, and although he must be every day of sixty-eight, she has recently had a child by him. I feel sure he would not like his family and his fellow church-wardens at Berkhampstead to know that, and will much prefer to resign, having first put forward a resolution himself that for one member of his firm to have a seat on the Board will in future be considered sufficient. A member of the Brotherhood will be elected in his place.

'Next I shall deal with Embledon and Smith. Both will be asked to resign on account of their advanced age. If either or both refuse, appropriate steps will be taken. It is laid down in the Trust that should any Trustee fail to attend meetings for six consecutive months he thereby automatically forfeits his Trusteeship.

'At present both of them stagger up to London twice a year to fulfil this minimum requirement. However, a quite simple ritual, performed by myself, will be sufficient to ensure such a rapid deterioration in the health of these recalcitrant gentlemen that they will be compelled to exceed the limit. No excuses will be accepted, and that will be that. They will be replaced by two further members of the Brotherhood; and I shall then govern six seats out of eight.

'There remain Rootham and Bartorship. Both have been granted a special dispensation from attendance at meetings for the duration of the war; and I think the war will go on for quite a long time yet. By the time they do eventually return, my position will be impregnable; but I think, all the same, that they will both have to go. It could be arranged for Bartorship's firm to have been found negligent in some matter; and if six Trustees demand a change of Accountants to the Trust, he will have no option but to retire.

'Brigadier Rootham presents the most difficult problem, because he still has copies of all our papers sent to him, and I don't think he will like some of the transactions upon which we shall enter. He is an intelligent and determined man, so it is probable that he will come back spoiling for trouble. If he does he will be signing his own death-warrant. A Chapter of the Brotherhood will have to perform a more serious ritual, to bring about his liquidation before he has a chance to ask too many awkward questions.'

I listened to this programme of trickery, blackmail and murder with cold horror. Even in my worst imaginings of Helmuth engineering such a plot, I had counted on Rootham and Bartorship going fully into matters when they got home, and insisting on coming to see me; which would provide a chance for me to secure release from captivity. But he had evidently given the matter more thought than I had, and got the whole set-up taped.

'So you see the situation, Toby,' he went on. 'It will be easier for all concerned if only you will be sensible, and sign the papers that I intend to put before you on your birthday, without further argument. That would save me a lot of time and trouble, you a most unenviable fate, and several of your Trustees a considerable amount of pain and grief. But in the long run whether you do or don't will not make the slightest difference; because the Brotherhood will assume the direction of the Jugg enterprises, anyway. And there is nothing you can do to stop that.

'My "conditioning" of you produced exactly the results I intended. I knew that you would try to get Julia and Paul, and probably some of the other Trustees, down; but I didn't intend to let you succeed in that till I was ready for it. I stopped your letters because I wanted you to get really boiled up and desperate before there was a showdown. I *wanted* you to suspect that I was at the bottom of the trouble, and make all sorts of wild accusations against me that you could not prove. My only concern was that things should not go off at half-cock; in case you kept some card up your sleeve to play later.

'But you didn't. You gambled all out to break my hold on you, and you've gone down for a grand slam. Just as I knew I would be able to, I took every trick in the game. By priming Julia, I manœuvred you into admitting that you had become mentally unbalanced and that your accusations against myself were groundless; then agreeing to a reconciliation with me. I got you to decide for yourself that you could not do better than to remain in my care, and stay on at Llanferdrack. I even succeeded in scotching the visit that the other Trustees would normally have made here on the twentieth, by securing your consent to your official birthday being put off for a month.

'That will not prevent your inheriting, of course, and any document you sign from the twentieth on will be legally valid. But it has the twofold object of cutting your last possible lifeline to the outer world, and keeping the Board in being for a further period; so that, never having been dissolved, there will be no necessity to go through a complicated legal procedure to re-create it, should you continue to resist and so compel me to take steps which will result in your being certified as insane.

'If you do as I wish the Board will assemble either here or in London in five weeks' time, and formally hand over to you. If you don't, then you will simply have inherited for a short time without performing any act in connection with your properties; then the Board will learn that you have been pronounced medically unfit to handle your affairs, and automatically reassume control. So you see, I've got you either way.

'You can write to Julia or Paul now to your heart's content; or if you like I will have you carried downstairs so that you can rave to them over the telephone. But they won't believe a word you say. They will only think: "Poor old Helmuth; what a time he must be having, trying to keep secret the affliction from which that unfortunate boy is suffering."

'Last weekend you burnt your boats, Toby. You are my prisoner now, as much as if I had you locked up in Brixton Jail. More so, in fact, for you are mine to do as I will with body *and* soul. There is nothing you can do about it, and if you have a grain of wisdom left you will submit with a good grace.

'The choice is still yours. But either you sign the papers that I shall produce on the twentieth, and join the Brotherhood, or I shall have to step up the conditioning process just as the Gestapo do when they have reached the conclusion that a prisoner is of no further use. If you force me to it, I will drive you mad within a month.'

He walked to the door, turned at it, and added: 'I will come for your answer tomorrow night.'

Saturday, 13th June
I have entered on my fight. Helmuth's allusion to the Gestapo was more apt than he knew. In France, Holland, Norway, and lots of other places, there are hundreds of men of the Allied Nations, and women too, who are being put through the mill by those human beasts in black uniforms. Day after day they are appallingly maltreated and made to suffer the most degrading indignities. They have no hope of rescue or reprieve, but they don't give in lightly. Some of them crack before the finish; but many of them stick it out to the bitter end, and carry with them to an unknown grave the secrets that might aid the enemy.

One likes to think that none of us are given more to bear than we can manage to sustain provided that we muster the greatest degree of fortitude of which we are capable; and that then we are overcome by a merciful oblivion. Perhaps it is like drowning, in which people usually come to the surface several times before they sink for good and all. I went under last night; but I've come up again this morning, and I still have a bit of kick left in me. Perhaps, though, that is due to Sally.

Yesterday's entry took me a long time to write; because I wanted to make it as complete and detailed as possible, in order that it may prove the more damning as an indictment of Helmuth if it ever reaches the hands of someone who is prepared to call him to account. When it was done I had not the energy left to set down my reactions, and they were too depressing to be of interest, anyhow.

It is clear beyond all doubt that he is a Satanist, and that when he spoke of 'conditioning' me he was referring to the Thing that menaced me from the courtyard. It *can* only be a manifestation of embodied Evil, that he called up with the deliberate intention of undermining my mental control. And, as he also spoke of performing mysterious rituals with the most monstrous intent, I spent most of the afternoon and evening in abject wretchedness, wondering what further horrors the future held for me.

The one thing that did bring me a ray of comfort, though, was the thought that the operation of his Satanic powers appeared to be dependent on bright moonlight; and we are still in the dark period of the month. The last full moon was on the 30th of May, so the new moon will not rise until the 20th; and, even after that, it will not reach the degree of brightness that I have come to regard as dangerous until several days later.

Alas for my hopes. Late last night they were shattered, in part at least. I had been buoying myself up with the idea that I could count on a minimum of ten clear days before Helmuth would be able to resume his ghastly 'conditioning' of me. God knows, my attempts to escape have so far ended in the most pitiful fiascos, but it is said that 'hope springs eternal in the human breast', and it did in mine, to the extent of desperately searching my mind for a way to make yet another attempt before he could get to work on me in earnest.

I am still doing that, as my belief that I shall not have to face the final crisis until towards the end of the month has been confirmed. But I am not to be given any peaceful respite to plan in; and it is now a question as to if I shall even be able to hang on to my sanity till then, let alone succeed in a last desperate bid to escape.

Yesterday evening I waited for Helmuth with mixed feelings of angry defiance and nervous apprehension, but he did not come at his usual time; nor did he come after dinner. Naturally, I could settle to nothing, and those hours seemed to drag interminably. At last Sally and Konrad settled me down for the night and I was left in the dark, still wondering why he had not come for his answer.

At length I dropped into a light sleep, but a little before midnight I was roused by hearing the creak of the hinges on the heavy oak door. And there he was, framed in its entrance, the light from the lamp he was carrying glinting on his mane of white hair and powerful features.

Having closed the door and set the lamp down, he said quietly: 'Well, Toby. What have you decided?'

Gripping the sides of the bed with my hands, I heaved myself up into a sitting position, and replied: 'To put a counter-proposition to you.'

He shook his head. 'I am not interested.'

'I think you will be,' I insisted, 'when you hear what it is. I can quite understand what led you to join the Brotherhood and to work for it all these years. You love power and you are an ambitious man; but no good will come to you through seeking it this way. It is well known that the Devil always lets down his followers in the end. You would do far better to abandon the whole thing and find other channels for your energies. I can enable you to do that. If you will agree to have me sent to Queensclere, and to resign from the Board of Trustees, I will sign a document which we will have legally witnessed, promising to pay you the sum of half a million pounds within one month of my twenty-first birthday.'

With a laugh of contempt he brushed my attempt to bribe him aside. 'Really, my dear Toby, you must take me for a fool. I hold a high position in the Brotherhood, and its interests are identical with mine. Why should I be content with less than a thirtieth part of your fortune when I can have the whole of it for the taking? We need the control of your money to further the great work upon which we are engaged, and we mean to have it. The only question is, will you give it to us and thereby save yourself; or must we go to the trouble of taking it from you and, in the process, turn you from a man into a filthy, grovelling animal?'

'Get back to hell, where you belong!' I shouted at him.

He was careful to keep his distance, in case I grabbed him, pulled him to me, and attempted to strangle him; but he sat down just out of my reach on the end of the bed, and said: 'Since you insist upon it I must teach you a lesson. As you have rightly assumed, the irresistible force which we of the Brotherhood invoke is known to the vulgar as 'the Devil'; but much of my personal power is derived through the agency of the moon. You will already have guessed that from your experiences down in the library on bright moonlit nights. If you remain adamant in your decision, I shall have to perform a solemn ritual to Our Lady Astoroth, when the moon is full again towards the end of the month. Once I have invoked her there will be no going back on that. All who have studied the esoteric doctrine agree that her appearance must be terrible beyond belief; for no man who has ever looked upon her face has been able afterwards even to recall his own name.

'But I still hope that extreme measure will not be necessary; and there are many other recourses of the Great Art known to me which do not require the propitiation of the Queen of the Dark Heaven.

'It may interest you to know that just as all Roman Catholics profess a special devotion to either their name-saint or some other, so all members of the Brotherhood place themselves under the protection of one of the Princes who form the entourage of the Ancient of Days. Incidentally, he is so called because he is infinitely older than any of the false gods invented since by man. He existed before Earth was created, and was given it as his Province; so he is the true Lord of This World, and everyone in it owes him allegiance. For countless thousands of years primitive man knew no other Deity, and all the cults which have developed in historic times are heresies.

'Traces of the ancient religion are still clearly to be seen in the fact that all, so called, savage races are divided into tribes, each of which regards itself as related through remote ancestry with one of the Princes of the Satanic hierarchy, and venerates his symbol in the form of a totem. The Wolf, Leopard, Scorpion, Hyena and Serpent are examples of these; and today we who perpetuate the age-old mysteries also associate ourselves with one or other of these powerful entities. My own totem is the Spider.'

I could not suppress a start, and my hands clenched spasmodically. I now knew what it was that had thrown the Shadow. That round body and the six hairy, tentacle-like legs had been those of a spider without a doubt; but a spider the like of which has never been recorded in this world. The big tarantulas of the Amazon were like flies to a bumble bee in comparison with it. Each leg must have measured at least two feet, when fully extended, and its body had been the size of a fish kettle. Leaving aside its supernatural aspect it would have proved a most formidable beast for any man to tackle.

Helmuth smiled as he saw my face whiten. 'My mention of spiders seems to call up disconcerting memories for you. If you tremble and sweat at the thought of a shadow, what would you do if you were brought face to face with the Great Spider in the flesh?

'That is what he is, you know; the Great Spider. But I forgot. You would not know that as all non-human forms of life have only group-souls their collective astral is always much bigger than the species it represents. The Great Hound is as big as a horse, and the Great Rat as a panther.

'I will tell you another thing, Toby. If one has materialised an astral and wishes it to solidify, one must nurture it on rotting offal, excrement or blood. Once it has taken sufficient sustenance to form a fleshy body of its own, it can look after itself; but it still needs and seeks food. Spiders are by nature blood-sucking animals and when the Great Spider has assumed material form he would not hesitate to attack a child – or a cripple, Toby – to satiate his lust for blood. What would you do if, one night, I let him into your room?'

I was sweating in earnest now; but I tried to put a bold face on matters, by muttering: 'I'd tear the brute limb from limb with my naked hands; I'd smash it to a pulp.'

He shook his head. 'Oh no you wouldn't. You might try, but you would not succeed. The Great Spider only borrows his coat of flesh. For him it is a fluid substance to which he gives form by his will; and he is indestructible. Your grip could squeeze but not injure his body, and if you tore off one of his legs it would immediately join itself on to him again.'

After pausing to let his horrible conception sink into my mind, Helmuth took a piece of candle from his pocket. It appeared to be made of black wax and was only about two inches long. He placed it in the centre of an ashtray which was well out of my reach, and said: 'I think that one night, before I call upon Our Lady Astoroth to destroy your mind utterly, I must introduce you to the Great Spider. I would not let him kill you, of course, but his embrace might bring you to your senses, or, alternatively, render an invocation to the Moon Goddess unnecessary. But to start with I will perform a minor magic for your edification.

'You will, no doubt, recall the story of the Pied Piper of Hamelin. He piped all the rats out of the city, and then, because the citizens would not pay him the promised fee, he lured away their children. That is not fiction. It is an account of an actual happening in the remote past that has come down to us through folklore. The Piper was a Mage, and one of considerable power, since he was able to entice the children of a whole township from their parents; but what concerns us is that his totem was the Rat, and it was that which enabled him to order the rats to follow him.

'But to return to ourselves. As I have already told you, my totem is the Spider. All spiders of every kind are my little brothers, and they will do my bidding.'

He lit the piece of black candle, and went on: 'This is made out of bear's grease, sulphur, pitch and the fat of a toad. To use such ingredients in making a candle may sound to you the most childish nonsense, but, believe me, it is not. All material substances have astral qualities and when consumed by fire procure certain results owing to immutable laws which govern the relation of the natural to the supernatural. You will probably find the smell somewhat nauseating, but it will burn for some forty minutes and give you enough light to see by. I am now about to leave you. When I get back to my room I intend to send all my little brothers who inhabit the old ruin to pay you a visit. I hope the experience will prove to you that I am not to be trifled with further.'

A moment later he had picked up his lamp and gone. I was quite calm, but as I stared round the room I felt extremely un-comfortable. All he had said had seemed quite logical at the time, but a swift reaction now made me feel that much of it was the product of a distorted brain. It seemed impossible that he really had the power to summon all the spiders in the Castle to plague me; yet I had seen the shadow of the Great Spider, *and felt* the sickening, soul-shaking waves of evil that radiated from it. That vile memory was real enough, and if he could materialise a demon such as that, where lay the limit to his potency for working these hideous miracles?

The candle burned with a steady blue flame, casting long shadows on the walls that reached up to merge into the darkness that still obscured the high, vaulted ceiling. The stench that came from the melting fat was most repulsive, and after a minute or two the fumes of the sulphur made my eyes water and got into my throat, making me cough.

Anxiously, I peered from side to side, watching for the first sign of movement which would indicate that he was succeeding in carrying out his fantastic threat. I gave a swift glance at my bedside clock. The hands stood at fourteen minutes to one; it had been just on twenty to when he left me. Another minute passed; another and another; still nothing happened.

I tried to figure out how long it would take for Helmuth to get back to his room and perform the incantation, then for the spiders to reach me; but two of those three factors were imponderables; so the answer might be anything from ten minutes to half an hour. All the same, I felt that a quarter of an hour should really be enough for him to set moving any spiders that were in my immediate vicinity; and when the minute hand of my clock had passed five to one I began to hope that either he had tried to hypnotise me into seeing what he wished me to see, and failed, or had attempted a ritual which had proved too much for him.

As each additional minute ticked away I grew slightly more optimistic; yet I did not relax my vigilance. Quite automatically I had dropped into the old, familiar, steady head-roll that was part of the drill for a Fighter-Pilot when searching the skies for enemy aircraft. My glance went down to the floor at my left, slowly upwards, across the opposite wall, down to the floor at my right, and back again across the bed. Now and then the beastly sulphur fumes caused me to break the rhythm in a fit of coughing, and each time that happened I looked at the clock. At one minute to one I saw the first spider.

It was a small red one; but there was no mistaking what it was, as it was actually on the clock and stood out clearly against the white clock-face.

After that things began to happen quickly. I spotted another, of the kind that have a tiny round body and very long legs, on the left-hand bottom corner of my counterpane. A third ran swiftly across my bedside table and disappeared behind my cigarette box. There came a little 'plop' on my pillow, and jerking round my head I saw that a big, hairy compact brute had fallen there from the ceiling. I made a swipe at it, and in doing so dislodged another that had just appeared over the edge of the bed. A tickling at the back of my neck caused me to clap my hand to it and at that moment a newcomer ran up the other sleeve of my pyjama jacket.

Within another minute the place was swarming with them. Minute little insects; things whose leg-span would have covered half-a-crown; round-bodied, oval-bodied, wasp-waisted, long-legged, short-legged, some hairy, some smooth, black, red, greyish, brown and mottled with nasty whitish spots; they came in scores, in hundreds, from every corner of the room, until the bed, the table and myself were spotted with them as thickly as a summer night's sky is with stars.

Frantically I beat at them to try and drive them off. Here and there my slaps caught and killed one, causing it to fold up in a little ball and roll away; but the great majority were agile enough to evade my flailing hands, or seemed to protect themselves by taking cover in the folds of the bedclothes. In a dozen places at once I could feel them crawling over me; they ran across my face and got tangled in my hair.

There was nothing supernatural about them but, all the same, it was a beastly experience, as the irritation never ceased for a second and there was something loathsome about the feel of their cold little bodies coming in contact with one's skin. Somehow, too, the longer it lasted the worse it became. For the first few minutes my mind was fully occupied by my angry attempts to fight off the little pests; but it suddenly dawned upon me that my efforts were both futile and exhausting. They were too many and too agile, and for all my wild slapping I had not succeeded in hitting more than a dozen or two. So I gave up, and endeavoured to remain still. But I found I simply couldn't for more than a few seconds at a time. It was then that my nerve began to give way.

I suppose it was pretty wet of me to allow a lot of harmless little insects to have that effect; but it was partly the impossibility of sitting still while they crawled all over me and the equal impossibility of getting rid of them; and partly, I think, the horribly disturbing knowledge of how they came to be there. Anyhow, after a quarter of an hour, that seemed to last half the night, I broke down, and began to weep with rage and distress.

Helmuth came in a few minutes later, to see how I was taking things, and he must have been extremely gratified by what he saw.

The stinking bit of black candle had burnt down to a quarter of an inch. He snuffed it, put the heel in his pocket, then went over to the terrace door and opened it wide for a few moments till the rush of cool air had driven most of the smell out of the room. Next he pronounced several sentences of what sounded like gibberish, but were, I suppose, a magical formula from some dead language. On that his legion of spiders immediately left me and scuttled away out of sight through the cracks in the wainscoting.

Holding his lamp aloft, he looked at me and said: 'Perhaps after tonight's experience I shall find you in a more reasonable frame of mind tomorrow. If not, I shall have to give you a sharper lesson. There is one family of spiders living in the ruins that I refrained from sending. They are not poisonous but their bite is painful, and if I send them to you in the dark you will find it most unpleasant. You might think that over before you go to sleep.'

When he had gone I did think it over; and I was, and am, still determined to resist. Spider bites can be most unpleasant, but I can hardly believe that they will prove more painful than would a beating with thin steel rods by a gang of Gestapo toughs. And, so long as my mind remains unimpaired, I mean to stick any pain that Helmuth may inflict on me to the limit of my will.

Nevertheless, at the time, my nerves were still in a parlous state;

and, having already given way to tears, I let myself go again in a flood of self-pity. It was in that state that Sally found me.

I did not hear her come in, as my head was half buried in the pillow and my sobs drowned the sound of her footfalls. It was her voice, saying 'What is it, Toby? Whatever *is* the matter?' that made me start up and find her already leaning over me.

She was standing right beside my bed holding a torch. It dazzled me for a moment, but I could just make out that she was in a dressing-gown and had her fluffy brown hair done up in a lot of little plaits. They stuck out absurdly, like a spiky halo, but made her look very young and rather pretty.

'What is it?' she repeated gently. 'Why are you crying like this? Have you had some awful nightmare? I've just had one about you. It was horrid. You were in bed here, and there was a great black thing over your face. I couldn't see what it was, but I knew that you were suffocating. When I woke I was so worried that I felt I must come up and see if you were all right.'

'I – I had a nightmare too,' I gulped. It seemed the only thing to say. I could not possibly expect her to believe that Helmuth had done a Pied Piper of Hamelin on me with all the spiders in the place; but I snuffled out that I had *dreamed* that a hoard of them was swarming all over me.

'There, there,' she murmured. 'It's all over now, and you'll soon forget it. But I'm very glad I followed my impulse to come up, all the same.'

Then she perched herself on the edge of the bed, drew my head down onto her breast, and made comforting noises to me as though I were a small boy who had hurt himself.

By that time I had practically got control of myself again; but I must confess that I didn't hurry to show it. Perhaps Weylands made me rather a hard, self-reliant type; anyhow, circumstances have never before arisen in which I have been comforted by a girl. It was an entirely new experience and I found it remarkably pleasant.

After a bit I could no longer disguise the fact that I was feeling better; so she said she was going to send me to sleep. She has marvellous hands; strong yet slim, and very sensitive – as I already knew from her giving me my massage treatments. Having made me comfortable on my pillows, she started to stroke my forehead with a touch as light as swansdown. In no time at all I had forgotten about Helmuth and felt a gentle relaxation steal over me; a few moments later I was sleeping like a top.

Later

This morning Sally and I said nothing to one another about last night. I had half a mind to thank her for her kindness, but shyness got the better of me; and she probably refrained from mentioning the matter out of tactfulness, feeling that I wouldn't like it recalled that a girl had found me in tears.

All the same it did come up this afternoon. I was sitting in my wheelchair looking through one of my stamp albums – I have five altogether, and two of them are now completely interleaved with these sheets, but this was one of the others – and I found I was out of cigarettes. As Sally was near my bedside table I asked her to pass me the big silver box on it, so that I could refill my case. She did so, and opened it as she handed it to me. There was a dead spider inside.

'That's funny,' she said. 'When I was making your bed with Konrad this morning I found three dead spiders in it, and here's another. I wonder how it got inside the box?'

I knew the answer to that one. The box had been open when Helmuth had come in to me at midnight. Later, while slapping at the little brutes, I had evidently hit this one as my hand caught the lid and smacked it shut.

But, without waiting for me to reply, she went on: 'It was queer finding three of them in your bed, too. I've never seen any there before. Perhaps a nest of them has hatched out behind the wainscot. Anyhow I'm sure it must have been one of them running over your face that gave you that horrid dream.'

An almost overwhelming impulse urged me to tell her the truth; but I managed to fight it down. I'm very glad I did now, as a few dead spiders would not have been enough to convince her that I hadn't dreamed the whole thing, and that it was simply my old prejudice against Helmuth reasserting itself in my sleep.

All the same, I count her having found the spiders a great piece of good fortune, as it is one item of concrete evidence; and, although it may cost me pretty dear, if the next few days produce others the time may not be far off when I can spill the whole story and she will *have* to believe me. Sally is 100 per cent honest; I am sure of that; and if only I can convince her of the facts she will be 100 per cent for me. I have *got* to, for in her now lies my only hope.

As it was, I said: 'Yes, you're right. I can still feel the little devils crawling over my skin. But that doesn't explain your dream about me; how do you account for that?'

She shrugged. 'Perhaps I was worrying about you before I went to sleep. For a permanent invalid you are a wonderfully cheerful person, and in the early part of the week you were right on top of your form; but the past two days you've gone right off the boil. Naturally I've felt rather concerned about that.'

'I'm very grateful to you, Sally,' I said. 'And I'm particularly grateful to you for your kindness to me last night.'

Then an idea came to me, so I added: 'I think I can explain why I've been a bit under the weather recently. I sometimes get premonitions, and I had one about this spider dream that shook me up so. I've a feeling, too, that I'm in for another tonight. Would it be asking too much of you to sit up with a book this evening, and come in to see me round about twelve o'clock?'

She gave me a queer, half-humorous, half-annoyed look, then said a trifle sharply: 'Nothing doing, Toby Jugg. You were genuinely upset when I came in to you last night; but for a good ten minutes before I sent you to sleep you were shamming. Midnight visiting is not in the contract, and the proper relations between nurse and patient are going to be maintained. You needn't tell me that you never knew a mother's care, either; because I've heard that one before.'

I was so taken aback that I could not think what to answer. She was right, of course, but I had no idea that she had spotted my manœuvre. Evidently she thinks I was making up to her with ulterior motives; but she is quite wrong there. It was only that I have been rather starved of human affection and found comfort in the warmth of her evident concern for me. Since she assumes that by asking her to come to me again tonight I was contemplating making a pass at her, I find it distinctly humiliating that she should have shown so very plainly that she thinks me too poor a fish to bother with. Still, I suppose one can't blame her really – what healthy girl would want to start an *affaire* with a poor devil of a cripple?

Sunday, 14th June
Helmuth carried out his threat, and the result was pretty bloody. He came in to me about eleven o'clock. There was the sort of scene which it has now become redundant to record; I called him by a string of unprintable names and he retorted with variations on the theme that I was a stiff-necked little 'whatnot', whom he was determined to bring to heel.

The fun started half an hour after he had left me. As there was no hell-broth candle on this occasion, and the fire had practically died out, I had no immediate warning before the attack. Something suddenly scurried across the back of my neck and bit me on the ear.

I shook my head violently, clapped a hand to the place, then quickly hauled myself up into a sitting position. Nothing more happened for a while; but I don't mind admitting that as I sat there in the darkness I had no mean fit of the jitters.

I could not help visualising swarms of the little brutes coming at me from every direction, as they had the night before, but this time every one of them having a nip like a pair of tweezers and intending to make their supper off me.

Thank God, it did not turn out to be as bad as all that, and the period of nerve-racking anticipation was really the worst part of the business. But the realisation was quite bad enough. Helmuth's pet family of 'little brothers' turned out to consist of about a score of small, active and persistent horrors, as far as I could judge – although it was impossible to estimate with any certainty how many there were of them making darts at me in the darkness.

I think being in the dark made the bites seem more painful, as this morning there is not very much to show for them; but at the time each hurt like the cut of a small, sharp knife, and the shock of it coming without warning added to its intensity. It brought to my mind what I had read of a Chinese torture called 'the death of a thousand cuts' and, although of course I wasn't, I could not help believing that I must be bleeding in dozens of places from the bites on my face, arms, neck, hands and the upper part of my body.

How long the ordeal went on I don't quite know; but it must have been well over three-quarters of an hour with a fresh bite about every minute. For the whole of that time I was jerking myself about and slapping at my unseen enemies; so when at last the biting ceased I was sweating like a pig and thoroughly exhausted.

For a time I remained sitting tense and vigilant, waiting for the next bite to come; but when a considerable interval had elapsed without one I gradually relaxed, and began to wonder if Helmuth would soon appear to gloat over his blood-soaked victim. But he didn't, and some time later, still propped up against my pillows, I dropped off to sleep.

One good thing, at least, has come out of this last bedevilment. Sally found two more corpses in my bed this morning; and although there was no blood to show, my skin was red and slightly puffy where I had been bitten.

I twitted her, a little unfairly perhaps, on not having believed my prediction that I should be the victim of another 'nightmare'; but she took the matter seriously, and expressed contrition at having given me a raspberry instead of the benefit of the doubt.

At the moment, while I sit here writing this on the terrace, she is conducting a grand spider-hunt in my room, and is dusting insect powder into the crevices of the wainscoting behind my bed. That will not stop the spiders, if Helmuth decides to send them again, as they come from all over the place; but, now that she is so concerned about it, he may abandon this form of tormenting me from fear that she will start agitating to have me moved again.

She said this morning that proper sleep was an essential to my recovery, and that if we couldn't get rid of the spiders she would have to speak to Helmuth about it. Moreover, she volunteered of her own accord to come in late tonight to see that I was all right.

I reminded her that she was dining with Helmuth, and suggested, with what I fear must have been rather a forced laugh, that she might find his books and his conversation so interesting that she would forget all about me.

To that I got the tart reply that a few hours' relaxation had never yet made her forget her professional duties.

Let's hope that tonight does not prove an exception. It would be a great triumph for me if she came in while a spider-attack was in full progress, as I think that if I then told her the truth she might believe it. But will she come at all? She certainly won't if Helmuth gets really busy on her.

Later

I have spent a miserable afternoon. Not on account of any further threat from Helmuth, or my own situation – which, God knows, is desperate enough – but worrying about Sally.

I feel sure she has no idea what she may be letting herself in for tonight, and it would be futile to try to tell her. She would only put it down to a recurrence of the abnormal condition in which I am supposed to have sex on the brain, and I should risk disrupting to no purpose the excellent relations that now exist between us.

Sally has been here over a fortnight, and a cripple is naturally far more dependent than any other type of invalid on his nurse, so I have already spent many pleasant idle hours in her company. In fact, I have really seen much more of her than I did of any of the girls that I met casually, and ran around with for two or three months, while I was in the R.A.F.

I have come to like her enormously; and I am beginning to wonder if my intense repugnance to the thought of Helmuth getting hold of her is not partly inspired by jealousy. I have never been jealous of anyone before; the Weylands training eliminated that emotion in my make-up during my adolescence, and I thought it had done so for good; but now I am by no means certain.

Knowing Helmuth's attitude to women as I do, the thought of her spending a whole evening with him makes me squirm. I simply cannot bear the thought of his filling her up with drink, then pawing her about. Of course, she may not let him; but his personal magnetism is extraordinarily strong, and if he thinks she is likely to prove difficult he is quite capable of slipping something into her drink.

The terrible frustration that I am feeling, from being unable to protect her, can hardly be entirely attributed to a normal sense of chivalry; so I suppose there is no escaping the fact that jealousy must enter into it. If so it is a most hideous emotion; and, since jealousy of this type is a by-product of love, it brings me face to face with the question – can I possibly be in love with Sally?

As I have never been in love, I honestly don't know. I have always thought of love in this sense as an extra intense form of physical desire, and Sally has not so far had any profound effect upon my passions. She has a lovely figure, and, although she is not beautiful in the accepted sense, her face is so expressive that it gives her an attraction all her own. There is, too, a rich warmth in her voice, and she is altogether a very cuddlesome person; but I certainly would not jump off Westminster Bridge for the privilege of sleeping with her. On the other hand I think I would jump off Westminster Bridge if by so doing I could prevent what is likely to happen tonight. Which strikes me as very queer.

Monday, 15th June
I am in love with Sally. I know that now, and I wonder more than ever what ill I can have done in my short life for God to have inflicted such a series of punishments on me. To be made a cripple at the age of twenty was a life-sentence; to be left in Helmuth's clutches, with the end of the month approaching, and to date not even the germ of an idea for getting away from him, is pretty well as good as having added to the life-sentence that it shall be spent in solitary confinement; and now this!

Last night I went through purgatory. Sally gave me my massage early so that she would have plenty of time to change for dinner; then she told me that Konrad would settle me down at ten o'clock, and she hoped that I would soon get off to sleep; but she would peep in round about midnight, just in case the insect powder had not proved fully effective and some of the spiders were causing me to have another nightmare. After that she left me, and I spent five hours of unadulterated hell.

If this is love, God help every imaginative man or woman who falls into it, and ever has to remain inactive while knowing the person they love to be in the company of an unscrupulous rival. I knew both Helmuth and Sally, and the rooms in which they would pass the evening, sufficiently well to form a series of mental pictures, of their having cocktails together, dining, looking through his books, and of what might happen later.

Most of the time up till about half-past nine my personal television set was jumping ahead, with only occasional flash-backs to what was probably happening at the moment; after that hour my imagination ran riot, and my torture was intensified a hundredfold by sickening visions of what might be taking place downstairs while I was actually thinking of it. No doubt many of the situations that I conjured up, with which to flay myself, were grossly beyond the probable, but, since Helmuth was concerned, they were never outside the bounds of the possible.

I see that I have written of Helmuth as my 'rival', which, of course, he is not, since I have never made even the suggestion of a declaration to Sally, and, if I did, I have not the least reason to suppose that she would reciprocate my feelings. On the contrary, she has already shown that, far from desiring any advance from me, she would regard it as most undesirable, on account of her professional status.

I cannot think that many young nurses allow medical etiquette to weigh much with them if they feel an inclination towards a patient; in fact, although it was officially frowned on, in the R.A.F. hospitals where I spent ten months lots of chaps had affairs with the V.A.D.s; so Sally's attitude with regard to myself must be taken as a clear indication that she has no time for me. On the other hand, she has never made any secret of her admiration for Helmuth, and she may quite well have been hoping for the past ten days or more that he would make love to her.

I don't know much about girls' reactions, but everything in such relationships must depend on the point of view. If a man of 45, like

Helmuth, makes violent love to a girl of 22, like Sally, and she thinks him physically unattractive, she probably regards him as a 'beast', a 'dirty old man' and almost as a 'medical case who should have more control over himself at his age'; but if she is attracted to him she then regards his amorous assault as a compliment, and he becomes in her eyes an 'experienced lover', a 'real man of the world' and a 'connoisseur of women whom any girl of *her age* might be proud to have as a beau'.

If Sally's conception of Helmuth is on the latter lines, as well it may be, that would make the agonies I suffered last night all the more pointless and absurd. But they were none the less vivid and heart-rending. And what makes things worse is that I have no idea how the party really went, or ended, as Sally is hardly on speaking terms with me this morning.

That is partly my fault, as I blotted it again, and badly; and she could hardly be expected to guess that I did so mainly out of concern for her.

Helmuth did not come in to me after tea; so there weren't even any further threats to distract my mind from Sally; and I knew that he would be too much occupied with her to come up and start an argument with me after dinner. So the spiders and myself were both given a night off.

From ten o'clock, when Konrad took my lamp away, the time dragged interminably. I thought it must be at least half-past one, and that Sally had long since forgotten her promise to come and see that I was all right, when the sound of Great-aunt Sarah's footsteps, going down her secret staircase, told me that it was only just eleven.

She is as regular as a clock, and recently I have feared that Helmuth might hear her either coming or going on one of his late visits to me. If he did, he is quite capable of having her stopped out of pure malice, and it would be a wicked shame to interfere with the only thing that makes the poor old girl's life worth living; but, fortunately, he has never been here yet at the actual time she has passed. I thought more than once on both Friday and Saturday nights of calling her in to help me against the spiders, but gave the idea up from the feeling that it could not only be useless but scare her out of the few wits she has left.

Anyhow, her passing last night told me that I had another hour or so to wait for Sally, even if she came at all, and had not forgotten me owing to Helmuth's blandishments; or because she was lying half drugged and unable to think coherently. That hour seemed to stretch into an age-long night, yet I knew that it could not be more than two hours at most, because Great-aunt Sarah always returns from her self-imposed toil at one; and she had not done so when I heard footsteps coming up the stone stairs outside my door.

It was Sally, but Helmuth was with her, and she was tight.

He held the lamp as she stumbled into the room in front of him. I had never seen her properly dressed up before. She was not wearing full evening-dress, of course, but the sort of frock that girls use to dine out informally. Her eyes were abnormally bright and her face was flushed. My heart gave an extra thump as I suddenly realised that she can look damn pretty; but almost simultaneously I realised the state she was in, and I was filled with rage and apprehension.

Helmuth had knocked back his share of the drink. I could tell that by the slant of his tawny eyes; but he knows how to hold his liquor and, as usual when he is wearing a dinner-jacket, he looked very distinguished.

While he remained standing in the doorway, Sally came over to me with what I suppose she thought was a cheerful smile, but was actually a sick-making grin, on her face, and said: 'Well, I promised I'd come, and here I am. Any spiders?'

'No,' I said. 'You've brought the only one with you.'

Her face went stupidly blank, but Helmuth understood me and laughed. 'There you are! What did I tell you? Poor Toby's got them again. In an old place like this there are bound to be a certain number of spiders hatching out at this time of year, and because you found a few about the room he now thinks that I am one.'

'Silly boy!' She suppressed a hiccup. 'You mustn't get spiders on the brain. It's bad for you! I'm your nurse and I want you to be a credit to me. Be good now, and go to sleep.'

'It is you who need sleep at the moment,' I said sharply. 'And as you are now you are no credit to your profession or yourself. You're tight, Sally. Get to bed and sleep it off.'

I shot that line in the hope that it would pull her together, although I knew I was taking a chance that it might put her against me. It did, and came back like a boomerang on my unhappy head. She swore that she was not tight and called on the grinning Helmuth as witness to the gratuitous insult I had offered her. Then she called me an ungrateful little so-and-so for dragging her up here only to be rude, swore that she would never come near me after ten o'clock again, and flounced a trifle unsteadily out of the room. Helmuth gave

me a parting leer as he turned away to light her down the stairs; and
that was that.

What happened after that I have no idea. Up to the time that I
saw them, the fact that Sally was in such rollicking form showed
that Helmuth could not so far have tried anything on to which she
had not been a willing party. But there might have been a very
good reason for that. If she told Helmuth quite early in the evening
that she had promised to come up and see me at midnight, he is
shrewd enough to have realised that, should she insist on keeping her
promise, it would probably upset his seduction act just as he was
getting going; so he might have decided to spend the first part of the
evening filling her up with drink and hold the rough stuff till after
their visit.

All I do know is that she is looking like the wrath of God this
morning, and has one hell of a hangover.

Later

After lunch Helmuth came in to see me. He announced that he is
going away this afternoon and will not be back till Friday. The
surprise, relief and excitement that I felt on hearing this can well be
imagined.

The length of his proposed absence is accounted for by the
fact that he is going to spend two days at Weylands, and getting
from central Wales to Cumberland is a most hideous cross-country
journey. By road it is about three hundred miles, so could be done in
a day, but wartime restrictions make going by car out of the question,
and by rail there is no connection which makes the trip possible
without lapping over into a second day. He is catching the afternoon
train to Birmingham and spending the night there, as if he caught
the night train on he would only find himself marooned at Carlisle at
some godless hour of the morning; so he will travel north tomorrow,
spend Tuesday night and the whole of Wednesday at Weylands,
start back on Thursday after lunch and arrive here midday Friday.

He seemed to take a special delight in describing to me the object
of his journey. For a long time it has been one of his ambitions
to have the chapel here dedicated to his Infernal Master, and at
last the Brotherhood have agreed. The ceremony is to take place
on St John's Eve – that is, Midsummer Eve – Tuesday the 23rd
of June. Apparently it is the second most important feast in the
Satanic calendar, the first being Walpurgis, or May Day Eve – the
30th of April.

That, no doubt, explains why it was that I suffered the worst of the early attacks by the Horror in the courtyard on April the 30th. Evidently, too, it was not coincidence that it should have been on a 30th of April that I caught a glimpse of the Brotherhood gathering at Weylands, and had the fright of my young life on breaking open the old tomb. I am inclined to think now, though, that the tomb had nothing to do with it, and that I ran into some incredibly evil presence that the Satanists at Weylands had conjured up to protect their meeting from being spied upon.

Anyway, there is to be a full-scale Sabbath held here tomorrow week. Helmuth is going up to Weylands to arrange the final details and the Brotherhood is coming in force from all parts to attend it. So I know now why it was that when I looked through the grating I saw that instead of being half full of rubble the chapel had recently been cleaned out.

He asked me again if I had reconsidered matters, and on my replying in the negative, he said: 'That is a pity, as I should like to have taken north with me the news of your willingness to accept initiation. However, the Midsummer-night's ceremony will provide a perfect opportunity for that, and I still hope to induce you to see reason before then. If I fail, instead of your receiving initiation that night, we shall have to invoke the Lady Astoroth. The circumstances for such a ritual are not always propitious, but they will be on that date – and that will be the end of you. But I shall be back on Friday and able to give my entire attention to you over the weekend. By the twentieth the moon will be entering her second quarter; so if you are still recalcitrant I shall summon the Great Spider, and we will see what effect a meeting with him will have on you.'

Later

All the afternoon I have been desperately racking my wits for a way to take advantage of Helmuth's absence. It is a God-given chance to escape, and the last I will ever get. I have three clear days to work in, but even that is all too little to prepare for a break-out, and to pull it off.

The physical difficulties alone are immense. That morning when I was hauled back from the railway station, and Helmuth and Sally were discussing in the car how I could be prevented from getting away again, she was so right in pointing out that I am too heavy to be carried, so that even with help I could get very little distance without my wheelchair. And it is such a weighty contraption that it would take more than one person to get it downstairs. Then there is the problem of getting me down after it; and the whole job would have to be done at night without arousing any of the household.

Still, I've a feeling that I would find a way to surmount such obstacles if only I were not so utterly alone and tied. If I had someone to get me from my bed into the chair, and help me out of it onto the top step of the stairs, I believe the getting down could be managed. While they supported and guided the chair from behind, I could take its weight against the back of my shoulders and lever myself down in a sitting position, taking my weight on my hands, a step at a time. But it would be utterly impossible to perform such a feat on my own, and none of the servants ever come here, except Konrad. To hope for any help from him is out of the question. So the problem really boils down to, can I or can I not win Sally over before Helmuth gets back ?

Unfortunately she is sadly changed from yesterday; and goodness knows what Helmuth said or did to her, but he must now be very confident in her loyalty to him to go off like this leaving me in her charge. It was probably with his journey in view that he put off having a party with her until last night. That would be just like him. The odds are that he is not the least attracted by her, otherwise he would have done something about it long before this, but he decided that it was important to secure her allegiance, and that the best way to do so was to create a strong emotional bond between them, just before his departure.

He is also, no doubt, relying to some extent on my isolated situation, up here at the top of this spiral staircase, and on Konrad keeping an eye on things for him. But Konrad, although sly and cunning, is not overburdened with brains; so it should not be difficult to outwit him. Therefore it must be principally on Sally that Helmuth is counting to keep me a prisoner here, and prevent me from obtaining any outside help, during his absence.

The fact that she is like a bear with a sore head today, and has so far treated me with frigid abruptness, is partly due to her hangover and partly to her annoyance at my having seen her tight last night. But I have an uneasy feeling that there is also something else behind it from the way she avoids my glance. Perhaps Helmuth told her about how I hypnotised Deb and warned her not to look me in the face for more than a few seconds at a time.

Since she first arrived it has occurred to me more than once to try out my hypnotic powers on her, but I felt that Helmuth would be watching for such a move on my part and be certain to nip it in the bud. Later, after Julia's visit, there was no point in attempting it – until Helmuth came out in his true colours a few days ago. That was followed almost immediately by the first spider-attack, after which Sally came and comforted me. I am sure now it was that episode which led up to my present feelings for her, and there seems to me something definitely wrong about attempting to impose one's will by such means on a girl with whom one has fallen in love.

An attempt to bribe her is equally repugnant; but my situation is so desperate that I am positively forced to try one means or the other. Of the two, to offer her a bribe seems the less unpleasant course, and the one more likely to succeed. At least she could not afterwards accuse me of having interfered with her free will, and if Helmuth has primed her against my hypnotic powers I might find it impossible to make any impression on her – except, if she guesses what I am at, to make her more prejudiced than ever against me.

Even if she did become Helmuth's mistress when she was tight last night, she may be regretting it by now. But, in any case, I can hardly believe that in an *affaire* of such short duration he could have secured such a hold over either her affections or her mind as to make her completely oblivious to her future interests.

Sally is much better born than I am. She comes of a long line of Naval people, one of whom was a Cavalier who commanded a ship in Charles I's time. She was brought up to understand and appreciate nice things, although her family has fallen on hard times and lost nearly all their money. She is quite philosophical about the fact that she would have to earn her own living even if the war did not make that compulsory; but at times I am sure she thinks it a little hard that she should have to, while all her ancestors for many generations back have enjoyed the comfort, elegance and freedom to live as they chose, which was the natural birthright of the English gentry.

I could give her all that, and with no strings attached. If only she will get me away from Llanferdrack I'll be as rich as Croesus this time next week. However right Helmuth may be in his prediction that the Socialists will reduce the whole nation to the level of beggary in a few years time, the Jugg millions are still mine at the moment to do what I like with, if only I can get my hands on them. I'll offer to make over to her a sum which will keep her in luxury for the rest of her life. But I have no time to lose. I must tackle her tonight, after dinner. She is bound to accept; she would be mad to refuse.

Tuesday, 16th June

Last night I was stymied. When Konrad brought my dinner up he told me that Nurse Cardew had asked him to say that she felt a little indisposed, so she was going early to bed and would not be coming up again.

Poor Sally. I love her so much that I could not help feeling sorry for her, despite the annoying setback to my own plans. She certainly had a packet the night before, and even I don't know quite how big a one it may have been; it was very natural that she should feel that she wanted to sleep the clock round.

Perhaps, after all, so far as I am concerned, it is all to the good that I should have been compelled to postpone my offer to her of a thundering fat bribe. She is in a much better mood this morning and, although still a bit stand-offish, at least civil to me.

I have decided not to rush my fences, but to be on my best behaviour all day, so as to try to win her back to a really friendly mood; then take the plunge just after tea, when we do my second daily standing exercise.

We haven't got very far with that. I can just bear my own weight for about a minute, but I fear it will be quite a time yet before I can take even a single step, as, directly I attempt to lift one foot from the ground, the other leg crumples up. Still, Sally remains extremely persistent and quite optimistic about me; and, as she regards this business as her own special contribution towards my recovery, she is always most patient and sympathetic during our sessions at it. I shall do my very damnedest this evening to show some progress, so as to please her; then offer her a life of a luxury for the rest of her days to become my ally.

Later

I have bogged it. I don't think it was my fault. The exercise was a success. I stood erect for two minutes by Sally's watch without support, and she was delighted.

As soon as I had recovered from the effort, I put the matter to her as tactfully as I could. I did not go into a long speech about Helmuth, much less make any apparently wild statements about his possessing occult powers derived from the Devil and having deliberately wished the spiders onto me. I simply said that, mad or sane, I was thoroughly fed up with Lanferdrack, and had come to the conclusion that it was bad for my nerves to remain here.

I added that, if I could get to London, I was perfectly prepared to go straight to the Air Ministry and ask to be taken back into one of their hospitals; and that as I was one of their own types, and a D.F.C. to boot, I felt certain they would take me – provided I was willing to pay my own expenses. That seemed to me a pretty reasonable proposition.

Then I went all out, and mentally transporting Sally to the mountain top, spread all the riches of the earth before her. For several minutes I dilated on what an ample supply of money could still do in the world for a personable young woman. Freedom from work and care, the opportunity to meet an endless succession of men with charm, ability and wealth; clothes, beauty-treatments, furs, jewels, travel, horses to ride in the country and parties to go to in town, winter sports in Switzerland and sunbathing in the West Indies, but she did not let me get as far as making the actual offer.

Having listened to me with an intent expression for a bit, she suddenly got what I was driving at; and, coming to her feet with a jerk, she told me to 'Shut up'.

But I went through with it; I had to, as things I value more than my life depend on my getting away from here before Helmuth gets back.

She went red in the face, stamped her foot, and declared that nothing in the world would induce her even to consider such a proposition. Looking back on it, I realise that she presents the most adorable picture when she is flushed and angry; but I was in no mood to think of that at the time. I told her that she was crazy; and that for her to reject such a future out of loyalty to Helmuth could only mean that he had bewitched her.

She replied that Helmuth had nothing to do with it, apart from the fact that he had engaged her and she was responsible to him. Then she got on her high horse about having been left in charge of me, and her honour as a professional nurse.

Again, looking back, I really believe she meant that; and, when one considers the temptation I was holding out, one does not have to be a born cynic to believe that very few young women would have shown such splendid integrity. Whether she is still a virgin, or has been Helmuth's mistress and had a dozen lovers before him, weighs as nothing in the scales against such a flat rejection of a colossal bribe; and I know now that I am very right to love her as I do.

But, at the time, my bitter disappointment, and the awful sense of impending fate that now weighs upon me all my waking hours, over-mastered all other emotions. My filthy temper got the better of me again, and I cracked at her: 'Oh, be your age; and stop talking hot air about your professional honour! You won't have any honour of any kind left if you have much more to do with Dr Helmuth Lisický.'

Her blue eyes blazed, and she retorted: 'If you were not, one – a cripple; two – my patient; and three – suffering from erotomania, I would slap your face.'

Wednesday, 17th June

I have blotted it again. Last night I decided that since there seems no possible chance of securing Sally's conscious aid, I must attempt to hypnotise her, and force her into helping me unconsciously. The idea was intensely repugnant to me, but desperate ills call for desperate remedies; and if ever a man was desperate, I am.

This morning, after we had been out on the terrace for about ten minutes, I tried the trick that had worked so well with Deb. I said that I had got a fly in my eye, and asked her to fish it out.

In an instant she rounded on me, called me an 'unscrupulous young brute' and proceeded to flay me with her tongue. I suppose that before Helmuth sacked Deb he got out of her particulars of how I had gone to work in her case. Anyhow he had told Sally about it the first night that she dined with him and warned her to be on her guard in case I attempted the same trick on her. Worse, he inferred that I had not only used the hypnotic control that I succeeded in acquiring over Deb to force her to help me to escape, but had used it before that to secure her unwilling cooperation in indulging my immoral aberrations.

Of course I hotly denied it; but that got me nowhere; and I don't wonder now that Sally takes such a dim view of me. She said that she would have thrown up the case and gone back to London days ago if she had not realised that when these fits seize me I am not responsible for my actions. So all I have succeeded in doing is to strengthen her conviction that I am an erotomaniac, and, this morning, made a most despicable attempt to make her my unwilling victim.

By this afternoon Helmuth will have been gone two days; and that is just half the period of grace that I have been granted. I have shot both my bolts with Sally, and have not another round of any kind left in the locker.

Later

It was Sally's afternoon off and she went down to the village; but there is nothing much to do there, so after tea she came up to sit with me. She was in a much more pleasant mood and, without exactly apologising, she inferred that she was sorry about having flared out at me as she did this morning. She said that I am so normal most of the time that she is apt to forget that my mind is unbalanced, so goes off the deep end when these occasional evidences of my malady occur, instead of calmly ignoring them. So I think her early return to keep me company was partly a gesture of the *amende honorable* variety.

I accepted it as such only too willingly, and after we had talked of trivialities for a bit, she said: 'I met your ex-nurse, Deborah Kain, in the village post-office this afternoon.'

'Did you?' I exclaimed. 'I thought she had gone back to London.'

'No. I gather that she is engaged to the village schoolmaster, a man named Gruffydd, and is staying with him and his mother.'

'What did you think of her?' I asked.

Sally smiled. 'Rather a flashy type, isn't she? I mean not at all the sort of person one would expect to find in these parts; or anyhow, not dressed the way she was. Her off-smart clothes, silk stockings, high heels and hair-do might have looked all right in Oxford Street, but they were a bit startling for Llanferdrack. I had no idea who she was until she came up and introduced herself. I suppose somebody had pointed me out to her as your new nurse. She asked me how I was liking it up at the Castle.'

'And what did you say to that one?' I smiled back.

'Oh, I was very non-committal,' Sally shrugged. 'I'm quite good at minding my own business, and other people's. I said that Helmuth was charming and you were a pet – which is by no means true all of the time – and asked her why she had chucked up such a pleasant job. That shook her rather; but she took refuge in the fib that, although she had liked both you and the Doctor immensely, when she had become engaged her fiancé had insisted on her leaving so that they could be together more often.'

We laughed a lot over that, as it was so absurdly far off the facts; but it suddenly occurred to me that Sally did not know the real truth about Deb's relations with Helmuth and myself – only a small part of it, with a number of entirely false additions given her by Helmuth. I knew that it was useless to give her my own version, as she would never believe me, and only get in an ill-humour again from supposing that I was once more attempting to blacken Helmuth in her eyes. But there *was* one way which, if it did not entirely convince her of the respective parts we had played, might at least arouse doubts in her mind about Helmuth's veracity.

'Sally,' I said, 'can you keep a secret?'

She nodded.

'I mean *really* keep it,' I went on. 'To me this one is of vital importance. I want you to give me your word that in no circumstances whatsoever will you disclose it to Helmuth or anyone else without my permission.'

'I'll give you my word, then,' she agreed. 'All this sounds very mysterious.'

'No. It's very down-to-earth, really.'

While I had been speaking the idea in my mind had swiftly developed. I realised that if I was to make this final bid to convince her that Helmuth was a rogue, to give her only the part that Deb had played in the story would be like producing a single slice of a large cake. So I decided to go the whole hog, and went on: 'Ever since the beginning of May I have been keeping a journal. You must often have seen me scribbling away with one of my stamp albums open on my knees. But I was not making long notes about water-marks, perforations and freak issues, as I pretended; I was entering up my diary, which now runs to over three hundred loose sheets.

'You believe me to be mad; but you admit that for much the greater part of the time I am perfectly sane, so the great bulk of my writing must have been done when I was normal. My reason for writing the journal was because *I* believe myself to be the victim of a conspiracy to *drive* me insane. I hoped that if the conspiracy succeeded, and I was put in a lunatic asylum, some honest person might come across my papers, realise the truth, and take steps to get me out. That is why I have taken considerable pains to prevent anyone here knowing of the existence of this document. You see, they might destroy it; and I regard it as my only remaining lifeline.

'If you read what I have written you may consider much of it to be the ravings of a lunatic; but it will tell you a great deal about me that you don't know, and of which independent proof is easily available. It will tell you all about my family and my early life; of the part that Helmuth played in it and of the great financial issues that hang upon the question of my sanity or madness; of the strange school, at which Helmuth was a master, where I was educated, and of how much he has to gain by making people believe that I am mad.

'If I told you this story myself I'm afraid you would think that I was making great chunks of it up as I went along; but you won't be able to think that of this account which has been written day by day as a record of events, and of the hopes and fears which have made my life one long battle for these past two months.

'If I give you these papers will you read them through this evening, and, whatever conclusions you come to, promise faithfully to let me have them back tomorrow morning?'

'Yes, Toby,' she said. 'I promise. And whatever I think I won't give away what you have been doing. I'd like to read the biographical part especially, as it may help me to help you to get well more quickly if I know more about you. If there are over three hundred pages of it though, it is going to take a long time to read, so perhaps I had better take them downstairs and start on it now.'

I asked her to get me the albums, extracted the pages I have written in the last few days so that she should not read the entries in which I have confessed my love for her, and gave her the rest.

Looking rather sweetly serious, she took them off with her, while I settled down to make this record of our conversation.

Was I, perhaps, inspired to start this journal before I even knew of her existence, so that she should one day read it? The workings of Providence are sometimes very strange; but perhaps Sally is the 'honest person' who will see the truth through the web of lies that Helmuth has spun, and set me free.

Thursday, 18th June

Anyone can imagine the state of suppressed excitement in which I awaited Sally's verdict this morning. Her face told me nothing when she came in shortly after Konrad, to help me with my morning toilet.

As soon as we were alone together for a moment, I asked her if she had read it all, and she nodded.

'Fortunately your writing is pretty legible, except in a few parts which were evidently written when you were overwrought, so I managed to get through it; but it took me till two in the morning. Konrad will be coming up with your breakfast in a moment, though; so I think we had better wait to discuss it until we are out on the terrace.'

So I had to contain my impatience for another hour; but as soon as we were comfortably settled in our corner of the battlements, she said: 'It is an extraordinary document, Toby. I was tremendously impressed; but, honestly, I don't know what to say about it.'

'The point is,' I said a little abruptly, 'having read it, do you consider that it is the work of a man who is sane or insane?'

'Honestly, Toby, I can't answer that.' Her voice held an unhappy note. 'Whether you imagine things or whether you don't, there can be no doubt about it that you have been through absolute hell. I cried in places, I simply couldn't help it.'

I think that is the nicest thing she has ever said to me. It almost made having gone through it all worth while, to have touched her heart like that. But the third day of Helmuth's absence was nearly up; he will be back by this time tomorrow, so the paramount need for action forced me to say: 'Thanks for your sympathy, Sally. I'm very grateful for that; but as I am situated it is not enough. I'm afraid I have placed you in a rotten situation. I wouldn't have done so from choice, but I had to; because I am a prisoner here and you happen to be my goaler, and there is no-one else to whom I can appeal for help.

'If I am still here when Helmuth gets back I am going to be sunk for good. You know that, from what you have read of his threats to me. If you consider that those threats are entirely the product of my imagination you will be fully justified in ignoring my plea. But if you feel that there is even a grain of truth in them you are now saddled with a very weighty responsibility. By helping to detain me here against my will you are not only aiding and abetting a criminal conspiracy, but doing something which you know to be morally indefensible.'

She took that very well, and agreed in principle that I was right; but she continued to declare that as she had nothing but my written word to go on it really was impossible for her to judge whether I had invented the more fantastic parts of my story or not. So for an hour or more we argued the matter, passing from the general to the particular, as I strove to convince her that every episode recorded was cold, hard fact.

There were two points in my favour. She had known a girl who had been at Weylands, so had some idea of the amoral principles that are inculcated there – which helped to lower Helmuth's stock – and she was not at all sceptical about ghosts or the more usually accepted supernormal occurrences. Moreover, she admitted that my whole conception of the motive for a conspiracy was built up on sound logic. But she simply could not swallow the fact that Black Magic is still practised today, and that Helmuth has been employing Satanic power with the object of reducing me to a gibbering idiot.

'All right, then,' I said at last. 'Let's leave the Brotherhood, and the Great Spider, and the question of Helmuth being a servant of the Devil out of it. If I can prove that he has told you a pack of lies, and slandered me outrageously, in connection with one particular episode, will that convince you that he has an ulterior motive in keeping me here, and induce you to help me get out of his clutches?'

After a moment she nodded. 'Yes. If you can do that, it would satisfy me that he really is plotting to get hold of your money, and whether he is using occult power to aid him, or not, becomes beside the point. Either way it would be up to me to do what I can to protect you from his criminal intentions. But I don't see how you are going to *prove* anything.'

'I may be able to,' I replied; 'but I shall need your help. Getting you to read the journal at all only arose through your running into Deborah Kain in the village yesterday, and because I wanted you to know my side of that particular story. If you will go down to the village again, and get her to come up here, I'll find a way to make her tell the truth; then you'll see if it is Helmuth or I who has been lying.'

'I can find her easily enough, because I know that she is living with the Gruffydds; but whether I can persuade her to come up here is quite another matter.'

'If you tell her that Helmuth is away until tomorrow, so there is no chance of her running into him, I think I can guarantee that she'll come back with you,' I said with a smile. 'I will write a little note for you to give her, and when she has read it I shall be very surprised if she does not agree to play.'

'You mean to hold some threat over her?' Sally frowned suspiciously.

'I do,' I admitted. 'But only to get her up here. After that you shall see for yourself that I won't use threats on her to get the truth.'

Turning my chair, I wheeled myself back into my room, got a sheet of notepaper and wrote on it:

MY DEAR DEB,

I am anxious to ask you a few questions, and it is of the utmost importance that I should put them to you at once; so would you be good enough to accompany Nurse Cardew back to the Castle.

In view of all you told me of your early life and political persuasions I am sure you will agree that it is much better that I should have this chat with you than to have to ask Mr Gruffydd to come up to see me.

I addressed the envelope, then wheeled myself back to the terrace and showed the letter to Sally. When she had read it she said: 'I remember, now, all that business about her being a Communist, that you got out of her when you had her in a hypnotic trance. You're threatening to tell her fiancé. That is blackmail, you know.'

'My dear Sally!' I exclaimed impatiently. 'I don't care if it is theft, forgery, arson, and all the other crimes in the Newgate Calendar. I'd commit the lot to get out of here; and since you insist on my proving my words before you will help me to escape, it is you who are driving me to commit this one.'

'I'm sorry, Toby.' Her voice had become quite meek. 'You're right about me forcing you into this; but I've got to know the truth, and the sooner the better. It is nearly twelve o'clock now, and it's a good bet that she'll be at the Gruffydds' house at lunch-time. If I borrow a bicycle from one of the servants and start right away, I shall be down in the village well before one. I'll have a snack myself at the tea-shop, then if all goes well pick her up afterwards and be back here soon after two.'

So off Sally went, and at any moment now I am expecting her to return with Comrade Deborah Kain.

Later

I've won! But what a session; and what a revelation! I am writing his now only to fill in time, as, anxious as Sally and I are to get off, it would be madness to make a start until Konrad is out of the way for the night. And our interview with Deb is well worth recording.

When she arrived she was pretty sullen, which was hardly surprising; but she became almost pleasant when I apologised for having troubled her, and said that I only wanted to ask her some questions, to set Nurse Cardew's mind at rest about certain things which it was suggested had happened here. Then I said: 'I want you to tell the truth, even if it appears to be unfavourable to myself, and if you do so I give you my word that I will say nothing to Owen Gruffydd of what I know about your affairs. Now; while you were here, did I at any time make any amorous advances to you?'

She looked very surprised, gave a quick glance at Sally and said: 'No. As a matter of fact I thought you were rather stand-offish. You were always quite polite, but you hardly seemed to notice me as a person at all.'

'Right!' I said. 'When Dr Lisický discovered that on several occasions I had hypnotised you, and had an explanation with you about that which led to your leaving, did he reveal to you, or even suggest, that I had taken advantage of you while you were in a trance state?'

'No; he never said anything of that kind.' Her eyes widened as she added: 'Did you – did you do that?'

'Certainly not,' I replied. 'But he seems to have given Nurse Cardew the impression that I did. Now, about the Doctor himself. Did he make amorous advances to you?'

'No,' she said firmly. 'He did not.'

Her denial took me by surprise, as it seemed quite pointless in view of all I knew, and the fact that Helmuth had thrown her out bag and baggage.

'Come, Deb!' I admonished her. 'I am not threatening you, and Nurse Cardew will promise not to repeat anything you may say to your detriment; but we want the truth. Dr Lisický told me that you were his mistress, and you confirmed that to me yourself, while you were in a trance. You can't deny it.'

She stubbornly shook her head. 'What I said in a trance you may have put into my mind; and if he said that of me it is because he is a vain and boastful man. He was lying.'

I saw that I was up against it, and there was only one thing to do. I said: 'All right; I will believe you, if you look me in the face and swear to that.'

She fell into the trap. The second she had her eyes fixed on mine I shot out my right hand, pointed my first and second fingers at them and gave the order: 'Sleep, Deb! At once! Go to sleep this instant!'

The old formula worked like magic. There was barely a flicker of resistance before her eyes began to glaze and the heavy eyelids drooped over them.

'Good,' I said, after a moment. 'Now we will start all over again. I am still not threatening you, but I order you to disclose the naked truth that lies in your subconscious. Were you telling the truth just now about me?'

'Yes.' Her voice had gone dull and toneless. 'You never laid a finger on me.'

'Were you Dr Lisický's mistress?'

'Yes.'

'I want details about that. I want Nurse Cardew to hear from your own lips the full particulars of your *affaire* with the Doctor, and how, having first taken, and then neglected you, he took you back again to spite Owen Gruffydd. You had better tell the whole story as you told it to me that day in the summer-house; with any additional details which may show how badly the Doctor treated you.'

It all came out in about twenty minutes' monotonous monologue; and when she had done Sally expressed herself as entirely satisfied that I had put no part of it into Deb's mind; her story included things that I couldn't have known, and it branded Helmuth as both a sadistic brute and outrageous liar.

I turned back to Deb and asked her, purely out of curiosity: 'Why did you seek to protect the Doctor before I put you in a trance? Why didn't you tell us the truth then?'

'Before I left he told me that I was never to mention that I had had an affair with him to anyone. And that if I was ever asked, I was to deny it.'

'But as you were leaving anyhow, he could no longer hold the threat of dismissal over you; so why should you take orders from him? Was it because you were afraid that he might tell Owen Gruffydd something about you that you did not want Gruffydd to know?'

'No. It was because I should have been severely punished if he found out that I had disobeyed him.'

'Who by?'

'By the Party.'

I drew in my breath. 'Do you mean then that Dr Lisický is also a Communist, and a member of the Party?'

'Of course, and a very high one. He is a Commissar.'

Sally and I took a swift look at one another. The reply had electrified us both. Later, I realised that I should have considered the possibility of Helmuth being a member of the Communist Party before. Deb had disclosed that Miss Smith, who ran her nursing organisation, used it as cover for a Communist centre, and Helmuth had told me himself that Miss Smith was an old friend of his – hence his pull with her to send him not only good-looking, complaisant nurses, but ones who were also 'trustworthy'. The tie-up was pretty clear, and I ought to have spotted it. By 'trustworthy' it was now clear, too, that he had meant girls who were members of the Party, whom he could order around, and who would keep their mouths shut if they suspected him of the filthy game he was playing on me. What a heaven-sent blessing that Miss Smith should have gone off for the weekend and the nurse she had selected to replace Deb had injured her ankle, so that dear Sally was sent instead!

But Helmuth a Commissar! I would never have suspected that. And what a field of speculation it opened up about the real activities of the Brotherhood!

When I had had a moment to recover from the bombshell that Deb had so unwittingly thrown, I said to her: 'Did you ever hear anything about occult forces being used by members of the Party to gain their political ends?'

'We are taught to use whatever means we regard as most suitable,' she replied. 'In some cases people who are interested in the occult can be led on through it to do things which they would not like others to know; then they can easily be blackmailed into doing as we wish.'

'But have you ever known a member of the Party actually to practise Black Magic himself?' I asked. 'I mean, one who cast spells, and used incantations to call up evil entities from the other world to help him in his work?'

'Only Dr Lisický,' came the toneless answer. 'He did not tell me very much about it. But I know that the reason he would not allow your blackout curtain to be lengthened, in the room downstairs, was so that the moonlight could continue to show under it. He needed the moonlight as a path for something to come into your room.'

I looked at Sally again, and I knew that as far as she was concerned I now had Helmuth completely in the bag.

Under hypnotic influence Deb had done her stuff, and more; so I woke her and reassured her that I would say nothing to Owen Gruffydd. Then Sally took her downstairs and got rid of her.

When Sally came back she could not have been more generous about not having believed me before; and for a little time I allowed myself the luxury of basking in her sweet sympathy about this ghastly time I have been through. But there is only tonight before Helmuth gets back, so we soon got down to brass tacks and started planning our getaway.

She was all against my idea for getting the wheelchair down the staircase, as she says it would be much too great a strain and might do me serious injury, even if I didn't collapse before we reached the bottom. But after a bit she thought of a better idea.

The far end of the battlement along the terrace is in partial ruin already, and the rest of the stones can easily be pushed over. It is only a fifteen-foot drop to the grass verge beneath, which is about two yards wide, having the chapel on one side of it and the edge of the lake on the other. With a twenty-five-foot rope, or even that length of stout knotted cord, we could take a hitch round the nearest sound castellation of the battlement and lower the chair to the ground.

Fortunately Sally is very strong for a girl, so she is going to take me down the stairs in a semi-piggyback. I'll have my arms round her neck, and my feet dragging, but each time she takes a step down, I'll be able to take my own weight off her for a moment.

There is a side door just down a passage from the bottom of the stairs and we shall go out through that. She will be able to get me along the passage, and round the outside of the Castle to my chair, in the same way as we mean to go down the stairs. We tried it out this afternoon, and found that I could get across the room quite easily that way.

She has gone down to the village again to buy the length of stout cord, and also to order a car to meet us at the bridge at the lake end, at midnight; so she won't have far to wheel me.

I think I can hear her coming up the stairs now; so she has lost no time on the job. What a blessed, merciful relief all this is.

Friday, 19th June
Those footsteps coming up the stairs were Helmuth's. As the door opened and I saw him the thought leapt to my mind that he must be the Fiend in person. Or, at least, that only by Satanic means could he possibly have learned of our plan to escape, and have returned eighteen hours before he was due back in order to prevent it.

Then, thunderstruck as I was by his unexpected appearance, common sense told me that, barely two hours having elapsed since Sally had agreed to help me, he could not have known of it earlier, even by a thought wave; and, if he had stuck to his schedule he would then have been in the train coming south from Carlisle. In so brief a time nothing short of a magic carpet could have whisked him from a station en route, back to Llanferdrack; and I put that beyond what even the Devil could do for his agents in full daylight.

I was right about that, but nevertheless it transpired that his psychic powers had hastened his return. For a moment he stood in the doorway, looking at me searchingly and almost seeming to sniff the atmosphere. Then he said abruptly: 'Well? Have you made your choice?'

Consternation, anger, hatred and fear all struggled for first place in my emotions following the shock; but, by a miracle, I managed to retain enough of my wits to realise that now Sally was on my side all was not entirely lost, and that my one hope was to play for time. So I shook my head.

'No. I've been giving my mind a holiday. The events of the week before you left put such a strain on it that I found I couldn't think coherently; so I decided not even to try to face the question till a few hours before you got back. And you said you wouldn't be back till after lunch tomorrow.'

'I know,' he said; 'but last night I felt an impulse to – er – as you would put it – consult the oracle. The stars were by no means propitious, so the portents proved unusually obscure. That does happen occasionally, even to the most gifted practitioner of the art. However, on one point I received guidance. It was to the effect that my plans might be endangered if I failed to keep you under my personal observation; so I caught the first train south this morning and hired a car to bring me from Birmingham.'

With a shrug of my shoulders I pretended an unconcern that I was far from feeling, and muttered: 'So long as I am kept in this glorified cell with Nurse Cardew and Konrad to act as my gaolers I shouldn't have thought you had much cause to worry.'

'In any case, I haven't now that I am back,' he replied. 'And now that your mind is rested you had better do a little serious thinking.'

That admonition ended his brief visit, and I was left to savour the gall and wormwood of my most promising attempt to escape having been nipped in the bud.

I was almost weeping with vexation, but my futile mental rebellion against this unforeseen blasting of my hopes was soon submerged by a specific anxiety arising out of the new situation. The question that made me sweat blood was – would Helmuth run into Sally on her return and find out that she had gone over to me in his absence? If he did he would sack her instantly, and I should never see her again. The thought was torture.

Half an hour after he had left me, that immediate anxiety was relieved by her reappearance. She was flushed with excitement, laughing, a little breathless, and carrying under her arm a brown-paper parcel containing the length of stout cord for lowering the chair. She had not seen Helmuth.

In a few words I told her what had happened. For a bit she was terribly upset – not frightened, but angry and disappointed. Then we discussed the possibility of carrying through our plans, but agreed that Helmuth having returned in such a suspicious mood our chances would be far better if we postponed our attempt for twenty-four hours, anyway.

Before we had time to go into matters further Konrad came in with my dinner, and Sally had to go downstairs to have hers.

While I ate I was again the prey of harrowing speculations. It suddenly struck me that Helmuth was almost certain to learn of Deb's visit. If he tackled me about it, what explanation could I invent that would not involve Sally? And when he tackled her was there one chance in a hundred that her explanation would tally with mine? That passage in our activities was obviously dynamite.

Later, Sally told me that she had been equally perturbed on the same point; but she did not dare to come up to me again till half-past nine, in case Helmuth should suspect that we had been getting together while he was away. She had seen him and reported my attempt to bribe her. That was clever of her, and had gone with a swing, as few things could have been better calculated to convince Helmuth that she still regarded him as her boss and was capable of resisting all attempts to undermine her loyalty to him.

Fortunately he still seemed to know nothing of Deb's visit, as he had not alluded to it. We discussed that, and decided that if he asked Sally about it, she should say that she had met Deb on the bridge on her way up here; that Deb had introduced herself, spoken of her forthcoming marriage, and – as one nurse to another – disclosed the fact that she simply did not know which way to turn to raise the money for her trousseau; and had had the idea of appealing to me either to give or lend her a hundred pounds as compensation for having been the cause of her losing her job. Upon which Sally agreed to let her see me and brought her up here; but what happened at the interview she does not know.

We were rather pleased with the story we concocted, as it covered Sally's having brought Deb to the house, and is really very plausible, since nurses are notoriously ill-paid and Deb, having no family to help her, may well be up against it for cash to buy nice clothes for her wedding.

Sally and I had only just agreed on the above when Konrad came in, and, after the usual drill, they both left me for the night.

I felt terribly tired, as Helmuth's return having baulked me when I was within an ace of getting free had exasperated me almost beyond endurance; and, added to that, I had gone through some four hours of nerve-racking fear that he might find out about Sally's change of attitude and sack her. But that danger seemed over for the moment if we both kept our heads, and it was up to me to make yet another plan; so I endeavoured to shake off my mental fatigue and get to grips with the problem anew.

The results of my effort were lamentably poor. Helmuth had clearly been in a highly suspicious mood on his return, but having found everything as he had left it, and particularly Sally having told him of my attempt to bribe her, must have done a lot to reassure him. So the best I could hope for was that if nothing occurred to cause him to take special precautions, we might have a decent chance of making our escape tonight.

The devil of it is that he will come up this afternoon, or evening, for his answer. I am determined not to give in, but if I defy him there is the dreadful possibility that he may carry out his threat to employ the Great Spider.

God knows how I will ever bring myself to face that fearful Satanic beast, and the touch of it may well drive me insane. But Helmuth must know that, and such a possibility seems to be the only card that I have left. If he *does* drive me insane he will have burnt his boats as far as the short, easy way of getting control of the Jugg millions is concerned. He will get hold of them in the long run, but that will take a considerable time, and an immense amount of skilful intrigue would be required before he could oust the Trustees that might oppose his plans, and achieve absolute control of the Board. Whereas if he can get me to sign a power of attorney he will have achieved complete victory by a single stroke of the pen. So I must play on that. The Sabbath, at which I take it the Brotherhood mean to celebrate a full-scale Black Mass in the chapel here, is not to take place until Tuesday – five nights hence – so I must temporise to the utmost of my ability in the hope of winning another two or three days' grace.

If only I can get him to postpone extreme measures until Sunday or Monday, Sally may be able to get me away before then. But there is no guarantee that he will not issue an ultimatum to me this evening; and as I lay in the dark last night, realising that in another twenty-four hours I might have to face the Great Spider, the thought alone was enough to make me sweat with terror.

It was casting frantically about in my mind for a means to defend myself that made me think of Great-aunt Sarah. What effect, if any, a bullet would have on a supernatural beast I have no idea, but I do know that I would feel considerably more courageous with a firearm in my hand if I am called on to face it.

I doubt if there is a pistol in the Castle, unless Helmuth keeps one somewhere, and, even if he does, it would be impossible to get hold of that; but there must be several shot-guns and ammunition in the gun-room, and it occurred to me that I might get Great-aunt Sarah to bring me one tonight.

In consequence, when I heard her going down the staircase in the wall behind my bed, I rapped on the panel and called her in. After making polite enquiries about the progress of her tunnel, I told her what I wanted her to do for me and, thank God, without even asking me what I meant to do with a gun up here, she readily agreed to my request.

This is a great comfort, as if I don't need the gun tonight I can hide it behind the back of my bed; then I'll have it handy and, in the last event, I'll be able to fill Helmuth full of lead

Later

It rained this morning, so Sally and I were not able to go out onto our terrace as usual; but we had a long talk here in my room. I gave her a full account of Helmuth's conversations with me during the few days before he went away – as I did not let her have the latter pages of my journal when she read the rest of it, because they contained several passages referring to my love for her – so she is now up to date with the whole situation and, thank goodness, she no longer doubts any part of what I told her.

She was, once more, sweetly sympathetic about the hell I have been through, and when I had finished, she said: 'You must have done something pretty frightful in one of your previous lives to be landed with a packet like this; but at least you have the consolation of knowing that you are paying it off, and that whatever happens now you will go forward witn a much cleaner start in the future.'

I looked at her in surprise. 'Do you honestly believe that this is what the Hindus call Karma; and that there really is something in Reincarnation?'

'Why not?' she smiled. 'It is the only creed which provides a logical explanation to any and every human experience; that is, if you believe that the power which created the world, and us, is both intelligent and just – and if you don't believe that, then the whole scheme of things does not make sense.'

'Not to believe it would be to argue that God is an inferior being to men,' I replied; 'so one must.'

'Then if He is intelligent He would not permit the destruction of His property by wars, starvation and disease, pointlessly – or allow us to be the victims of all the other ills that inflict us in this life, needlessly – but only for our own ultimate good as a part of a great pattern. And if He is just, He would not condemn any-body to suffer for all eternity because they had failed to make good in the infinitesimal fraction of a second, which by comparison is all that anyone gets in even the longest of human life-span. However much evil might have been crammed into that single life the punishment would still be out of proportion to the crime; and that is not justice.'

I nodded. 'You're certainly right there. Do go on.'

'You will remember the famous bit in the Bible about the "sins of the fathers" and God venting His wrath on those who had displeased Him "even unto the third and fourth generation". Well, what could be more flagrantly unjust than punishing innocent children for the faults of their grandparents?'

'Yet it happens, in the form of syphilis,' I murmured.

'Of course it does; and lots of children are born with T.B., although there is no taint of sin about their grandparents having caught that. But it doesn't follow in the least that because a child starts life with an hereditary disease it is through God seeking to revenge Himself upon someone who may already be dead. To accept that puts God on a par with a criminal lunatic. But look at it a different way and you'll see that the disabilities with which many children are born result from a just and logical process.'

'Oh, come, Sally!' I cocked an eyebrow at her. 'You're going to find it difficult to make a case for that.'

'Not at all,' she replied quietly. 'I believe that in the course of ages the real meaning of the Bible text became obscured and was then lost altogether. I think it was originally a warning that people who led evil lives would have to pay for it "unto the third and fourth generation" of *their own personalities*. That is, if you take it that each time our spirit is reborn in a new body we *inherit* the mental and physical disabilities – and, of course, all the good things too – that are due to us as a result of the good or ill that we did in our previous lives. If, in one life, a man forces some poor girl into prostitution with the result that she contracts syphilis, and in the next he is born with it himself, you wouldn't consider such a punishment either illogical or unjust, would you?'

'You've certainly made your case,' I smiled. 'But does the punishment always fit the crime?'

'Always. It is never a fraction more or less than you deserve.'

'How about my back; what do you think I did to deserve that?'

'It may be that you were due to learn patience as a cripple; or simply that the Nazi was paying off an old score, because long ago you had broken his back with a battleaxe, or something.'

'Then will I have to break his again in some future life, to punish him in his turn? It seems a stupid game to go on playing tit for tat like that through all eternity.'

'Oh no. You will be given the chance; and if you care to take it you will be in the clear, as you are entitled to give back what you get. But not a fraction more, mind. And if you are wise you will refrain from taking your revenge. It is by suppressing one's anger, and turning the other cheek, that one achieves spiritual progress.'

'If I did that he would get off.'

Sally shook her head. 'No, he wouldn't. If you denied yourself the temporary gratification of sloshing him, he would still have to pay up for having sloshed you; but it would be through some other agency. He might have his back broken in a mine disaster, or by some scaffolding falling on him while he was walking down a street. If you *did* break his back first you are now even, on the old eye-for-an-eye and tooth-for-a-tooth principle, so he has nothing to worry about; but if this was the first round between you he has got it coming to him in some form or another.'

'How about the other thing? These hideous ordeals that Helmuth has inflicted on me?'

'I think it's pretty certain that you must have put up rather a special black to have earned those.' She smiled a little wickedly. 'Until people learn that it does not pay they are always exchanging blows of one kind and another – and a lie which does harm, or doing anyone an ill-turn of any kind, is just as much a blow as an actual slap in the face – but this is something different. I can only suppose that at some time or other you must have been a powerful Black Magician yourself, and have caused a great deal of misery and terror by your evil practices.'

'That sort of thing hardly goes with wielding a battleaxe,' I demurred.

She shrugged. 'One does not pay all the debts contracted during one life off in the next; but one may settle old ones from several lives during one short period. That is probably what you have been doing recently.'

'If you are right, where does all this lead to?'

'It fits us for a higher sphere. We all start here on a very low level, as cruel, superstitious, barbarous savages. Gradually we learn this and that – to be gentle, generous, courageous in the right way, unselfish, wise, and to exercise control over all our appetites and passions. Eventually we become really fine people; we may live our last life on earth as great religious teachers, or pass it in comparative obscurity doing a great deal of good – it is quite immaterial which – but when we have learnt all there is to learn here we join the great ones who have preceded us.'

'What happens if we fail to progress, or get worse and worse with each life we lead?'

'That is impossible. If we are pig-headed, and ignore all the sign-posts that point the way to our becoming better people, progress will be slow; and if we give free rein to our baser instincts we slip back a bit. That is a bore, as it may mean having to go through several extra lives before the lost ground is regained. But everyone realises their faults sooner or later and makes a determined effort to eradicate them. Even an animal has the sense not to keep on getting itself hurt in the same way over and over again.'

'What part do animals play in all this? You said just now that we all start as low types of human beings, but some religions teach us that souls have their origin in much humbler forms of life.'

'No. Mankind is a different and higher form of creation than anything in the animal world. We are individuals; they are not, so they have only group-souls.'

The word 'group-souls' instantly brought to my mind what Hel-muth had said when he was talking to me about totems – the Great Spider, the Great Serpent, and so on. With a quick look at Sally, I said: 'You seem very certain about all this. Where did you get it from?'

She smiled. 'I got it from a book called *Winged Pharaoh* by a woman named Joan Grant. At least that is where I got the basic principles. But somehow it rang such a bell with me that I have since been able to fill in additional little bits and pieces for myself. That is why I am so certain about it. Every other form of faith that I have ever met with has always seemed to me to demand a belief in not only a number of good things, but in all sorts of absurdities as well; whereas this is simply sound common sense.

'Hellfire apart, how could any God who was worthy of respect condemn the most wayward of His children without giving them a second chance? And how can our salvation possibly depend upon anyone but ourselves and our own actions? Going to church may be an excellent form of discipline, and a useful reminder that worldly success has no permanent value; but it is childish to think that any ceremony one attends on Sunday can cancel out meannesses, cruelties and betrayals committed during the week.

'We all know what is right and what is wrong without any telling from other people. The still small voice of our own spirit, which has lived with us through all our lives from the very beginning, tells us that. We may not always be strong-minded enough to follow its counsel, but in every crisis of our lives it is an infallible guide, and we need no other.'

Sally paused for a moment, then went on, her face glowing but in a low voice, almost as though speaking to herself: 'This belief of mine also abolishes all fear of death. Naturally as long as our spirits are chained to bodies we all fear the pain that proceeds so many forms of death, but most people seem to dread death itself even more. They are frightened at the idea of being parted from the little securities of family, home and money, that they have built up round themselves during their few years on earth; they are terrified at the thought of their soul going out into the dark empty spaces as a lonely wanderer, until at last it is called on to face some dread Being who will pronounce a final and irrevocable judgement upon it.

'Such thoughts have been instilled into them by generations of ignorant priests, who have blindly followed the teachings of churches that long ago became decadent and lost the light. Death is really a release from trial and hardship. Again and again we are sent here, like children going term after term back to school. Each time in a new body with new surroundings; sometimes as men, sometimes as women, sometimes to be rich and sometimes to be poor; we are given an allotted span of days and set certain tasks to learn in them.

'We have free-will and we can cut short that span in a variety of ways. If we do we only have to make it up by going through another part-life, as an infant or child who dies while still young. But we cannot increase the span by a single instant, whatever we may do. When the term is over we may go home with a bad report or a good one, and any trials that we have shirked we shall have to face again later on.

'But death is a holiday; and between our lives here, while our spirits are no longer imprisoned in a dull and heavy body, we are infinitely more fully our real selves, and have a far greater capacity for understanding and enjoyment.

'Unlike a school curriculum down here, the holidays are usually longer than the terms. As we have free-will we may decide that we wish to be born again almost at once, for some special purpose; but more often it is two hundred years or so before we feel impelled to enter on another trial; so it follows that a greater number of the friends we have made in many lives are always away from earth than on it, so we have the joy of being with them again. In what we call Life we are really only half alive, but constantly beset by troubles, sometimes by ill-health and often lonely; whereas what we call Death is really living to the full, without material worries or physical handicaps, and being happy in the company of those we love.'

Later

I had to break off because Helmuth came in. He mentioned Deb's visit at once, and to my great relief I learnt that Sally had already sold him our story; so I had only to add that since I had no money I had had to refuse Deb's request.

He then produced a lengthy legal document and said: 'Tomorrow is your birthday, Toby, and your signature to this document then will make it a fully valid legal instrument. Are you prepared to sign it?'

'I certainly won't until I've had a chance to study its contents,' I hedged.

He nodded, quite amiably. 'I thought you would say that; so with a view to avoiding unnecessary delays tomorrow I propose to give it to you now. You will have plenty of time to read it through this evening.'

I took it, but made no reply, as there seemed nothing to be said.

After a moment he went on: 'You have put up a good fight, Toby, and I admire you for that. It makes me all the keener to have you become one of us. You have brains and guts, so there is a great future for you in the Brotherhood. But it is both useless and dangerous for you to fight further. So don't try to back out tomorrow; because if you do I really shall have to turn on the heat – and you'll find that all you have experienced to date was only child's play compared with this next step. Instead, I want your birthday to be a happy one, marking the beginning of an entirely new treatment by which I believe we'll soon have you well again.'

As it is of the first importance that, for tonight at least, he should go happily to bed, believing that I am at the end of my resources and about to give in, I raised a smile and murmured my thanks. Then he left me.

So, without any effort on my part, I have gained the twenty-four-hour respite that I needed so desperately. It seems at last the 'Great Ones', as Sally calls them, have listened to my prayers.

Reverting to the fascinating conversation I had with her this afternoon. We talked a lot more about her beliefs, and they certainly ring a bell with me too. The more one thinks about them the sounder they seem. All the intolerable stupidities and injustices of mankind, which make so many people doubt the existence of a God, are explained by them. And if one accepts it that all the misfortunes and set-backs with which we meet are not blind, ugly chance, but obstacles to be surmounted from which lessons can be learned, and tests of our fortitude and courage, the struggle of life takes on a real meaning and becomes a great adventure.

She confirmed my own belief, too, that no-one is ever given a trial that is beyond his capacity to bear; and that, in conjunction with all she said about death not really being Death at all, but a return to a fuller, happier Life, makes me feel now as if I were encased in a suit of shining armour.

Sally is a wonderful person. What would I not give for her to feel for me one-tenth of what I feel for her; but to have won her friend-ship is in itself a triumph and a benediction.

Before we parted she agreed that we dared wait no longer, but must make our bid for freedom tonight. She went off to bicycle down to the village and order the car to be at the bridge again. Our worst fear was that Helmuth might send the Great Spider to me, and thus wreck everything at the last moment; but we decided that we must chance that. Mercifully that fear has since been removed; so I have great hopes now that on my birthday morn Sally will give me the splendid gift of freedom.

Later

I hardly know how to write it. This afternoon I was full of a splendid new courage; now I am near to tears. Sally is to dine with Helmuth.

She met him on her return from the village, and came straight up to tell me. I implored her not to; but she said that she must, otherwise he would become suspicious that I had prejudiced her against him while he was away, and that might put all sorts of ideas into his head – especially after she had allowed Deb to see me during his absence, about which, it seems, he spoke to her rather sharply.

I have never before dared to broach the subject of her last dinner with him, from fear she would resent it. But I did this evening.

She shrugged and said: 'It wasn't particularly pleasant, and, of course, you were right about him. He played his cards skilfully enough not to be offensive, but I soon saw which way the wind was blowing. That's why I got tight. I hate getting tight, as it al-ways makes me feel frightful the next day. But it seemed the best thing to do.'

I stared at her in amazement. 'Do you really mean that you delib-erately got tight so that you shouldn't care what happened?'

'Certainly not!' she retorted with a sudden flash of anger. 'You must have a very poor opinion of me to think that. If you want to know the truth, I am still a virgin; and I have not the least intention of throwing my shoes over the moon until my own good time – and then it will be with a man that I really love. But if you had ever tried to make love to a girl who is drunk you would know that it is neither easy nor pleasant – particularly when she ends up by being sick in your immediate vicinity.'

Her outburst both confounded and cheered me; and, blushing at the awful gaffe I had made, I muttered: 'I'm sorry, Sally. That was darned clever of you; but, all the same, I'm afraid he won't let you get away with that sort of thing a second time.'

'I don't expect him to,' she agreed frankly. 'And I am not looking forward to this evening's party one little bit. But I'll get by somehow. It may make me late in coming for you, but that can't be helped; and if the man with the car has given up and gone by the time we get to the bridge, I'll have to push you a bit further, that's all.'

'Oh, Sally!' I begged. 'Please, please don't dine with him. He is capable of any dirty trick. He may put a drug in your wine or try to hypnotise you.'

She shook her head. 'He won't do either. When he warned me against your attempting to hypnotise me I told him that an expert had tried it on me once, and failed completely, showing that I'm not a good subject. And in view of what happened before, I have an excellent excuse this time for refusing to drink anything.'

'All the same,' I argued desperately, 'he is horribly clever at getting his way with women, and absolutely ruthless. I implore you to pretend you are ill, or something, and cut it out. Even at the best it will mean your going through an absolutely beastly time for several hours, and if he gets really wrought up it may end in your having actually to fight him.'

Suddenly she stooped over my bed and kissed me lightly on the forehead, then she gave me a wan smile. 'Don't worry, Toby. Try not to think about it. And remember; none of us is ever given a trial that it is beyond our capabilities to bear. So help will be sent me if I really need it.'

I think the fact that she gave me that sisterly kiss makes things even worse. But Great-aunt Sarah should bring me that gun tonight. And if I learn tomorrow that Helmuth has hurt a hair of my darling Sally's head, I swear to God I'll kill him.

Saturday, 20th June
I am at my wits' end. Sally did not come last night. God alone knows what that swine did to her.

I have been awake all night, turning and twisting in the most frantic agony of anxiety that any man can ever have known. I am scribbling this by the early light, and I've got to get through another two hours yet before they come to call me. Till then I'll have no means of knowing if Sally's non-appearance was owing to an eleventh-hour decision by her that circumstances rendered any attempt to escape last night being doomed to failure, or if the poor darling was *in no state* to come to me.

Dante knew nothing about Hell.

Later

When I attempted to eat my breakfast, I was physically sick from rage, grief and impotence. It was knowing that my last surmise about Sally is correct.

Konrad came in to call me at the usual hour; but to my consternation Sally did not appear. When I asked him where she was, he said that she had been taken ill last night, and he understood that she would not be well enough to get up today.

That can mean only one thing. She must have used her wits to stall Helmuth off as long as she could, then dug her toes in. He is not used to prolonged opposition from women, and her resistance must have eventually made him see red. He has all the servants under his thumb, and whatever she said afterwards she would never be able to prove anything against him. He must have got really tough, and her being in bed today is the result of his vile brutality.

And I am tied here; unable to help or comfort her; unable even to lift a finger in her defence. I only wish I had the means to kill Helmuth. I'd like to shoot him in the stomach and watch him writhing in agony on the floor. But I haven't yet got that gun. Greataunt Sarah passed the panel near my bed without stopping, and I had to rap hard on it to call her back. The poor old nitwit had forgotten all about my request; but she promised to bring me a gun tonight. I only hope this second time of asking impresses it more strongly on her mind.

In the meantime I am tied here. I can do nothing against Helmuth unless he is stupid enough to come within my reach. I have no means of finding out how things are with my poor, sweet Sally. I cannot even send her a message.

Later

While I still have the sanity to do so, I wish to record that this, my twenty-first birthday, has been the most ghastly day of my whole life.

For years I have always visualised it as a day of joy, gaiety and rejoicing. Not for myself alone, but for the many thousands of people who are concerned in it. I saw it as a carnival of flowers, music, dancing, wine, and toasts to the long-continued prosperity of everyone – man, woman and child – who are connected with the Jugg enterprises. I expected many gifts, but I meant infinitely to surpass them by what I returned to my people in bonuses, special grants and unexpected pensions.

The war, and my having been rendered *hors de combat*, rendered the broad picture impossible of full realisation; but it might still have been a day of smiles and happiness. Instead it has been rendered a nightmare through that fiend Helmuth.

As it was, after my long hours of full and hideous wakefulness all through the night, I dozed a little in the mid-morning. But for the rest of the day my mind has never ceased to be harrowed by thoughts of Sally.

I have had no word from her, and Konrad could, or would, tell me nothing. I dared not ask him to take a message to her from me, as he would have carried it straight to Helmuth; and I still feel that it is imperative to conceal our friendship.

Just after I had finished my dinner Helmuth came in. Again, I did not dare challenge him openly about her; but I asked him at once what had prevented her from being on duty for the whole day.

He shrugged his broad shoulders, and gave his maddeningly sphinx-like smile. 'Our evening did not go quite so smoothly as I expected. She had a fall, in which she bruised herself and hurt her ankle. That's what has kept her in bed today; but it is nothing serious; and she will soon be about again. Anyhow, we have more important things to talk of this evening.'

That told me nothing. I did not believe his story of her having had a fall, for an instant; although she might easily have been badly bruised during the sort of attack in which I had good reason to believe she had been the victim. My hands clenched spasmodically beneath the sheets, and I had to lower my eyes to prevent his seeing the blazing anger in them. To have disclosed my feelings about her might have led him to suspect that I have told her what is going on here, and that she believes me. If he thought that it would bring her into grave danger.

He shook his mane of white hair back, and went on: 'Had we not decided to postpone the celebration of your birthday till next month, I should have come up earlier to offer you my congratulations on attaining your majority. But I have been particularly busy all day making arrangements for the ceremony on the twenty-third; so I thought I would leave it till this evening to bring you my unofficial birthday greetings. You will have read the document that I brought you yesterday. It remains only for you to sign it. Then we will hold a little private celebration. I have told Konrad to bring up a bottle of champagne that has been on the ice for a couple of hours, when he comes to take away your dinner-tray.'

On that score I was, at last, able to let myself go. Taking the document from my bedside table, I said: 'I haven't read this and I'm not going to. As for signing it, I'll see you damned first, you filthy, bloody Communist!' Then, exerting all the strength of my hands, I tore the tough paper through and through and flung the pieces at him.

He went pale with anger and snapped: 'I have another copy, and you shall sign that, yet. How did you know that I am a Communist?'

Throwing caution to the winds, I shouted: 'Your wretched cat's-paw, Deb, told me. When she was here on Thursday I put her in a trance again; and I got the whole disgusting truth out of her. You are a Commissar, acting under orders from Moscow, and you have been trying to get my money to finance a Communist revolution in Britain.'

His rock-like, leonine face broke into a fiendish grin that showed his eye-teeth gleaming ferociously, and his perfect colloquial English suddenly took on the heavy foreign accent that now reappears only when his emotions get the better of him. With all the fervour of a fanatic he flung at me: 'You miserable young fool! Since you now know so much you may as well know the rest. I am a Communist, yes; but only for a purpose. That you may the better appreciate all that you have lost by rejecting my offer to make you a member of the Brotherhood I will reveal to you the shape of things to come.

'Socialism is the easy slope which opens natural citadels to capture by Communism. The suppression of freedom which goes with all control of industry, and the nationalisation of public services, is the royal road to Totalitarianism. It gags and binds all individual opposition, while placing all power in the hands of a small group of politicians and highly placed civil servants. Then, it requires only secret infiltration of Communists into those key posts for the fruit to be ripe for the picking.

'In this country, when the word is given a *coup d'état* will take place overnight. The troops, the police, the B.B.C. and every department of State will be brought under control within a few hours. And the stupid British are so law-abiding that they will never question the orders of their *legal* superiors until it is too late.

'But to provoke a situation in which this country will accept a Communist *coup d'état* without a general uprising it will be necessary first to discredit the Socialist Government. Strikes, sabotage and the skilful manipulation of money will be used to bring about industrial and financial chaos. The Jugg millions are required by us to assist in that. The deterioration in the standard of living will condition the people to accept a stronger form of Government as their only hope. The ground for the *coup d'état* will be so carefully prepared that, when it does come, the average British citizen will regard it only as a welcome break from the tyranny of an outworn semi-dictatorship by the Trades Unions, and not even suspect that by it his country has finally lost the last shadow of independence.

'Britain will become a bond slave of Moscow, and the unorganised masses will be powerless to lift a finger to prevent it. A few scattered individuals – officers, judges, politicians, professional and business men, and Trade Union leaders – may realise what is happening, and that it is the end for them. But we shall know how to deal with such reactionaries. The opening of their mouths will be the signal for us to close them for good. It will all be very quiet and orderly, as suits this country. A few hundred people will be removed from their homes by night, and the opposition will be left leaderless.

'But that is not all. That is not the end; it is only a stage in the programme of the Brotherhood. Communism is the perfect vehicle for the introduction of the return of Mankind to his original allegiance. It already denies Christianity and all the other heresies. It denies the right of free-will and the expression of their individuality to all those who live under it. Communism bows down only to material things; and my real master is not Stalin but the Lord of Material Things; Satan the Great, the Deathless, the Indestructible.

'The priests of the decadent Churches, the pathetic modern intellectuals, and our little scientists who fiddle with power on the lowest plane, no longer believe in the existence of my master. Or at the most regard him as having been so idle as to become a nonentity during the past century, just because he has held his legions in check from manifesting themselves openly.

'But he has been far from idle. He saw in this movement, to give the most stupid and lazy equality with the most brilliant and active, a means to recover his sovereignty over all. He saw that if the masses could be induced to destroy their natural protectors they would be left as corn before his wind. Therefore he bent his whole energies to the fostering of Communism all over the world. He has taken the very word Communism as his new name, and he even mocks those who no longer believe in his existence by having them demonstrate in favour of rule by the Proletariat on the first of May. Have you never realised that that is *his* anniversary, and that it is born of May Day Eve – on *Walpurgis Nacht* – on which we celebrate *his* festival?

'The true Millennium is approaching. When the war is over Hitler's Europe will fall into chaos. It will be a forcing-ground for the rapid spread of Communism. Britain will be compelled to give India her so-called freedom. That will result in civil war and anarchy overwhelming a population of three-hundred-and-fifty million people; so the triumph of Communism is inevitable there. China's four-hundred-and-fifty million will be left hopeless and starving; but her great neighbour, Soviet Russia, will see to it that she is set on the right path. When Britain succumbs, her Dominions and Colonies will soon follow; and with three-fourths of the world under the red flag, the United States will not be able to stand out for long.

'So the glorious day is approaching when, through the agency of Communism, my master, the Ancient of Days, the Archangel Lucifer, the Prince of This World, will at last enter into his own again.'

After this long and horrifying revelation, Helmuth paused for a second, his yellow eyes gleaming like those of a great cat, then he added: 'You were offered what would have amounted to a Governorship in the hierarchy which will rule the new Satanic world; but you have had the folly and temerity to reject it. Tonight I shall send a Prince of the House of Satan, the Great Spider, to you. He could have been your patron and ally, and even at times your servant, to destroy others at your bidding; but he must come now as your enemy. You have brought this terrible thing upon yourself, and will have only yourself to blame if, through it, you become a poor mad creature, who for years to come screams with fear at the sight of the smallest spider or even its shadow.'

Sunday, 21st June

In the past ten hours I have been the plaything of such violent emotions that my mind is still reeling under their impact. Setting them down may help to reassure me that the thing which over-whelmed me really happened.

To get the whole picture in proper perspective I had better continue this record from where I left off.

Helmuth's fearful disclosures – *that the Devil's new disguise is Communism, and that for the past century he has devoted all his energies to wearing this dark cloak with which to blanket for ever the free-will of mankind* – kept him with me barely twenty minutes.

After his final threat he turned away to leave me, but almost collided with Konrad in the doorway. Helmuth had probably forgotten that in anticipation of his victory he had ordered up champagne. With a cynical smile he told Konrad to leave the bottle with me, as I might 'need it in the night'. Then they both went downstairs.

To keep my thoughts off the ordeal ahead of me I spent the next hour and a half writing the last entry in my journal. At ten o'clock Konrad returned, settled me down and removed my lamp.

It was a fine night, the moon was up and threw the pattern of the grating on the floor; but only faintly, as the late summer twilight still lingered and reduced its power.

Gradually, as the last light of day disappeared outside, the big oblong with its criss-cross of black bars grew brighter. I tried not to look at it, dreading what I might see, and endeavoured to comfort myself with my last remaining hope.

I thought it unlikely that the Evil would appear much before midnight and at eleven o'clock Great-aunt Sarah would be going down to her tunnel. I prayed, as I have never prayed before, that she would not have forgotten again her promise to bring me a gun.

At last I heard her footsteps, and I rapped sharply on the panel. It slid back and she stepped out into the room. With an awful sinking of the heart I saw that she was not carrying the weapon. Her poor old mind is evidently incapable of retaining any thought permanently, except that of rescuing her lover from the Lady of the Lake.

For a moment I thought of trying to keep her with me, but I realised that would have been a futile as well as a wicked thing to do; so I let her go off to the strange task that will end only when she becomes bed-ridden, or at her death.

My hopes of obtaining the shot-gun having been dashed, I cast about for the next best thing with which to defend myself. The reflection from the moonlight now lit the room faintly, and on glancing round my eye lit on the bottle of champagne. Failing a fire-arm or a cutlass few things could have suited my purpose better. The tapering neck of the bottle offered a perfect handhold, and its weight made it a first-class club. As my fingers closed over the gold foil I blessed Helmuth for his cynical gesture in leaving it with me.

Between my prayers I thought a lot about Sally, and the wonderful new faith that she had given me. Without it I doubt now if I would have had the courage to defy Helmuth. Somehow, having to face the ordeal took on a new aspect, as if what I had to go through was the paying off of an old debt that I had contracted during a life when I was myself a servant of Evil, or a test of courage which, if I passed it, would give me a step up the ladder of progress. I was very far from being unafraid, but I now felt that there was a definite limit to what either man or Devil could do to me; and that those friends of the long journey, of whom Sally had spoken, who were at present untramelled with bodies, were watching over me and would see to it that no permanent harm befell my spirit.

I tried to keep my thoughts off the Great Spider, but despite my efforts they kept reverting to it; and one thing that puzzled me greatly was the nature and consistency of my enemy. There could be no doubt that it was a Satanic entity and, since it came from another plane, it could have no *real* being here. Therefore, it seemed to follow, from what little I knew of supernatural manifestations, that it could be seen and, perhaps, heard, but not felt. If that was so, then I had little to fear, except the horror inspired by being forced to look at a terrifying and repulsive beast. And if I *knew* that it could not touch me or harm me there was really no reason to be afraid. On the other hand, Helmuth had spoken of it materialising, and having to sustain its *body* on blood and excrement; which definitely implied that at times it had the power to transform itself into a ferocious animal capable of biting and tearing at a victim with its strong, spear-pointed legs. So I did not know what to think.

Again, if it was only a form of spectre it would find no difficulty in passing through walls, or a pane of plate-glass; yet it had obviously been incapable of getting at me through the courtyard window. Alternatively, if it had a solid body, surely the same factor would prevent its getting at me up here as had prevented it from doing so downstairs. The grating through which I can look down into the chapel from my room has no glass in it; but the mesh of criss-cross bars make the open squares between them far too small for a brute even one-tenth of the size to squeeze itself through.

For a time I strove to draw what comfort I could from the assumptions that if it was a spirit form it could not harm me, and if it had a physical body it could not get in; then another idea came to me.

Perhaps it would come through the grating or the wall in its spirit form, and materialise a body for itself when it was inside the room. Yet Helmuth had said that it needed rotting offal, and such things, from which to form an envelope of flesh, and there was nothing of that kind here, except – yes, the thought was horrifying, but he had mentioned blood – my own blood.

With a shudder, I tried to thrust from my mind the appalling picture of myself lying there in bed, striking wildly with the champagne bottle at an intangible form which yet seemed to smother me, and gradually became a semi-fluid substance like reddish black treacle as it sucked at a vein in my neck.

I countered that unnerving vision by arguing that if it could enter and materialise in such a manner here, it could have done so equally well down in the library. But then again, perhaps, in those early stages of my 'conditioning', Helmuth had held it in check, whereas tonight he had no such intention.

My grim speculations got no further. At that moment I heard footsteps on the stairs; the door opened and Helmuth appeared.

I could not see him very clearly, as the moonlight hardly penetrated to that corner of the room, but it shimmered faintly on the strange garment he was wearing, and as he moved forward I saw that it was a ceremonial robe of white satin with a number of large black symbols imposed upon it. The folds of the robe prevented me from making out exactly what they were, but they looked like the signs of the Zodiac. Round his neck he wore a black stole heavily embroidered in gold, and on his head a curiously shaped flattish mitre. In his hand he carried a silver wand, at one end of which there was a crescent moon.

Without a word to me, or a glance in my direction, he walked past the foot of my bed. As he did so I could see the flattish mitre more clearly; it was really a toque of dark fur with two large red jewels in front; it was fashioned to appear like a big spider and the jewels were there to represent eyes.

Holding himself very rigid and moving with slow deliberation, as though he were in a trance, he advanced to the door that gives onto my little terrace, made the sign of the Cross the wrong way round with his wand, then unlatched the door and opened it a fraction.

The question I had been asking myself was answered. He had to assist the Great Spider to materialise itself by some hideous ceremony, and once it had acquired a body it could not pass through material obstacles. He had come up to let it in.

Turning, he walked slowly back towards the door that gives onto the staircase. I did not see him go. My eyes were fixed on the terrace door. At any second I expected to see it open and disclose the beast. As the other door shut behind Helmuth I had a wild impulse to call him back and beg him to spare me; but I managed to suppress it.

If I had not actually seen him unlatch the door to the terrace I would not have known that it was open. But I did know. It was just ajar, and it needed no more than a push of a child's hand for the heavy oak postern to swing slowly inward on its well-oiled hinges.

My hands were clammy as I stared at it, imagining that I could see it moving; but for what seemed an age nothing happened.

Suddenly my heart missed a beat. The door had not moved, but I knew that the beast was approaching. It was three weeks since I had felt that awful sensation, but there was no mistaking it. The perspiration that had already broken out on my forehead now chilled it as though snowflakes were melting there; my breath was coming faster yet catching in my throat, and I had a queasy feeling in my stomach that made me want to retch.

Still the door remained as Helmuth had left it. With the saliva running hot in my mouth I kept my gaze riveted on the old oak boards. The waiting seemed unbearable, and if at that moment I had been able to pray at all, I should have prayed for something – anything – to happen, that would end my agonising suspense.

The night was very still. It was close on twelve o'clock and I knew that all the Castle staff would normally be asleep. But even if any of them were awake and I had screamed for help, shut off as I was and at such a distance from their quarters, they could never have heard me.

All at once the eerie quiet was broken by a faint scuffling noise. The hair on the back of my head rose like the hackles of a dog. I could feel my eyes open wide with apprehension, and my ears seemed to start out from the sides of my head with the intensity of my listening.

The noise came again, louder this time. It sounded as if a boot was being scraped with quick, light jerks against rough stone. I still had my eyes fixed unswervingly upon the door; but a sudden flicker of movement just outside my line of vision caught my attention. Jerking my head round, I stared at the checkered patch of moonlight on the floor. Part of an all too familiar shadow sprawled across it. Slowly I raised my eyes; then I saw the beast itself.

It was peering through the left hand lower corner of the grating at me. I could not see the whole of it; only about three-quarters of the body, the head and parts of several legs, one of which was fully extended above it and measured more than the length of my arm. Its body was fat and furry; its legs thick, sinewy and covered with sparse stiff hairs each about two inches long. As it clung there, silhouetted against the bright moonlight that was now streaming through the grille, I could see every detail of its outline; but its face was obscured by shadow, and all I could distinguish of that were two reddish eyes, glowing luminously.

The room was now ice-cold, and filled with an appalling stench. There flashed into my mind a temporary morgue that I had once had to visit, where bomb-torn bodies were being preserved for identification on blocks of ice. The atmosphere was very similar, except that there the smell of putrefaction had been partially obscured by iodoform, whereas here it came undiluted in sickening waves from the pulsing body of the beast.

After a second it shifted its position. The movement was so swift that I only glimpsed its action. One nimble sideways slither and it was still again, spreadeagled right in the middle of the grating.

I was no longer capable of any coherent thought. All I could do was to keep muttering 'This is it! This is it!' while my brain subconsciously absorbed certain physical facts about the Horror.

It was as big as a fully fledged vulture. Its skin and hair were black, but splotched here and there with patches of a leprous-looking greyish-white. It could easily have torn a cat limb from limb or made mincemeat of a hound. But there seemed no animal, short of the elephant, hippopotamus and rhino to whom the beast would not have proved a formidable opponent. Even a lion might have found himself bested by such a beast, had it sprung upon his back and, while he roared impotently, clung there, gnawing its way into his liver.

Suddenly it began its devil-dance, scampering to and fro across the grating. With chattering teeth I watched it; and slowly the fact penetrated to my mind that although it possessed immense physical activity its intelligence must be dull and sluggish. It could see the terrace door through the grille yet it made no attempt to test that way into the room; instead it kept at its frantic blind fumbling to find a means of getting through the iron bars.

For a good ten minutes it continued to leap up and down, back and forth, until I was dizzy with watching it; then, all of a sudden, it dropped from sight.

I was sitting up propped against my pillows, the champagne bottle gripped in one hand and my heavy silver cigarette box in the other. For a moment or two I remained with every muscle tensed, then I relaxed a little. The room was still very cold, and the stink of rotting offal remained strong in my nostrils; but I was beginning to have just a flicker of hope that Helmuth's plan had miscarried, and that I might yet come through unharmed – unless he had some means of communicating with, and directing, his foul emissary. I think now that must have been so.

It is impossible to estimate time with any accuracy in such circumstances. It may have been three minutes, it may have been ten, after the brute had dropped from sight, that I heard the scraping noise again. This time it came from out on the terrace.

I shuddered, swallowed hard, and tensed myself. The scraping grew louder; then there came a faint tapping, which might have been made by the brute's pointed feet. My eyes were starting from their sockets as they stared at the door. Slowly it was pushed open.

The door swung back without a sound, and there in the entrance stood the monster. Now that it was no longer between myself and the moonlight I could see it plainly. It stood a good two-foot-six from the ground and shimmered with a faint reddish radiance of its own It appeared to have no neck and its head was sunken, like that of a hunchback, into its obese body. Under a low, vulture-like forehead the two fire-bright eyes glared at me malignantly. Instead of the beak I had expected, its mouth was a horrid cavity surrounded by fringed gills, that constantly twitched and exuded a beastly brownish saliva.

In spite of the cold the sweat was pouring off me. I knew that in another moment this awful creature – a devil out of hell in the form of a gargantuan insect – would be upon me. But Sally's assurance, that none of us are ever given a trial to bear that is beyond our capabilities, came back to me, and strengthened my determination to fight the brute to the last gasp.

Something outside myself suddenly warned me that the monster was just about to spring. With all my force I hurled the cigarette box at it.

The box caught it full and square on the body, just below its slavering mouth. Even in that moment of terror I found myself observing the curious effect of my missile with surprise and interest. It did not go through the brute, as it would have through a spectre; nor did it land with a bump and then fall to the floor, as it would have on striking a flesh-and-blood animal. It seemed to sink right into the furry mass just as though I had thrown it at a great lump of dough. And the impact had some effect, as the beast wobbled uncertainly on its spindly legs, then backed a couple of paces.

I had no other missile in reach that was heavy enough to be of any value; so gasping out a pray for help, I transferred the bottle to my right hand and grasped it firmly by the neck.

It took me only a few seconds to do so, and in that time the monster had recovered. It sidled forward again to its previous position and gathered itself to spring. At that instant my prayer was answered.

I heard the staircase door open. There came the rush of flying feet, and I saw Sally race past the end of my bed. Without a tremor of hesitation she flung herself against the terrace door and slammed it to.

The beast had been half in, half out, of the open doorway. The impact threw it back onto the terrace, but the door closed so swiftly that it caught and cut off the lower part of one of the brute's legs. Sally, her eyes distended from the awful thing she had seen, and her breath coming quickly after her valiant effort, had turned, and was standing with her back against the door staring at me.

By her feet I could see the severed leg. It seemed to have a vile life of its own, and was wriggling like a snake; but I had seen too much during the past quarter of an hour to feel any surprise when it flattened itself into a ribbon and slid under the door to rejoin its monstrous owner on the terrace.

For what seemed a long time Sally and I said nothing. Both of us were rendered speechless from horror of the Thing we had just seen, and fear that it would yet manage to get at us. It must have been a good two minutes before we recovered sufficiently to feel that the stout oak door was really a strong enough barrier to keep it out.

At last Sally whispered: 'Are – are you all right?'

'Yes!' I gulped. 'But you? Oh, Sally, I love you so much! I've been in agony about you for the past twenty-four hours.'

She left the door and, coming over, stood beside my bed. 'Do you really mean that?' she asked slowly.

I nodded. 'Yes. I didn't mean to tell you that I loved you. It just slipped out in the stress of the moment. But I do – terribly. You won't mind my loving you, will you? I promise faithfully that I won't make a nuisance of myself.'

'No,' she said, and her voice seemed rather flat, 'I'm sure you won't make a nuisance of yourself; and I won't mind your loving me – not a bit.'

She was standing with her back to the moonlight, so her face was in shadow; but she turned it a little away from me, and then I saw that she was crying. The light glinted on a large tear running down her cheek.

'Sally!' I exclaimed. And I reached out and took her hand. As I did so, she openly burst into tears, crumpled up, and practically fell into my arms.

For a moment I thought that she was still frightfully overwrought from the sight of that fearsome beast; but as she clung to me she laughed a little hysterically between her sobs, and murmured: 'I won't *mind* your loving me! How could I *mind*? Oh, Toby! Haven't you guessed that I – I'm terribly in love with *you*?'

Over her shoulder I had been keeping an anxious eye on the door, but it was fast shut and no sound came from beyond it; so at those marvellous words of hers I ceased to think of the terror outside, and our mouths met in a succession of long, sweet kisses.

A little later she told me she had believed that I thought her both plain and stupid; to which I was able to reply truthfully that her dear face aroused a tenderness in me that I had never felt for any other woman, and that I *knew* her to have more real wisdom than any woman *or* man that I had ever met.

She still seemed to think it astonishing that I should have fallen in love with her, but I said that the boot was on the other foot; and that, anyhow, it was the most rotten luck on her to have developed those sort of feelings for a cripple.

'Why?' she asked. 'There is nothing wrong with you apart from the fact that you can't walk, and that does not make the slightest difference to your personality.'

'Perhaps not,' I said a little sadly. 'And I'm immensely grateful for this present blessing of your love; but I won't be able to keep it, because I can't ask you to marry me.'

She turned her head and peered at me in the moonlight. 'Does that mean that you are secretly married already and have a wife hidden away somewhere?'

'Good lord, no!' I exclaimed. 'But I couldn't ask a girl like you to tie yourself to a cripple for life. It wouldn't be fair.'

'Would you' – she squeezed my hand hard – 'would you, Toby, if you were strong and well?'

I smiled up at her. 'Of course I would. I've had quite a number of affairs, but I've never before met a girl that I really loved. You've read my journal, so you know that's true. And now I have, it's only natural that I should want her to be mine for keeps.'

She nodded; then, after a moment, she said: 'I shouldn't have asked that. It was my beastly vanity that urged me to. Please try to forget it. I feel awfully touched and honoured by what you said; and I'd like you to know that your being a cripple has nothing whatever to do with it. I would marry you tomorrow if it were only that; but well or ill, if you did ask me, I'm afraid I would have to say no.'

'Why?' I asked a trifle belligerently; then I added with an attempt at lightness that I did not feel: 'Perhaps you've got a husband tucked away somewhere?'

'No, it's not that. It's just that you are far too rich.'

'Too rich!' I echoed. 'What on earth has that to do with it?'

'A lot,' she replied seriously. 'When I do marry I want it to be someone who will really stick to me. I don't mean that I'd never forgive a slip-up; in fact, human frailty being what it is, I might need forgiveness myself some time – and if I did, I'd expect to get it.

'But I do feel that marriage should be something much more than two people agreeing to legalise a yen for one another, and after living together for a few years accepting it as quite natural that they should take another dip in the lucky tub. That is rather like starting to build a house without bothering to select a firm piece of ground, then abandoning the job halfway because the foundations have turned out to be rotten. I think one should try to make something really fine and enduring of marriage. In fact that it should be a sort of growing together in spirit, so that the joy of it should become greater, instead of less, with the passing of the years.'

'You're right about that,' I said softly, 'just as you are about so many other things. But I still don't see why having a lot of money should prevent two people making the sort of marriage you suggest.'

'Don't you? Well, just think for a minute. Mind, I'm not advocating poverty. That is tragic and hideous, and just as bad the other way. But surely you've noticed that couples who are not very well off generally make a much better thing of marriage than the rich. It is all the little difficulties that they have to overcome in making a home and keeping it together, that act as the cement for the bare bricks of love. When one of them wants something, it is not just a matter of signing another cheque, it means that the other must forego something they would have liked to have had themselves. It is that give and take, the little willing sacrifices, the saving up out of a not very big margin to buy one's love a present, that really binds people together.

'But for the rich it is all too easy. They have their fun while it lasts and then there is nothing left. Their homes are not the centres of their lives, but only beautifully furnished settings which they occupy from time to time when they have nothing more exciting to do. They have few real friends but a legion of acquaintances, so they are always running into new people who may attract them physically, and it is an accepted thing that they should flirt just as lightly as they go to the races or play cards. And almost always one of those flirtations becomes a new craving that they feel they must satisfy at all costs. Money is no obstacle so they get expensive lawyers to arrange matters, and with very little fuss or inconvenience to anyone concerned one more divorce goes through.'

After a little pause, Sally went on: 'It is sweet of you to say that I am beautiful; but I know that I am not. I believe that I am passably good looking; and I think that I could hold my own with most girls who have had my type of upbringing, but I am not in the same class as, for instance, your Aunt Julia. I'm not being catty, either, when I say I wouldn't want to be. It's just that I'm different, and I like my own type best.

'But women like Julia Jugg make an art of beauty, and they bowl men over like ninepins. Just one slinky look from a woman like that will often do something to a man that a girl like myself can't bring off in a month of Sundays, however much she loves him. When you get better, Toby darling, as I'm sure you will, and things are normal again, you will lead the sort of life in which you'll meet dozens of women as beautiful as Julia, only younger; and because you are a millionaire they will all make a dead set at you. Well, I'm not competing. It would break my heart if I tried. That's why I wouldn't marry you, Toby.'

I was silent for a moment. I saw the sound sense of her reasoning, and admired her more than ever for her strength of character in scorning the sort of marriage that most girls would have given their eyes to make. Then I said: 'As I am still a cripple, and likely to remain one for a long time to come, the question does not arise. But if I were fit I'd never rest until I had persuaded you to think differently, as far as I am concerned. I am different, you know, from most young men who have had riches thrust upon them. I am different because my unusual upbringing disillusioned me very early. I know better than most people how utterly empty and worthless easy conquests always prove. You are the first girl that I have ever really fallen for, and I think you are underrating that a bit, by suggesting that a platinum blonde, dolled up in a Schiaparelli outfit and a new shade of lipstick, is all that is needed to make me lose my head.'

'I'm sorry, Toby,' she murmured. 'I didn't mean quite that.'

I kissed her again and made a joke of it. 'Anyhow, if I do get well there is always one way of getting over your objection. I can make all my money over to Helmuth; then we'll take a ten-bob-a-week cottage, where you can scrub the floors and do all the cooking.'

All this time she had been lying beside me on the bed, with her head pillowed on my shoulder. At my mention of Helmuth she broke from my embrace and sat up with a jerk, exclaiming: 'He mustn't find me here! I waited to come to you till I thought he was safely in bed; but as he sent that awful thing tonight he's certain to come up to find out what effect it had on you.'

As he had done so after he sent the legion of small spiders I thought the odds were on her being right, but I said quickly: 'Don't worry, sweet. If he does, you can hide while he is here.'

'Where?' she asked, with an anxious glance round.

'Behind the secret panel that gives onto Great-aunt Sarah's stair-case,' I replied, pointing it out to her. 'But there's another thing. He left the terrace door open slightly, and if he comes up he must find it like that, or open; otherwise, as I couldn't possibly have shut it myself, he'll know that I must have had a human visitor.'

She shuddered. 'I daren't open it again. That – that awful creature may still be out there.'

For the past twenty minutes my every thought had been of Sally, so I had not been conscious of the change in the atmosphere; but now I realised that, although the moonlight still shone brightly through the grille, the air was no longer foul with that awful stench and was once again warm with the balminess of the summer night; so I said: 'The brute has gone. I'm sure of that. It seems extraordinary that simply slamming a door on a powerful Satanic entity should have been enough to drive it off altogether. I should have thought it would have had another go at trying to get through the grating, but your presence seems to have worked a miracle.'

She shook her head. 'If it has gone, it wasn't anything that I did. It was *us*. The saying "God is Love" is true, you know. And the spiritual something we released when we discovered that we loved one an-other must have been terrific. It probably had the same effect on the Horror as its shadow used to have on you; and I wouldn't be surprised if it crept away somewhere to be sick in a corner.'

As far as the beast was concerned her theory sounded highly

plausible, but we did not feel that we could count on it also applying to Helmuth; and if she opened the door and left me there was a chance both that it might return, and that she might run into him on her way downstairs. We decided that she had better remain and we would keep our ears open for sounds of his approach. Then, if he did come up, she could quickly open the terrace door, and get into hiding behind the panel, before he entered the room.

So that no time should be lost I suggested that she should get the panel open. She slid off the bed and, as she stepped forward, gave an 'Ouch!' of pain.

'What is it, darling?' I asked anxiously.

'My ankle,' she explained. 'I sprained it last night. That is why I wasn't able to come up to you all day.'

'So Helmuth wasn't lying about that,' I murmured. 'Last night I was half crazy with worry about you. How did you manage with him?'

She laughed, a little ruefully. 'I overplayed my hand and this is the result. Before dinner I thought out what I meant to do. If a girl has just ricked her ankle badly and is in considerable pain it is just as much out of the question to make love to her satisfactorily as if she is disgustingly drunk. He was as charming and interesting as ever over dinner, and I'm sure he thought that he had really got me going.

'Afterwards we went upstairs to look at his books. That main staircase is so highly polished that it is rather a death-trap anyway. Halfway up I slipped on purpose, pretended to clutch at him, missed and went tumbling down to the bottom. Unfortunately I was wearing high heels, the right one turned over and gave me an awful twinge. It wasn't a case of shamming any longer and in a few minutes it had swollen to the thickness of my forearm. He put a cold compress on it, and offered to help me undress; but I said I could manage all right, and by half-past nine I was safely in bed.'

'That was darned clever of you, darling, but the most filthy luck. Is it still giving you a lot of pain?'

'It is now, rather; as I had to put all my weight on it when I ran across the room to slam the terrace door. Of course, its swelling up like that made it impossible for him to doubt that I really had hurt myself; so I don't think he has the least suspicion that I was deliberately holding out on him; but the infuriating thing is that as long as I can hardly bear my own weight on it I can't possibly get you downstairs on my back; and now that Helmuth is taking extreme measures it is terribly urgent that you should escape.'

As she finished speaking we caught the sound of footsteps on the stairs. Limping a bit Sally ran across the room, opened the terrace door, then ran back and slipped into her hiding-place, sliding the panel to after her. Meanwhile, I quickly disarranged the bedclothes, so that it would look as if a struggle had taken place on the bed, and wriggled down flat with my head lolling over to one side. I let my right arm hang right out of bed and, under cover of a trailing corner of the sheet, I once more grasped the champagne bottle; then I let myself go limp, as if I was unconscious.

I heard Helmuth come in, cross the room to the terrace door and shut it. Then he turned and walked over to my bed. My eyes were a fraction open and I could just see him under my lowered lids. He was still in his ceremonial robes and the moonlight glinted upon the white satin. He spoke to me. I made no reply, so he leant over and shook me.

That was my opportunity. Jerking up my arm I struck at him with the bottle. It did not, as I had hoped, smash in his nose, but caught him on the side of the face. Even so it was a fine bash and may well have cracked his cheek-bone. With a guttural cry he staggered back and fell to the floor.

For a few moments he lay moaning there, then he picked himself up. I had hoisted myself into a sitting position and, still clutching the bottle, was praying that he would come near enough for me to get another swipe at him; but he did not even look at me. With one hand held to his face, he tottered towards the door, fumbled his way out and banged it to behind him.

As soon as the sound of his uneven footsteps had died away I rapped on the panel and Sally came out. From the noises, she had guessed more or less what had happened, and I gleefully gave her details of that marvellously satisfactory come-back on our enemy.

'I can't help hoping that it is hurting him like hell,' she smiled, 'and I think in his case you must have a pretty big margin in your favour; but when you are tempted to hit people in future, don't forget that unless you owe them the blow already the time will come when they'll give it you back.'

'You give me a kiss, and I'll give you that back,' I laughed, and we were in one another's arms again.

Later we opened the champagne and drank it; the empty bottle will still prove a useful weapon.

Sally stayed with me till the moon had gone down and the first light of dawn was coming through the grating. It was an unforgettable night and, from her arrival in my room onwards, would have been one of unalloyed happiness, had it not been that my battle with Helmuth is now rapidly approaching its final crisis, and Sally's ankle makes it impossible for us to get away for another twenty-four hours, at least.

We felt that if she rested all today, the ankle might be well enough for her to get me downstairs tonight, or anyhow tomorrow night, which is the last before the Midsummer Night's meeting of the Brotherhood; but that in the meantime we positively dared not take a chance on her being able to do so, and must take any other measures we could think of which might possibly spike Helmuth's guns.

Naturally my thoughts reverted to Julia and Uncle Paul, and I suddenly realised that now Sally had come over to my side it should not be difficult to get them down here. After our last meeting, and my reconciliation with Helmuth, they would be certain to regard anything I said in a letter to them as the outcome of a worsening of my mental state, so it was most unlikely that they would make an immediate response to an SOS from me. But there was no question about Sally's sanity, so if she got in touch with them and told them it was absolutely imperative that they should catch the first train for Llanferdrack, it was a hundred to one that they would agree to do so.

A letter would take too long, so we agreed that Sally should either telegraph or telephone to Julia as soon as she could today. The trouble is, though, that her ankle makes it out of the question for her to bicycle down to the village; and, as she is officially *hors de combat*, we could think of no reason she could give which would be even remotely plausible for asking for a car to take her there and back. So, unless she has a brainwave, she will have to telephone from the house; and while she is supposed to be sitting in her room with her foot up, it will be far from easy for her to snoop on Helmuth until he leaves the coast clear, without his spotting her.

I very much doubt if Sally's ankle will be sufficiently better for us to make our attempt tonight, but whether it is or not she is going to come up to me a little before midnight, in case Helmuth decides to summon the Great Spider again.

It is now nearly dinner-time and he has not so far been up here today, so I still have no idea if he thinks that my attack on him was the result of his spider driving me frantic, or if he suspects that his abominable scheme broke down in some way and that I simply took the chance that came my way to slosh him.

I hope that his non-appearance can be taken as a sign that the blow

I dealt him has put him temporarily out of action. Anyhow it has spared me further immediate anxieties, and as Sally has not been up here either – apart from Konrad's routine appearances – I have spent the whole day in solitude.

Thank God, once again, for this journal, as writing this long account of my twenty-first birthday night has taken me all day, and has kept me from worrying too much about the possibility of Helmuth catching Sally while she is telephoning to Julia my own still horribly critical situation.

In the past twenty-four hours I have known the extremes of terror and happiness. Strange as it may seem I have already almost forgotten the former in the warm glow from the latter. I can still hardly believe it true that Sally loves me, but my head goes swimmy at the very thought of her sweetness, courage and wisdom. I can hardly bear to wait until she comes to me again.

Monday, 22nd June

Helmuth left me alone last night, but my sweet Sally came in to me about a quarter-to-twelve. As she had not got her outdoor clothes on I knew at once that she had decided that she was not yet up to attempting to get me out. She was using a stick to take the weight off her foot and, as I feared, sufficient time has not elapsed for her ankle to show very much improvement.

Recently Rommel seems to have been having it all his own way in Libya, and the worst news so far came in yesterday. Tobruck has fallen, without any siege at all. Sally told me about it and we talked of the campaign for a few minutes. It seems a terrible thing to have happened when it held out so long and gallantly before. We must have some rotten Generals in Africa now.

After Sally and I had kissed a lot and said many tender things to one another, she told me that she had found it impossible to telephone Julia.

In the morning, soon after the maid had brought in Sally's breakfast tray, Helmuth came to her room. He had a glorious black eye and the rest of the left side of his face was one huge purple bruise. Having briefly explained how he came by his injuries, he asked her to bandage him up.

Thank goodness it did not occur to him to go to her right away, as he would have found the room empty and, if he had waited there, no normal excuse could have explained her absence, as she did not leave me until nearly six o'clock.

Anyhow, she sent him out while she got on a dressing-gown, then greased his hurts and swathed his head in lint. During the process he told her that the waxing moon seemed to be having a worse effect on me than ever, and he had come to the conclusion that the only thing to do was to have me put in a strait-jacket. Then he went on to say that unfortunately he could give no more time to me at the moment, as the 'Ancient Society of Christian Druids' were to meet here on Tuesday, and he still had all the final arrangements to make.

About eighty people are expected and, according to Helmuth's story, a midnight service is to be held in the chapel, after which the congregation will remain to witness the rising of the sun. As the visitors will be up all night none of them will require beds, but accommodation has to be provided for them to change into their ceremonial robes and refreshments to sustain them both on their arrival and before their departure in the midsummer dawn.

No extra staff is being taken on, as they will wait upon themselves; but it is quite an undertaking to get together enough food for such a crowd, and every hire-car for twenty miles around will have to be mobilised to bring them from the station and fetch them again the following morning. So Helmuth, with a very sore jaw, was about to begin a trying day, during most of which he expected to be glued to the telephone.

The Christian Druid idea certainly provides very good cover for this sinister meeting; as Wales was the last refuge of the ancient Druids, and I believe the genuine modern ones still meet at places like Stonehenge and Avebury to watch the rising of the Midsummer Day sun; while the Christian touch gives a plausible reason for their first holding a service in the chapel.

Such villagers as hear about the party will undoubtedly take it to be a form of Eisteddfod, and the small permanent staff here are so completely under Helmuth's thumb that if he orders them to bed at their usual hour none of them would dare to risk staying up with the idea of spying on the proceedings. And, anyhow, if the curiosity of some bolder spirits overcomes their fear of him, they will probably meet with the same type of horrifying experience that I had near the Abbot's grave, at Weylands.

Sally knew that as it was a Sunday there was not much chance of Helmuth going out on estate work, and that had been rendered even less by the battering I had given him. The additional factor that he had all this telephoning to do had decided her that her chance of getting a trunk call through to Kent, without his finding out what she was up to, was pretty near to zero.

However, my Sally is not the type to throw her hand in; so she wrote out a long telegram to Julia, pinned a pound note onto it, and wrote a letter to the local postmaster asking him to send it off at once if he could, or, if regulations forbade sending wires on Sundays, first thing this morning. Then she put the lot in an envelope, addressed it, gave it to the maid when her lunch tray was brought up, and tipped the girl five bob to take it down to the village. As the postmaster is the grocer, and lives above his shop, there can hardly be any hitch about her delivering it to either him or his wife; so by this time Julia should have it.

Sally says her telegram ran to nearly a hundred words, so there is no possibility of Julia misunderstanding it or failing to appreciate its urgency; moreover, it suggested that to satisfy herself fully about my condition it would be a good thing if she and Uncle Paul brought a doctor with them. I feel confident that they will not ignore such an SOS from my professional nurse; so they may be here tonight, or, at all events, not later than midday tomorrow.

My darling Sally had slept all the afternoon, so she was not a bit tired, and we talked until early this morning. She lay on the bed beside me all the time and it was absolute bliss. If only I can get well I swear I'll make her marry me. She is unique, superb, adorable and I am absolutely crazy about her.

Later

All is well. Sally's telegram did the trick. Julia and Uncle Paul arrived shortly after tea. With them they brought a Dr Arling. Helmuth was out when they arrived so they first went to see Sally, then they came up to me.

Uncle Paul looked nervous and unhappy, but Julia was as sweet, competent and sympathetic as ever. Apparently Sally had thought it better not to go into details in front of a strange doctor about Helmuth practising the Black Art; she confined herself to saying that she was convinced that I was 100 per cent sane, and that when I had told them my story she would confirm the essential parts of it.

I felt, too, that it would be asking too much of a completely strange doctor to expect him to believe in the Great Spider at a first inter-view, and that it would only serve to prejudice him unfavourably about the state of my mind. So I told Julia that I would like to have a private talk with her later, to put her *au courant* with what had happened here since her last visit, and suggested that to start with the doctor should put me through a preliminary examination.

'That was what we had in mind, darling,' she agreed. 'Then if Dr Arling finds that Nurse Cardew is right about you, it may not be necessary to bother him with the sort of accusations you made against Helmuth before. We can take you away with us and sort all that out later.'

Such an arrangement suited me all right, and the doctor went ahead. He is a tall, thin middle-aged man with a sharp nose and a big, bulging forehead that gives him the appearance of having an outsized brain. He seemed to know his stuff, too. For nearly an hour-and-a-half he questioned me about my early life, upbringing, habits and appetites; and it was no random questionnaire either, as the whole of the enquiry was aimed at ascertaining my mental reaction in scores of different circumstances.

At length he said: 'You will appreciate, Sir Toby, that most mental aberrations are periodic, so I could not give you a clean bill except after prolonged observation; but your mind does not show any signs of disturbance at the moment. If, while in your present state, you express the wish to be removed from Dr Lisický's care, I feel it that those responsible for your well-being would not be justified in refusing such a request.'

Nothing could have been more satisfactory; for, of course, Uncle Paul and Julia at once agreed, and said that they would take me away with them.

As it was getting on for my bath-time, I asked Julia to come up again when she had finished dinner, so that we could have a heart-to-heart; but she said that after the shock of Nurse Cardew's telegram, the business of having to get hold of a brain-specialist of Dr Arling's status at a moment's notice, and the long journey from Kent, she felt terribly done up. So would I mind very much if she went to bed directly after dinner and we had our chat tomorrow?

Now it is definitely settled that I should leave here with them, there is no longer any great urgency about our going into Helmuth's criminal conduct, so it was decided that she should come up about half-past ten in the morning, and we would have a long session then.

I was simply dying to tell Sally the great news of our triumph, so I asked Julia to give her a message that, if her ankle was well enough, I should very much like her to come up and sit with me after dinner.

Helmuth will be mad with rage when he hears that Sally and I got the best of him after all. He will be still madder tomorrow night when he finds that as the owner of Llanferdrack I have the police here to take the names of all his 'Christian Druids' on arrival, as trespassers; and have forbidden the use of the chapel for their abominations.

Obviously, this is no case in which I can prosecute him for his conspiracy against me. At the moment I can do no more than give him the sack. But I do not mean to let matters rest there. I am determined to hoist his infernal Brotherhood with their own petard. They meant to use my money to foster Communism in Britain, and now I am going to use it to drive them out of the country. I am prepared to spend a million, or more if need be, on the job.

If the police can get me their names for trespassing tomorrow night that will enable me to open a dossier for each of them; and if that fails I can always start my investigation by listing the staff at Weylands. I will employ half-a-dozen detective agencies, all working independently, to watch these people in secret and uncover their private lives. Sooner or later I'll get enough evidence against a number of them to have them brought to trial for blackmail, industrial sabotage, and communicating official secrets to a foreign power; and I'll make things so hot for the rest of them that they will be glad to take refuge with their brother thugs in Moscow.

By the time I've done my stuff I shall be quite content to leave Helmuth to the tender mercies of his Infernal Master. Unless I am much mistaken, for having started all this, the Devil is going to be very, very angry with Dr Helmuth Lisický.

Later

I hardly know how to write this. A terrible thing has happened. One that I would not have believed possible. It has shaken my faith in all humanity.

Sally has just left me and in a few minutes Konrad will be coming up to settle me down for the night. That is why I am scribbling this now. If I don't, and am not able to re-read it in my own writing tomorrow morning, I shall believe that I dreamed it – that it was part of a nightmare – or that I am beyond dispute a madman who is subject to the most ghastly hallucinations. But it happened only a quarter of an hour ago. There is no shadow of doubt about it. This thing is beyond words appalling, and my mind is still numb with the shock. I cannot yet make any attempt to analyse how the fact I have discovered is likely to affect my own situation – except that in a general sense it menaces me with black disaster. I only know that I am overwhelmed with grief and misery – and that it happened. It really happened. It is true.

After dinner Sally came up to me. We made love. We talked; mainly of the visitors. After three days' rest her ankle is better, but still far from strong; and she was greatly relieved that it would not, after all, be necessary for us to take a gamble on its bearing up during an attempt to get me away tonight.

As the summer dusk deepened we suddenly noticed that artificial light was mingled with it. Sally pointed to the grating and said: 'Helmuth and Konrad must be preparing the chapel for tomorrow night; there are lights on down there.'

For a moment we sat in silence and the faint sound of voices drifted up to us, confirming her surmise. Getting up she limped quickly over to the grille. Its lower edge is over five feet from the floor, but being tall for a girl she could easily see over it and down into the chapel.

'Well?' I asked. 'What's going on?'

'Something I think you ought to see,' she replied in so low a voice that I only just caught her words.

I threw back the bedclothes and did the wriggle that throws my useless legs sideways, so that they dangle over the edge of the bed. Sally came across to me and helped me to my feet. For a few seconds I took my own weight while she turned round so that I could put my hands on her shoulders; then, step by step, I followed her over to the grating.

My first glance down into the chapel showed me that considerable activity was going on. A broad strip of red carpet had been laid down the centre of the nave, and on either side of it there were fifteen or twenty mattresses and scores of cushions, which, presumably, had been collected from all over the house. In the side aisles some men were erecting long trestle tables. The scaffolding round one of the pillars that support the roof interfered with my view, so I could not see them very plainly; but it was easy to pick out Helmuth, as one side of his face was still bandaged.

A woman in a dark cloak, who wore a red scarf tied round her head, was decorating the altar – but not with flowers. The candles on it gave ample light to see that she was making her artistic tribute in a medium that the Devil might well be expected to approve She was arranging garlands and bunches of deadly nightshade, toadstools, hemlock, ivy, tares, pigweed and nettles.

She stepped back to admire the effect; then she turned towards me. It was Julia.

Tuesday, 23rd June
It is still very early in the morning, and I am writing this by first light. Fortunately I slept all yesterday afternoon, so although I have not slept at all during the night, I do not feel particularly tired. Anyhow, I can still get in a good couple of hours' sleep before Konrad calls me, and God alone knows what will happen tomorrow – today I mean – so this may be the last chance I'll have to make an entry in my journal, and I wish to record the splendid courage and devotion that Sally has shown in the desperate turn of my affairs.

The sight of Julia decorating an altar to Satan – even the thought of it now stuns me afresh – left me dumbfounded, stricken to the heart, hardly able to credit what I had seen with my own eyes, yet forced to because Sally had seen it too; and I knew inside myself that it explained all sorts of little things about Julia that had vaguely puzzled me in the past. Yet, at first, I could not bring myself to accept it as a fact, and the upheaval in my mind robbed me of all initiative. So Sally took charge.

As soon as she had got me back to bed, she said that she was terribly sorry for me, but that from what we had seen there could be no doubt at all that I had been 'sold down the river' by my own people.

She had spotted Dr Arling among the men who had been helping Helmuth to erect one of the trestle tables, so he was in it too. Clearly my relatives were members of the Brotherhood, and the doctor was also a member. He had been brought down to pull the wool over my eyes and, no doubt, to remove me to a private asylum in due course. They were all actively abetting Helmuth in his criminal plot.

Sally's view was that my only chance lay in her getting me away that night. Her ankle was still paining her but she declared that she would manage somehow. It was already half-past nine so we had very little time to plan in before Konrad came up to take away my lamp.

Her main anxiety was whether she would be able to get me around the outside of the Castle. She thought she would be able to semi-piggy-back me downstairs, but it was going to be a terribly long haul from the side door to the place under the terrace to which we meant to lower my wheelchair, and she feared that her groggy ankle might not stand up to it.

I was still too bemused by my recent discovery to think of any possible alternative, and it was she who had the idea of using Great-aunt Sarah's secret staircase. It could lead nowhere except straight down to the chapel, and we knew that a flight of about twenty steps led up from the chapel floor to a side entrance, which gave onto the grass verge of the lake within a dozen yards of the spot where the chair would be.

That route was barely a third of the distance we should have had to cover along our old one, down the spiral stairs, along the passage and halfway round the Castle. Even allowing for the extra strain of getting me up the stone steps inside the chapel, the total effort required would be nothing like so great. I pulled my wits together sufficiently to produce the only snag I could think of – that the door at the bottom of the secret staircase might be locked, and its bolts rusted in with long disuse, so that we should not be able to get it open.

Sally countered that by saying she could get hold of some oil, a hammer, a small saw and other tools from the garage machine shop, and that she would bring with her candles as well as a torch; and that even if it took us an hour to get the door open we would still have ample time to be out of the grounds well before dawn. She also pointed out that another advantage of going by the secret staircase was that we could be certain of not running into anyone on it; so there would be much less danger of our being caught.

I had no further objections to offer, and time was getting short; so I kissed her and blessed her and, after promising to be back shortly before midnight for our eleventh-hour bid for freedom, she left me.

The entry I made in my journal took me only a few minutes, and I had hardly completed it when Konrad arrived. After he had gone the time of waiting passed with extraordinary swiftness because, I am ashamed to say, my mind was not really on the job ahead, but occupied with the most wretched speculations about Julia.

On Sally's return the first thing we decided was that she should reconnoitre the secret stairway, to make certain that there was a door at its bottom and that it would be possible to get it open. She had brought quite a large bag of tools and, taking them with her, she disappeared through the panel, closing it after her.

Going into such a place alone at dead of night must have taken more courage than most girls possess, particularly when one knew of the evil things that lurked in the vicinity; but Sally never hesitated, and somehow I did not feel afraid for her, only rather humble at the thought that I should be loved by a girl with such a valiant heart.

But as time went by and she failed to reappear I did get worried. I endeavoured to convince myself that she had found the door and was working on it; but I could not help imagining that she had met with some accident, and I began to pray frantically for her safe return.

She must have been down there over three-quarters of an hour, but at last I heard her coming back and, dusty, begrimed, dishevelled, she stumbled, still panting, through the panel opening.

'It's all right,' she said with a smile. 'Luckily the bolts are on this side. I managed to get one of them back, but the other needs a stronger blow with the hammer than I can give it. The lock will have to be cut out too. I've bored the holes for that and sawed down one side, but my wrist got so tired that I thought I had better come back and get you down there to help me.'

'Thank God you did!' I murmured, pulling her to me and kissing her cheek where it was smudged with dirt.

Limping over to the staircase door she shot the bolt, so that we should not be interrupted. Then she helped me to dress and got me into my chair. Next she opened the terrace door and wheeled me out to the far end of the terrace, where the battlement is crumbling away. I helped her to push over a number of the big, loose stones until we had made a gap about four feet wide. To get out the lower ones needed all the strength of my arms and I had to lie on the ground to exert sufficient pressure, but after about twenty minutes we had the gap clear to the bottom, so that the chair needed only a push to run over.

We tied the stout cord to the backrail of the chair, took a double hitch round the nearest castellation, and I hung on while Sally wheeled the chair over the edge. She supported part of its weight for a moment, so that the jerk should not snap the cord, then I cautiously lowered away. Two minutes later the cord abruptly slackened, and we knew that we had accomplished that part of the job all right. The moon was just showing above the tree tops on the far side of the lake and on peering over the battlement we could make out the chair standing right way up fifteen feet below us.

It had been easy enough for Sally to get me out of the chair onto the ground but it proved a much harder task to get me up again. On previous occasions when she had got me to my feet I had always been sitting on the edge of the bed or in my chair, but now she had to kneel down so that I could clamber on her back, then, with a great effort, she lifted me bodily.

Once I was upright we were able to go forward slowly. She took most of my weight on her shoulders, in a semi-piggy-back, but I was able to take some of it on my feet, and with each of them dragging alternatively we made our way forward a few steps at a time. It took us ten minutes to get back to my bed. There we rested for a bit, and while we were doing so we heard Great-aunt Sarah come up the stairs behind the panel, so we knew that it was one o'clock. When her footsteps had died away, by a further five minutes of strenuous effort Sally got me through the secret panel.

The light from her torch showed the staircase to be much broader than I had expected. It was a good six feet wide, and lofty, with a vaulted ceiling. The air inside it was warm but had none of the stuffiness that one associates with secret passages; and for that we soon saw the reason. About every five feet down the outer wall there were shallow embrasures with long arrow-slits, through which the moonlight percolated faintly.

After another short rest we essayed the descent. Before we were halfway I could feel the perspiration wet upon poor Sally's neck, and from the way she flinched each time she now put her bad foot one step further down, I knew that it must be hurting her like the devil.

I insisted that we should make longer pauses, but she said that did not really help, and that when we got to the bottom there would be plenty of time for her to rest her foot while we were getting the door open.

Between the bottom step and the door there was a short section of passage, only about eight feet in length, the floor space of which was partly encumbered by square blocks of stone. I saw that these had been removed from the left-hand wall, in which there was a big hole some four feet high and three feet across, and I knew it must be the entrance to Great-aunt Sarah's tunnel.

The blocks of stone now came in handy as they were from twelve to eighteen inches square, and were not too heavy for Sally to lift with an effort. By piling them up she made a seat for me, so that while she held the torch I could get to work on the lock.

It is no light task to cut through a three-inch-thick panel of ancient oak, and after I had been at it for a little while I marvelled that Sally had managed to get as far as she had in the time. Nearly two hours elapsed before I had completed the square round the lock, and by the time I had hammered back the remaining bolt it must have been three in the morning.

Having brushed ourselves down, we made ready for the next stage of our arduous journey. Sally put her shoulder against the door and heaved. With a loud groan of rusty hinges it gave, and reluctantly opened a couple of feet. As it did so I felt a chill draught come through from the chapel.

Instantly I knew that all our labours had been in vain; for at the same second a wave of nausea flooded through me. I was still seated on the pile of stone. As I leaned sideways to look past Sally I heard her give a sob; then I saw what she had already seen, and knew that my fears were only too well founded. The Great Spider was crouching in the middle of the aisle.

The moonlight streamed through a rent in the roof right onto the monster. Between its forefeet it held a dead cat, and it had evidently been making a meal off the cat's entrails, as they hung out from its torn stomach onto the floor; but the noise of the opening door had drawn our enemy's attention to us. Flinging aside the dead cat the black, hairy brute bounded in our direction.

Simultaneously, Sally and I grabbed the door and hauled it shut again. Then, falling on her knees beside me, she gave way to her distress in a flood of bitter tears. It was hard indeed to find our escape route barred by that hideous sentinel and, although I tried, there was little I could say to comfort her.

Afterwards, it did occur to me that if we could have gone boldly out into the chapel hand in hand the strength of our love might have created an aura that would have driven the brute back. But I could not stand alone for more than a moment, and I would not have let Sally face that incredibly evil thing with me dragging along behind her. At the time, to beat a retreat seemed the only possible course open to us.

When Sally had recovered a bit we began the ghastly business of getting back up the stairs. The eighteen or twenty steps that we had meant to go up on the far side of the chapel to its lake-shore entrance would have proved a bad enough ordeal, but here there were more than double that number. Leaning on Sally's back, I had been able to come down a step at a time, but I was much too heavy for her to carry and it was beyond my powers to take a single step upward.

We started by my clinging to her waist while she dragged me behind her, and got up about ten steps that way. But the strain on her was frightful; and when she could no longer suppress a loud moan from the pain in her ankle, I refused to let her pull me any further.

I tried pulling myself up, but as there was nothing ahead of me to grip except the smooth stones, and my knees were useless, I had to abandon the attempt. Then, turning round, I used my arms as levers to lift myself backwards from step to step. By the time I was halfway up I felt as though my arms were being wrenched from their sockets, and I could not possibly have got much further had not Sally come to my assistance. She went up backwards, too, behind me, and, stooping almost double, got her hands under my armpits so that she could heave every time I lifted. We managed that way, and at last she got me back to my room, but the final effort of supporting me to my bed proved too much for her, and as I flopped onto it she fainted.

She slipped to the floor near enough for me to sprinkle water from my bedside carafe on her face, and to my relief she soon came round sufficiently to pull herself up onto the bed beside me. We remained like that for a while, getting our strength back and wondering miserably what we should do next.

To attempt our original plan, of going down the spiral staircase, was out of the question. We were both dead-beat already, and Sally's ankle was paining her so much that she would have fainted again before we were a quarter of the way down it. So there seemed nothing for it but that I should resign myself to remaining where I was, and facing whatever was coming to me.

Suddenly I remembered that we had lowered my wheelchair over the battlements. It was much too heavy for us to pull up again, and I could not possibly have got it down to the lakeside by myself. When that was discovered – as it must be first thing in the morning – it would be realised that someone had aided me in an abortive attempt to escape; and suspicion could point only to Sally.

When I told her my new fear she laughed a little bitterly. 'You poor sweet; don't fret about that. Surely you realise that I have burnt my boats already. By sending that telegram to Julia I disclosed the fact that I am on your side. But she is not; and she only brought Dr Arling to hear what I had to say this afternoon to keep *me* from suspecting that they are both in this plot against you. Since we have failed to escape it is certain now that they will prevent my seeing you again, and do their best either to bribe or browbeat me into acknowledging that I was quite mistaken about your being sane.'

That gave me furiously to think. I felt convinced that Helmuth and Co. were capable of going to any lengths to ensure that Sally held her tongue. The business of the chair would give it away that her interest in me was not merely one of wanting to assure fair play for her patient; but that she was actively endeavouring to get me out of Helmuth's clutches. That presupposed that I had told her the whole story, and that she believed me. In that case they could not possibly afford to let her leave Llanferdrack, and, therefore, she was now in grave danger.

I told her that, and added: 'There is only one thing to do, darling. You can't get me out, but you can get out yourself. You must go downstairs, collect the few things that you feel you will be able to carry, and slip away before daylight.'

She shook her head. 'I'm damned if I will, Toby! What do you take me for? I love you; and I'm going to stay and fight these bloody people with you.'

For a quarter of an hour we wrangled fiercely over that. I alternately begged and ordered her to leave me; she refused to listen to my arguments and insisted on remaining. At length we agreed on a compromise. She should not return to her room, where she might find herself at their mercy, but lead them to suppose that she had got the wind up and cleared out. Actually she would retire into hiding behind the secret panel, so that she could hear all that went on in my room and render me any assistance that she could.

By the time the issue had been settled it was after four o'clock. The moon was down, so Sally lit a candle. The sweat had dried on us, caking the dirt, and we looked like a couple of sweeps. Anyone who saw me would have known at once that I must have been burrowing in some dirty hole, and the last thing we wanted was for Helmuth to start hunting for a secret passage. So Sally helped me to undress and got me properly back to bed, then brought me the basin and ewer from the washstand.

We made a cross on the water to prevent bad luck and washed our faces and hands. She threw the dirty water out onto the terrace, shut the door and unbolted the one to the spiral stairs.

Before she left me we arranged that if I gave one knock on the panel that would be the danger signal; she would know that I had heard someone coming upstairs and that she must remain quite still in case they heard her. If I gave two knocks that would be the signal that the coast was clear again, and I would knock three times if I wanted her to come out.

On my insisting she took some of the clothes from my wardrobe and a couple of cushions to make a couch to lie on; then we parted with mutual exhortations to have courage, and with great tenderness.

The grey light of dawn was already throwing the criss-cross bars of the grating into relief, so I started to scribble this; but I hope that my sweet Sally has been sleeping for the past hour or more. I am now feeling very tired myself, so I will snatch a couple of hours' sleep before Konrad comes to call me.

God alone knows what fresh ordeals the coming day will bring. I am alone in a dark world, but for the beacon of Sally's love. That must and shall sustain me.

Later

If I were not so desperately afraid of what may happen in the next twenty-four hours to Sally and myself, I should be laughing at the comedy that has just taken place.

Within a few moments of entering the room Konrad noticed the disappearance of my wheelchair. I had only just woken, so I had not got my wits fully about me; but I think my subconscious must have been concerning itself with the problem during my two-hour sleep, since I replied without hesitation: 'The Archangel Gabriel appeared to me last night. He said that I no longer required it, and he took it away. I think he threw it in the lake.'

Konrad's pale blue eyes almost popped out of his head. This cunning Ruthenian peasant is terribly superstitious. He would, I am sure, have bullied me unmercifully during these past three weeks had I not taken a leaf out of Helmuth's book. H. scared Taffy by telling him that I had the evil-eye. I told that story to Konrad soon after H. made him my gaoler-bodyservant. Since then he has done his job with as little fuss as possible. He is still 100 per cent Helmuth's man, but he has been mighty careful not to give me offence.

My quiet, unemotional statement about the Archangel having visited me, threw him into a paroxysm of terror. The chair was no longer in the room and he knew perfectly well that I could not possibly have disposed of it myself, so it was not altogether surprising that he should accept the suggestion that it had been removed by a supernatural agency.

He had already dumped my breakfast tray on my bed-table; and, instead of proceeding as usual to hand me my toothbrush and the basin, he gave me a shifty glance then sidled quickly out of the room.

I gave three knocks for Sally. A moment later she almost tumbled through the panel opening, still half asleep.

'Quick!' I said. 'Help yourself to a cup of coffee, and take some toast and fruit; then skip back to your hiding-place. Konrad has gone to fetch Helmuth and they will be up here in a few minutes.'

She poured the coffee, made a face as she gulped it down, took a handful of cherries off the plate, gave me a swift kiss on the nose, then stumbled back through the opening like a large sleepy child. I longed to call her back and put my arms round her. She is absolute heaven.

Konrad returned with Helmuth five minutes later. It is the first time I have seen him since I hit him with the bottle. He had the bandages off this morning but his eye is still black and blue.

I maintained my story about the Archangel, and for a moment I saw fear in his tawny eyes. Then his suspicions overcame his credulity. He went out onto the terrace, saw the gap in the battlement and, on looking over, the chair down by the lakeside. Striding back to me, he shouted: 'That great hoyden Sally Cardew must be responsible for this! It was she who telegraphed for Julia. And now she's tried to help you to escape; but it proved too much for her. I'll teach that young bitch to double-cross me like this!'

'Do, if you can find her,' I mocked him. 'But you won't; because she's gone back to London. And in due course she will bear witness against you in a criminal court.'

'She won't get the chance!' he snapped. 'I'll soon have her traced and stop her tongue. The Brotherhood has plenty of ways of dealing with stupid or indiscreet people. It may interest you to know that Deborah Kain will be sailing from Cardiff in the hold of a tramp steamer today. If she does not die on the voyage round Africa she will eventually reach Persia, and be sent through to Russia. She came here to see you against my orders, and in the Soviet Union they know how to punish the servants who have failed them.'

Glad as I was to know that Britain was nurturing one less viper in her bosom, I could not help feeling sorry for the wretched Deb, as it was largely my fault that such a fate had overtaken her. But Helmuth was going on: 'As for anyone bearing witness against me in a criminal court, you must be really mad if you think you will ever be in a position to prosecute me. After the dance you've led me I'm in no mood to show you further mercy. Tonight I mean to finish your business once and for all. The Brotherhood will invoke the Lady Astoroth to visit you here, and she will destroy your reason.'

Turning on his heel he flung out of the room, and I was left to contemplate anew the really desperate situation in which last night's failure to get away has placed me.

I had continued to put a bold face on matters in front of Helmuth, but I am feeling very far from bold. Sally's love, and her faith in the inevitable triumph of good over evil, alone sustained me. But I am powerless to help myself and I do not see how she can help me further. Moreover, while I now fully accept her wonderful teaching, it is a long-term policy; it may well be that in a past life I once drove someone mad, and in this one must pay the penalty by being driven mad myself.

I have only one weak straw to cling to, and that is Julia. There can be no question about her being in with Helmuth. If further proof were needed, he gave it himself by disclosing that she had told him of Sally's telegram, thus giving it away that Sally had come over to my side.

If Helmuth is with her at the moment, and mentions his disclosure, she will realise that I now know her to be in league with my enemies, and she may be ashamed to face me. But if she does not yet know that I know of her treachery she should be coming up to see me as she promised, quite soon now. If she does, there is just a chance that I may be able to save myself through her.

Later

It is afternoon. I am writing the following only because it is absolutely vital that I should do so. This time tomorrow I expect to be insane and my testimony will then be valueless.

I hereby make solemn declaration that I am now in my right mind; that the following is the truth, the whole truth, and nothing but the truth, with regard to the death of Julia Jugg.

I murdered her. Nurse Cardew was an accessary but an innocent one. She acted in defence of her crippled patient, in the belief that she could help to save him from a gang of criminals. The very fact that I shall not attempt to conceal the part she played is in itself testimony that she was innocent of the actual crime. What she did was done by my orders and the responsibility for Mrs Paul Jugg's death is entirely mine.

This is what occurred; so help me God.

A little after ten-thirty this morning, Tuesday the 23rd of June, 1942, Julia came up to see me as she had promised. Her demeanour was affectionate and unabashed. She sat down beside my bed and, after talking trivialities for a few moments, by a casual question I extracted the information from her that she had not seen Dr Helmuth Lisický since last night; as she had breakfasted in bed, only just got up, and had come straight up from her bedroom to me. I knew then that she knew nothing yet of my abortive attempt to escape last night, or that I realised that she was involved in the conspiracy against me.

I asked her when we were going to leave Llanferdrack.

'Not till tomorrow, darling,' she replied. 'Dr Arling wants to examine you again tonight in the moonlight to see if the moon really has a bad effect on you. But whether it has or not Paul and I mean to take you back with us to Queensclere tomorrow morning.'

Stretching out my hand, I took hers. Then I said quietly: 'You are lying, Julia. You have been plotting with Helmuth to drive me mad tonight, so that Dr Arling can take me away to some private asylum tomorrow.'

Her great eyes suddenly showed fear and consternation. She shook her head and struggled violently to drag her hand from my grasp; but I had a firm grip of it, and I went on: 'It is useless to deny it, Julia. I saw you last night arranging those poisonous herbs and stinging nettles on the Devil's altar. That was the most awful thing that has ever happened to me. It was like losing a limb. It was worse than when I was told that my back was broken and the odds were against my ever walking again.'

I paused and added in a husky voice: 'Even now, terribly as you have hurt me, I hate having to hurt and bully you. But I've got to; because only you can save me from Helmuth, and only by regaining my freedom can I save you from the ghastly web in which you have enmeshed yourself. I suppose you were blackmailed into becoming a Satanist. I want to know the truth about that. Then we'll make a plan to trick Helmuth at the last moment. Once I am free I mean to smash up this evil Brotherhood; but whatever you have done I'll find a way to save you from them. You see, I want to help you to become clean and free again. So you must tell me the whole truth.'

'I won't!' she moaned. 'I won't! Let me go! Let me go!'

'Oh yes, you will,' I said. 'If you won't talk freely I shall have to make you.' Then I caught her glance and held it.

'Let me go! Let me go!' her voice grew louder, and tearing her glance from mine she wailed: 'You beast! You're trying to hypnotise me!'

I knew then that even at the price of giving Sally's – Nurse Cardew's – hiding-place away I must have help, otherwise my forlorn hope was doomed to failure. Stretching across Julia I rapped thrice sharply with my free hand on the secret panel.

In leaning over I had momentarily to loosen my grip on Julia's hand. As the panel slid back and Sally came out Julia wrenched her hand from my grasp. Turning, she ran towards the door.

'Quick, Sally!' I cried. 'For God's sake catch her, and bring her back. I've got to hypnotise her by force. It's our only hope.'

Sally darted after her and caught her in the middle of the room. For a few moments there ensued a horrid scuffle. The two women fought like tiger-cats. Julia's long nails tore three furrows in Sally's grimy cheek; then she got hold of a handful of Sally's fuzzy hair and wrenched it out, while kicking violently at her shins. But Sally was much the stronger of the two. She hit Julia hard in the face, grabbed one of her arms and twisted it behind her back, then hurtled her across the room and forced her face down onto the bed.

I seized Julia by the shoulders, but by that time she had begun to scream for help; so I transferred my grip to her throat and, much as I hated having to do it, choked her into silence.

She was now sprawled over sideways on the bed and face upwards across my middle. Stooping over her, I stared down into her eyes and ordered her to sleep.

But she shut her eyes firmly, so I had to get Sally to turn the lids back and hold them open.

Even then, Julia put up a terrific resistance, and after we had held her like that for a quarter of an hour she still had not given in. I had always heard that it is terribly difficult to hypnotise anyone against their will, but I was determined to go through with it.

I had been holding her down by the throat the whole time, and I began to choke her again, with the idea that if I reduced her to semi-consciousness that way she would no longer be able to exert her will, and her resistance would give way. Her lovely magnolia skin began to go red in patches and her black eyes bulged from her head. Sally warned me to be careful, but I disregarded her advice. I eased the pressure a little, now and then, but kept my thumbs digging into Julia's neck each side of her windpipe. It was horrible; but it worked.

Her eyes took on that curious look of the somnambulist and I knew that she had passed into an hypnotic sleep. I released my grip at once and Sally got her into the chair beside my bed. We gave her a glass of water and a few minutes to recover; then I started on her.

'Now Julia,' I said, 'I want the truth. When did you become a Satanist?'

'When I was seventeen,' she replied hoarsely.

Her answer staggered me; but details of my reactions to her story are irrelevant now.

'How did it happen?' I asked.

'An old peasant woman in our village took me to a Witches' Sabbath in the Alban hills.'

'Did you go willingly?'

'Yes.'

'Why?'

'I wanted all the things which were mine by right, but of which I had been cheated. She promised me that if I became a witch I should make a rich marriage.'

'But you had great beauty and you were a daughter of the noble Roman house of Colona, so why shouldn't you have made a rich marriage anyhow?'

'No. My father was a Colona, but he was not married to my mother; that is why I felt myself to have been cheated. She was a peasant girl on his estate outside Rome, and I was brought up by her in a cottage that was almost a hovel.'

'What happened after the Sabbath?'

'My father rarely left the big house when he visited his estate, but one day soon after the Sabbath he came down to the village. He saw me washing clothes in the stream, and struck by my beauty he enquired who I was. When he found that I was his own daughter he expressed a wish to do something for me. He sent me to school for two years, but after that I suffered a bitter disappointment. I had expected to become one of the family, but all he did was to make me his wife's lady's-maid.'

'Was that what you were when you met Uncle Paul?'

'Yes; and he was the rich husband I had been promised. He was not rich then, but he was a gentleman, so he could lift me by marriage to the status that was mine by right of blood; and while he was courting me he told me all about the Jugg millions. I realised that he must be the husband that had been sent for me by the Old One, and I felt certain that once I was married to him I would be able to get hold of a share of those millions.'

'What happened after you came to England?'

'I thought that if I could cure Paul of his bad habits, your grand-father would forgive him and make him a handsome allowance. That was the object of the séances at Kew. By means of them I was able to frighten Paul out of drinking so much. When he got tight I used to send a ghoul to give him the horrors. Sometimes it used to get out of control for a while and appear in the house unbidden. That is how you came to see it the night you thought you had run into a burglar on the stairs.'

'Soon after that we moved to Kensington Palace Gardens and Queensclere, and you had everything you could wish for. Why did you continue to be a Satanist after that?'

'I didn't. And your coming made a lot of difference, Toby. I was very happy looking after you, and I became very fond of you. I didn't want you to be mixed up in that sort of thing; so after we left Kew I had nothing more to do with it.'

'Why did you take it up again then? And why did you send me to Weylands?'

Julia's big dark eyes were suddenly suffused with tears, and they began to run down her cheeks; but she made no motion to brush them away and, in her trance state, she probably did not know that she was crying. She made a pitiful spectacle, as she went on tonelessly: 'I had to. One of the Brotherhood came to me a little over a year later. How he found out about me I've no idea; but he knew all about my past. He told me that the time had come when I must pay for my riches or lose them; and that you were the price. I was too weak to refuse. I simply could not bring myself to face poverty again, so I agreed to send you to Weylands. But I hoped that later on I would find a way to prevent them making you one of us.'

'But Helmuth got the better of you, eh?'

'Yes. He did not arrive on the scene until you were about thirteen; but within a week of his coming to stay at Queensclere as your tutor, he became my lover. I had had others – ever since I was seventeen. Paul was never anything to me, except the vehicle for my ambitions; and he soon became the complacent husband, content to show me off and let me manage his affairs. But Helmuth was a landmark in my life. I became as wax in his hands, and have been so ever since.'

'That time at Weylands when you and Uncle Paul came up to see me, and I had that horrible experience. I take it that you had not been to a friend's house, or run off the road in the car, at all. When you found me at the bungalow had you just returned from a Black Mass in the crypt of the ruined Abbey?'

'Yes. Paul had been initiated that night as a lay-brother. He is not a type out of which a potent Satanist could be made; but as you were growing up, it was considered advisable to bind him to the Brotherhood, so as to ensure his taking his future orders from Helmuth without question, and working to get him the next vacant seat on your Board of Trustees.'

'You knew all about the conspiracy to drive me insane, in order that the Brotherhood could get control of my fortune?'

The tears welled from her eyes again. 'I knew their intention, Toby, but not the details. Helmuth knows how fond I am of you, and he did not altogether trust me. He feared that if I learned too much about the methods he meant to employ I might rebel, and try to save you. That is why he intercepted all your letters to me, and would not let me come down to see you until he gave the word.'

'Yet you came at once in response to Nurse Cardew's telegram?'

'Paul and I were coming anyway for the Black Mass tonight. When I got the telegram I telephoned Helmuth and asked him what I was to do. Directly he realised that he could no longer trust Nurse Cardew he feared that she might help you in another attempt to escape, last night. So to make you believe such an attempt unnecessary he said that Paul and I must come down at once to reassure you, and that we were to bring Dr Arling with us.'

That was the whole awful story of how her ambition for riches and luxury had led her to betray a child that she had brought up with loving care as a younger brother. There seemed nothing further left to ask her, so I said: 'Now Julia, I freely forgive you for all you have done, and intended to allow to be done, against me. It is never too late to mend. Somehow, I will get you out of the clutches of these vile people, and we will forget the whole horrible business. I still want to repay you for all the love and happiness with which you surrounded me when I came to you as a little orphan, and so long as it lies with me you shall never lack for money. But you have got to do as I tell you.

'I am going to write a letter to the district Inspector of Police. I shall tell him about the meeting that is to be held here tonight; but I shall say nothing about Satanism, or a Black Mass. I shall simply say that these people are meeting in the chapel without my consent and I have good grounds for believing that they intend to use it for sacrilegious and immoral purposes. As the owner of this property I have the right to invoke the protection of the law against this unwarranted and scandalous trespass. I shall ask that a squad of police be mustered in the grounds at ten o'clock, in readiness to take the names of the trespassers and expel them at the signal of the Inspector; and that he should come to me here at that hour in order to see for himself through the grating all that takes place in the chapel.

'I shall also draw a little sketch plan of the Castle, showing the position of the side-door which is at the end of the passage at the bottom of the spiral staircase, and enclose it with the letter.

'When I have written the letter I shall give it to you. Then you will go downstairs, beg, borrow or steal a car, make any excuse you like, and drive into the village. There you will go to the Police Sergeant and he will tell you where the nearest Inspector is stationed. You will drive on to the Inspector and give him the letter with your own hand, remain there while he reads it, make certain that he fully understands the urgency of the matter, and intends to do as I wish; then return here and come up to report to me. Lastly you will be at the side-door I have marked on the plan, yourself at ten o'clock tonight, to let the Inspector in and bring him up to me here. Is that all clear?'

She said that it was. Sally got me my pen and paper. I wrote the letter, drew the plan, put them both in an envelope and gave it to Julia. Then I gave her my instructions a second time and made her repeat them after me.

When she had done so I told her that she was to say nothing of what had passed between us to anyone except the Inspector, and woke her from her trance.

As her full consciousness came back she stared at me wide-eyed, stood up, turned to look at Sally, then clutched at her heart. Suddenly she let out a piercing scream, pitched forward and fell flat on the floor.

The echo of her scream had hardly died away when I caught the sound of footsteps on the stairs. Almost instantaneously they broke into a run. Too late I remembered that I had neglected to tell Sally to bolt the door, so as to secure us from interruption. After one look at Julia she had hurried over to my washstand to get water. As she picked up the jug Helmuth and Dr Arling burst into the room.

There is little point in giving a detailed account of what happened, after that. The secret panel was closed, so Helmuth still does not know how Sally came to be in my room when he thought she had gone to London; but she could not get back into her hiding-place without revealing it. As cold water failed to revive Julia, Helmuth and Dr Arling carried her out onto the terrace, hoping that the fresh air might do so. A few moments later Helmuth came back and announced that she was dead – that she had died of heart failure.

There was no disguising the fact that the two women had had a fight. The bloody scratches on Sally's face showed that, and the doctor had found some strands of her hair still adhering to Julia's fingernails. They had also come on my letter addressed to the Inspector of Police.

Helmuth took Sally's arm with one hand and waved the letter at me with the other, as he said: 'Your writing to the Inspector of Police seems to have been prompted by a forecast of events. I will save you a stamp, as I mean to telephone him now. It will be my unpleasant duty to hand Nurse Cardew over to him on a charge of murder.'

In vain I cursed him and swore that it was my doing. He took Sally downstairs to lock her up. A few minutes later he returned with a sheet; then he and Dr Arling carried Julia's dead body, draped in its awful final whiteness, in from the terrace and through my room.

The above is the truth. By Almighty God I swear it. How, I cannot think, but I hope to get these papers to Sally for her defence. Should I fail, I implore anyone who may come across them to take them to the nearest J.P. Blessed be the person who does. Cursed for all eternity be anyone who reads this and fails to act upon it.

It is the truth, the real truth. I swear it by all I hold holy. Sally did no more than catch Julia for me. It was I who choked her and threw so terrible a strain upon her body and mind that it proved too much for her heart.

Oh, Sally! Sally! That your love for me should have brought you to such a pass is terrible beyond belief. Had I the power to save you by dying at this minute I would do it; and gladly, rather than they should harm one hair of your sweet head.

Later

At three-twenty this afternoon I signed away my fortune.

Helmuth came to me with a duplicate copy of the deed that he showed me some days ago. He said that there was a clear case against Sally for wilful murder. That, bedridden as I am, I could not have killed Julia, and that there was ample evidence that she had died as a result of Sally's assault.

He went on to say that the Brotherhood were above the petty laws and shibboleths of this world, and was not the least interested in bringing offenders to the so-called justice of the British courts. Their only interest was the immediate furtherance of their own concerns, of which obtaining control of the Jugg millions was one. By signing the document he produced I could spare them much trouble and delay in achieving this particular item in their plans. If I would do so, Dr Arling was prepared to sign a certificate that Julia had died a natural death, and there would then be no occasion to call in the police.

I attempted to make some other stipulations, but he would not listen to me. He insisted that it should be a plain one-clause bargain. Either I signed or Sally went to the rope.

He had me in a corner. There was no option. I signed.

Later

This is the end. Sally was telling me the other day what she believes to be the true interpretation of the conception that 'the unforgivable sin is to blaspheme against the Holy Ghost'. She said that it is not a matter of mere words, but the act of suicide; because we all carry a particle of the Holy Ghost within us, and to drive our spirit out of our body before the time ordained for it to go is not unforgivable – nothing is unforgivable – but it is the most heinous crime which it is possible to commit.

Yet had I the means I would be sorely tempted to take my own life tonight.

It is after nine and I am writing this by the failing light. My lamp has not been lit, nor will it be, as Konrad will not be coming up to me again. Helmuth has just paid me a final visit and he told me that before he left.

He came to gloat, and render my last sane hours unendurably hideous by disclosing the way in which he had tricked me; and, infinitely worse, tricked my beloved Sally.

Julia is not dead. It was only a heart attack she had, and she is now little the worse for her seizure. The inspiration to *say* that she was dead came to Helmuth when he and Dr Arling had her limp body out on the terrace. He realised that Sally and I were in love, and saw that by causing us to believe that we had killed Julia he could bend us both to his will.

He led me to believe that, as Julia and Sally had clearly had a fight, it was Sally who would be charged with the murder, unless I signed away my fortune as the price of Dr Arling giving a certificate that Julia had died a natural death.

He led Sally to believe that he knew the fight to have been only incidental, and that the marks on Julia's throat showed that she had really died from strangulation – and that it was I who had strangled her. He threatened to hand me over to the police unless she would do as he wished; and, believing it to be the only way to save me from hanging, she agreed.

He told me that having signed the document would not now save me from mental destruction tonight, because I had not signed it with resignation – only under extreme pressure. He said that my prolonged and bitter opposition showed that I could never be made a useful member of the Brotherhood, and would always be liable to make trouble.

Therefore, at a quarter-past one in the morning, when the moon is at its highest, they will invoke the Lady Astoroth. She will appear here in my room, and tomorrow I shall be found a raving lunatic. Dr Arling will remove me to his private asylum, and after I have spent some time there the official Board of Lunacy will examine and certify me.

I only pray that a merciful God will allow my mind to be blotted out entirely. If I were certain of that I think I could resign myself to this miserable fate. But nothing could make me resigned to what is in store for Sally.

Helmuth stood well out of reach at the end of my bed. Leonine, rock-faced, sardonic, he grinned at me with unutterably evil malice as he told me about that.

He says that Sally knows too much to be allowed to depart in peace, and that steps have to be taken to stop her tongue once and for all. That could be done by making her a lay-sister of the Brotherhood, as, after even the lowest degree of initiation, she would never dare to risk the appalling fate reserved for a member who betrays them – there is no recorded case of anyone ever having done so yet. And she has agreed to accept initiation, believing that only by doing so can she save my life.

Helmuth said that the initiation will take place at midnight, and that although I shall not be able to see it I shall hear enough of it through the grating to imagine what is going on. Sally does not yet know what they mean to do to her, but Helmuth took fiendish delight in describing to me what will happen, in order that I could better imagine the scene when it takes place.

He is to act as the officiating priest. Sally will be spreadeagled naked on a bed of nettles before the Devil's altar. He will then do to her what he has failed to do so far. The excited cries of the congregation will inform me when the ritual is being accomplished, and the completion of the act will be the signal for a general orgy.

I do not think that when the Lady Astoroth appears to me at a quarter-past one I shall know much about it. I shall have gone mad by midnight. May God have mercy upon dear Sally, and upon my soul.

Wednesday, 24th June

This old Castle must have seen many strange and terrible events, but it can have seen none stranger or more terrible than those which occurred here last night. It is now the scene of catastrophe and death; yet, despite everything, I am still sane.

That I am so after what I endured between nine o'clock and midnight last night is in itself a miracle.

No sound came to distract my agonising thoughts until a little after ten; then I heard people moving in the chapel. Gradually the noise increased. I heard the clatter of plates and the clink of glasses; so I knew that the Satanists had begun to feast at the tables set up in the side-aisles.

The voices grew louder and more distinct. There came the drinking of healths and raucous laughter. That went on for well over an hour, so it must have been about half-past eleven when the service started.

There was music, but music the like of which I have never heard before and hope never to hear again. It had no tune or any kind of beauty, but was a series of hideous discords, rising at times to a wild cacophony of sound interspersed by catcalls, shouts and animal noises.

I knew that those beasts in human form were working themselves up into a frenzy of abandon, the better to satiate their vile lusts when the time came.

The night was stiflingly hot, and the fumes of strange and horrible things that were burning down there came up to me through the grating. The chapel was brightly lit, and the grating stood out sharply; a great rectangle of light criss-crossed with its black bars, which illuminated the whole room almost as brightly as though it were day.

I had thrown off the bedclothes, and swung myself round so that my useless legs were dangling over the side of the bed. From time to time, as midnight approached, I tried to stand, but I could not do so for more than a minute without having to grasp the head of the bed for support.

I prayed as I have never prayed before – violently, unceasingly – supplicating God to spare Sally, or at least grant her oblivion, so that she might be spared the knowledge of the abominable things those beasts meant to do to her. I prayed aloud, and I was raving. I called on God and the Virgin Mary; on all the Powers of Good and Light and Love that there had ever been in the world.

The sweat was pouring off me. It ran into my eyes and they grew misty. I could no longer see even the brightly lit grating clearly. My effort was so intense that I was shaking all over. I tried to throw my spirit forward out of my body, and down into the chapel to protect Sally. I cried aloud my defiance of Satan and all his works.

It was then the miracle happened. God had heard my prayer. I found that I was standing up, and that I was walking towards the panel.

I seemed to be buoyed up and supported by unseen hands. Without any effort I climbed through the panel opening onto the secret stairs. They were faintly lit by the moonlight coming through the arrow-slits. I walked slowly but surely down them till I reached the door at the bottom. I thrust it open and entered the chapel.

The scene was one which will remain stamped on my memory until my dying day. There were about eighty people present, all wearing fantastic costumes. Many of them were women, some nude to the waist, others dressed in eccentric arrangements of veiling through which their bodies could be seen, or which left their sexual parts exposed. The men were in gorgeous satins and velvets, and each wore a head-dress in the likeness of some wild animal or poisonous reptile.

Like a reredos, behind the altar, there spread a vast web which seemed to have been spun from liquid silver. It extended to both sides of the chapel and right up to its roof. In the centre of the web, about twenty feet up, sat the Great Spider.

In front of the altar stood Helmuth. He was wearing his white satin robe with the black signs of the Zodiac on it, but the robe was now hitched up so that he was naked from the waist down. Two women, one of whom was Julia, knelt at either side of him in attitudes of adoration. In front of him two assistant priests were standing, and between them they held Sally by the arms. She was dressed in the fashion of a nun, except that her single garment was of magenta veiling, through which one could see her white body.

Konrad was stationed quite near me, with five other men. They were all clad alike, in red with long hose and horned head-dresses, in imitation of the Devil; and evidently formed a Satanic guard, as they stood in a line in front of the main door of the chapel and each of them was holding at rest long tridents with barbed points.

It was Konrad who first saw me. He must have thought that I was an avenging spirit. Pointing at me, he let out a howl of terror, then fell to the ground and lay grovelling there a dozen paces from my feet.

At his shout the whole congregation turned in my direction. Sally

alone could have known how I had got into the chapel, and that by
some extraordinary means I had managed to get down the stairs. She
gave a loud cry, broke from the men who were holding her, and came
running towards me.

Helmuth and the rest must also have thought that I was a spirit
sent to disperse their diabolical gathering, as they either remained
rooted where they stood, their faces aghast with fear, or cowered
away from me. The Great Spider had begun to run frantically up and
down its huge silver web. Then, just as Sally reached me, I found
myself with my right arm outstretched again, hurling defiance at
the Devil.

As I did so I could feel the power streaming into me and out
through my pointing arm like an electric current. Suddenly the
Great Spider stopped its dance, quivered violently as though struck
by lightning, and began to disintegrate. In a matter of seconds it had
dissolved into a cloud of evil-smelling black smoke.

Consternation seized the Satanists. They began to run senselessly
in all directions, covering their heads and screaming with fear. I
waited no longer, but grasped the edge of the door behind me and
made to pull it open.

I had it about a foot open when it stuck. At that moment something must have clicked over in Helmuth's quick brain. He had not
seen me come through the door and was probably unaware that it
even existed until he saw it partly open. He must have guessed then
that behind it lay a secret staircase up to my room: and that what he
had thought to be an apparition was really myself in the flesh.

Above the din, I heard him bellow: 'There's nothing to be afraid
of! He is only a man! Stop them! Stop them! Catch them before they
get away!'

A sudden hush, all the more marked from the previous clamour,
fell on that weird assembly. For a moment they hesitated, and in that
moment I got the door wide open. It gave unexpectedly, and swung
right back.

'Stop them, damn you! Stop them!' Helmuth yelled again; and as I
thrust Sally through the doorway, the brief hush was succeeded by a
new pandemonium. With howls of rage and hate the Satanists came
charging towards us.

We were up about four steps when the first of our enemies reached
the door. Helmuth was among them, and from the maniacal glare in
their eyes I knew that if they got us they would tear us limb from
limb. It was an awful moment – perhaps the worst that night – for we

had so nearly got away, and I knew that only God's help could save us from being dragged down before we were halfway up the stairs. But He extended His merciful protection to us once again.

It was then that there came the second miracle of that unforgettable night. I heard a rumbling sound. It increased in volume to the noise of thunder before we were up another couple of steps, drowning the fierce cries of the mob that pursued us.

Suddenly a great torrent of water burst from the entrance to Great-aunt Sarah's tunnel. It hit the opposite wall of the passage like a tidal wave, drenching us to the skin; then turned and roared into the chapel. A second later I glimpsed the old lady's frail body as it was whirled out of the tunnel and through the open door.

Night after night for over forty years she had laboured for love's sake, and an inscrutable Providence had decreed that the culmination of her efforts should exactly coincide with the desperate need of two other lovers who were in dire peril. Her own ordeal, too, was over. At long last she had burrowed her way to the lake bottom, and in so doing had rejoined her Lancelot in a better way than she could ever have done in life.

As the first violent spate of water receded we saw that it had swept the advancing Satanists below us from their feet. They were now a flailing mass of legs and arms struggling in the torrent. Helmuth alone was still standing framed in the doorway, breasting the tide as it raced past on either side of him. For a moment he stood there hurling imprecations at us, then a screaming, half-drowned woman was thrown against him by the rushing water. He lost his balance and plunged beneath it, to be swept away with the rest.

Thousands of gallons were pouring down from the lake to the lower level of the chapel in a steady flood. But for that unholy congregation worse was yet to come. Within a few minutes of the first inrush the water took hold of the half-ruined pillar bases and the temporary structures that were shoring the building up. Beams cracked and snapped. Above the roar of the water we could hear the louder roar of great chunks of masonry giving way. The Satanists were trapped there, owing to the main door on the chapel floor level being held fast shut by the weight of water pressing against it.

After Helmuth had been swept away, Sally and I continued to stand on the stairs watching the horrific spectacle through the open doorway. It was as though Samson had come again to pull down the pillars of the temple upon another host of Philistines. We saw one forty-foot column collapse upon the screaming crowd that struggled waist-deep in water. Then big sections of the roof began to fall in, burying them beneath water-logged debris.

We were cut off from the chapel by the flood, so there was nothing that we could do to help; no act of mercy that we could perform. The chapel was soon full of water to the height of the top of the tunnel, but it still continued to rise, as I knew it must until its level reached that of the lake outside. Step by step we retreated up the stairs, until the swirling waters, now quiet, had reached the top of the door, and our last glimpse of the débâcle within was cut off. Then we turned and went slowly up to my room.

There, side by side, we gave thanks to God for our merciful deliverance from Evil, and vowed to devote our lives to fighting Evil in all its forms. Nor did we forget to pray for the happiness of that spirit which for a little time lived in the body of Sarah Jugg – who yesterday was old and mad, but today is young and sane again.

****

Monday, 3rd July, 1945
It is now over three years since that terrible night when God overwhelmed the Satanists at Llanferdrack.

The following morning Sally found the document I had signed for Helmuth in his study and destroyed it. That afternoon we left for London in an ambulance, and this is the first time since that we have visited the Castle.

My back caved in soon after I got back to my room, and for a time the specialists thought that my miraculous walk had placed so severe a strain upon the healing ligaments prematurely that there was little hope of my ever setting foot to the ground again.

It was then that Sally insisted on marrying me; because, as she said, with all the money in the world, I would have to be good and could not be got at by designing hussies, as long as I remained a permanent invalid.

All the same, she always maintained, against the opinions of the doctors, that I would get well in the end; and I owe it to her loving care that by the end of the year I was able to walk a few steps, and can now walk a mile without crutches.

But no designing hussy has got at me yet, or is ever likely to. Sally and I are gloriously happy and eighteen months ago she had two of the loveliest babies in the world. I mean, of course, that she had twins. They are girls and alike as two peas. They've got Sally's eyes but they are red-heads like me, and delightfully naughty.

These past three years I have been far too busy with my Companies even to think of my stamps. But on coming back here yesterday I went straight to my albums and extracted the scores of closely written pages that I had hidden in them. Sally and I read them through last night, and they recalled the time we spent here as though it had only ended yesterday.

I am going to have them bound up for her; and now that the war is over she wants me to have them published. We shall not mind if some people cannot bring themselves to believe the terrible and wonderful things that they reveal. We shall only be sorry that such people are still bound in Darkness and shut out from a realisation of the Eternal Verities. We know it all to be true, and it is our testament that Evil can never triumph over the power of Love.